HANNAH

and the

HIGHLANDER

HANNAH
and the
HIGHLANDER

SABRINA YORK

St. Martin's Paperbacks

This is a work of fiction. All of the characters, organizations, and events portrayed in this novel are either products of the author's imagination or are used fictitiously.

HANNAH AND THE HIGHLANDER

For information address St. Martin's Press, 175 Fifth Avenue, New York, NY 10010.

ISBN: 978-1-250-06969-6

Printed in the United States of America

St. Martin's Paperbacks edition / September 2015

St. Martin's Paperbacks are published by St. Martin's Press, 175 Fifth Avenue, New York, NY 10010.

10 9 8 7 6 5 4 3 2 1

This book is dedicated to Monique Patterson.
Thank you for everything.

ACKNOWLEDGMENTS

My deepest appreciation to Barbara Wild for her copy-editing genius, to the St. Martin's Art Department for such a beautiful cover, and to Alexandra Sehulster for all her guidance.

My heartfelt appreciation to my fellow writers for their support along this journey. Especially Cherry Adair, Pam Binder, Sidney Bristol, Ann Charles, Cerise DeLand, Wendy Delaney, Delilah Devlin, Tina Donahue, Laurann Dohner, Sharon Hamilton, Mark Henry, Desiree Holt, Elle James, Jennifer Kacey, Gina Lamm, Delilah Marvelle, Rebecca Zanetti, and so many more.

And of course a shout-out to my amazing support team, Linda Bass, Crystal Benedict, Stephanie Berowski, Crystal Biby, Kris Bloom, Monica Britt, Kim Brown, Sandy Butler, Carmen Cook, Celeste Deveney, Tracey A. Diczban, Shelly Estes, Lisa Fox, Rhonda Jones, Denise Krauth, Barbara Kuhl, Angie Lane, Tina Leuthardt, Chris Lewis, Rose Lipscomb, Jodi Marinich, Loraine Oliver, Tracey Parker, Laurie Peterson, Iris Pross, Tina Reiter, Hollie Rieth, Pam Roberts, Regina Ross, Sandy Sheer, Kiki Sidira, Sheri Vidal, Sally Wagoner, Deb Watson, Veronica Westfall, and Michelle Wilson, as well as the shy ones, Christy, Elf, Fedora, Gaele, Lisa, Nita, and Pansy Petal.

To all my friends in the Greater Seattle Romance Writers of America, Passionate Ink and Rose City Romance Writers groups, and the Pacific Northwest Writers Association, thank you for all your support and encouragement.

CHAPTER ONE

May 1813
Barrogill, Caithness County, Scotland

She should look away. Really, she should. But Hannah Dounreay could not tear her gaze from the sight of the enormous man striding onto the field of combat like a warrior of old. It could have been the glorious fall of inky black curls riffling in the breeze, or the breadth of his shoulders, or the sharp cut of his chin . . . or the rippling muscles of his bare chest, swathed only with the Sinclair plaid. But something had captivated her attention.

He stood, tall and proud, bare legged in the traditional kilt, head and shoulders above the other men. He was even taller than her father and Papa was not a small man.

Hoots and hollers rose from the throng as he surveyed the pile of logs—taunts from his competitors, who, one and all, wanted to break his concentration. They did not. His biceps bunched as he braced his thick legs and hefted a caber. Hannah sucked in a breath at the undeniable evidence of the sheer power of this man. An unfamiliar flutter danced deep in her core.

It was a shame he was too far away for her to make out the details of his face.

His body stilled, his energy hummed, as he studied the clutter of tossed cabers and took his aim. The catcalls rose. He ignored them and heaved back. With a great growl, he let fly. The log wheeled through the air like an arrow, arcing past all the others to fall with an enormous thud that shook the earth. A plume of dust rose, along with the cheers of the crowd.

Though she wasn't a fan of male posturing and ridiculous, archaic games such as this, Hannah couldn't deny she was impressed. This man had easily trounced all the others.

Her father approached him and clapped him on the back in congratulations. Papa said something and the tall, striking man threw back his head and laughed.

Hannah's heart hitched. The sound was like music, rising above the cacophony of the fair-like atmosphere, dancing on the wind to her ears. He turned then, and she caught a glimpse of his face. Hard. Harsh. As craggy as the moors. But, lit with his grin, striking.

Ach. She really should look away. But she couldn't.

"Husband shopping?"

Hannah whirled to frown at Susana. Heat prickled at her nape. First of all, because she'd been caught ogling. And second of all, she was tired of her sister's teasing about her reluctance to settle on a suitor.

Susana excelled at teasing.

And on the topic of suitors, there was much fodder.

"I have no idea what you mean." Hannah tried not to speak in a defensive tone but failed.

Susana smirked. "He's a fine bonny lad. I couldna blame you for drooling."

"I wasna drooling." And he wasn't a lad. He was a man.

"Although he's hardly your . . . type."

Hannah snorted. She had no "type."

"I mean, look at him." Too late. She already was. Again. That Susana was now ogling him as well sent an odd ripple of annoyance through her. "Tall. Powerful. Domineering. It's written on every line of his face. *That* is a man you could never control."

"I doona need to control everything." A mutter.

There was no call for Susana to laugh as she did. Uproariously. The sound captured the attention of every male on the field. But then, it would. Of the three Dounreay sisters, Susana was by far the prettiest, statuesque and curvy. Her hair, a riotous fall of red, was her crowning glory. Lana, the youngest, was very pretty too, with honey-blond curls and sweet, delicate features. They each took after their father, but as they had had different mothers, they were very unalike in looks and temperament.

Beside them, Hannah felt like the cuckoo in the nest. She'd inherited her mother's coloring of dark, black tresses and pale white skin. Her eyes were too large and her mouth had a crooked slant. She was hardly stunning. *Plain* was a better word for it. Aside from all that she was, well, plumpish. Perhaps it was a blessing that, as the eldest, she also came with the fertile strip of land and bustling fishing village.

Likely, without that she couldn't catch a husband at all. Certainly not the kind of husband she would want.

It was quite lowering to be desired only for one's orchards. Well, there was the castle too. And the loch. And the lucrative salt mining.

Though it was naïve in this day and age, and probably ludicrous given what she saw in the mirror, Hannah reviled the prospect of marrying a man who only wanted her land. Deep in her heart she longed for a man who might want her for *herself.*

And, if she had to marry, she wanted what Susana had had with Gilley.

But she was not Susana. She was naught but a pale shadow in comparison. She was hardly a woman to engender blind devotion. When she married, her husband would, no doubt, see her as chattel, as a broodmare. He would expect her to follow his orders rather than issuing her own.

She'd never been adept at following orders and she'd certainly never met a man to whom she would willingly surrender her freedoms. And a husband would expect that, she supposed. The thought made her shudder.

Hannah frowned and turned her attention back at the field, where other men were now stepping up to try their luck. She winced as her gaze tangled with *his*. Indeed, he'd been watching her with a scorching stare that was fierce and assessing, almost hungry. And Susana was right. As attractive as he was, he was not what Hannah was looking for in a husband. Not that she wanted a man she could control. Above all things, she craved a sweet and romantic man, one with whom she could share confidences, laughter, and late-night chats. A man with whom she could have a *connection*.

This man was a warrior. There was probably not a romantic bone in his body.

Still . . . that body. Heat blossomed on her cheeks at his frank survey and she yanked her attention to something else. Anything else.

Unfortunately, it landed on Niall Leveson-Gower, who was also staring at her. His attention made her uneasy. Then again, Niall always made her uneasy. He offered a toothy smile and she nodded in response but quickly looked away. She didn't want to encourage him. Niall was one of her suitors. His father, the Marquess of Stafford, had made no secret of the fact that he wanted to acquire Reay, a feat that could only be accomplished through marriage. To her.

Aside from the fact that she found Niall physically revolting, there was a greater peril to consider. The marquess had followed the example of the southern lairds and cleared his land, evicting his tenants to import sheep; should Reay fall into his hands, he would, no doubt, do the same there, destroying everything her family had built for generations.

She owed her people far too much to allow that to happen.

"Ooh," Susana gusted. "Now *there* is a fine figure of a man." She waggled her brows, which should have served as a warning.

Hannah glanced at the field just as Olrig waddled up to the caber toss. She grimaced. Another of her suitors, Olrig was as wide as he was tall, which she didn't mind as much as the fact that he tended to spray when he spoke. And then there was the farting.

It was unfortunate that Olrig bent over to survey the logs. The bright flash of twin fleshy moons nearly blinded her. "Good lord," she murmured.

"Such a tempting target." Susana fingered the bow draped over her shoulder; she was rarely without it.

"Nae doubt Olrig would object to an arrow in his hindquarters," Hannah advised her sister.

"Do ya think?" Susana's green eyes sparkled, but then, they always did.

With something between a screech and a bellow, Olrig tossed his caber. It didn't go far, clattering into a pile of the others and rolling even farther back. He grumbled and kicked at a hummock, as though blaming the earth for his shortcomings.

"Just think. One day, all *that* could be yours." Susana excelled at a dry tone.

But Hannah excelled at glares. She affected one. "I would rather marry a rutting pig."

Susana's shoulder rose. "Same difference. But his lands, merged with yours, would make an enviable holding."

True, but when it came to choosing a husband, a man's lands were her last concern. If she was going to bind herself to a man, give herself to a man, she wanted *something* in the bargain. *Love, passion*, a tiny voice within her whispered, but she silenced it. Love was a fool's dream. And passion? A hopeless hope.

Without conscious thought, Hannah scanned the crowd for another glimpse of that dark warrior, the one who made her body warm in a way it never had—though she would have denied it had anyone asked. Her mood drooped when she realized he was gone. "I think I've had enough of this," she said. There was no point in staying if there was nothing truly impressive to see.

"Oh, doona go," Susana cooed. "Olrig might bend over again."

"Precisely." Hannah swallowed a laugh. Once a decade was often enough for that view. Too often. "I think I may go visit the castle library."

"There's a shock."

"Do come with me."

Susana wrinkled her pert nose. "Stare at a room full of dusty tomes? I'd rather watch the games."

"And imagine how you could defeat them all?"

"Hardly a flight of fancy." It wasn't a boast. Susana had an aim so true, she could shoot a bird from the sky. Hannah couldn't hit the broad side of a castle. Unless, of course, she was aiming for something else. Likely Susana could outshoot every man in attendance. A pity she would not be invited to do so.

The gathering was for the men. Leaders from all over the region and their families had converged on Barrogill for this important meeting. The tiny village was no match for such an influx and the castle could hardly accommodate them all, so most of the lairds had set up tents on the lands surrounding the castle. The result was much like a festival. The games this afternoon would be followed by the convocation of lairds, to which none of the ladies had been invited.

Papa had dragged her to this gathering of the clans in

hopes that she would settle on a husband, but the up close and personal inspection of the contenders had done nothing but harden her heart against them all.

She glanced at her sister, whose attention was fixated on the field. "I'll see you later then?"

"Hmm." Susana didn't even look up. The archery competition had begun.

Hannah sighed and started up the path leading through the assembled tents to the castle, which was perched on the top of a rise overlooking Pentland Firth. Though the keep was very old, dating back three hundred years, it had been well tended. It rose like a sparkling jewel, surrounded by a verdant swath of green lawn.

It was rumored to have a superb library.

And ghosts. Lana would have loved that. It was a pity she had not come to the gathering. Lana didn't care for crowds and had stayed home with Susana's daughter, Isobel.

Now Isobel? Isobel would have loved this. She was far too much like her mother.

The sounds of laughter and music faded behind her as Hannah made her way through the sprawling gardens, glorying in the stiff, salt-tinged breeze and the desolate vista of the churning sea beyond. The sun slanted in the sky, bathing the trees and flowers with a soft, peaceful glow. A kestrel wheeled overhead and she paused to watch its flight. She loved nature, in all its glory, and nothing was more glorious than an afternoon in Scotland on a lovely day in May. It was—

"There ye be."

Hannah's step faltered as a deep male voice wafted toward her. She turned and raked her hair from her eyes; the wind had kicked up, dancing her tresses about her face.

Oh, bother. Niall had followed her.

Skating a look around the garden, she realized, with a

tightening in her gut, no one else was about. Likely, they were all watching the games. She sucked in a breath and braced herself for his presence. Part of her mind began planning the excuses she might offer to slip away. Of all the people she'd like to meet in a deserted garden—however pleasant it was—Niall was at the bottom of the list.

He stumbled as he scampered up the rise and then he stumbled again as he came abreast with her. Even without those clues, she would have known he'd been drinking. He stank of whisky.

"Niall."

He fixed a thin grin on his face as he dabbed the sweat from his brow. "Ye walk fast."

A complaint? Hannah didn't care. She hadn't wanted his company to begin with. She glanced toward the castle, where the legendary library awaited . . . and sighed. Perhaps she could see it another time. It didn't seem wise to venture there with a drunken Scotsman by her side.

When she turned to head back toward more populated surrounds, he skittered to keep up. "Hannah." A gasp. "I wanted to talk to you."

"Aye?" She didn't stop. Indeed, she walked faster. Something about him set her teeth on edge, and the vast solitude that had been so pleasing a moment ago was now unnerving.

He halted her with a hard hand on her arm. She frowned at him. He didn't take the hint. "I said I wanted to talk to you," he said sharply.

The thread of command in his voice irritated her and the avaricious glint in his eye made the hairs on her nape prickle. "You can talk as we walk."

"Nae." His grip tightened.

"Niall, let me go." She tried to jerk free but couldn't.

His brow furrowed; anger simmered in his eyes. "I've

offered for you twice," he said. "You denied me both times. Why have you not accepted my suit?"

Hannah tugged impatiently. "I haven't accepted anyone's suit."

His eyes narrowed to piggy slits. "I'm hardly just *anyone*. My father is a verra powerful man."

"Yes, well, I wouldn't be marrying your father, now would I?"

She should have known better than to taunt him. He was petulant and childish and a bully. His grip tightened to the point her fingers went numb. There would, no doubt, be a bruise. He leaned closer and hissed, "It willna go well for you, and your family, if you refuse me."

A threat? Fury rose within her and she yanked at her hand. He did not release it. "I will marry when I am damn good and ready. Now let me go."

He looked her up and down with a sneer. "Yer practically on the shelf."

Charming. Granted, at twenty-two she was well past the age most girls wed—indeed, Susana had married years ago—but Hannah was hardly on the shelf. Aside from which, if she was to marry it would not be this man. It would never be this man.

"Niall . . ." A warning tone.

He was not warned. He edged closer. "I willna be denied, Hannah." His breath was fusty and foul as he spat, "Perhaps you need some incentive."

Ach. She didn't like the sound of that at—

Her thoughts scattered as he yanked her toward him, whipped her around, and slammed her against a tree. Then he pinned her body with his and smothered her with his mouth.

She nearly retched. For one thing, she didn't like being manhandled—she never had. For another, he tasted sour.

Without thought she plowed a fist into his soft gut. He

doubled over with an *oof*, releasing her. She spun away, to sprint back to safety.

But he snatched at her skirts and caught her. She reached the end of her tether, as it were, and the impact caught her off guard; she tripped over her own feet, falling to the ground. The air whooshed out of her as she landed hard and smacked her chin against a stone. The impact dazed her, so she didn't move away quickly enough. Before she realized it, he was on her.

With a snarl he flipped her over onto her back and covered her, his hard groin an uncomfortable pressure against her belly. He fisted his hands in her hair and held her still as he pressed yet another kiss on her mouth. She thrashed from side to side to escape the noxious fumes, bellowing at him as best she could around the gag of his tongue.

"Shut up," he snapped, leaning up to work at something at his waist. With horror, she realized he was undoing his breeks. She tried to bring her knee up into his crotch, as she'd been taught, but he sidled between her legs, pinning her with her own skirts. When she flailed him with a series of blows to the head, he caught her hands and pinioned them with one of his.

He hovered over her, staring at her hungrily. His avid expression made something unpleasant slither through her. She knew—just *knew*—what would happen next if she didn't stop him. The prospect sickened her.

Frustration, anger, and revulsion slammed through her with every beat of her heart.

"My father is going to kill you," she hissed. And he would. If Susana didn't do so first.

Niall just laughed and tried to kiss her again. She turned her head away. Undeterred, he landed slobbery busses along her jaw. "Ye'll be ruined. Ye'll have to marry me."

"I'll never marry you."

Probably not the best thing to say to such an ardent

suitor. It only infuriated him more. His eyes narrowed. A red tide crept up his face. "I will have ye," he muttered, wriggling around to yank up her dress.

And then he froze. His entire body went still.

At the same moment, a wolfish growl rippled through the garden. It danced on the skeins of air, making the little hairs on the back of her neck stand up.

She peeped to the left and her pulse leaped.

A tall man stood over them with a sword—what looked like an ancient claymore. It was nested between Niall's legs, right where it counted. The glare of the sun blotted out the man's features, but his silhouette, broad, bulging, and shimmering with rage, was that of an avenging angel. He shifted then, just a tad, and his face became visible.

Hannah's breath caught. It was *him*. Her warrior.

Ah, God, he was magnificent. A trill of relief and an unaccountable excitement shot through her.

He was still dressed in the plaid he'd donned for the games, but this close he was even more impressive. His belly was flat and hard and layered with thick muscle, his arms bulged as he flexed, and his legs, in a wide stance, were rooted like tree trunks.

But his face . . . *Ach.* His face.

He was savage and fierce. He had a ferocious look about him, with rawboned features, a broad brow, high cheekbones, and a long blade of a nose. A ragged scar tracked its way down his left cheek.

And he was angry. His jaw bunched.

"*Shite!*" This from Niall, and naught more than a peep. He skittered away from the sharp tip of the sword and rolled to the side, which was a relief; without his weight on her, Hannah could breathe again. He scrambled to his feet and forced a laugh, though his eyes were locked on the fat sword. "We were just . . . having a chat."

The warrior's lip curled. His gaze narrowed.

"Well, we were—" Niall's throat worked.

A growl. Nothing more than a growl—low-throated and expressive beyond words.

Niall caught his meaning at once and *eeped*. Then he turned tail and ran.

While Hannah had watched this vignette with something akin to amusement, when Niall left and she was suddenly alone with this intimidating behemoth it didn't seem so funny. She didn't know this man, and he was very large. His eyes blazed with intensity.

She could well have leaped from the pan into the fire.

But before she had time to consider this, before a new fear had the opportunity to sprout, he sheathed his sword and knelt at her side.

Knelt.

His heat surrounded her. His presence enfolded her. The lines of his face dazzled her. His gaze . . . paralyzed her. There were flecks of gold in his creamy brown orbs, she noticed of a sudden, and his lashes were unnaturally long. And his lips . . . my, they were fine-looking, lush lips. . . .

When he lifted a finger, she didn't flinch away. He touched her chin, right where it still throbbed, but with a heartrending gentleness. He quirked a brow; his question was clear.

"I-I'm f-fine," she said, though her tongue barely worked. Or perhaps it was her brain that had seized. All she could think about was . . . those lips. Those exquisite lips.

His expression warmed and he nodded, and then he stood and reached out a hand.

She took it.

Purely on instinct.

She took it, and he raised her up onto her feet, holding her steady when she wobbled. Though her knees were weak, it wasn't due to the reaction of Niall's attack. It was because the sensation of this man's palm scraping over hers was dizzying.

She should have been mortified to collapse against his rock-hard chest—she was hardly a collapsing kind of girl—but she wasn't mortified. Indeed, it was quite pleasant. His heat, his scent, surrounded her.

He gazed down at her in silence—as she gazed at him, thinking about those lips. When his head lowered, an unholy thrill shot through her.

He was going to kiss her.

Oh, yes, please.

Where the prospect of Niall's kisses disgusted her, there was an entirely different kind of emotion raging through her now.

Want. Need. Probably a result of reaction, of the blood pumping in her veins, but she could not deny it.

Ah, but he didn't kiss her. Not really. With a murmur, he touched his lips to her chin, so softly, barely a whisper, brushing against the growing bruise.

It was a sweet gesture. A tender buss.

And absolutely not what she had in mind.

So she tipped her head, just slightly . . . and captured his lips.

The feel of him, the taste of him, shocked her. Earthy. Warm. A hint of velvet and mint. There was another flavor too, one she couldn't identify. It was distinctly him, and it was irresistible. She pressed closer.

To her surprise, he lurched back, eyes wide, nostrils flared. Her gut tightened at his retreat; she hadn't been finished exploring. Indeed, she could explore this man all day.

He stared down at her, his attention fixated on her mouth. His fingers on her hips flexed. The moment hummed between them. She knew—she just *knew*—he was going to kiss her again. Her breath hitched as exhilaration flared. Knowledge. Recognition.

This was a man who incited that illusive passion she'd always craved but thought beyond her reach.

This was a man to whom she might be tempted to surrender all.

The thought should have concerned her, frightened her, stopped her wayward thoughts. It did not. He was—

Her elation deflated in an instant, replaced by a howling wash of chagrin, when he released her and stepped away. In his absence, a cold wind rushed in. His features went taut, a muscle bunched in his cheek, and he gave a tiny shake of his head.

Hannah was no fool. She recognized rejection when she saw it. Something bitter tickled the back of her throat. Heat raked her. Mortification raged.

Damn and blast.

He had saved her from an overzealous suitor, as any chivalrous man would. He had touched her cheek in sympathy for her injury. He had done or said nothing to encourage her to *crawl up his body* as she had.

She should have known. A man like this would never be interested in a mousy, bookish woman with too-large eyes and a crooked mouth. A man like this would want a bold, beautiful warrior princess like Susana. They all did.

No doubt women clamored for his kisses. No doubt he had to fight them off with a stick. No doubt her kiss had been naught but an annoyance from yet another dewy-eyed lass.

She shouldn't have kissed him—though she couldn't regret that she had.

"I'm—" *No.* She would not apologize. She cleared her throat and waved back at the spot where Niall had so nearly ravaged her. "Um. Thank you. I dinna realize he had followed me until it was too late."

He nodded.

Silence sizzled between them. "I'm Hannah Dounreay." She thrust out a hand.

He stared at it.

"And you are . . . ?"

She waited for his response on bated breath, aching to know his name. Raw embarrassment still scorched her and discontent raged within her breast at the reminder that she could never attract a man like this. It would help, a little, knowing his name. At least she would know what to call him when she thought of him in the years to come. And she would.

His Adam's apple made the long slide up and down his throat. His lips parted. Hannah stared at them, trying very hard not to think about leaping on him and kissing him again. It was difficult. Something about his scent, his aura, his presence, tugged at her soul. Filled her with an unfamiliar *hunger.*

But he didn't give her his name; he wouldn't even grant her that tiny sliver. Without a word he bowed to her, spun on his heel, and strode away.

Hannah gaped at his receding form, raging emotions tumbling through her in a maelstrom. Few were pleasant. Had that been what it had seemed? A complete and utter cut direct?

How rude.

As embarrassing and dreadful and delightful as this entire debacle had been, for some reason outrage trumped all other feelings. Fury railed her. Though he was physically perfect, tempting, and . . . *tasty*, she never wanted to set eyes on him ever again.

Whoever he was.

CHAPTER TWO

Alexander Lochlannach, Laird and Baron of Dunnet, clenched his fists as he made his way back to his tent. Damn, but the touch of her lips, the dab of her tongue, had been sublime.

Hannah. Her name was Hannah.

At the thought of her, something ephemeral and enticing bubbled in his breast.

He couldn't help but notice her as he'd prepared for the caber toss, didn't miss the fact that she watched him with a gleaming interest. Indeed, he'd felt her gaze like a raging firestorm. A spear of lust.

His first glimpse of her had stunned him. She'd been laughing, with her head thrown back and her eyes alight, her hair like a river of black silk streaming down her back. She was a tiny thing with lush curves and alabaster skin. Her large brown eyes made her appear vulnerable, like a frightened fawn, but he knew better. There was strength in her, a spine of steel. The set of her chin left no room for wondering about that.

Aye, he'd wanted her on sight. He'd been *compelled* to follow her when she'd sauntered away from the festival. He'd been enraged to find her on the ground, pinned by that worm Niall Leveson-Gower.

Niall was lucky he still had his man parts. The only thing that had stayed Alexander's hand was the fact that maiming the marquess' son would probably have started an all-out war. Alexander's relationship with Stafford was rocky at best, and it was unwise to provoke a man who had the ear of the Prince Regent.

He'd considered it, though. For Hannah.

When she'd told him her name, he'd nearly laughed out loud. Some inappropriate amusement twined with bone-deep relief. *She* was the daughter his friend Magnus Dounreay, Laird of Reay, had been urging him to offer for. He could kick himself for not taking Magnus up on his invitation to visit Ciaran Reay and meet her.

Why had he resisted?

Aside from her gorgeous face, her mouthwatering form, she came fist in glove with a swath of prosperous lands. Lands any man would be honored to claim as his own.

Ah well. He knew why he'd resisted. Any lass with eyes in her head would espy his ruined face and run for the hills.

But she hadn't run for the hills. She'd *kissed* him. Kissed *him*.

And damn. He should have kissed her back.

Hell. He should have given her his name.

But when he'd stared into her mesmerizing amber eyes, his mind had seized, his throat had locked, and a familiar panic had scorched him.

He hated his curse. He always had, but never more than now.

Alexander didn't have a pretty face or a silver tongue like his brother, Andrew. And unlike other men, Alexander's wounds were not easily hidden. They taunted him daily. Every time he glanced at the glass. Every time he opened his mouth.

He tried, very hard, not to do either with any regularity.

His brother had no trouble whatsoever issuing seductive whispers to entrancing ladies. No trouble at all offering something as simple as a name. And though Alexander had worked hard to overcome his challenges, every once in a while they rose up to best him. At those times, each word, each syllable, was a torment. But he fought, fought like hell, to make sure, when he spoke, his words were bold and clear.

He resolved, the next time he saw her, he would be more prepared.

Hannah.

Aye, he'd been captivated by her at first glance, and intrigued when she told him her name and he realized the breadth of her dowry. But it hadn't been until their lips had brushed that he'd known—*known*—she was his. It had hit him like a fist to the gut.

Now that he'd held her, tasted her, he wanted her. With an unruly passion.

It was a damn shame he hadn't kissed her back. He could have shown her with his actions that which he found so difficult to say.

But he would have her. Have her he would.

His determination swelled and he changed direction, striding through the crowd, searching for Magnus. Now that Alexander had made up his mind, there was no reason to delay. Aside from which, he knew Hannah had many suitors. He would not lose her to one of them. Not now.

His steps stalled as a booming voice called his name. He fought back a grimace. *Blast.* Olrig. The last person he wanted to see right now. Ever, really. Olrig was the laird of the land to the east of Dunnetshire and through the years they'd had more conflicts than Alexander could remember—mostly because Olrig was an ass, determined to fill his coffers at all costs. He saw reeving as a game, a right of Highland lairds, and didn't flinch at sending men over the border to steal cattle, raid crofts, and cause mayhem.

Aside from that, Olrig reminded him of someone he had detested. Alexander tried not to let the resemblance prejudice him, but it was difficult when Olrig insisted on *acting* like Dermid as well.

He considered pretending not to hear, walking faster in the opposite direction, but if he knew Olrig, and he did, the man would hound him to the ends of the earth if he wanted something. Best get this over with. With a sigh Alexander turned and watched as Olrig hastened toward him.

It was slightly amusing watching Olrig hasten. He was hardly a sprightly man. Indeed, his face was red and his breath hard as he approached. Whatever he wanted to discuss must be important for him to bestir himself so.

Alexander didn't know the reedy man at Olrig's side, but there were many here he'd not met.

"Ah. Dunnet. There you are," Olrig huffed.

Alexander fixed him with a dark look.

Olrig did a credible job of hiding his flinch and forced a smile. Alexander could tell it was forced because it didn't meet his eyes. "Dunnet, have you met Scrabster?" Olrig waved to the bony man.

Ah. This was Scrabster, Olrig's neighbor to the west. Scrabster's lands bordered Reay. Though they had never met, Alexander had heard of him. None of the stories had been flattering, though they were in keeping with his constantly shifting beady eyes. Scrabster gave a brief bow. "A great pleasure to finally meet the legendary Wolf of Dunnet," he wheezed.

Alexander narrowed his eyes. He disliked the moniker.

Scrabster paled and took a step away and Olrig laughed. He clapped the slender man on his back with a force that launched him forward. "He looks ferocious, but I assure you, he is quite tame."

Where Olrig had reached that conclusion was a mystery. "Aye," Alexander said through his teeth. "Quite tame. Until someone raids my mill."

Olrig laughed again, but there was a thread of alarm in the sound. "Och, Dunnet. That was all in good fun."

"It willna be fun when winter comes and there is not enough grain in the stores to feed my people."

"I have people too," the bastard said with a shrug.

Alexander stifled a growl. Or perhaps not. "Stay off my land, Olrig," he said. "And tell your minions I will gut the next man who crosses our borders with mischief in mind."

"Well, there's nae reason to be huffy," Olrig said. Huffily.

For some reason Alexander's fist wanted, rather mightily, to plant itself into a bulbous nose. He reminded himself of his vow to control his temper; he didn't want to be the kind of man who lost it with frequency. Though with certain people controlling it was more of a challenge. It took some effort, but he managed to uncurl his fingers.

"Surely we can look past these petty squabbles," Scrabster said in a lofty tone, and Alexander's glare rounded on him. His features arranged themselves into something he probably thought was an encouraging smile. It dimmed when he caught Alexander's expression. "Ahem. I mean, I, we . . . We wanted to talk to you, Dunnet."

Ah, bluidy fooking hell. Impatience simmered. He had no time for this. He was eager to find Magnus and make his offer at once. "Aye?"

"Before the meeting," Scrabster added.

Alexander arched a brow. "About what?"

Perhaps his irritation was plain on his face or perhaps it was the ferocity of his expression, but the men exchanged pained glances and eased back. Then Olrig collected his courage, sucked in a breath, and gusted, "It has to do with Stafford."

Alexander narrowed his eyes. *Really?* Had Niall run to Daddy already? The marquess was one of the most powerful men in the region and something of a bully, but Alexander didn't care if he ran afoul of him. What his son had tried to do was heinous and—

"He has a proposal ye will want to hear," Scrabster whispered.

Now this was surprising. Although any proposal from Stafford would, no doubt, be abhorrent. The rumors and reports coming from Sutherland, where he had his seat, were sickening. Stafford was in the process of clearing his land, though they called it Improvements—evicting tenants and importing sheep to make a profit. The trouble was, the tenants had nowhere else to go and those who resisted were beaten, sent to the colonies, or killed outright. The practice had created bands of roving thieves who ravaged the Highlands, and hordes of homeless refugees. It unraveled the fabric of the clan system that made Scotland what it was.

And all for profit.

Stafford was a grasping bastard, and the worst kind of grasping bastard. One with no conscience whatsoever.

"What kind of proposal?" Alexander spat.

Perhaps he shouldn't have asked. It had the unfortunate effect of encouraging Olrig. His face lit with enthusiasm. "Come and hear him out. He's waiting for you in his tent."

Alexander's gut rippled. He had no intention of meeting with Stafford. He couldn't imagine the man having anything of interest to say. With a snort he shook his head, then turned away.

"Wait!" Olrig grabbed his arm; his hold was far too tight. Alexander glanced at Olrig's hand and growled a little in his throat. Olrig blanched and released him. "Listen, Dunnet. These are changing times. You will want to be onboard for this."

Something in his tone made Alexander's blood go cold. "What do you mean?" He ground out the words through clenched teeth.

Olrig leaned closer. The stench of his sweat engulfed Alexander like a cloud. "As you know, Stafford is . . . close to the Prince Regent."

"Aye."

"The word is, the prince will soon give him the title of Duke of Sutherland."

Alexander frowned. He didn't know why this would affect him. His lands were not in Sutherland County; his overlord was the Duke of Caithness.

"Rumor has it, when Stafford receives the title, the prince will gift him Caithness' lands as well."

It was hard not to gape. With both counties, Stafford would hold all of northern Scotland. Including Dunnet. Alexander set his teeth. "And what of the Duke of Caithness?"

He didn't like Olrig's grin. "We doona need to worry about Lachlan Sinclair."

The little hairs on Alexander's nape prickled. Lachlan Sinclair, the aforementioned duke, Alexander's ancestral overload and Chief of the Clan, had been an absentee laird for decades, eschewing his homeland for the frolics of London. He had recently returned to Scotland, though he hadn't bothered to attend this convocation of his lairds.

A huge mistake.

Still and all, he was the laird of all baronies in the county. And a duke. Alexander owed him his fealty. "So, what does Stafford want from me?"

Olrig clapped him on the back. "See, I knew you would be interested." He wasn't, but it behooved him to know what machinations were happening around him. "Stafford knows, if he receives the blessings of the barons, the prince will be more inclined to gift him the land when Caithness dies. It makes sense, as Caithness has no heirs."

Alexander's first reaction was revulsion at the thought of giving Stafford his *blessing* to claim Dunnet. No doubt he would raze the crofts and burn out the villages as he had on his own land.

But a darker thought supplanted Alexander's annoyance. *When Caithness dies? Holy hell.* Was this treason? It sounded like it. He crossed his arms and fixed Olrig with a narrow-eyed stare. "But Caithness is young." Thirty, if that.

Scrabster snorted. "All the Sinclair men die young. And from all accounts, the duke is ailing and weak. The Prince Regent knows this. Stafford knows this."

And, no doubt, Stafford would be willing to help the duke along on his journey, should the opportunity arise. No doubt Stafford wouldn't quail at murdering a peer if it meant taking ownership of every scrap of land from Scourie to Wick.

Alexander had never even met his overlord and all of the baronies had suffered as a result of their overlord's negligence, but that fact didn't dampen the loyalty he felt for Caithness' office. As a Scotsman Alexander held a fierce devotion to the clan system—despite its recent decimation. He would remain loyal to Caithness regardless of his failings, and he would never budge on that.

Not ever.

This whole conversation sickened him.

Without a word he turned his back on Olrig and resumed his hunt for Magnus.

"Dunnet! Dunnet!" Olrig bellowed. "Stafford is waiting for you."

Alexander ignored him. Stafford could rot.

And, for that matter, so could Olrig, Scrabster, and their ilk.

Fury savaged Alexander as he made his way through the festival grounds. He was aware of the wide-eyed glances he received and the fact that men scuttled to remove themselves from his path, but he paid them no mind. While he didn't like being feared, he allowed it. Because a man would think twice, or three times, or more before threatening that which Alexander held dear. And, at the moment, he was not in the mood to weave through the crowd.

Being frightening did have its advantages on occasion.

He found Magnus near the lists watching a mock battle that had all the earmarks of turning very real. It was never wise to give Scotsmen weapons and an opportunity to work out old grudges on a field of combat, even if it was supposed to be for fun. There was more than one nose streaming with blood.

Magnus' eyes lit up as he spotted him. He clapped Alexander on the shoulder and boomed, "Ah, Dunnet."

"Sir, I would like to speak with you if I may."

"Certainly."

"In . . . private."

Magnus studied him for a moment, his smile dimming. Then he nodded. "What do you say to a spot of whisky in my tent?"

Alexander nodded, though it was not whisky he was after, and the two men turned and made their way through the milling throng. Though his resolve had not wavered, Alexander's nerves roiled. He'd decided to make the biggest step of this life and take a bride. This was the most significant meeting of his life. He hoped to God his friend would look favorably on his offer. More than that, he hoped that Hannah would.

Magnus held open the flap to his tent and Alexander bowed his head and stepped through. It was one of the larger tents here and was set up with a sitting area in front and sleeping quarters in back. He couldn't stifle the riffle of awareness that *this* was where she slept. It took some effort, but he pushed the thought from his mind and concentrated on the matter at hand.

Negotiations.

As Magnus headed for the whisky set on the table in the sitting area, he sighed. "I canna tell you how relieved I am that you are here, Dunnet. A rational head amidst fools." Aye, he and Magnus saw eye to eye on many issues, unlike some of the other barons. It was one of the reasons Alexander respected the man as much as he did. "You wouldna believe the conversation I had with Scrabster today."

Alexander took the proffered drink and sat in one of the chairs. "Did it involve Stafford?"

Magnus snorted. "What on earth is he thinking?"

"He's thinking he will rule the entire northern coast."

"Bah. And he will too, if the rumors are true." They shared a dark glance. Neither of them savored the thought of having Stafford as an overlord. "The problem is, we're in the back of beyond. The prince doesna give a tinker's damn about the Highlands and, unfortunately, neither does Caithness."

"He is still our laird."

"True. But you and I may be the only two who see it that way. Why, even Morac was *blethering* this nonsense." Magnus took a generous sip of his drink. "Nae doubt they are all anxious to end up on the side of the victor."

"And you think that will be Stafford?"

Magnus shrugged. "He is powerful. And present. Until recently, Caithness hasna set foot in Ackergill since he was a lad. How can a man demand fealty from barons he's never even spoken to? If that boy had a brain in his head, he would hie to each holding and whip these barons into shape. They've been allowed to run amok for far too long."

It was true. And with the ill winds blowing across Scotland, misdeeds and mayhem were all too common.

"Ah, but enough about politics. What did you want to discuss?" Magnus pinned him with a piercing gaze and all of a sudden Alexander's throat locked.

He swallowed heavily and stiffened his spine. "Sir, I—"

When Magnus smacked him on the leg, it derailed his thoughts and he sputtered into silence. The old man waggled a finger. "That's the second time you've called me sir. This must be serious business indeed."

Aye. It was.

Alexander sucked in a deep breath and began again. "Sir . . . I would like to talk to you about your . . . daughter." The reluctance of the words to flow smoothly irritated him, but he forced them out.

Magnus' eyes widened and then he barked a laugh. "Ah. Clapped eyes on my Susana, did you? I should have known. She's a right beauty. And every man has that reaction. But I warn you, she is a stubborn one."

Alexander stared at him. *Susana?* "Nae."

"Nae?"

"Not Susana. Hannah." *Ah.* It felt so right, speaking her name for the first time.

He had no earthly idea why Magnus gaped at him. "Hannah?" He shook his head. "Are you sure you doona mean Susana? With the red hair?"

"Nae." Long, inky tresses. Wide brown eyes. Thick lashes. Lush lips. "Hannah."

"Oh." Magnus studied him for a moment and then his face broke into a grin. "Oh."

"I . . ." *Damn it.* Why did this always happen when he needed to say something important? "I should like your permission to offer for her."

"Excellent." Magnus clapped his hands together and leaped to his feet. "Excellent choice. I think this calls for a drink." He hummed to himself as he filled two more glasses. He appeared to be surprised when he returned and saw Alexander already had one and it was untouched. With a shrug, Magnus set the new drinks next to the one he was working on.

"Magnus . . . Do you think Hannah would be . . . amenable to an offer?"

Magnus tapped his lip. "Hard to say. Hannah is my eldest and nearly as stubborn as Susana. But then, all my girls are stubborn in their own way, truth be told. Comes from not having a mother, I'd wager. Wouldn't you?" Alexander didn't respond. He had no idea why women were stubborn. "But she's a good girl, an exceptional catch, make no mistake about it. Strong and willful. Sturdy."

Sturdy?

Not the word he would use to describe her. *Ravishing* came more to mind.

"She has her share of suitors, mind you, given her properties." Magnus waggled his brows. "She's rebuffed them all. I do admit I've been despairing the girl will ever choose a husband." He sighed and fixed his gaze on Alexander; his smile tweaked again. "But I do believe the two of you would suit and, frankly, I would be delighted to have a man like you in the family. Tell you what. You send an offer and, in the meantime, I will work on her." He winked. "With any luck, she will see sense. But I warn you, she is stubborn."

"Aye. You did . . . mention that."

"But she has to marry sometime, does she no'? And frankly, I canna think of a better man." He pressed his hands together and glanced toward the heavens. "Pray God she sees it that way."

It warmed his heart that Magnus held him in such high esteem, and as Alexander left his tent he couldn't stop the trickle of anticipation sifting through his bowels.

She might be a stubborn woman, but he could be stubborn too. Once he set his mind on something, he did not change it.

And he'd set his mind on Hannah. And her land.

CHAPTER THREE

Hannah settled herself on her favorite bench in the garden and opened the long-awaited book with a sigh. It had been impossible to read on the bumpy ride back from Barrogill. Aside from which, her mind had whirled with thoughts of *that man*. Her ire had only grown.

She'd tried to discover his identity, but it was difficult to do so without exposing her interest to her father. Such a revelation—that she had an interest in *any* man—would lead to disaster. Though surely it wasn't interest. She merely wanted to know who he was. So she could avoid him in the future.

That she'd dreamed about him did not signify.

With great resolve she thrust all thoughts of him from her mind and attempted to focus on a fascinating treatise on crop rotation. Her concentration was shattered when an arrow whizzed past her head.

It wasn't often an arrow whizzed past one's head when one was reading a tome on agronomy in the garden, but when it did it behooved one to investigate. She closed the book on her finger and stood.

A mistake.

The next arrow was far closer. She felt the kiss of air on her cheek as it flew by.

She spotted her nemesis. Indeed, the archer was difficult to miss. The startling white-blond hair was like a beacon.

"Isobel Mairi MacBean. Please do stop shooting at me!"

This she called loudly, as her niece had a vexing tendency to ignore things she didn't want to hear.

Isobel nocked another arrow in her tiny bow. A tiny bow for a tiny body, but the arrows were still sharp. Hannah thought it prudent to duck. Once the arrow had been loosed, thankfully at a long-suffering tree, Hannah charged through the flowers to her niece's side. Where she was less likely to offer an easy target.

"What are you doing, darling?" she asked, forcing a light tone but taking the precaution of snatching the remaining arrows from the quiver.

Isobel blinked at her in surprise, as though Hannah had appeared from thin air. "Oh, hullo, Aunt Hannah. I'm practicing. Mama said I should practice."

Honestly. What was Susana thinking, giving her five-year-old daughter a bow and setting her loose on the denizens of Reay? The parish would never be the same.

"But not in the garden, dearest." When people were reading.

Enormous blue eyes widened. Long lacy lashes fluttered. "Would the library be a better place?"

"Good God, no." She could only imagine it. All of her favorite books, bristling with arrows like so many hedgehogs. Hannah tried to scowl, but she really wasn't very good at scowling and Isobel's glee was infectious. "You very nearly skewered me."

Isobel leaned in and whispered, "I missed you on purpose." She grinned then, an irresistible mix of mischief and mayhem. And dimples. Hannah had no clue where Isobel had gotten her dimples. They were probably on loan from the devil himself. "May I have my arrows back?"

"You absolutely may not." She was lucky Hannah didn't snap them in half. " 'Tis time for breakfast. I'm sure your mother is wondering where you've gone off to."

Isobel readjusted her empty quiver and snorted. Oddly, much like her mother might snort. "She's still sleeping."

"Nae doubt you exhaust her." Hannah tried to take the bow, as well as the arrows, but Isobel tightened her grip. *Ah well.* Maybe next time. If she was diligent. The bow definitely needed to disappear. Maybe they could blame it on the Grey Lady.

Castle ghosts were convenient for things like this.

"Come along," Hannah said, wrapping her arm around her niece's slender shoulders and leading her back inside. As always, when Hannah's gaze hit the rose stones of the ancient battlements of her home her heart hitched. Particularly now, in the early-morning light, kissed by the tender lips of dawn, it was stunning.

Merciful heavens, she loved it here. She loved everything about it, from the village of Ciaran Reay to the outlying crofts. She loved the tacksmen, the shopkeepers, and the fishermen. She loved the scent of the sea in her nostrils and the smell of newly mown hay in the harvest. She loved the taste of crisp Reay apples and the sweet bite of heather honey. She loved managing the land and overseeing the work of her people.

And she loved her family. Her *life* was here.

She didn't want to leave.

If she married, she would have to. Brides did cleave to their husbands. Or at least that was what she'd been told.

Papa was already seated in the morning room when they entered; he was surrounded by piles of letters. He paused in his work to tug Isobel into an enormous hug. She wriggled away and scampered to the sideboard to peruse the buffet, where she proceeded to *touch* everything. Hannah ripped her attention from the disturbing sight of Isobel licking a scone and then setting it back on the plate when Susana burst into the room like a summer shower.

Susana always burst into rooms. She was a force of nature. She hung her bow on the back of her chair, and ignoring their father's scowl—as he didn't approve of weapons at the table—she sauntered to the sideboard and selected her breakfast.

"Good morning, all," she breezed as she sat next to her daughter, dropping a kiss on Isobel's soft white curls. Isobel, glutting herself with cakes, ignored her. Susana didn't seem to notice. "What a lovely day!" she gusted.

Hannah fixed a stern expression on her face. "Isobel was shooting in the garden again." It was probably bad form to tattle and indeed Isobel glowered at her, but something had to be said. Someone could be skewered.

Susana beamed at her daughter. "Excellent. Did you hit anything?" she asked.

"She almost hit me," Hannah grumbled, but they both pretended not to hear.

"I almost hit a rabbit."

"Ach, my wee warrior. You'll get it next time."

Isobel grinned. The devil's dimples rippled. She probably would get it next time.

Poor rabbit.

"I wouldna mind some rabbit stew," Papa murmured, and Hannah frowned at him. One should not be inciting a child to mayhem.

Then again, Isobel required little encouragement.

Hannah considered renewing her objections to being barraged with arrows before breakfast but decided it was pointless. Also, it reminded her she'd not yet had breakfast. Her stomach growled at the thought. She made her way to the sideboard, attempting to find some sustenance that had not yet been licked. She settled on eggs and a nice slice of beef.

As she was finishing up, Lana drifted into the room.

She paused in a shaft of sunlight and her body, willowy and lithe, was imbued with an angelic glow. The rays danced off her golden curls.

It was probably beneath Hannah to entertain that lance of envy; she tried to ignore it, but it was a trial to do so. Between the two of them, her sisters often made Hannah feel . . . inadequate.

But then Lana smiled at her and her discontent dissolved. Lana had a magical smile, a calming, soothing spirit that made every person in her presence feel embraced. Lana was a special soul, with a special gift, and although Hannah couldn't claim to understand it, she did her best to support her sister's . . . eccentricities. "Good morning," she said softly as she made her way to the buffet and piled her plate high with bacon.

Hannah wished she could eat a plate of bacon, but she lacked Lana's svelte physique. If Hannah ate what she wanted, she would probably have to be rolled from the room.

That in itself was terribly unfair. Life often was.

Upon second thought, Hannah selected a cake—though it had probably been licked—and turned back to the table.

Papa gored her with a gaze sharper than any arrow. "A new offer has come, girlie."

She endeavored not to wince. A sense of dread clogged her throat.

She always hated when new offers arrived, as each was more depressing than the last. As a general rule, her suitors were less than inspiring. Dirlot had a forest of sprouting ear hair, Olrig was a rather squatty sort, with a distinct waddle to his walk, and Brims was eighty if he was a day. He also had a rather alarming propensity for hacking up phlegm.

Not that she minded phlegm, but, as a rule, not in her soup.

"Ooh," Susana cooed, buttering a bannock. "Who is it this time?" She sent Hannah a minxish grin. And why not? Susana knew she was safe. As she was a widow, there was no pressure for her to marry. None at all.

"Stafford again?" Lana asked with a frown.

"I hope not." Hannah shuddered at the memory of Niall's kiss; aside from the fact that he had tried to overpower her, he kissed like a trout. She couldn't imagine living with him, much less kissing him again. She did hope for a husband she wanted to kiss on occasion. Especially now that she knew what a kiss could be like—

The memory of a bold, harsh face surfaced. Prickling with annoyance, she forced all thoughts of that magnificent, infuriating man away and focused on the conversation. Or tried to, at least.

"It is from Dunnet." Why her father chortled she had no clue.

"Dunnet?" Susana pierced her poached egg. She was fond of piercing things. The yolk bubbled up and oozed out and she sighed as she watched it flow. And then her brow wrinkled. "The boozy old fart?" Her grin at Hannah was evil. "Quite in keeping with your retinue."

Hannah forbore from sticking out her tongue, but barely.

"That was the uncle." Papa's lip curled. "Never liked that man. He died, oh, several years back. Got himself drunk one night and tumbled from the castle battlements. This is *Alexander*." This he said as though it *meant* something. "He's a good man. Not much for words, but a good man." He waggled his brows at Hannah. "You would suit. Of all the barons, he is one of the few who have spoken out against these damned Improvements."

"I doona know how they can call them Improvements," Lana gusted. "Evicting tenants and importing sheep?"

Isobel nodded, nibbling her cake. "Sheep are stupid."

"Aye, they are." Hannah couldn't help but agree. "But

political beliefs canna be the sole standard by which I choose a husband."

Susana narrowed her eyes. "*Is* there a standard by which you choose a husband? Because from what I can tell you have rejected them all . . . summarily."

"Hardly summarily." Hannah bristled. "I am being *prudent*."

For some reason, Lana found this amusing. Her laugh rippled through the room.

Hannah frowned at her. "What's so funny?"

"You," Lana said. "Describing yourself as prudent."

"I'm always prudent."

Snorts—a quartet of them—rounded the table.

"I am."

"You're impulsive," Susana proclaimed.

Lana patted Hannah's hand. "Impetuous."

"Reckless." This from her niece, in a warble.

Hannah grimaced. "*Et tu*, Isobel?"

The demon grinned widely.

Papa gusted a dramatic sigh. "Think on it, lass. Dunnet has profitable lands and a strong following. Practically an army of warriors at his beck and call. Even the Marquess of Stafford would hesitate to stand up to him. And he's a robust, hearty lad. Not decrepit like the others. You would make fine sons together."

"I've never even met him."

"You've probably seen him. He was at Barrogill." For some reason, Papa's eyes glinted.

It sent a prickle up her nape. "He was?"

"Aye. He won the caber toss. Verra impressive, that."

"He-he . . . won . . . ?" Hannah's pulse throbbed; her mind whirled. Heat crept up her cheeks as the image of *that man* flickered.

No.

Surely it couldn't be him.

And why was it suddenly so difficult to breathe?

Susana shot her a sharp look. Her lips quirked. "Dunnet, eh? Is he tall, with dark curls? Broad shoulders and fine muscled legs?"

Hannah could have throttled her.

"The one with the scar?"

The vision of *his* face filled Hannah's mind, as though it had been burned there. *A scar? Aye. He'd had one.* It had done nothing but make him more savagely attractive.

Papa's eyes lit up. "Aye. That's the man. Did you see him?"

See him? She'd *kissed* him.

And then he'd rejected her. He'd stormed away without so much as a word. Every time she remembered it, her humiliation grew. And now . . . Now he was offering for her?

Why?

Her breakfast churned in her belly.

Oh heavens. She knew why.

Though her kiss had clearly revolted him, he'd somehow discovered she came with a fat dowry and decided he wanted her after all. Apparently, the enticement of Reay lands was far too strong to resist. Certainly strong enough to compel a man to take a bluestocking antidote he couldn't bear to kiss into his marriage bed.

Fury rose and roiled. And there, twined with it, a ribbon of pain. "I am not marrying that man." Hannah hadn't intended to blurt the declaration; she opened her mouth and it spilled forth as though forced out by the pressure welling in her chest.

The disappointment in her father's eyes gouged at her. "You're going to have to choose one of them, lass. I'm not gonna live forever and the vultures are circling."

"Of course you're going to live forever," Susana said, patting his hand.

He ignored her. “Hannah. My wee lass. You’re going to have to choose one.” This he murmured softly in a thready, tired voice.

Hannah’s heart thumped once and then went still at the bone-weary expression on his face. “Papa. Are you . . . all right?”

“Strong as a bear.” A gruff boast. “But time is running out.” He squeezed her hand with an intensity that frightened her. “Promise me you will choose soon.” A whisper.

“I will.” *Ah, merciful heavens.* The hardest words she’d ever spoken. But the best, perhaps, for the worry faded from his brow and he smiled around the table. “Good. Good. Now, what are your plans for today, my girls?”

“I’m going shooting,” Isobel chirped.

“Hopefully not in the library,” Hannah murmured.

Susana sent her a befuddled glance but didn’t comment. “I’m planning to work with Torquil in the apiary.”

Hannah wrinkled her nose. She loved honey, but bees had an unfortunate habit of stinging. “Do be careful.”

Susana waved her hand. “I’m always careful.”

A boldfaced lie.

“I fancy a walk in the woods.” Lana winked at Isobel. “Please try not to shoot me.”

Isobel grinned. “I shall *try*.”

“And you, Hannah?” Papa asked. “What mischief will you be up to?”

Nothing as adventurous as mischief. “A ride, I think.”

Isobel blew out a breath and Susana chuckled. “There’s a surprise.”

“Beelzebub needs exercise. The grooms were too frightened to ride him while we were away.”

“Small wonder.” Papa’s brows rumpled. “That beast is a menace.”

“He’s magnificent.” He was. And she’d missed him. In fact, she was itching for a ride. Hannah stood and kissed her father on the top of his head. "Have a wonderful day, Papa," she said as she breezed from the room.

"T'will be a wonderful day indeed when you choose a husband!" he called after her.

Hannah sighed. As always, it was best to let him have the final word.

As she made her way to the stables, she resolved to enjoy her ride, even if that meant *not* thinking about her suitors, not even once.

And Alexander, Laird of Dunnet, was the last thing on her mind. Really. He was.

~

Beelzebub chomped at the bit as Hannah approached to greet him. "Hello, my darling," she cooed. He tossed his head and showered her with a wet spray. "Impatient, are ye?" He truly was a magnificent stallion, all glossy black from tip to tail, and aye, he was something of a terror, at least to those who didn't understand him.

Hannah adored him. He was wild and unrestrained and he ran like the wind. She never felt more glorious, never freer, than when she was on his back.

"My lady." Rory tugged at his forelock. "He's ready and waiting."

"Thank you, Rory. Did he give you much trouble?"

The groom's blush was telling. She tried not to chuckle as she led the beast to the mounting block.

"Would you like an escort?" Rory asked, his brow wrinkling with concern as he watched her mount. He knew better than to offer to help.

She shot him a grin as she settled into the saddle. He asked each time she went for a ride. They both knew the answer. Without hesitation she set her heels to the stallion's flank and he shot from the stable yard into the bailey, his muscles bunching with pent-up energy and the anticipation of a good hard run. As they pounded over the cobbles and under the portcullis, chickens scattered and sheep scuttled out of the way with plaintive *baa*s. And then, once they reached the open road, they flew.

It was splendid.

It was a lovely day for a ride. The breeze was cool and the sun shone down through the spotty clouds overhead in a soft, watery light. There were some shadows in the sky. No doubt it would rain later, but for now the road leading toward the loch was dry and spattered with colorful blooms. Some would call them weeds. But Hannah was not some; she loved every flower, weed or no.

Because it had been so long since she'd ridden, Hannah decided on a ride around the loch. Enough to give Beelzebub a much-needed outing, warm his muscles, but not enough to exhaust him. Though she knew he would run and run like the wind as long as she allowed it. Aside from that, she loved to take the curving road as it wound in and out of the woods. It was much more exciting than the straight stretch to the east.

Hannah bent low over Beelzebub's neck and urged him on, exulting in the feel of the wind in her hair and the taste of adventure. In tandem with the churning dust kicked up by Beelzebub's heels, her thoughts roiled. They tumbled through her mind like water through a burn, nearly too fast to capture.

Not the least of which was the realization that once she settled on a husband there would be no more reckless rides like this. No doubt a husband would want to fetter her freedoms, chain her up and lock her in. She'd seen more than one of her carefree friends tender their independence for a ball and chain.

Other thoughts ran rampant as well. Most of them circled around a certain tall, silent, simmering man—the kind of man for whom she had yearned, except for his rudeness, and the fact that he'd offered for her. She was torn between a bothersome tug of longing . . . and irritation.

Above all things, she wanted warmth in a husband. Someone who would laugh with her and share ideas. Someone who would accept her as an equal. Should he prove to be malleable, well, so much the better.

Dunnet, that hard, dark warrior, was nothing of the sort.

Beyond that, she couldn't thrust that kiss from her mind. Or, more to the point, the fact that he'd ended it so abruptly. Ended it and then reared back and stared at her with that *look* in his eye.

What had it been? Disgust? Revulsion?

Regardless, it made an uncomfortable heat prickle on her skin. *He* made heat prickle on her skin. And she didn't like it.

Papa made a good point about Dunnet's following, though. Of late there had been a rash of raids on the outlying crofts, reevers and thieves. It would be nice to have additional security in the upheaval caused by the Clearances to the west. *Damn Stafford anyway.*

But how foolish would she be to marry him? A man who made her *feel* the way he did . . . when he saw her as no more than a chunk of land—

Beelzebub reared and Hannah's heart leaped into her throat. Madly she grasped at the reins to keep from being thrown, then sawed back to bring her mount under control. As Beelzebub danced, she glanced up and stilled. Something curled in her belly.

Three men on horseback blocked the road. They were men she did not know.

Hannah frowned. She'd spent her entire life here. She knew everyone, but there had been a flood of strangers coming to Reay of late, usually under the cover of night and usually up to no good.

As she calmed her mount, she felt for her dirk. When she found the hilt, tucked in her belt, her panic eased. If they were bent on mischief, at least she had a weapon.

"Who are you?" she called.

The largest one smiled. It was not a pleasant smile. "It's her," he said, and Hannah's unease flared again. "He said she'd come this way."

He? He who?

"What do you want?" Hannah clenched her knees, telling Beelzebub to be ready to wheel and run. His muscles quivered. He whinnied and shook his head. His eyes rolled back toward her.

With a prickling at her nape Hannah glanced over her shoulder. Her heart dropped as two more men emerged from the woods behind her, effectively blocking her in.

And one of them was Niall.

Hannah narrowed her eyes and spun her horse around. She glared at Niall. "What the hell are you doing here?" she snapped.

He tipped his head to the side and tsked in a manner that made irritation skitter up her spine. She hated being patronized, and tsking infuriated her. "Honestly, Hannah. Did I not warn you?"

"Warn me? What are you talking about?"

"I told you I was determined to have you."

Oh lord in heaven above. Hannah blew out a breath. "Niall, I'm not marrying you."

"O' course ye will, girlie." The man next to Niall smirked. "Ye could be a marchioness."

"I doona give a whit for titles."

"My father is a powerful man," Niall said. "He will be a duke one day. And from all accounts, your da is weak. Ailing. He canna stop my father from taking what he wants. And he *wants* Reay."

Niall edged closer, far too close for comfort. As his

mount approached, Beelzebub danced restlessly. Hannah knew, if Niall didn't, Beelzebub hated to be closed in; he'd been known to attack horses that got too close. Still, she didn't warn Niall, because now that he'd moved there was an opening between the two men. Not a huge one, but enough for her to charge through if the chance presented itself.

"Papa is not weak."

"He is. He's weak and he's old. And his forces are laughable. You know that croft that burned down last week?"

Hannah stilled. The fire had been a tragedy. The family who lived there had not escaped. Husband, mother, and child had perished in the blaze. "What about it?"

Niall's response was an oily smile. "Such a pity."

"Are you saying *you* caused that fire?" Horror curled in her gut.

"And the cattle that have been disappearing? With regularity?"

A cold fist gripped Hannah's heart. Prickles rose on the back of her neck. *Bloody hell. Was it him? Was it all him?*

"It will only get worse, Hannah, unless you marry me now. It would be a damn shame if your granary caught fire. Or your sister . . . disappeared." He leaned closer. His fetid breath gusted over her face. "Or if your poor da should take a tumble."

Hannah's skin went clammy. Sweat beaded on her brow. The thought of Papa, Lana, Susana or Isobel in danger appalled her. "You are a bastard," she snarled.

He had the temerity to look put out. "Is that any way to speak to your husband?"

"Jesus, Mary, and Joseph, Niall. How many times do I have to tell you, I'm not marrying you!"

"You will, actually. In fact, if that bastard Dunnet hadn't interfered in Barrogill, we'd be married already."

Not hardly.

Niall glanced around at his men. They all urged their mounts closer. "We're here to make sure of that. Today. You might as well make this easy on us. Come along peacefully." He flicked his reins and his horse eased forward. Beelzebub nickered and pawed the dirt, but Niall was oblivious. Niall was a fool.

Without warning he grabbed for her, fisting her sleeve. She lunged back and the sound of tearing fabric rocketed through the glen.

Fury raged. She made a sound. Something like a snarl.

This was her favorite dress.

He leaned in again, to make another attempt to get hold of her, but Hannah whipped out her dirk and swiped at him. He lurched out of range, but at the same time Beelzebub did what he'd been wanting to do for a while and nipped at Niall's horse's rump. The beast wheeled away with a scream. The momentum, and Niall's wild lunge, knocked him from his seat. He fell into the dirt with a warbled curse.

Hannah saw her chance—a wide berth through which she could charge—and she took it. With a feral growl she hunkered down over Beelzebub's neck and surged forward, through the breach. The man who had been beside Niall made a grab for her as she passed, but Hannah saw his hand coming and met it with the swipe of her dirk.

She didn't tarry to see what damage she had done. She set her heels and gave Beelzebub rein. The men followed her, of course. She could hear the pounding of the hooves twining with their furious shouts, but no horse could outrun Beelzebub, so she quickly outpaced them.

No doubt, her fury gave her wings.

Beyond all that, outrage boiled in her veins.

Niall thought to make a show of her father's weakness in an attempt to force her hand? Making her people suffer to bring her to heel? Aside from the fact that she would die before submitting to such a man, Hannah hungered for the opportunity to thwart him.

This land belonged to *her*, not the Marquess of bluidy Stafford or his son.

And damn them to hell! How dare he try to kidnap her and force her into marriage? This act of outright villainy must not go unanswered.

But what could they do? Theirs was a small holding amongst small holdings. Their overlord, the Duke of Caithness, didn't give a fig about their well-being. They could send a plea to him or to the Prince Regent himself, but Hannah doubted either would bother to respond. The English thought the Scots all savages anyway.

Standing alone against Stafford was no longer an option, either. This much was clear. Her father had many fine men beneath his banner, but not nearly enough to fight Stafford. Not even enough to scare him.

It was up to Hannah to protect her people from further incursions. The only way to do that was to unite with a man who would give Stafford pause.

And only one such man, amongst the legion of her suitors, came to mind.

So he only wanted her for her land.

So he was dour and rude.

It no longer mattered.

When she arrived at the castle, she leaped from the saddle and tossed the reins to Rory, then she stormed into her father's office. He stared at her with his mouth agape; his gaze settled on her shredded neckline and then flicked to her tousled hair. "Hannah? What happened?"

"Send a missive to Dunnet at once," she commanded before her courage fled. "Tell him I have accepted his suit and intend to marry him with all haste."

She didn't imagine her father's lips quirked into a smile. Then again, he didn't bother to hide it.

CHAPTER FOUR

So. Damn. Satisfying.

Alexander brought his sword down on his opponent's with a resounding clang that echoed through the meadow. The blades tangled and then the other man's arm weakened; his stance collapsed. He whirled and came at Alexander from another angle, but he was ready for him and blocked the strike.

And then Alexander advanced, battering the brigand with one hard whack after another, driving him back. The man stumbled over a hummock and fell on his arse, his weapon clattering to the ground. He stared up at Alexander with his eyes wide. Desperation flickered over his features. It was clear he was convinced the end was nigh. But Alexander didn't intend to kill him—though he deserved it. He just wanted to teach the blighter a lesson.

Alexander tossed his sword to the side and wrenched the man up by his collar.

"Stop," he said, handing a blow to the man's midsection. "Stealing." Another blow. "My cattle." With a final punch, this time to a pointy chin, he let the man go. He tumbled into the dirt and lay there, moaning.

"Well," a too-chipper voice came from behind Alexander. "That was fun to watch."

Alexander whirled, his blood still high. He'd been furious to ride up on yet another raid in progress, determined to make a statement here and now.

Dunnet lands and people would be protected with ferocity.

He frowned at his brother. "You could have helped."

Andrew shrugged and set his hand on the hilt of his sword. His *sheathed* sword. His blue eyes twinkled; his dimples danced. "You were having too much fun. I dinna want to ruin it for you." His grin was slightly crooked, and mischievous. It usually was.

They were like two sides of a coin, the brothers, Alexander dark and silent and Andrew bright and lighthearted. His face was chiseled like a Greek sculpture, flawless in every respect, and his hair, a startling shock of white, caught every lady's eye. Though they were both big men, well-muscled and strong, with the blood of ancient Norsemen coursing through their veins, Andrew had gotten all the good looks in the bargain.

Alexander should resent him for the ease with which he breezed through life, but he couldn't. The bastard was too damn charming for anyone to begrudge him his gifts. Also, he was the only family Alexander had in the world and he loved him so much it made his chest ache sometimes.

Hiding his sudden swell of emotion, he bent and picked up his sword, wiping off the dirt. "Well, thank you for nothing," he grumbled.

"It wasn't nothing. It was an enormous sacrifice." Andrew blinked innocently. "Do you have any idea how much it cost me to exert such restraint? I would have loved to trounce that bastard." *Aye.* Andrew did love swordplay. And trouncing people. It was something of a sport for him. "But I let you have the pleasure."

"Again, thank you?"

"You needed the distraction."

Alexander set his teeth. "What do you mean?"

"Seriously?" Andrew barked a laugh. "Ever since you returned from Barrogill you've been a bear."

He had been. Even more surly than usual. "I've been . . . preoccupied." Since he'd sent his offer to Magnus, he'd had one thing and one thing only on his mind.

Hannah.

He'd been lashed with dueling bouts of excitement and dread. She'd refused every man who'd offered for her hand. It was quite possible she could refuse Alexander as well. Now that he'd made up his mind about marrying her and adding the Reay lands to his holdings, he couldn't countenance the prospect that she might say no. Beyond that, he couldn't evict the memory of her sweet lips and her sweeter form.

And that kiss . . .

God in heaven above. That kiss. Shivers skittered down his spine at the memory. Surely that boded well for his suit. It had nearly blinded him, the innocent passion in that simple buss. It bemused him still.

It wrapped him in the coils of fantasy and hope, battered him with thoughts about the ebony silk of her hair and how it would feel twined in his fist; or her rosy lips, or her amber eyes. Or her body, lush and full and oh, so soft.

She crept into his mind more often than he should allow.

Especially at night, when all his work had been dispensed with, when he lay in the cold clutch of his enormous bed . . . alone. He thought of her. Dreamed of her. And at those times, the desire within him rose.

And discipline evaded him.

Even the fear that she could reject him didn't dampen his obsession.

She might say no, but she might say yes. The prospect thrilled him to the core.

"Aye. You have been preoccupied," Andrew said. His expression sobered. He looked away. "Hopefully you will hear back soon."

"I hope so." The wait was untenable.

The man on the ground stirred and then, with a leery glance at Alexander, scurried away. The two brothers watched as he ran.

"Should we chase him down?" Andrew asked.

Alexander responded with a shake of his head, "Nae. Let him run. Let him return to Olrig and explain why he has arrived empty-handed." Let Olrig know the Laird of Dunnet would no longer tolerate these petty attempts to needle him.

"Do you think Olrig is behind this?"

"Aye." Indeed, since their heated altercation in Barrogill conditions on the border had deteriorated. As though Olrig had given orders to pester him into submission.

The bastard should know better.

Alexander would not be pestered. Or cowed. Or bullied into joining Olrig's coalition of lairds. He could not be compelled to commit what was, in his mind, treason against his overlord.

"Shall we continue on?" Andrew asked.

Alexander nodded and headed back to Wallace, who stood patiently on the rise nipping tufts of grass. He waved to the men in his company to collect the purloined cattle and return them to the farmer from whom they had been stolen, and he and his brother resumed their rounds.

They stopped at several crofts, checking in on the crofters, and made a side trip to visit Agnes, an aged widow who lived on the border. Technically she was Olrig's vassal, but Alexander always made it a point to stop by when he was in the area and slip her a mutton chop or a chicken. The poor woman was nearly bedridden and but for her son, who stopped by to work her fields each day, she lived alone.

It was likely only a matter of time before Olrig remembered her. And when he did, he would evict her. Alexander wanted her to know, when that happened, she would be welcome in Dunnet.

With their rounds completed, the brothers headed back to the castle. As they clattered over the moat bridge and into the bailey, Fergus, Alexander's factor, hailed him, scuttling over the cobbles. His brow rose. Fergus never scuttled.

"My lord," he huffed as he ran up.

Alexander leaped from the saddle and fixed his attention on Fergus' face, steeling himself not to wince. Though his factor's visage was familiar and dear, it was difficult not to wince whenever he saw that scar. It brought back memories he longed to forget and incited far too much guilt. Determinedly he thrust all that from his mind. "Aye, Fergus?"

The factor's lips curled into something that might have been a smile. With the puckered skin tugging at his features, it could be difficult to distinguish a smile from a frown. "It has come, my lord."

He stilled. His muscles clenched, nerves hummed. "What has come?"

"The letter, my lord. The letter from Dounreay. It has come."

Holy God.

As Alexander stared at the letter lying on his gleaming desk he idly scratched Brùid behind the ears. The beast, his fierce protector and ever-loyal friend, nipped him when he stopped. Alexander chuckled and riffled Brùid's fur again.

There was something soothing about petting a dog when one's mind was in a welter. He was torn between the desire to rip the missive open and devour its contents . . . and the fear to do so. Why his pulse skittered so he didn't know.

Or maybe he did.

As he contemplated the scrap of parchment, his fate, he washed down an oatcake with a liberal gulp of coffee. He tossed a bite of it to Brùid, who caught it mid-air . . . and then spat it out.

Alexander could sympathize. He didn't care much for oatcakes, either, but Morag took such pride in her recipe—*handed doun from cook tae cook through time immemorial*—he felt, as laird of the manor, he was obligated to eat at least one each morning. He would much rather be tucking away kippers or a great slab of salt pork or a pudding of some sort, but such were the sacrifices of a laird. It was a damn shame his dog refused to help him out.

With a harsh movement he shoved Dounreay's letter back and focused on the rest of his mail. Surely that wasn't a cowardly thing to do. He had many responsibilities, many matters weighing on his shoulders. Still, it took all his concentration to focus.

He worked his way through the tasks with diligence. At long last, he reached the letter on the bottom of the pile. It was a report from his factor in Lyth detailing a conflict that would require the Justice of the Peace.

Alexander sighed. As he was the laird, resolving such conflicts was his responsibility. This meant he would need to carve out time in his schedule for a trip to the village to hear the complaints. He could send Andrew, but Alexander preferred to be a visible presence with his people, so they knew they had his support and, more important, so *he* knew he had their loyalty. Loyalty was all that held them together anymore, and even that was a tenuous thread.

The last such trip had taken a week, but it had been well worth the time. Judging from the facts laid out by his bonnet laird, this was a simple issue of land rights tangled by interwoven marriages and ancient feuds. Passions were riding high, so Alexander would need to attend to this immediately.

With his docket thusly cleared, he had but one letter left.

The letter from Dounreay.

With trembling fingers, he picked it up. While he dreaded what the letter could hold, he knew it was best with such things to make it a quick death. If things didn't go his way, it might not be entirely painless, but at least it wouldn't linger.

God, he hoped things went his way.

He ripped open the seal and scanned his friend's familiar script.

Alexander's heart stalled. His breath caught.

All dread, all worry, all fear, flew. An indescribable waft of joy, like the first green breath of spring, blew through his soul. Little ripples danced over his skin as his nerves shivered, a maniacal dance.

He set the letter down and rubbed his eyes. Then he picked it up and read it anew. Just to be sure. Just to be sure it said what he'd thought. What he'd hoped. What he'd dreamed.

She has accepted your suit.

He read each word. One at a time. Then blew out a breath. A laugh. A whoop.

She has accepted your suit.

Excitement flooded him, sang in his veins.

She would be his. And she was coming soon.

He grimaced as he realized how little time there was

to prepare. And on top of that, he had this trip to Lyth to contend with. There was no time to waste and there was much to do. Hurriedly he pulled out a pile of parchment and began scratching out orders to his staff. First and foremost, the baroness' chambers, which connected to his, would need to be completely redone. He barely knew his bride, but he was fairly certain the jonquil color scheme would not do.

Hannah didn't seem like a *yellow* sort of woman.

He briefly considered moving into his late uncle's much grander suite of rooms, but it was a brief flicker of a thought. He had no desire to sleep in Dermid's bed. Though the man was long dead, Alexander still carried the weight of his detestable memory. Aside from that, Alexander preferred the view from the west wing and he felt certain Hannah would as well.

But what color should he select? With much thought, he decided on an amber brown. Something warm and welcoming, like the color of her eyes. That decided, he moved on to the details of the wedding. Hannah would probably want to have a say in the arrangements, but Alexander had no intention of giving her an opportunity to change her mind or delay the ceremony. He intended to have everything in place the instant she walked through the door.

He quickly wrote out a note to the parish priest and added it to the pile. It would be helpful to have a clergyman on hand. With any luck, Father Pieter would eschew the whisky and attend sober.

The letter to Hannah took more time. How did one greet a bride? Alexander had little experience with this. He knew it was, of all of them, the most important message, for it would set the tone for his and Hannah's dealings.

While the written word rarely failed him, with this he

did struggle. He tried one letter filled with flowery prose and then, upon reading it back, balled it up and tossed it in the wastebin. The second attempt read like a business agreement and met the same fate.

After five more attempts, he settled on something brief and curt.

I am pleased to welcome you to Dunnet. Our wedding shall take place forthwith.

Not overly flowery, but not unnecessarily indifferent. And it got right to the point.

Alexander liked things that got to the point.

With great satisfaction, he scrawled his name and affixed his seal, setting the letter on the pile with the others. That done, he wrote out another missive for her, to be delivered when she arrived, welcoming her once more and advising her to ask Fergus to see to her needs. As Alexander didn't know how long his business in Lyth would take, it seemed prudent. He wouldn't want her to arrive in his home with no welcome from her groom.

It was essential that they started out on the right foot.

He was just scratching her name on the front and affixing his seal when Brùid growled. It was a lazy growl, the grumble of an interrupted drowse more than a warning.

Alexander's hand stilled as he sensed a presence at his side. Slowly, he turned.

Large, dark eyes, set in a small, solemn face, peered up at him.

Alexander's heart swelled. Fiona McGill was a wee thing, one of the orphans who had come to Dunnet for shelter last winter, having been tossed out of their homes into the snow by a cold-blooded laird to the west. Her poor mam had been wracked with fever and died at the gates.

Very few people ventured up the three hundred steps

to his sanctuary in the turret tower, and Alexander liked it that way—he preferred quiet when he worked—but he was always happy to see Fiona. He had an affinity for the girl, and not only because they shared the same affliction. Her presence was calming to him, a balm. A reminder that he could, in fact, protect someone.

Her lips worked, and his gut clenched. He knew the feeling of dread, the ache of attempting to force out words that would not come. He waited, patiently, as she struggled.

"What-what are ye d-doing?" she managed at length.

"Working."

Her small smile faltered. *Shite.* He had not meant his tone to be so clipped. Not with her. He winked at her in recompense and reached down to lift her onto his lap, issuing a great groan, as though she weighed as much as a boulder, though, in truth, she was like a feather.

She giggled and nestled against him.

Something squeezed his chest. How he ached for a child of his own. Until today it had been a hazy dream, but now he would be married and all that would change.

Soon he could have *sons.*

Fiona picked up his quill and made marks on the parchment. She shot a proud look up at him. There was a hint of uncertainty in that glance, so Alexander patted her on the shoulder. "Fine. That's fine work."

"You-you-you write a lot."

"Aye. 'Tis easier than speaking." Truer words he'd never uttered.

Her chin firmed. "I . . . sh-should . . . like to l-learn to write."

"So you shall. When . . . you're older." He pressed a quick buss to her dark curls and lifted her down. While he enjoyed her presence, he had much left to do today. "Here." He handed her his quill. She stared at the feather as though he'd handed her the royal jewels. "Practice."

She nibbled at her lip and, though she tried to hide it, a radiant grin broke free. She nodded once and, clutching her treasure, scampered from his office.

Alexander stared after her, unable to hold back his smile.

A great, glorious thrill washed through him. Now that Hannah had agreed to be his wife, he would soon have children of his own. He would do everything in his power to give them a wonderful life, secure and filled with love and laughter. He would sacrifice anything to make sure his sons did not suffer a hellish childhood like his.

CHAPTER FIVE

"Oh dear." Hannah tried to hold Lana's cat on her lap, but when the coach lurched to the side the creature squirmed and hissed and scratched until she let him go. "Whyever did you insist on bringing him?"

Lana tossed back her head and laughed, a sweet and merry lilt.

Then again, why not? Nerid never scratched her.

Nerid *liked* her.

In fact, the little monster leaped across the carriage and settled in her lap. Lana stroked him gently. "He fancied a journey. And I dinna want to be lonely in Dunnet."

Hannah gaped at her. "*I* will be there."

"I know. But you will be spending most of your time with your new husband." Hannah couldn't repress her shudder at the thought. "Besides, Lady Braal thought he should come."

Hannah nodded and fixed her gaze on the passing heather, trying not to blow out a breath. Lana had frequent long-winded conversations with Lady Braal. She didn't seem to mind that Lady Braal had died centuries before.

It mattered not to Lana that no one else could see or hear the Grey Lady, and she absolutely didn't care that some people thought she was mad. There was a certain courage in that, being who you were, despite what the world thought. In that Lana was the bravest soul Hannah had ever met. And the dearest.

Poor thing.

She'd never been the same since the fever that had almost killed her.

And while Hannah didn't understand her sister's eccentricities, she accepted them. Still, when the oddness surfaced it took her by surprise. Each and every time.

Long ago, Hannah had learned to placate Lana and play along, but today she didn't have the energy to do so. The journey to Dunnet had taken several days and it had been tiring; their outriders had set up a grueling pace, and the cat had been . . . difficult. On top of all that, Hannah's nerves were on edge.

For one thing, it had been so difficult, leaving home, especially with Papa too ill to travel along. He'd promised to come and visit soon, but Hannah knew it would not be soon at all.

It had broken her heart to say good-bye to everyone she loved, especially Isobel and Susana, the latter of whom had actually produced tears. Susana was hardly a weepy sort, and though she'd agreed that Hannah marrying Dunnet was the best course for all of them, her anguish at losing her sister had been clear.

Hannah had shared the feeling. She'd spent nearly every day of her life in Reay, nearly every day with her sisters at her side. Leaving had been harder than she'd expected. Thank heaven Lana had insisted on coming with her. With Lana's calm, familiar presence, Hannah didn't feel so very alone.

She reached across the carriage and squeezed Lana's hand, ignoring the swat from Nerid. "I am so pleased you came with me," she said . . . speaking to her sister. *Not* the cat.

Lana's eyes glimmered. "How could I not come? Someone from our family had to see you wed the Wolf."

Hannah winced. "Oh, please doona call him that."

"Why not? That is what they call him, is it not?"

"It is. But heavens. It makes me . . ."

"Makes you what?"

Hannah shuddered. "Terrified."

Lana chuckled. "You? You're not terrified of anything."

"I'm terrified of a lot of things."

"I think we both know only one thing makes you quake in your boots."

Hannah narrowed her eyes. "And what is that?"

"The prospect of not having complete and utter control over everything."

"That is ridiculous." But in her heart she couldn't deny the truth of it.

Lana lips quirked, as though she saw Hannah's denial for what it was. Utter ballocks. "But other than that tiny thing, you are fearless. Nerid thinks you're fearless too, do you no', my wee beastie?" He was hardly a *wee* beastie. She lifted the cat to her face and nuzzled his fur, placing noisy smooches on his muzzle.

By some miracle, Nerid allowed this. If Hannah had dared to do such a thing, she would have lost an eye.

Hannah crossed her arms and tried not to glower. Neither Lana nor Nerid deserved to bear the brunt of her foul mood.

Well, maybe Nerid.

But she held her tongue and tried to calm her skittering nerves. For she had spoken the truth. She was terrified. At least a little. She would see *him* again, and soon. Her intended. Her groom. She hoped to God she had not made a monumental mistake.

Oh, certainly he was pleasant to look at and he smelled wonderful and he kissed . . . Well, she didn't quite know how he kissed, but she certainly knew how he tasted—hunger simmered at the thought. However, simply because she found the man passably attractive didn't mean they would suit. She knew so very little about him. He could be surly and mean, or he could be domineering like Meg Taggart's man. He could be jealous or cold. And her greatest fear? He could certainly refuse her the liberties she'd so enjoyed at home.

She was far too independent a woman to live under some man's thumb, but in her observations of so many married women that was exactly the case.

The fact was, until she met him, spoke to him, she couldn't make a determination on what kind of husband he would be.

His note to her was not forthcoming.

I am pleased to welcome you to Dunnet. Our wedding shall take place forthwith.

Forthwith.

The word made her hackles rise.

The entire missive annoyed her. It was far too commanding, for one thing. Beyond that, it was cold, clipped, dispassionate. Well in keeping with the man she'd met, she supposed, which was a little distressing, because, in truth, she didn't want a cold and dispassionate marriage.

She hoped with all her heart that they would suit, but she feared they would not.

According to Papa—whom she trusted—Dunnet was a good man. He was strong and handsome and not terribly old. He would not be onerous to bed. But there was no doubt this was a marriage of convenience. She'd agreed to wed a warrior to protect her people and he'd chosen her to expand his fortunes. It was unrealistic of her to expect anything more. She resolved to face this marriage with a positive outlook and be happy with what she got. To be very careful not to expect too much of him.

And as for those wayward desires his touch incited? Those she would keep to herself.

Rory rode by and peered into the window. His smile at Lana made Hannah's stomach clench. While she was delighted her sister had come along on this journey, Hannah couldn't help but feel . . . responsible for her. Not that she was being controlling. She wasn't. She absolutely wasn't. But Lana was her baby sister and far too innocent and trusting. It was up to Hannah to shield her from the harsh realities of the world.

In Hannah's estimation, Rory's too-ardent attention was one of those realities.

She issued a growl and he yanked his focus from Lana's face to Hannah's. His smile dimmed at her expression. "I, ahem . . . We're close now," he said.

A new tension coiled within her. It was clear from his tone he had no idea of the maelstrom those simple words set up in her heart and soul. She sucked in a breath and tightened her hold on the straps. With another glance at Lana he spurred his mount forward.

Hannah nibbled on her lip, wondering if she should say something to Lana now or later. It was a conversation that needed to be had. But the decision was taken from her as Lana leaned forward to peer out the window and gasped. "There it is," she said.

Hannah followed her gaze and her heart stalled as the full force of Lochlannach Castle hit her.

Dounreay was an attractive keep, but this was stunning. The castle rose, grand and glorious against the backdrop of a robin's-egg-blue sky. Hewn of granite, the high walls gleamed a smoky silver. Tall turret towers flanked all four sides, connected by ramparts decorated with crenellated stone. While they had kept the ancient fortifications in place, there had also been modernizing work. The windows glittered with new glass. Bright banners, bearing the Wolf of Dunnet, flapped in the breeze.

"Oh, look!" Lana cried as they crossed a bridge over a

picturesque lake, bespeckled with swans as it was. Lana had always had a fascination with swans, although why Hannah couldn't say. Hannah found them irritable and fierce. More than once, she'd been chased by the cygnets roosting near Dounreay. She made a mental note to avoid strolling by this loch. "Isn't it lovely?" Lana said.

Hannah grunted an assent. Everything was a wondrous discovery to Lana—it was part of her charm—but at present Hannah wasn't in the mood to be charmed. Her heart thudded and tension sizzled through her.

She would see *him* again soon.

Her breath caught as the carriage rolled beneath an ancient portcullis into an enormous bailey, large enough to house an entire village. Every stone was in place, every cobble swept. There was no doubt Lochlannach Castle was very well kept. Some lairds neglected their ancestral homes and let them fall to rack and ruin. Some tore them down. It was clear that generations of Lochlannachs had loved this place.

As the carriage pulled to a stop, a trumpet sounded and servants flooded from the entrance and into the bailey.

Hannah steeled her spine and peered out the window, searching the faces for her betrothed. When she didn't see him, her mood plummeted.

Where was he?

This was one of the most important occurrences in her life, her welcome to her new home. The least he could have done was *be here.*

A tall behemoth with blond hair bounded through the crowd and wrenched open the carriage door. His gaze landed on Lana, sitting there with Nerid on her lap, looking like a princess, and his face split in a too-charming grin. "Welcome, my lady," he said with a little bow.

Annoyance riffled through Hannah's belly. Of course he would assume *she* was the laird's betrothed. Next to her,

Hannah looked like a dowdy companion. She cleared her throat. "I am Hannah." She tried to keep the irritation from her voice but failed miserably.

The ripple of glee at his dismay was probably beneath her, but she enjoyed it anyway.

"My apologies, my lady." He affected yet another bow, this time in her direction, although his gaze lingered on Lana. It was far too ardent.

Hannah frowned meaningfully at him, but he pretended not to notice. Instead he smiled again—at both of them—and said, "I'm Andrew Lochlannach, Dunnet's brother. Welcome to Lochlannach Castle." He held out his hand to help her down.

"Thank you," she said as she stepped from the carriage onto the soil of her new home. "I'm Hannah Dounreay, and this is my sister Lana."

"Ah." Turning his back on her, he reached for Lana with far too much zeal. Displeasure flared; Hannah narrowed her eyes as he handed Lana from the carriage. She wasn't a fool. She'd seen the way Andrew was ogling her sister and she didn't like it. Not in the slightest. She resolved to keep a close watch on him while Lana was here. Not that she was being controlling. She was simply being prudent.

Once they were both on terra firma once more, Andrew turned to the assemblage and launched into a pretty welcome speech, after which everyone burst into a round of applause.

Hannah was not pleased. It shouldn't be Dunnet's brother offering this welcome. It should be her groom himself. "Where is he?" she asked, but Andrew pretended not to hear.

He was quite good at pretending, she decided.

Blissfully unconcerned with her displeasure, Andrew introduced her in turn to the housekeeper and the cook and the butler and the upstairs maids (there were ten of them) and the downstairs maids and the footmen and—Mercy, there were a lot of them.

More servants than they'd ever had at Dounreay.

She had to wonder what she would do here, as there appeared to be a person for every job.

She would ask Dunnet.

If she ever saw him.

She would see him at some point. Wouldn't she?

Her heart stilled and she forgot her worries as a clutch of adorable children rushed up, thrusting bunches of wildflowers into her arms. "Welcome, my lady," one of the older ones said with a gap-toothed smile.

Hannah couldn't help but smile back. She loved wildflowers. And children. "Thank you," she said. Then she leaned over to Andrew and whispered, "Who are they?"

"The orphans."

Her smile dimmed. "The orphans?"

"Of the Clearances. We took them in, of course."

This revelation warmed her heart and eased her trepidation. How a man treated the helpless was a good measure of his mettle; it was a telling clue to Dunnet's character. These children were plump and clean and looked very well. The mischievous glimmers in their eyes spoke volumes about their contentment here.

But—

Through the sea of smiling young faces, her attention snagged on a glower. One child who wasn't content in the slightest. In fact, she seemed very put out.

One of the smallest girls, a tiny thing, glared at her with arms crossed.

Hannah knelt before her. "And who are you?" she asked.

The girl pressed her lips together.

"That's Fiona McGill," one of the boys said. "She doesna t-t-talk much."

Fiona's ears went red.

The boy laughed and the some of the others laughed too, but the older girl jabbed the boy with an elbow and barked, "Doona make fun of her." And then said, to Hannah, "Fiona has trouble speaking sometimes."

"Oh, darling. That's all right. We all struggle with something," Hannah said, tucking a curl behind a tiny shell-like ear. "But why are you so unhappy?"

Fiona's eyes narrowed.

"She thought the laird would marry her," the brash boy crowed.

Hannah silenced him with a frown, but it was too late. Fiona whirled on him and kicked him in the shins before scampering away. Hannah stared after her, clutching her flowers and ignoring the pounding thud of her pulse. Why that adorable little face had touched her so she couldn't say.

Perhaps it was because Fiona was an orphan. That was heartbreaking in itself. Or perhaps it was because she was Isobel's age and reminded Hannah of her beloved niece. But most likely, it was because the poor mite was besotted with an aloof and surly man. That was a dismal fate indeed.

Hannah decided, once she was settled into her new home, she would find Fiona and try to make friends with her. The last thing she wanted to do was begin her new life here with an enemy.

Oh, certainly Fiona was only five, but Hannah knew well what mischief five-year-olds could wreak. She had one at home.

As Hannah stood, a man in an austere tunic with a bleak expression stepped forward and pinned her with a cold gaze. She didn't wince, but just barely. Aside from his inhospitable air, the man had a savaged visage. The entire right side of his face was a puckered burn scar, so tight it tugged the tip of his eye downward and froze his mouth in a permanent scowl. But it wasn't the scar that startled her; it was the hostility in his eyes.

Incongruously, Andrew clapped him on the back and offered a broad grin. Apparently, Andrew had failed to notice the daggers. "Ah, Fergus. There you are. This is the Honourable Hannah Dounreay, soon to be Lady Dunnet. My lady, this is Fergus, our factor here in Dunnet."

"Miss Dounreay," he said with a tight bow. "Welcome." His tone implied anything but.

"Fergus manages the running of the castle and much of the estate," Andrew explained, smiling as though the factor wasn't trying to murder her with his glare.

"I see."

"You may feel welcome to ask him anything."

That word again. Did they understand what it meant?

Hannah nibbled her lip. "Ask him anything?"

"Of course. Anything." Andrew fixed his intent blue gaze on her.

"Where is Dunnet?"

Andrew blanched. "I . . . ah." His gaze whipped to Fergus.

The factor's throat worked. "He's . . . sleeping, my lady."

Hannah's eyes widened. *Sleeping?* When his bride arrived? She wasn't sure if she should be infuriated or insulted. Or both. Nae, this didn't bode well for their marriage. Not at all.

"He left orders, my lady," Fergus said, as though it justified a nap . . . in the middle of the day. "I'm to show you to your room, and introduce you to your lady's maid who shall prepare you for the wedding."

Hannah's heart gave one dull thud. *Ah.* The wedding.

She swallowed heavily. This was it. Her new home. For the rest of her life. She glanced around at the milling throng, all of whom were watching with glimmering interest.

Fergus noticed her attention on them and frowned. He clapped his hands and bellowed, "Everyone back to work!" and, in a trice the staff melted away. Hannah set her teeth. That was not how she would have handled it. The barked command was far too gruff and dictatorial. She made a mental note to speak with Fergus about his demeanor with the staff as soon as she found her bearings.

It was probably too early for a lecture at this juncture, but there would be one. If she was to take over the management of the castle, she would not have her people barked at.

Andrew offered a too-charming grin. "Shall I leave it to Fergus to show you your rooms while I get your men settled?" he asked.

"That would be lovely." She and Lana were both exhausted from the long journey. "And can you see my horse stabled?" she asked. Beelzebub had been restless on the journey, likely annoyed to be tied to the back of the carriage when she was not riding on him. "He prefers oats to hay and . . . you should probably not stable him near the mares."

Andrew's eyes widened; they sparkled as well. "An irresponsible boy?"

"He does tend to knock down walls to get what he wants. And you might want to let Rory handle him." She ignored Rory's sigh. "He does like to nip strangers."

"He likes to nip everyone," Rory muttered. But when Hannah glanced at him he tugged his forelock and cautiously approached Beelzebub's tether.

Andrew bowed to them both with a chuckle and turned

to greet the men who had accompanied them while Fergus led Hannah and Lana—holding Nerid—into the castle.

Hannah tried to take in every detail, but it was almost too much to process. The intricately carved front doors opened on to an expansive hall with gleaming wood floors and a grand curving staircase. Hannah's breath caught at the sheer splendor of it all.

Had she worried that Dunnet was marrying her for her money? For her paltry castle? For the Reay salt mines?

What a fool.

Which begged the question . . . why was he marrying her? A woman he couldn't bestir himself to greet as she arrived at his home for the first time? Sadly, she knew the answer. For some men, there were not enough riches in the world. She attempted to swallow her disappointment. She had hoped for more from him.

Fergus didn't allow her and Lana time to gape at the hall. He whisked them up the staircase and down a hall, to the left into another wing, and up another flight of stairs. She was beginning to despair she would never find their way back when he stopped before a set of double doors. "These," he pronounced, "are your chambers. His Lordship had them redecorated just for you." With a great flourish, he flung open the doors.

Hannah stood on the threshold and stared.

It was a spacious room with north-facing windows and a huge four-poster bed. An arrangement of comfortable chairs arched around the hearth, in which crackled a cheery fire. To the left, another door opened to a parlor.

She should have been pleased. She reminded herself of her earlier resolution to attempt to be so.

But delight was beyond her.

The bedroom was . . . hideous.

Oh, it had been redecorated—the carpets and the furniture all had a newish scent—but the color scheme was atrocious. In point of fact, it was brown. It was all brown. Everything from the wall hangings to the coverlet on the bed to the carpets. Brown.

And not just any brown. It was the color of a turd.

The room was, at best, depressing. And at worst . . . turdy. It would be like sleeping in a barnyard. Or a privy.

She shot a look at Fergus. "He had these rooms redecorated?"

"Aye, my lady."

"For me?"

"Aye, my lady." He seemed so proud Hannah didn't have the heart to tell him she thought the rooms were ghastly. But they were. Perhaps, at some point in the future, she could arrange for a fire.

She forced a smile and murmured, "Delightful."

The lie was worth the effort. For the first time, his harsh demeanor faltered and his expression softened. His ears went pink and he bowed effusively. "Excellent, my lady. Excellent. The footmen will bring up your trunks shortly." He waved at a girl, standing in the corner with her hands folded; so beset had Hannah been with the horror of her new rooms, she hadn't even noticed her. "This is Senga. Your lady's maid." Disquiet flickered over his features. "Unless you would like to choose someone else?"

The girl winced, but only slightly, and sent Hannah a hopeful glance.

Hannah had no need for a maid, but she couldn't bear to crush that fragile hope. "Senga." She nodded. "It is so wonderful to meet you."

The poor girl nearly collapsed with relief.

"Senga will fetch you a tray . . ." Fergus paused, his face puddling. "Unless, of course, you doona want a tray?"

Hannah had the sudden inkling the man's previous harshness had probably stemmed from nerves. At least, she hoped this was the case. She tried not to sigh. "A tray would be verra nice." Though how she could eat, staring at these walls, she didn't know.

The girl curtseyed several times and bowed her way from the room, as though Hannah were the Queen of Sheba. How very tiring. Granted, she would be the new baroness, but she wasn't used to such deference from her staff. And she didn't care for it.

"I think we would like to rest and get acclimated now, Fergus." If nothing else, she needed a moment, or six, to get used to the disagreeable colors of her room. Doubtless, she wouldn't be spending much time here.

"Of course, my lady. Your sister's rooms are across the hall. His Lordship thought you might like to be close."

Well, that, at least, was thoughtful.

"Thank you, Fergus." Hannah tried not to herd him from the room, but a sudden exhaustion had descended upon her. She wanted nothing more than to wipe the insipid smile from her face and collapse.

But at the door, he stopped so abruptly she bumped into him.

"My lady. I almost forgot." He reached into his pocket and pulled out a letter, stamped with the seal of the Dunnet Wolf, and handed it to her. "From His Lordship."

Hannah took the letter with numb fingers. She exchanged a glance with Lana, who shrugged.

Hannah's mind reeled. Not only had he not bestirred himself to greet her—sleeping through her arrival—he'd also sent a letter.

A letter.

A part of her wanted to rip it open and read it immediately. Another part of her wanted to rip it to shreds and toss it into the fire. She nodded at Fergus and closed the door on him, though he seemed loath to leave. Then she dropped into a chair and glared at the offending parchment. "Can you believe this?" she said to Lana, who sat across from her and settled Nerid in her lap. The cat leaped down and started exploring the room. No doubt, looking for a good spot to contribute to the brown.

"It's a verra nice room," Lana murmured. "Much larger than your rooms at home."

"That's not what I mean, and you know it. The color—" *Dear lord.* She couldn't even say it.

Lana nibbled on her lower lip as she surveyed the drapes. "It's quite brown."

"Indeed."

"But it all . . . matches."

Repulsively and revoltingly, but aye, it did. It was like an endless sea of bilious brown.

"He redecorated just for you."

"Indeed."

Lana glanced at the letter and Hannah realized she was mangling it. She made a great show of flattening it on the table.

"Are you going to read it?"

"I suppose."

"It was verra thoughtful of him to write you a letter, do you no' think?"

No. She didn't think. "I would much rather have a conversation with him."

"He's sleeping."

Hannah's belly roiled at his sheer arrogance. There might have been a trickle of excitement as well, but she resolved to ignore that and focus on her irritation. Sleeping in the middle of the day. When his *bride* arrived. How like a man.

She set her teeth and ripped open the letter. It was short and to the point. She wasn't surprised.

Hannah,
Welcome to Dunnet. I sincerely hope you will be happy here. If there is anything you require, please doona *hesitate to speak to Fergus. He will happily see to your every need.*
Alexander

Anything she required?

She required a conversation. With *her groom.*

Just one, she hoped, before they became man and wife. Was that too much to ask?

"What does it say?" Lana asked, and Hannah handed her the parchment. She read it over and sighed. "That is sweet."

Was it?

It was probably irrational of her to be aggravated. Then again, maybe not.

He was to be her husband. Was it too much to ask that he speak to her in person?

Lana yawned hugely, though she tried to hide it.

"Darling, it's been a long day for both of us. Why do we no' find your chambers so you can settle in as well?"

After a thorough and unproductive search for Nerid, they made their way to the rooms across the hall. Hannah tried very hard not to be piqued that Lana's bedroom was decorated in a delightful crème with an eyelet comforter and lacy curtains. Hannah would have liked, very much, to stay here, but Lana shooed her out, insisting she needed to rest as well.

However, she found, when she was back in her execrable chambers, she couldn't sleep. And it wasn't just the color that battered her vision whenever she opened her eyes.

She was a bundle of nerves, beset with worries.

Would they suit?

What would her role be here in his bustling barony?

And, most important, *why* had he offered for her?

To calm herself, she explored her rooms, which consisted of her bedchamber, a privy, and the parlor. There was another door to the far side of the parlor. Without a thought she pushed it open. And froze.

Oh heavens.

It was *his* room.

She should have suspected it.

A flash of annoyance curled through her at the realization that his chamber was done in an enchanting heather green, a hue she found quite pleasing, but her exasperation didn't last long. It was quickly supplanted by a sizzle of illicit excitement at the sight of *him*.

For there he was, sprawled out on his bed, a panoply of hard muscle—naked. She swallowed as she stared at him, taking in the glorious vision of his thick thighs, sprinkled as they were with dark hairs, his chest, which was broad and hard and spattered with a dark mat as well. One arm draped over his eyes, and even in his slumber the muscles of his arm bunched. Thank heaven the sheets covered his groin, or she might well have fainted.

And then she nearly did.

Because even as his snore rumbled through the room, so too did a deep-throated growl.

Slowly, and with menace, a creature arose from the bed, an enormous ferocious furry beast, a wolf surely. His gleaming eyes narrowed and the hackles on his neck rose. With teeth bared, he stepped toward her.

And then he sprang.

CHAPTER SIX

Alexander shot up in bed, awakened by a snarl, a squeal, and the slamming of a door. He hadn't thought he would sleep at all, but he must have. After settling the issue in Lyth—which had taken far longer than he'd wanted—he'd ridden straight home and worked through the night, finalizing details for the wedding and making arrangements for a company of his men to leave at once for Reay to provide the protection his contract with Hannah required.

After that, and catching up with the work that awaited him upon his return from Lyth, he should have fallen straight to sleep, but he hadn't. Instead he'd lain awake with Brùid by his side, thinking of her.

As a result, he hadn't slept well and now, when he awoke, he was groggy. So it took him a while to realize what had roused him from a dead sleep. Someone had entered his chambers. Brùid was poised by the door to the parlor, his hackles up, growling low in his throat.

Alexander frowned. Brùid rarely growled, unless he wanted food . . . or there was some threat. He levered off the bed and padded to the door, pulling the dog back so he could open it and see what was on the other side.

He didn't expect the hound to rip free and tear into the parlor. He certainly didn't expect to see Hannah standing there in the middle of the room. His pulse lurched at the sight of her. A wash of excitement spiraled through him. She was here? Already? How long had he slept?

But there she stood, her hair like an ebony curtain curling around her delicate face, her hands clasped before her, her eyes wide . . . with fear. Her lips parted and another squeal wrenched forth as Brùid bounded across the room toward her, his teeth bared.

"Brùid, heel!" Alexander bellowed, but his usually obedient dog ignored him. His heart lodged in his throat as the hound charged the woman who would be Alexander's wife. Time slowed down. Panic traced a cold finger along his spine. His gut tightened into a hard knot.

Would he lose her before he'd had her?

And to the jaws of his beloved Brùid?

But Brùid did not attack her.

He knocked her down, though, and then barreled past her and through the door into her bedchamber.

Alexander's relief was brief. Because then rose the symphony from hell. Thuds and crashes. A hideous screeching yowl. Wolfish snarls and a low, rumbling growl that made the hairs on the back of his neck stand up.

Hannah glared at him and bounded to her feet, running into the bedchamber. Alexander, perforce, followed.

He stopped stock-still at the sight of his dog—his painstakingly trained and disciplined wolfhound—dancing like a pup before the hearth, tail whirling like a windmill, as he barked and bayed at the ball of hissing fur perched on the mantel.

The urge to laugh bubbled up within Alexander. He wasn't a man who laughed with much regularity, but this . . . this was funny.

Then he caught Hannah's eye and flinched.

All right. Not so very funny.

"Call him off," she howled over the ruckus. "He's scaring Nerid."

"Brùid. Heel." Alexander's dog had been trained almost from birth. He had always responded to commands with a satisfying immediacy. However, in this instance he ignored his master utterly, in favor of the delights of treeing a cat. Or manteling a cat. Whatever one called it.

Alexander stormed across the room and grabbed Brùid by the scruff of his neck, and though he whined and bayed a few more times, he allowed Alexander to tug him back toward the door. It was a struggle. Alexander could only hope she appreciated his efforts.

When he lifted his gaze to her face, to check, to see if she indeed appreciated his efforts . . . he froze. Because she was gaping at him with an expression of combined horror and fascination.

It didn't take long to realize why.

He was used to sleeping in the buff. It hadn't even occurred to him that he was completely naked when he'd leaped from his bed. His man parts were certainly not new to him.

They were, apparently, new to her.

Which, on the face of things, was good news—given her habit of kissing strange men.

But lord, he really had not intended to frighten her.

Certainly not on their wedding day.

He hunched down, so his dangly bits were somewhat obscured by the wolfhound, and her attention flickered to Alexander's face. Her jaw hung slack. She swallowed. With great effort.

He should say something. *I'm sorry.* Or *Forgive the intrusion.* Or *No, it's not usually quite so dangly.* But he found he couldn't find the words. Even if he could have found them, he couldn't have formed them.

So he settled for a quick bow and, holding Brùid at a fortuitous angle, backed from the room.

Not a promising start to their union.

Not promising at all.

~

Oh. Holy. God.

Hannah stared at the door as it closed behind her betrothed.

Her *naked* betrothed.

He'd been utterly unaware of his nudity, like Adam in the garden, beautiful, perfect . . . enormous. As he'd leaped across the room and wrangled his hellhound, her gaze had been locked on one thing, and one thing only.

Enormous.

A shiver rippled through her.

She knew much about animal husbandry. She'd read several books on the topic. She'd seen horses mating. She'd listened in when the matrons of Ciaran Reay thought she could not hear their whispers. She felt as though she was somewhat educated on the topic. She knew how things *worked.* But *that* had shocked her.

For one thing, the sheer size of it . . .

No matter how she wrapped her mind around it, she couldn't imagine how it would . . . fit.

The other thing that shocked her was the scalding sizzle of heat that had settled in her belly. The force of it had weakened her knees, sent her pulse to pounding, made her mouth go dry.

It was all the feelings she'd had upon kissing him . . . and more.

Was this what lust felt like? True lust? Not the girlish excitement of a quick kiss but a rampaging fire that threatened to consume her from within?

Visions of being tangled in those long, lean limbs, of being touched by him, wrapped in his arms, swirled through her mind and the heat rose again, prickling at her temples. She gusted out a breath and her head went light.

Nerid issued a plaintive cry, recalling her to the moment. She reached up and lifted him down from the mantel, holding him close and calming him. Though they both shook, it was for very different reasons.

She wasn't certain if she should be excited or afraid.

But she did know one thing.

She was very glad she wasn't marrying Olrig.

Her opinion on the matter shifted slightly when, less than an hour later, she received another letter from Dunnet. That it was delivered by his gloomy factor didn't help.

Please prepare yourself, it said. *The wedding shall take place forthwith.*

Hannah's teeth clenched. She was really beginning to hate that word.

"Everything is in place, my lady," Fergus said with something that might pass as a smile. "The priest is here—and sober." What that meant she had no clue. "And the laird is awaiting you in the chapel."

Hannah blinked. "Now?"

"Oh, aye, my lady. Now."

Well, for heaven's sake. She wasn't even dressed. At least, not for a wedding. Although, as this was a marriage of convenience, a mere sealing of houses, that hardly mattered. She thrust the letter back at him. "Some warning would have been nice."

Fergus' brow rumpled. "Some warning, my lady?" His tone made his meaning clear. *Were you not aware the purpose of your visit was a wedding?*

Hannah set her hands on her hips. Had Dunnet given her the courtesy of a word or two, she wouldn't have been so exasperated. He'd been naked in her room once today after all. He could have said something.

Aside from which, she was not marrying the man until her concerns about the union were addressed. Surely her delay had nothing to do with the trepidation that lashed her whenever she recalled the vision of him—his . . . member dancing around—as he hauled his hound back into his room.

As fascinating as that glimpse of his naked body had been—and as curious as she was to know what making love with him would be like—she was not consummating this marriage until she had a face-to-face conversation with him.

With actual words and everything.

And on the topic of his hound . . . would they sleep with him? Every night?

Hannah didn't savor the thought.

Another question to ask Alexander, no doubt.

"Please tell Dunnet I wish to speak with him."

The factor's lips moved, but no sound issued forth. Mutely he handed her the letter once more.

With a snarl Hannah ripped it in half.

He watched the scraps flutter to the ground, his horror intimating she'd just shredded something akin to the Magna Carta. His throat worked. "I, ah . . . The laird awaits your . . ." He trailed off and pointed to the parchment on the ground. "Why did you do that?"

"I'm tired of letters from him," Hannah snapped. "I would like to speak to him."

Why Fergus blinked, like a bemused owl, was a mystery.

"People do speak to him. . . ."

"Ah . . . Nae. Not really."

"Nae?" She narrowed her eyes. "He's the laird of the manor. How can he manage business without speaking to his people?"

Numbly, Fergus bent down and picked up the scraps of paper, holding them out. Apparently, he felt this was answer enough.

"Oh, bother." Hannah took the pieces and shoved them in her pocket. Not that she'd read them later. She'd never read another letter from Dunnet again.

She crossed her arms over her chest and fixed Fergus with a recalcitrant glare. "I willna marry a man with whom I have yet to share a conversation."

His lips flapped. "But-but . . . everything has been arranged."

"Then unarrange it. And notify Dunnet we will wed when and only when I decide we shall suit."

It was clear her adamant stance was not appreciated. Hannah didn't care. Dunnet might as well understand from the very start that he was marrying a strong and stubborn woman. One who couldn't be bullied into doing something she did not wish to do. And she would not be rushed.

With no remorse Hannah closed the door on the sputtering factor.

She would be married when she was damn good and ready, and not an instant sooner.

Where was she?

Please God, let her not have changed her mind. He couldn't bear it. He couldn't.

Ignoring the impatient and rustling crowd—all of his people had crowded into the small chapel to see him wed—Alexander paced, running a finger around his collar. Why the hell was it so tight?

He was racked with worry that she would back out or delay the proceedings or—given the expression on her face at the sight of his naked form—run in horror. He could only hope she hadn't seen the scars on his back.

He shot a glare at Andrew, who shrugged, and then, for good measure, Alexander glared at Father Pieter, whom he caught taking another nip from his flask.

If she didn't arrive soon, the clergyman would be insensate. He was already starting to list to the side.

Please God, let her hurry.

Immediately upon dressing in formal kilt—which included his jacket, waistcoat, hose, ghillie brogues, *sgian dubh*, and formal sporran—he'd rushed downstairs and issued a flurry of orders for the wedding ceremony and the subsequent celebration dinner. When all was in place, he'd sent the note to Hannah notifying her that the time for their wedding was nigh.

Not that he was anxious to have it done, but he was.

He had so wanted this day to go smoothly, but from the instant he'd awakened, much later than he'd intended, it had been a disaster. He hoped this wasn't an omen regarding the success of their marriage.

But it probably was.

Fergus had been gone far too long in fetching her; it made his hackles rise. Made sweat pop out on his brow. Made his throat close.

He had no idea why.

Perhaps it was because he'd never felt such . . . was that desperation?

Odd, that. He'd always stood strong and faced the world alone. Never wanted or needed anyone, aside from Andrew. Now that Alexander's marriage was imminent, he found his wish to acquire her lands had been supplanted by something deeper. Certainly, he deeply desired *her*, but beyond that, he found he no longer wanted to stand alone. He craved a partner by his side. He craved her by his side.

Except, of course, that she wasn't here.

He growled at Father Pieter when he pulled out his flask once more. The priest paled and slipped it back into his pocket.

Alexander was about to spin on his heel and storm to her chambers and demand—*demand*—she attend her own wedding when Fergus appeared in the doorway with a pained expression on his face.

Alexander sent him a speaking glare. It said, *Where is*

she? and, to his horror, Fergus shrugged. With a narrow-eyed glance at Andrew, Alexander hastened to the back of the chapel. "Well?" he barked. A trickle of remorse flitted through him at Fergus' flinch, but it was only a trickle. Alexander was far too nervous to pay it any mind.

"My lord . . ." the factor began, and then he stopped to clear his throat.

Something in Alexander's gut clenched. That Fergus wasn't meeting his gaze made his skin go clammy. "Where is she?" he hissed.

"She, ah . . . She wishes to *speak* to you before the wedding."

His blood went cold. "*Speak* to me?" *Holy hell.*

Had she changed her mind?

As he followed Fergus back into the castle, his mind awhirl, a horrifying prospect occurred. Hannah was a delicate flower. A young, innocent girl. She'd arrived at a new home, to marry a man she barely knew—and promptly spotted him buck naked. No doubt that had been a shock.

No doubt he'd frightened her to death.

All he needed to do was reassure her, although how he might accomplish that without appearing like a stuttering idiot he didn't know. But now that she was here, now that he had seen her again, his conviction to have her as his wife had solidified.

It was not the only thing that had solidified.

Ever since he'd burst into her room, ever since her gaze had locked on to his cock, he'd been possessed by the memory of that brief kiss they'd shared. It was only natural for him to entertain thoughts of stealing another. To plot said theft.

Perhaps this was the time.

Perhaps he could ease her concerns about the earthy aspects of their marriage with actions rather than words.

He lifted his hand to knock on her door and then realized Fergus was still by his side. Ever since he'd been a boy, the factor had been there for him, his protector. But Alexander didn't want his protection now. He certainly didn't want any witnesses if this discussion didn't go well. He shot the man a frown; he paled, nodded, and backed away.

Once he was gone from sight, Alexander took a moment to collect his thoughts, steel his spine, and straighten his plaid. Once he was ready, he knocked.

The door opened immediately, as though she'd been standing there waiting. At the sight of her, his heart stalled and his throat tightened. She had this effect on him each and every time he saw her. God, she was so beautiful.

Her eyes widened, as though she was surprised to see him, which befuddled him, because she'd asked him to come. Then her gaze raked him. He liked to think that look in her eye was a glimmer of appreciation. "Dunnet," she said. "You're . . . dressed."

Aye. Dressed for a wedding. He couldn't help but notice she was not.

"Lady . . . Hannah." He bowed. "You wanted to . . . talk?"

She nodded briskly and opened the door wider, stepping back to allow him to enter. He did so and closed the door behind him. The click was deafening. It was not lost on him that he was in her bedchambers. His gaze flicked to the bed. It was slightly rumpled. That made him feel slightly rumpled as well.

This was not the time for his passion to rise.

It did.

"Thank you for coming," she said, turning away to pace. "I know you are prepared to marry . . . *forthwith.*" He had no idea why she emphasized the word as she did. "But before we exchange our vows, I have some things that I need to say."

He nodded, even as relief gushed through him.

She hadn't changed her mind.

And if she had things to say, he should probably stay silent. And listen.

"You and I need to have an understanding."

"An . . . understanding?"

"Aye." His hope was supplanted by a hint of disappointment when she said in a very businesslike tone, "We both know this is a marriage of convenience."

His gaze snapped to her face. Ernest though her expression was, it lacked the dreamy, romantic tinge a groom might hope for. In fact, she set her chin and shot him a very unromantic glance.

A marriage of convenience? A cold, heartless, distant union? Denial howled. Suddenly, to his surprise, he found he wanted something very different. He longed to respond, to cry out his dissent, but his throat locked.

"There is no reason to pretend this is something other than it is. I agreed to marry you because Dounreay needs your protection and you agreed to marry me for my lands. We are marrying for no other reason. Aye. I understand that. *We* understand that."

Nae. We understood nothing of the sort. There was another reason he was determined to marry her, did she but realize.

He *wanted* her.

"Regardless, Dunnet, my wish is for a peaceful union."

Peaceful. Aye. Peaceful was good.

"I should like for us to work together as a team. In partnership."

Aye. He had a partnership in mind. . . .

"If I'm going to pledge myself to a man forever, I need to know that he will respect me. That he will honor my wishes. I need to know he will take my counsel into account." She fixed Alexander with a steady gaze, as though she expected a response. So he nodded.

She was so beautiful, so earnest. So tantalizing.

He stepped closer, intent on his target.

Her eyes widened as he neared. Her hand on his chest stalled his approach and her brow wrinkled. Her gaze flicked to his mouth and her tongue peeped out, wetting her lips, igniting a flame in his belly. With great effort, she ripped her gaze away and frowned at him. "Do you agree to my terms?" she asked.

He cupped her cheek and angled her head up. Her breath caught. Her features froze as she realized his intent. "Aye," he said. "Aye." And then he did what he'd been thinking about for weeks. What he'd been obsessing over all day. He kissed her.

And it was glorious.

∾

A shiver rippled over Hannah's skin as Dunnet took her mouth. His taste, his scent, infused her. It was a light kiss, a testing foray, but it sent an unholy thrill through her and left her wanting one thing. More.

She had wanted this chance to speak with him privately, to receive his assurances that their marriage would be a partnership, to set her mind at rest, and he'd done that. But if she was being truthful . . . something like this had been on her mind as well, skulking there behind her noble intentions, a roiling hunger. A curiosity. A need.

She'd kissed him before and he had turned away. She desperately needed to know if, in his heart, he had any passion for her whatsoever.

He lifted his head—way too soon—and stared down at her. "Hannah . . ." he murmured.

Even as she attempted to rein in her disappointment at

his withdrawal, his hold on her cheek tightened, his eyes narrowed, and he issued a noise, something gruff and deep, something that sent a lick of exhilaration through her.

He yanked her closer. The feel of his body against hers, rigid and unyielding, made her head spin. His fingers threaded through her hair and he held her steady as his head descended again. She sucked in a breath, quivering with anticipation.

And *ah. Ah.*

This kiss was different.

This wasn't tentative in the slightest. It was a taking. A mad, starved consummation of her mouth with his, a melding of lips and tongue and need.

This was as wild as the windy squalls off the coast. As tantalizing as the fairy wisps at dusk. As scorching as the forge where razor-sharp steel was tempered and formed.

And it cut through her like a screaming wind, an enticing magic, a warm blade.

Scuttles of heat rose in her womb. Rivulets of excitement danced in her veins. His taste filled her senses, her mouth, her soul.

When he lifted his head, a glimmer danced in his eye. It was the look of a conquering hero, a savage Scotsman, a man whose hunger had been sated but ignited at the same time.

Oh heavens.

Exultation whipped through her. Her knees were weak and her body melted.

Damn her reservations.

Damn her fears.

Damn her doubts about whether or not he really wanted her.

She wanted him. And she would have him.

It was gratifying to see that he was not unaffected. His breath came heavy and hard and there was a slight tremble in his voice when he spoke. It was one word and one word only, forced out and wreathed in a growl, but it was enough.

"*Mine.*"

Alexander stared down at Hannah. Her expression was soft, her lips damp. Need coiled in his belly. He ached for her. Now. But he was aware that all the town and half the clan was gathered below. Waiting for them. As much as he wanted to lay her down on the bed by the window and show her the depth of his passion, he couldn't.

Not now. Not until she was truly his.

He would wait to have her until after the wedding. Tonight. Soon. Anticipation skirled through him. He gestured toward the door.

She stepped back. Blinked. The dewy expression on her features faded, replaced by something that could have been intransigence.

Unease riffled at her retreat. Had she not been as befuddled and bewildered by their exchange as he had? Was she not as anxious as he to seal their bond?

"My lady? The . . . wedding?"

Ach. Ah. She frowned at him and crossed her arms. Intransigence indeed.

"Dunnet, surely you doona expect me to get married in this?" She gestured to her dress with a huff of disgust. He stared at it. It was a dress. Just like every other dress. And it looked charming on her.

He opened his mouth to respond but didn't know what to say.

With a snort she pushed past him into the hall and rapped on the door to her sister's suite. A delicate blonde with large blue eyes answered. She smiled at Hannah, but when her gaze landed on him her smile widened. "Is it time?" she whispered.

"Aye."

"Nae."

He and Hannah responded at the same time. She frowned at him and then hooked arms with her sister and tugged her toward her room. "Come and help me prepare," she said.

"P-p-prepare?" Alexander burbled. She looked just fine. In fact, she looked amazing. He took a step to follow her and make his case, but she shut the door in his face.

"Trouble in paradise?" Andrew's chuckle rippled down the hall.

Alexander turned to see his brother leaning against the wall. He gestured at the closed door. "She wanted to change her dress," he murmured in a bewildered tone.

Andrew grinned. "Women do that."

Alexander's brow rippled. "But everyone's waiting."

His brother levered off the wall and came to clap him on the shoulder. "It's her wedding day. No doubt she's nervous. She wants to look fine."

"She looks fine." She always looked fine. She would look fine wearing nothing.

Alexander's mind stalled on that thought.

"Come along. Give her some time to ready herself." Andrew led him back toward the stairs. "You'll be leg shackled soon enough."

His brother laughed and Alexander tried to force a smile as they headed back to the chapel, but it was a halfhearted attempt. His bowels were knotted and his muscles clenched. Sweat prickled his brow. All he could think of was the fact that his wedding was nigh . . . as was the wedding *night*.

~

It took her forever to dress, or at least it seemed so. Alexander occupied himself by wearing a rut in the stone floor of the chapel. When Auld Duncan creaked to his feet and the plaintive wail of the bagpipes, heralding the bride's arrival, sounded, Alexander's heart shot into his throat.

He whirled. His breath caught. His pulse thrummed.

She was here.

And she looked beautiful.

A murmur went up through the crowd as Hannah and her sister stepped into the chapel.

Hannah's hair was caught up in a tantalizing confection of ebony silk and pearls. She wore a dress of emerald green that set off the alabaster tones of her skin. Her décolletage made his mouth water. As custom demanded, she wore a sprig of white heather pinned to her lapel. In her hands, she clutched a bouquet of . . . were those weeds?

He ignored this incongruity and flicked his attention to her face.

Her expression was tight and wreathed with fear, but when her gaze landed on him it softened; her eyes glimmered. He thought she might have sighed.

Alexander swallowed the knot in his throat and bowed as she approached the altar. As she came to stand at his side, her scent rose to engulf him and his knees locked.

He straightened his plaid and took his place beside her, nodding to Father Pieter.

Alexander had prompted the priest on how the ceremony should go—short and sweet—but that was before the flask of whisky. As it was, Pieter had a tendency to be somewhat long-winded. And he was now, babbling on about fealty and ancient vows and God's plan for man and wife until Alexander had the urge to give him a swift kick.

He was nervous enough as it was without all this falderal.

He wanted the vows and nothing more.

He gave a low growl.

Pieter halted mid-word, gaping at him with wide eyes. Then Pieter cleared his throat and opened his book.

Why he needed a book for such a familiar ceremony Alexander had no clue, but Pieter quickly got to the meat of the ceremony and that was all that mattered.

"Do you, Hannah Dounreay, take Alexander Lochlannach to be your husband, and in the presence of God and before these witnesses, do you promise to be a loving, faithful, and loyal wife, for as long as you both shall live?"

She hesitated before answering, which gave Alexander cold chills, but when he glanced at her and their eyes met she nodded and murmured, "I will."

A bolt of satisfaction slashed through him. His heart thudded. But then, when the priest spoke again, she looked away. Alexander forced himself to pay attention, so he would respond at the proper time—and without delay. He'd been practicing this for days, the most important two words he would ever say. He was determined they would come forth with ease and perfection.

"Do you, Alexander Lochlannach, Laird of Dunnet, take Hannah Dounreay to be your wife, and in the presence of God and before these witnesses, do you promise to be a loving, faithful, and loyal husband to her, for as long as you both shall live?"

He drew in a breath. His gaze met hers again as he spoke. "I—"

His throat locked.

A frown flickered on her brow.

Panic snaked through him.

I will.

Simple words.

They wouldn't come.

Father Pieter, apparently satisfied, or eager to finish his flask, slapped his book closed. "Excellent. I now pronounce you husband and wife."

Holding up the ring, Alexander glared at him.

"Ach. Oh, aye. The ring."

With a sigh, Alexander slipped the Lochlannach Knot onto her finger. It was a ring that had been in his family for centuries, a symbol of his clan and his promise. Then, having done that, he gestured to Andrew, who approached with the Lochlannach sash. He smiled down at Hannah as he draped the sash over her shoulder and pinned it with the rosette. Then, as tradition demanded, he kissed her.

There was no reason for Alexander to clench his fists as he did.

Tradition also called for Father Pieter to kiss the bride.

Tradition was far too annoying at times. And the priest was far too enthusiastic. The kiss went on and on. Perhaps there was a reason for the clenched fist after all.

Alexander issued a snarl and the priest staggered back, having the good grace to flush.

But when it was Alexander's turn to kiss her, Hannah turned her cheek.

He tried to ignore his flash of disappointment.

Their first kiss as husband and wife.

On the cheek.

When he eased back and she glared up at him, he knew something was wrong. Terribly wrong.

Pity he had no idea what it was.

∾

As she followed her new husband from the chapel Hannah fumed, barely aware of the skirling wail of the pipes as they celebrated the new union. Barely cognizant of the cheers of the crowd—with the exception of Lana, all people Hannah didn't know.

A single thought circled in her mind.

One word.

He'd said one word.

Aye.

Do you take this woman to be your wife?

Aye.

Not *I will* or *I do.* Simply *Aye.*

That blasé response made her hackles rise.

Beyond that, their conversation before the wedding had been somewhat less than satisfying. Although he'd agreed to her terms, he certainly hadn't had much to add. He'd stood there, the great lummox, and stared at her through most of it.

And then he'd kissed her.

While it had been a wonderful kiss—it still sent chills through her body—she couldn't shake the suspicion that he, like all men, felt that when it came to women, only one form of intercourse mattered.

Granted, she'd married him for her own purposes and he had done the same. But heaven help her, she wanted more. She so desperately wanted more.

In a daze, she watched as he scattered coins before the assembled children, barely noting that he saved one for Fiona, the tiny girl with the enormous frown—although she did smile at *him.* One of the boys stepped forward and handed Hannah a horseshoe, the traditional symbol of fertility and good luck.

She offered the boy a smile in exchange for the token, but it might not have been a smile—a baring of teeth, perhaps—judging by the way his eyes widened before he slunk away.

Without a word, Alexander led her back through the walkway, into the castle proper, and to an enormous hall decked out with flowers and tables groaning with food. It seemed as though every resident of Dunnet followed them in for the Ceilidh, the wedding reception.

Hannah should have been elated. She should have been thrilled. She should have had an appetite, but she did not.

All through the dinner, her husband sat silent at her side. She tried to engage him in conversation several times, but his responses were confined to a smile, a nod, or a stare. She had to turn to his brother for reprieve. Andrew was in good spirits, but that might have been the whisky, which was flowing freely. He chattered gaily about the lands and the clan and the history of the Lochlannach family—all of which should have come from her husband.

As for Dunnet, he didn't drink much, only a sip with each new toast, and barely that, but it hardly mollified her. When he met her gaze and then looked away, Hannah lifted her finger for another glass of wine.

She'd had no intention of partaking as much as she did, but she found it useful to abate her brittle mood. She could only hope being married to such a stone would not drive her to drink.

By the time the wedding cake arrived, she was feeling somewhat mellow and had arrived at a resolution. So he didn't want to talk to her? She wouldn't talk to him.

It would make for a peaceful union. A quiet one, at least.

It would be a challenge for her, holding her tongue, but she could do it. She was certain that burn in her belly was determination and not the desire for reprisal.

Morag, the cook, beaming with pride, bustled in after the footmen carrying her cake. Indeed, it was a stunning creation of fruitcake steeped in brandy, and quite large. Though it would need to be, to accommodate the crowd. The first piece was served to Hannah's husband with two forks—apparently, they would share, while the rest of the top tier was pieced out to the guests. The bottom tier would be saved to celebrate the birth of their firstborn child.

She tried to ignore Dunnet's heated gaze as he fed her the first bite of cake but couldn't. There seemed to be a wealth of meaning in that look, in the slight quirk of his lips, but Hannah couldn't interpret it. Obediently, like a baby bird, she opened her mouth and allowed him to feed her.

As delectable as the confection probably was, it tasted like dust in her mouth. She chewed and swallowed and then fed him a bite as well.

She had thought they would finish their cake, or at least make an attempt to, but as soon as he'd swallowed his morsel he stood and tugged her up by his side.

"Ladies and gentlemen!" Andrew cried. "The Laird and Lady of Dunnet!" The assemblage cheered.

When Dunnet whipped her up into his arms, the crowd went wild. Hannah's *eep* was swallowed in the roar. She shot a panicked glance at Lana, but she responded with a delighted grin.

There would be no respite from that quarter. Nor any other. As Hannah's husband carried her from the room the denizens of Dunnet crowded around them, and the throng stood at the bottom of the steps calling out their good wishes as he bounded up the stairs and down the long, long hall to his chambers. As their cheers faded, Hannah's trepidation rose.

She was beset by a welter of sensation. Not the least of which was the flurry of his movements as he strode with great speed, whisking her away from the party. Then there was the feel of his arms around her, cradling her. The warmth of his chest. The tang of his scent as it curled around her.

Oh dear. She really shouldn't have had so much wine. At the very least, she should have eaten more.

He leaned down to open the door to his bedchamber and then carried her over the threshold. Gently, he set her to her feet, kicking the door closed with his heel. She could feel his gaze on her face, but she couldn't meet his eyes. Heat walked up her cheeks.

They were alone. Absolutely alone.

In his bedchamber.

She glanced at the bed.

It was enormous. Four thick posters flanked the corners. It was rafted with fat pillows. The sheets were turned back.

Egads.

She opened her mouth to speak—to state her unwavering assertion that this would be an excellent opportunity to continue their chat—when he lifted her hand. His lips were warm, his breath damp, as he tenderly kissed the ring he had placed on her finger.

And then he knelt before her.

She had to look at him then. Had to stare at him, and once she did her consciousness was ensnared by the vision. In the traditional Highland dress, he was heartbreakingly handsome and there, on his knees before her, irresistible.

Holding her gaze, he lifted her hem. And kissed it.

No words could express what that simple gesture conveyed. It shafted through her soul, truer than any arrow.

My wife, he'd said. *I am your servant.*

In a flash her aggravation with him crumbled, like a sand castle consumed by a rushing tide. In a flash her hunger for him rose again. It filled her veins with a scorching heat. Uncomfortable prickles throbbed throughout her body.

Maybe it was the wine she'd had or the fact that she hadn't been able to eat much, but her head spun. Her heart raced. A mad, dizzying rush engulfed her.

To hell with conversation.

She wanted him and she wanted him now.

CHAPTER SEVEN

Beautiful.

She was absolutely beautiful. With her cheeks flushed, her eyes shining, her lips parted.

Alexander trembled as he stared up at her. He could hardly believe the time was here. Finally. Finally they were husband and wife. Finally they were alone. He'd barely been able to contain himself throughout the Ceilidh. The speeches, the endless toasts, shaking countless hands. When it had been time to sweep her into his arms and carry her away, a great welling elation had encompassed him.

And now they were here. He wasn't sure how to proceed. Making love to a wife was a new thing for him, but he knew what he wanted to do.

He wanted to worship her.

Every inch.

With knocking knees, he stood and stepped behind her, releasing her hair from its knot. It tumbled over her shoulders in a silken fall. He spread it out, sifting his fingers through the soft strands.

Then he unfastened the rosette and removed the plaid his brother had bestowed upon her, folding it carefully and setting it on a chair. Next, he unfastened the white heather from her lapel and set it aside, next to his.

He should have kept going. He should have slowly unbuttoned her bodice and removed her dress, but he couldn't. Nae. He needed to taste her. It had been far too long since he had.

When he tipped up her chin, it trembled. There was a hint of apprehension in her eyes. He knew he was large and she was small, but he didn't want her to fear him. He would be gentle with her, always. This he vowed.

So as he set his mouth on hers, he murmured the words in his heart. "Hannah. *Mo bhean. Mo ghraidh.*" *My wife. My love.* Though the last of it might have been muffled as their lips touched.

Then again, his brain might have been muffled.

Because as he touched her, tasted her, all thoughts flew asunder.

Heat rose in him and he deepened the kiss, pulling her closer and delving in. She moaned and pressed into him, which enflamed him. This was their first true kiss as husband and wife. She was warm and fragrant and he ached to have her.

Though she responded sweetly, kissing him back, threading her fingers through his hair, he stepped away.

He would worship her, he reminded himself.

Not pounce upon her like a savage.

He would show her with his body that which he found so difficult to say.

Though she frowned at him, he led her to the chair by the fire and sat her down. Then he knelt once more and removed her slippers. Her eyes widened, but she didn't demur. In fact, she didn't make a peep.

She did peep, though, when he stroked the delicate arc of her instep. And she peeped again—well, more of a squawk—when he kissed her there. A laugh bubbled from her lips and she tried to squirm away, but he didn't allow it. Rather, he continued tracing the lines of her foot, her toes, her ankle, relishing each touch.

And each touch he followed with a buss.

Her eyes widened when he pushed up her hem and began exploring her calves.

"Oh dear," she murmured.

He put a finger to his lips. "Shhh."

She nibbled her lip—a sight that poleaxed him, but he forced himself to continue, paying special attention to the backsides of her knees, because it caused her to moan and wriggle and he did enjoy that very much.

By the time he reached her thighs, he was hard as a rock. His cock thrummed with every beat of his heart. Hunger for her, his wife, rolled through him in waves. Slowly, he eased up her skirt until it pooled in her lap, then drew his fingers over the silky skin, amazed at how creamy and flawless it was.

It humbled him that she—this exquisite creature—would deign to allow him to touch her. To hold her. To have her. He expected that at any moment she might leap to her feet and stop him, but she did not.

When he raised her hem the final bit and a downy triangle of jet-black curls came into view, his breath stalled. He nearly swallowed his tongue when her thighs shifted apart. Only an infinitesimal bit, but it was enough to enrage his senses.

Her heat, her scent, her soft sighs, surrounded him like a swirling fog.

He scudded his palm over the tops of her thighs, inching closer and closer. Her breasts rose as she sucked in a breath.

When he touched her there, every nerve in his body sizzled. Easing through the down, he found her pearl.

It was damp.

She was damp.

His vision blurred.

Worship her, he reminded himself, repeating it like a mantra in his head.

The urge to take her, wildly, brutally, savagely raked him. But he could not. Would not.

He had vowed. And a Lochlannach never broke a vow.

Though he might die trying to keep it.

His tongue dabbed out to wet his lips and she gasped, drawing his attention to her face. It stalled there.

Had he thought her beautiful before?

Was he mad?

Nothing was as enthralling as her expression as he stroked her most intimate center. Her eyes were glazed; her lips parted, her breath came in small pants.

When he stilled—only for a second, but it didn't matter to her—she sank her nails into his scalp and gripped him tightly. "Doona stop." A guttural command. One with which he was delighted to comply.

He opened her with his thumbs and stared at her. *God. God in heaven above.* He could gaze at this sight forever—

But no.

When she lifted her hips and tightened her grip, he knew he couldn't gaze at that sight forever.

He was not a patient enough man.

He wanted, needed, to *taste* her.

Now.

Hanna's body clenched as Alexander lowered his head. Her chest ached until she remembered to breathe. Every muscle quivered. How was it that such a simple touch, the mere skim of his hand, could cause such havoc?

Feelings she'd never known raced through her. A tightness at her core, a welling dampness between her thighs, and an emptiness, a restlessness that lashed at her body and mind.

The matrons of Ciaran Reay had certainly never mentioned *this*.

She wanted to push closer but dared not. She couldn't

bear to miss a second of this—whatever he was doing. It was far too heavenly.

When he lapped her, she nearly swooned. And she was not a swooning kind of girl. Pleasure, intense and delicious, shot through her as he drew his velvety tongue along her tender crease and dabbed at the bundle of nerves at the center of her being. He made a sound, a strangled groan, one that rumbled through her with a heady hum. The vibration sent new delights dancing over her skin, through her flesh.

She couldn't stop herself. She closed her thighs on his head and arched into the bliss.

Thank God he didn't stop. *Thank God.* Instead his lips closed around her and—dear heavens—he sucked.

Something took her. She wasn't certain what it was, but it was wondrous. Lights danced before her eyes; a great tide welled within her; a series of mindless quivers and quakes shook her.

As marvelous as it was, it engendered within her only a desire for more.

Nae, more than a desire. A raging need.

She took hold of his ears—ignoring his yelp—and wrenched his face to hers, and she kissed him. She knew that strange taste was the flavor of her own arousal, which only excited her more. That he leaned into the kiss, that he covered her mouth with his and consumed her, thrilled her to the core.

The weight of his broad chest against hers was a delight. The scrape of him as he moved over her, brushing against the swollen tips of her breasts, was nearly unbearable.

But ah, she would bear it.

Especially when he closed a hand on one sensitive mound and squeezed.

Rivulets of pleasure spread out, fomenting new flames of passion.

It frustrated her that she didn't know what she wanted, didn't know what she needed. But he seemed to know. As he toyed with her breast, he continued to stroke between her legs, bringing her to higher and higher glory until the peaks melded together into one long ripple of unending sweetness.

He leaned back to gaze at her. The hint of regret made clear his intention to retreat, to stop. She nearly wailed.

"Not . . . here." His voice was gruff, harsh.

"Aye. Here." She didn't want this to stop. Couldn't bear for it to stop. Not even to move over to the bed.

She tugged him back, taking his mouth with hers and raking his neck with her nails. Unable to still her restless hands, she stroked his shoulders, ran her fingers through his hair. As she scraped her palms over the great slabs of his back, unexpected ripples captured her attention. Curiosity scoured her. She traced one and then another. And then, fascinated, she began exploring them all.

When he realized her intentions, his muscles bunched. He stilled, lifted his head, and looked down at her, his brow furrowed. "Hannah . . ."

"Are these scars?"

"Hannah . . ."

"How did you get these?" It seemed there were many. They covered his back.

He huffed a laugh. "They're nothing."

"Nothing?"

"It was . . . long ago." He bent and kissed her again, with a wild passion, possibly to silence her questions. Possibly because he felt the need as strongly as she did. His mouth burned a path over her cheek and down to the crook of her neck, where he nested. His reaction made it clear he didn't want to talk about the scars. Which was fine. Because this new barrage was such a tantalizing sensation, it filled her consciousness. She gripped his head to hold him there, just so.

Apparently, he was as needy as she, for he sank back into her, resumed his delightful forays beneath her skirts and his assault on her aching breasts. When he dipped his head to suck one of her nipples into his mouth—and even through the fabric of her gown it was nearly more than she could take—she arched into him, pressing her groin against his.

His hardness shocked her. Delighted her.

She rubbed against him and he shuddered. "Lord, have mercy," he murmured. Or something like it. It was difficult to tell, with the pulse rushing in her ears. She couldn't help undulating against him again. This time he reared back, his eyes red, his nostrils flared, his lips tight.

He closed his hands on her thighs and yanked her forward.

His ferocity thrilled her. She tendered a smile; it was probably a wicked smile, judging from his reaction. A snarl, a curse. He lifted his kilt and fisted his cock. Hannah's attention was snared by the sight and her heart lurched.

Oh, not in fear. In an agony of want.

She spread her legs farther—surely she must, to accommodate him. As large as he'd seemed before, he was larger still and stiff as a pike. The tip gleamed; a droplet clung to it. The sudden urge to lap him there possessed her. Perhaps, later, she would.

He waited until she met his gaze and then he nudged forward, guiding himself to her entrance.

She sucked in a breath as he touched her, dragging the fat head up and down her slick center. And then—heaven help her—he eased in. There was a slight burn as he pushed past her barrier and then nothing but the most agonizing delight as he sank deep.

He moved slowly, though she could tell it cost him.

Hell, it cost her. She wanted more. More.

"Ah, God!" she cried as he filled her, impaled her. All her senses danced and sang at the fullness, the heaven, of this intimate touch.

He made a noise too, something feral and wild and twined with bestial satisfaction. And then another, a grunt, as he pulled out.

Hannah nearly smacked him. She didn't want him to pull out. She wanted—

Ah! But then he plunged in again and the excitement curling in her belly tightened like a fist. The whirlwind that had besieged her before began to spin again and, as he took her, faster, harder, deeper, as his own frenzy grew, she feared it might snatch her away.

She clung to him for purchase, wrapped her legs around his waist and her arms around his neck, and held on as tight as she could, sinking her nails into the muscles of his back, running her restless fingers over the fabric of his shirt. Relentlessly he worked in and out of her, even as a new delirium descended, taking her, sending her flying and skittering like a leaf on the wind.

Her entire body seized, a series of delightful quivers over which she was helpless, and pleased to be so.

As she closed around him, he thrust harder. His strokes became more frenzied Shorter. Harder. His breath came out in harsh huffs. His features tightened. The scar on his cheek went white. Hannah stared at his face, fascinated, deluded, bemused by the tick of his pulse in his neck.

She couldn't resist a lick. A suck. A nibble.

And her husband, her silent, whispering wolf, bellowed so loudly the walls shook.

His cock surged inside her. A warm wetness flooded her. He thrust again, and again and again.

Then, with a groan, he collapsed on her, nesting his face in the crook of her neck.

Boneless, replete, and exceedingly pleased with how much she had enjoyed this, Hannah held him close and stroked his hair as he recovered.

He didn't speak much and he had an aggravating penchant for writing letters when a conversation would do quite nicely. But heavens. Could he make love to a woman.

She might be very pleased with her marriage after all

Bluidy fucking hell.

He had bollixed that up but good.

He'd intended to worship her. To make slow, sweet, passionate love to her for hours until she was on the knife's edge of desire, panting and begging for him. Not fall on her like a lust-flown fool.

He'd only gotten as far as her thighs before he lost all reason.

It was probably her scent. Or her mewls. Or her *presence*. But he'd lost all reason and completely forgotten the worshiping part.

He'd taken her. In a chair. Like an animal.

That animals didn't make love in chairs hardly signified.

No doubt she hated him. Thought him a savage at best.

However, this wasn't the time to castigate himself. No. This was just the beginning of their marriage. The beginning of their wedding night. He would be gentler next time.

Next time being now.

With that resolution, he lifted her gently and carried her to the bed.

She was boneless in his arms, which he took as a good

sign. She sighed and wrapped her arms around his neck and tangled her fingers in his hair, but in a dreamy way, as though she wasn't quite aware she was doing it.

Setting her on the mattress, he edged in beside her, pulled her into his arms, and kissed her, but it was only to distract her, so he could make his way down the row of buttons along her back. He gave the same teasing strokes he'd lavished on her legs to each swath of skin he revealed. She was warm and soft in his arms, a handful of heaven, and as he explored her shoulders, and the exposed vee of her back, she explored him.

His heart stuttered when she tugged at his kilt.

Damn it all to hell. He was wearing too much. Too much for what he intended to do.

He stood and held her gaze as he unwrapped his plaid, delighting in her avid attention. Without a care, he dropped it to the floor. Then, slowly, he pulled off his shirt. She gasped as his bare chest was revealed. Her eyes flickered over his body in a hungry rake. His knees went a little wobbly when her tongue peeped out.

Her entire body stiffened when he stroked his belt.

Again with that damn tempting tongue. His pulse jumped as she dabbed at her lip. As though she wanted to taste him.

And damn, he wanted her to taste him.

He unbuckled his belt, undid the snaps, and let his kilt fall, baring everything to her fervent stare. Her focus locked on to his groin, which sent a sharp thrill cutting through him. The beast stirred. Rose.

Hanna's nostrils flared. Her body went on point. She rose up on her knees, and with that movement the loosened bodice of the dress fell, pooling at her waist. The dusky circles of her aureoles were visible through the sheer fabric of her chemise, inciting his ardor. Alexander's mouth watered. He swallowed heavily.

As his cock lengthened, her eyes widened. Her lips parted.

Her gaze flicked to his and they connected, touched. Something sizzled between them.

"Your . . . dress." It was all he could manage, but thankfully she understood his command. His need.

She lifted the frock over her head, tugged it off, and then tossed it behind her. The chemise followed.

The vision of Hannah, naked, perched on his bed, gutted him.

Holy God. He'd just had her. He'd just been sated. He'd just sworn to take it slowly this time—to show her how glorious passion could be when a man took his time.

He was in dire peril of breaking that vow.

When she opened her arms to him, he knew he was lost.

He wrenched off his boots and then, without even taking the time to remove his stockings, he joined her on the bed. They faced each other, on their knees, each rapt in their own examination of the other's body. She set a hand on his chest, then dragged it slowly up and over his shoulder, murmuring to herself, testing his flesh, and occasionally scraping him with her nails.

As she explored him, he explored her.

Her breasts were irresistible. Like a bee to a perfect, fragrant flower, he honed in on them, cupping each in a questing palm. Warm and soft and oh, so sweet. Tantalizing, alluring, a perfect handful. A perfect fit. He thumbed a nipple. Ripples danced over her skin. She moaned. Wriggled in an enticing dance.

He couldn't stop himself from lowering his head and tasting her. Her nipples were thick and tight, enticing targets for his attention. Showing the full force of his discipline, he lapped at them and whirled his tongue around the peaks for at least a full minute before he sucked one into his mouth.

She shuddered and wailed and he drew harder. Her fingers fisted in his hair; brutally she held him in place, barely even allowing him to release one for the other. As he feasted, he skimmed his hand down her bare flank. The silk of her skin registered on his brain with a scorching heat. His senses swam at the smell of her, her taste, her essence.

Hannah. His Hannah.

He wanted to taste her everywhere.

He planned to do so.

But she had other plans.

When she pushed him away, his heart plunged. She reared back and stared at him, a fierce expression on her delicate features. She pushed at him once again, this time harder. Denial raged through him. Denial and confusion.

Ah, but the third time she pushed, her intention became clear.

His desolation was replaced with a rampant surge of white-hot lust. Because she pushed him onto his back and she surveyed him the way a starving woman surveys a banquet, laid out before her.

On a bed. Naked. Aroused.

Wearing nothing but stockings.

She ignored his stockings.

He was oblivious to them too. Especially when she leaned closer. Her hair fell onto his chest, a lacy whisper, a silken caress. Then she cradled his face in her hands and kissed him. Not his lips, as he would have liked, but the tip of his nose, his forehead, his cheek. She sent a series of tiny kisses along the length of his scar. When he tried to stop her, when he tried to take charge, she captured his wrists and set them above his head, splaying him out for her delectation. When she shot him a warning look, he understood her perfectly.

Don't move.

Holy fook.

Had he thought to tease *her*? To bring *her* to the knife's edge of anticipation?

He was there already, and she'd barely touched him.

He could not last. He would not last, and he knew it.

But he would bear it, this innocent, heinous exploration. He would bear it as long as he could. Because *she* wanted it.

That above everything else—above the incredible sensation of her fingers riffling through the springy hairs on his chest, the slight tickle of her teeth as she nipped at his beard, the sharp rake of her nails over his belly—moved him.

She wanted *this*.

She wanted *him*.

When her journey of discovery led her lower, toward his hips, his cock strained up to greet her. Alexander was aware of the dizzying effect of her touch, her breath, her murmurs. He was also very well aware of the pressure in his balls, the hard, hot thrum of his pulse along the length of his cock. The simmering urge to plant himself in her again. The need to release.

So when she did it, when she wrapped her fingers around his turgid length, he nearly came out of his skin.

With a yelp he rolled up and caught her wrists, stopped her. He had to. He was far too close to disaster. She had no idea, this wee bundle of torment and curves. She had no idea what she was doing to him.

Or perhaps she did.

A sizzle of excitement whipped through him at the glint in her eye. The tweak of her lips.

With great resolve, she pushed him back down on the pillows and arranged his arms above his head once more. She waggled a warning finger in his direction, one that made her meaning plain.

Do. Not. Move.

He groaned and squeezed his eyes closed but then wrenched them open again when he realized he didn't want to miss a second of whatever she had planned.

Because he had a pretty good idea what she had planned. And he didn't want to miss a second.

She curled her hand around his cock and gave it a testing pump. He hissed in a breath through his teeth. And then—God help him—she lowered her head. It was nearly overwhelming, watching her mouth close on him and feeling it at the same time. His breath stalled in his lungs. His pulse kicked into a manic rhythm and his head spun.

Delirium, mindless pleasure, and a clawing need for more raged through him. He threaded his fingers through her hair, reveling in the sleek slide, and then, ultimately, tightened, holding her in place.

She suckled him, sending skeins of agony through to his gut. Her teeth grazed at his sanity, but then she opened wider and took him deep, enrobing him, encasing him in a grip of torment and pleasure.

Her tongue lashed his sanity. Her lips worked in a wet frenzy. The suction nearly drew his soul from its earthly anchorage.

The storm within him raged, edging up, higher and higher, constricting into a torturous grip until he thought he might expire, implode.

When she added a wicked stroke to her torment, caressing him while she worked him with her velvet kiss, he lost all control.

Bliss rode over him, like a wild stallion, rampant and free and uncaring of the desolation it incited. Shivers and shudders, quivers and quakes racked him as his being narrowed down to that single point. That point where their bodies merged.

With a feral howl he came, sinking into her, taking her

mouth, filling her with all he had. She took it all. Every drop.

She left him with nothing.

Weak, drained, and still beset with shimmers of delight, he collapsed.

Hannah crawled up his body and lay on top of him, a heady weight. Despite the pleasure she'd just drawn on him, he didn't think he'd ever known such contentment as *this.* Skin to skin, from chest to groin, they were sealed. He wrapped his arms around her and held her.

She murmured a sigh and nestled closer, tucking her face into his neck. He stroked her back as he fought for purchase.

Bone-deep gratification, bone-deep gratitude, coursed through him and he sent up a prayer of thanks that he'd found her. That she'd wanted him. That they were wed. That she was his.

Every night could be like this, he told himself. Every night.

He was almost asleep when it hit him. When he remembered.

Damn it. He'd forgotten, once again, that he was supposed to be worshiping her.

Not the other way around.

CHAPTER EIGHT

Hannah awoke from a pleasing dream and stretched, enjoying the ripple of soft sheets on her skin and the embrace of a warm nest. The memory of last night drifted through her, along with a pleasant pinging ache between her legs.

Ah. Her wedding night.

She'd loved every moment of it.

She snuggled deeper into her pillow.

She'd heard tales from the married women of Ciaran Reay, tales intimating that the first time was painful, but Hannah had not experienced that. There'd been nothing but heaven. Nothing but the desire for more.

Most specifically she'd been possessed of the urge to taste him, as he'd tasted her.

And he'd allowed it.

She didn't know if this was something married women did; the matrons of Ciaran Reay had certainly not mentioned that, but she had enjoyed it. Loved the feel of his smooth skin between her lips, the taste of him, the scent of him. His shivers and groans.

The best part, of course, had been tormenting him to the point where he lost all control and bellowed her name. *Bellowed* it.

She bit back a smile and rolled over, hoping to wake him and, maybe, try that again.

But her hand landed on cool sheets, long deserted. He was gone.

She pouted down at his pillow, next to hers, dented with the shape of his head but empty.

Well, not empty. There was an envelope on it.

Hannah recognized the parchment and something in her belly curled.

A letter?

Another letter?

With a frown, she picked up the note and opened it. His script was crisp and precise and, if she was being realistic, not romantic in the slightest. Certainly not as *loverly* as a night like the one they had shared should command. It said, simply:

Hannah, Wife,
I dinna want to wake you. Please enjoy your first day as the Lady of Dunnet. Fergus will be available to give you a tour and introduce you to your people.
Yours,
Alexander

No prose or poems about the beauty of their joining—although she certainly had not expected that. But she'd expected *something*. Something more.

And he'd signed it *Alexander*. Not *Dunnet*. Was this an invitation to call him by his given name?

Short of asking him, there was no way to know.

She sighed and collected her wedding dress and the plaid he had given her and padded through the parlor to her hideously hued room. She saw a covered tray set on the table in the parlor and paused to investigate. A pot of tea—still warm—and a plate of oatcakes.

Hannah wrinkled her nose. She wasn't a fan of oatcakes, but she was hungry. She took one and nibbled on it as she continued on to her room and dressed for the day.

Thusly fortified, she crossed the hall and scratched on Lana's door.

Hannah's sister greeted her with wide eyes. Lana caught Hannah's arm and tugged her into the room. "How was it?" her sister asked in a whisper, as though someone else might overhear.

Hannah's response was naught but a blush. It had been marvelous—until she awoke to find him gone—but she didn't want to share the details with her sister, who was a maiden, no matter how curious she was.

Hannah shot a glance at the bed, where Nerid lounged in a truly undignified arrangement, his back leg lifted high. He shot her an offended glare and then proceeded to resume grooming his fur with furious licks. It was nice to see he had weathered his kerfuffle with Brùid with his usual aplomb.

Something captured her attention then, something that wiped all thoughts of the cat, of her absent husband and the night they had shared, from her mind.

"What is that smell?" she asked.

Lana waved at a tray on the table next to her hearth.

Hell. A full breakfast. With eggs and cheeses and . . . "Is that bacon?"

Lana nodded and snagged the last piece, crunching into it with relish.

"How did you get bacon?"

A slender shoulder rose. "I asked. Morag is a dear, you know. She and her sister Una have served as Dunnet's cooks forever and a day." Lana poured two cups of tea.

Hannah picked up a fork and helped herself to some of the fluffy eggs and then ate them all, despite Lana's frown. "All I got were oatcakes."

"Hmm. I told Morag they make me ill." A mischievous grin. "You should try that."

"Perhaps I shall." She glanced at her sister, sitting there

in the soft morning light looking so sweet and innocent and pure, and something rippled in her belly. It felt like concern. Though she'd been distracted last night at the feast, she hadn't been so distracted that she'd been oblivious to Andrew's hungry glances at Lana. Though Hannah knew she should hold her tongue, she couldn't.

"Lana?"

She smiled; her face glowed with it. "Aye?"

"I . . ." She sighed. "I canna help but worry. . . ."

Lana quirked a brow and took a sip of tea. "Worry? About what?"

"You."

A laugh. "I'm fine. Doona worry about me."

"I canna help it. You are here, under my charge. I would never forgive myself if . . ."

"If . . . what?"

"If anything happened."

Lana tucked her chin and fixed Hannah with a puzzled glance. "What are you talking about, dear?"

It had to be said. And bluntly. "Andrew."

"What?" Lana blew out another laugh, this one of incredulity.

"I've seen the way he looks at you, watches you, as though you were a plump rabbit and he a hungry fox."

"Are you saying I am plump?"

Hannah narrowed her eyes. "You know what I mean. He intends to seduce you. I can see it."

Lana tapped her lips. A mischievous light danced in her eyes. "He is verra handsome."

Hannah clenched her fingers. "Aye. He is an attractive man, but I've met his sort before."

"His sort?"

"The kind of man who flits from flower to flower, taking what he wants and then dances away."

Lana's brow rumpled. "So am I a rabbit or a flower?"

"Both." A growl. "You should keep your distance from him. Papa would slay me if I allowed you to be compromised."

Her delicate chin firmed. "Hannah, if I'm to be compromised, or rather when, as I do hope it will happen at some point, it willna be you who allows it. It shall be my choice."

"Men like Andrew can be verra convincing."

Lana reached over to pat Hannah's hand. "Darling, doona worry about me. I know how to handle men like that."

Hannah's eyes flared. "What?"

"I'm not a complete innocent," she said with a sniff.

"What-what-what are you saying?" Hannah's heart thrummed.

"I know how things work."

Och, Hannah did not like that *knowing* look. It was far too . . . knowing. "*How* do you know how things work?"

Lana lifted a shoulder. "I eavesdropped on the matrons while they were carding wool."

"Lana Dounreay! You dinna!" It was easy to ignore the ripple of guilt that Hannah had done the same. This was a completely different circumstance. This was *Lana*.

Her innocent lips curled into a wicked smile. One that made Hannah's bowels seethe. "I discovered many things." A wink. *Holy hell. A wink!* "Besides, I've been kissed before."

"*What?*" Hannah gaped at her sister. "Who? Who kissed you?"

Lana pinkened. "Rory for one."

"Rory?" *Good God.* Hannah would flay him.

"And Torquil."

"Torquil? The beekeeper?" Hannah gaped. Torquil had *nostril hair.*

"Is there another Torquil? And Angus and Ewan and—"

"Oh, do stop." A ghastly thought occurred. "Lana, you havena . . . I mean there hasn't been . . . You dinna . . ."

Lana's laugh was incongruous and a little irritating. "Of course not, Hannah. Doona be silly. They were all just kisses. Only kisses."

"Kisses can easily lead to something else." She knew. Och, aye, she knew.

"Doona fash yerself, Hannah. While I find Andrew rather attractive, and I wouldna mind a kiss from him—"

Hannah *eeped*.

"I prefer a man with dark hair." Her eyes twinkled. "A man who isna . . . prettier than I am."

Aye. Andrew was pretty. And he knew it.

"I still must ask you to guard yourself around him."

Lana studied her for a moment, taking in her concerned expression. "All right, Hannah. If it will make you rest easy, I shall." Relief gushed through Hannah . . . until Lana added, "But I wouldna mind a kiss from him."

"Lana!"

Her laugh echoed through the room. She patted Hannah again, though she was not mollified. "So tell me, Hannah, what are your plans for today? Your first day as a wife?" It was a clear attempt to change the topic, and Hannah allowed it. She didn't respond, *Keeping you from kissing Andrew Lochlannach*, as she wished.

She was very proud of her restraint.

"Dunnet has notified me that Fergus is prepared to give me a tour of the castle." She tried very hard not to allow a bite in her tone. "Would you like to come?"

"I would love that." Lana refilled their tea. "So Dunnet finally spoke to you?"

Hannah sniffed. "Another letter." She added honey and stirred with a clang that bespoke her irritation.

"He does like those letters."

"Humpf."

Lana chuckled. "Why do you snort like that?"

"I hate those letters."

"You hate them?"

"Darling, he's spoken but a handful of words to me in the entire time I've known him. And that man is my husband."

Lana waggled her fingers. "Words are overrated."

"Humpf."

"Is it not true that a man is measured by his actions, not his words?"

Hannah glared at her sister, and not only because she was parroting back a maxim Hannah herself had often spouted. It was rather annoying to be in a fine fettle and have some logical and rational person attempt to calm one down. "That is hardly the point."

"It is precisely the point."

"Is it too much to ask that I have a conversation with my husband?"

"If you want to speak to him, well, speak to him."

"In point of fact, I shall." Hannah rose and brushed out her skirts. "Shall we go and find him?"

"That would be lovely." Lana hooked her arm in Hannah's and they headed for the door. "I quite like him, by the way," Lana murmured.

"Oh? Has he spoken to *you*?"

"Of course not." Lana patted Hannah's hand. "You know I see things differently." It was true. When Lana described people she'd met, she spoke in terms of colors surrounding them, rather than their physical persona. Hannah had never understood that, but Lana was usually right in her assumptions about people and once she decided she liked someone she never changed her mind.

Maybe Lana should have married Dunnet.

Or maybe not.

"Why do you like him?"

"He is verra strong. Loyal. Brave." Lana's brow wrinkled. "I have a sense he's been through great hardship."

"This is Scotland." Everyone had been through hardship.

"You should be patient with him."

"I've never excelled at patience."

Lana didn't respond. Probably because she knew this was true.

With the help of a footman, they found Fergus in the morning room, a charming east-facing salon speckled with elegant Chippendales and comfortable divans. The factor was overseeing the work of a pretty young maid who was dusting a breakfront. Andrew, Hannah's new brother-in-law, was with him.

Apparently, it took the oversight of two grown men to assure the girl's work was up to par.

When Andrew spotted the sisters, he ceased his mooning at the maid and proceeded to moon at Lana. It was all Hannah could do not to growl.

He affected a bow. "Good morning, my lady. Miss Dounreay."

"Good morning, Andrew. Fergus."

The factor bowed. "My lady. I have orders to give you a—"

"Aye. A tour of the grounds." Hannah had received those orders as well. "Do you know where my husband is?"

Fergus frowned. "At this hour? Most likely in his study."

"Aye. And where is this study?"

Fergus blanched, except for his scar and the tips of his ears, which showed a hint of pink. "Oh, ye canna go *there*."

Hannah blinked. A whisper of outrage skulked through her. "I would like to speak to him."

"He shall emerge by lunch." Fergus attempted a smile. An unsuccessful smile.

"I would like to speak to him now."

Fergus' lips flapped. His gaze whipped from her to Andrew, who shrugged. The factor's chin firmed. "No one interrupts the laird when he is working. And no one is allowed in the study."

"No one is *allowed* in the study?" Irritation bubbled through her. She'd never liked being told no. Never in her life had she been *forbidden* from doing something, especially something so . . . simple. She didn't like the prospect of being prohibited from visiting a room in her new home, and on her first day in residence, no less. She shot a glare at Lana, whose eyes widened. She might have mouthed the words, *Oh dear.*

"Alexander is a verra busy man." Andrew offered a much more successful smile, but likely he'd had more practice. "When he's not checking in with crofters, he spends most mornings closed up in the study getting through the bulk of the work. We've all learned not to bother him until later in the day. It is best if you wait for him to be available. In the meantime, may I show you around the castle?" He extended an arm.

While Hannah was not pleased, she sensed the men would not budge on this. And the castle was so enormous, if she attempted to find this mysterious study on her own she would probably get lost. Clearly, the best approach would be to take the offered tour and discover the study along the way.

It would, most likely, be the one room they didn't show her.

"I would love that. Thank you, Andrew."

Apparently, her brother-in-law was more devious than she gave him credit for, or perhaps he had deduced her intentions. For as he showed her around her new home, with Fergus trailing along, interjecting the few facts her husband's brother had omitted about this room or that, there wasn't so much as a glimpse of the mysterious study. There were certainly no rooms they skipped.

But the castle was old, a meandering warren of hallways and wings. It would have been easy to deliberately skip one section or another with a visitor being none the wiser. Beyond that, Hannah had the distinct impression Andrew was leading her in circles. She resolved that she would make herself a map of the sprawling building and conduct a search on her own at some point in the future.

She would discover Alexander's secret hideaway and she would beard him there.

When they finished with the tour of the castle—or, at the very least, when Andrew had tired of the roundabout—they moved on to the castle grounds. As Lana skipped toward the stables with Fergus in her wake, Hannah held back a bit. Andrew, perforce, slowed his pace as well, though it was obvious he very much wanted to hie after Lana.

Too bad.

Not only was Hannah determined to scuttle any opportunities for those two to be alone together; she also wanted to talk to Andrew. If she couldn't speak to her husband, she could learn more about him from his brother. She hooked her arm in his and smiled up at him.

He blinked in surprise. Why he blinked in surprise was a mystery. She had not been precisely curt to him this morning.

Well, maybe a little.

"Thank you so much for giving up your time for us this morning," she purred.

His Adam's apple worked. He scuttled a glance around them and tried to untangle his arm. She didn't allow it. "It, ah, it was my pleasure, my lady. We all want you to feel at home here."

"Hmm."

"And do you?"

"Do I?"

"Feel at home?"

She studied him for a moment. "It is far too early to tell."

His lashes flickered. "Alexander has gone out of his way to make you welcome."

"I'm sure he has." Redecorating her rooms, for one thing. "On that . . . May I ask you a . . . personal question?"

Though the stable was shaded from the sun, cool and welcoming, Hannah didn't step inside. Lana gave out a squeal as she discovered a clutch of newly born puppies squirming in one stall and rushed for it. Hannah preferred to remain where she was. This conversation was far too important.

"You may ask me anything." He said this without hesitation, but his cheeks went a little pale.

"Your brother . . . he doesna speak much."

"Ach." Andrew gusted a laugh and scrubbed his face. "That. Nae, he doesna. He never has."

"He writes me letters. About everything."

"He is far more at ease with the written word."

Her brow wrinkled at that, but she let her curiosity go in favor of her indignation. "I'm his wife."

"I'm his brother. I still get a letter every morning."

Hannah paled. She had this to look forward to? "Every morning?"

Andrew grinned. "You'll get used to it, I'm sure."

"I would much prefer a conversation."

"You may find it one-sided. Alexander is not a man of many words."

"So I've noticed." She pursed her lips.

Andrew's chin firmed. "But doona make the mistake of confusing his silence with indifference. He cares. Verra deeply. About everything."

"I'm sure he does." Remarkably, lightning did not strike her dead at the lie. Nor did the stable burst into flames at the dryness of her tone. *Astonishing.*

Andrew set his hand on her shoulder. "Be patient with him. Alexander is a complicated man."

Now this was true.

"Will he ever speak to me?"

"Of course. As he relaxes. As he gets to know you. But he will never *blether* on. He's not much of a *bletherer.*"

That was some consolation, she supposed. She'd never cared much for *blethering.* But the occasional chat would be nice.

As Lana finished snuggling the puppies and they moved on to inspect the mill, another question nagged at Hannah.

"Andrew?"

"Aye, my lady?"

"Why did he marry me?"

Andrew's friendly expression closed down. "That, my lady, is a question you shall have to ask him."

It took great effort not to growl at Andrew's disobliging response.

Still, the sound she made, deep in her throat, could easily have been interpreted as one.

Alexander's fingers tightened on the sill as he stared from the window of the turret down at the stable yard. His office was situated in the old solar of an ancient Lochlannach baron and took up the whole of the top floor of the tower. The room was circular and had windows on either side, so the laird could survey the north and south.

Unfortunately, that meant he had a clear view of the stable yard. And Andrew. With Hannah.

It was illogical for Alexander to be jealous of his brother as he guided his new wife around the castle grounds. *He* could have done as much—he was her groom, after all—but fear had sent him scurrying from her bed and up into his office.

Not that last night hadn't been the most splendid experience of his life. It had. She had sated him in ways he'd not known he required sating.

He'd awoken at dawn and stared down at her delicate features, stroking the lines of her face with a gentle finger, frightened to death that she would awake. That those eyes would flutter open and she would gaze up at him and *speak*. If she spoke to him, he would have to respond. The prospect made his blood go cold.

Frustration and rage lashed at him. He hated the demon that clung to him with sharp, hoary claws. How he would love to be free of it, but he didn't know how to break the chains.

In his naivety, he'd thought after having her, loving her, the ball in his throat would dissolve, the words would flow. He had imagined that once they'd joined, they would be as one.

That had not happened. The opposite, in fact. The closer he'd come to her, the more his emotion and need for her flowered, the worse his affliction had become.

Ah, how he wanted to be with her, spend every moment with her. But therein lay the danger. He couldn't guard his words forever. Sooner or later he would slip. Sooner or later she would discover the truth, or suspect it. He was frightened to death that when she found out about his past, his weakness, his curse, she would be revolted. She'd married him thinking he was a strong, indomitable protector. He dreaded the day when she discovered what he really was.

So he'd slunk away to his tower office—a room that had once been his sanctuary but right now felt very much like a prison. Or maybe his fear was the real prison.

He'd slunk away to hide from her, this magnificent woman who had so completed him the night before. He'd left her, ostensibly to work.

But the work, or his concentration, at the very least, had evaded him.

He could only think of her.

And when he'd wandered to the window for a breath of fresh air, there she was, in the bailey, with Andrew. Chatting. As though conversation was not the most difficult thing in the world.

Then again, to the two of them, it wasn't.

Alexander wanted nothing more than to spend time with her.

And he feared nothing more.

Facing an enormous man wielding a tremendous sword? Not a problem.

Grappling with the tangled and bitter spats of his people? Simple.

Figuring out a way to repurpose an unproductive field for a better yield? Child's play.

The prospect of *speaking* to his wife? A terror.

As ridiculous as it was to try to hide it, he dreaded her reaction.

Though they'd only been married a day, somehow suddenly he couldn't bear the thought of losing her respect. Someday, and someday soon, he would have to tell her. Tell her everything. But not today.

With a growl of frustration he turned back to his desk and stilled. A small bundle sat in his chair, swinging her legs. She grinned up at him and he couldn't help but respond.

"Fiona."

She knew she wasn't supposed to visit him in the mornings, but most days she did. He didn't have the inclination to tell her to stop coming. Her vulnerability made his heart ache. And he enjoyed her company.

Truth be told, his turret tower did get lonely on occasion.

Not bothering with a greeting, Fiona wrinkled her nose. "Wh-why did you . . . do it?"

"Do what?" Although he knew. Or he had a very good idea.

"M-marry her?"

"Ach. My wee lass." He lifted her up and sat in his chair, settling her on his knee.

"Wh-why?"

"She's . . . verra lovely."

Fiona's features scrunched up.

"It was time I took a bride."

"She's . . . *old*."

Alexander barked a laugh. "Old enough for an ancient creature like me?"

"You're not old." Fiona patted his cheek. "You-you're p-perfect."

"I'm too old for you, lass."

She didn't care for this in the slightest. "Do-do you like her?"

"I . . . like her verra much." More than he expected he would. More than he should, after one night.

Fiona humphed and wriggled off his lap. "Well, f-fine then."

"Will you . . . be nice to her? For me?"

She surveyed him somberly for quite some time and then, at long last, nodded. "I . . . suppose."

"I would like that. Th-thank you, my lady." With great pomp, he lifted her tiny hand and kissed it. She went beet red to the tips of her ears and ducked her face so he couldn't see her smile, but he saw it anyway.

A great and welling joy filled his heart.

He loved children. Ached for children of his own. And maybe, last night, he and his wife had made one.

He could only pray this was the case.

Fiona deserved a playmate.

Hannah's husband spent the entire day in his study—wherever it was. She tried not to let her displeasure reign. She spent the afternoon with Lana exploring the grounds around the castle and chatting with some of the people she'd met at her welcome; she found them all to be quite pleasant. To her delight, she discovered a broad terrace running the length of the castle in the back, which overlooked Dunnet Bay. The little town of Dunnet, which she could see from a distance, seemed charming as well. She looked forward to exploring it.

She had the sense that she could be very happy here. If, of course, her concerns about her husband could be set to rest. She had great hopes for dinner tonight.

As she and Lana descended the stairs that evening, the emotion seething within Hannah tasted a little like desperation. She attempted to swallow it down.

Fergus showed them to the sitting room. It was a charming chamber, wood paneled, speckled with comfortable chairs and lit by a welcoming fire, but Hannah hardly noticed. She was a bundle of nerves, anticipating the chance to finally speak to her husband at length.

Andrew arrived first, sauntering into the room like a conquering hero come to dinner. His gaze locked on to Lana and warmed. "My ladies." He bowed over both their hands, though Hannah noticed he lingered over Lana's. His attention, and something in his expression, made irritation riffle through Hannah. When their eyes met and he took in her speaking expression, he flinched and paled, but only a little.

He did, however, loosen his hold on Lana.

When Dunnet arrived, all thoughts of Hannah's annoyance with his brother faded. Her breath caught. Dunnet was so handsome in his plaid, so striking, it made her heart ache. As he approached her, her pulse rushed in her ears. When he took her hand in his and bent over it, a shiver ran through her. "My lady," he whispered, as his gaze locked to hers.

And then he kissed her.

Oh, only lips pressed to the back of her hand, but it sent a sizzle up her arm and straight to her womb.

Her mouth opened. Then closed. She couldn't form a word, or a cogent thought, to save her life.

Before Dunnet had a chance to sit, Fergus bustled into the room and announced that dinner was served in the small dining room. His tone brooked no denial and Hannah decided that while she would have preferred a chance to talk in this casual setting, a dinner conversation would do.

She was wrong.

For one thing, the small dining room was enormous. The table seemed to be leagues long and she was expected to sit at one end, with her groom at the other; he was so far away she could barely make out his features. The footmen showed Lana to a seat near the center, but she sniffed and moved her setting to Hannah's side. *Thank heaven.*

Still, conversation was awkward, so Hannah didn't bother as the footmen brought the first remove.

Andrew broke the clanging silence. "How are you finding Dunnet?" he asked from far, far away.

Hannah's annoyance rippled. She cupped her ear. "I beg your pardon?" Not a shout, but barely.

"I say, how are you finding Dunnet?" His question rang off the stone walls.

Lana glanced at her. The glint in her sister's eye was mischievous. "What did he say?"

"I have no idea. I'm certain he said something, but I couldn't quite make it out."

"Me either."

With exchanged looks and heavy sighs, Andrew and Alexander picked up their bowls and plodded down the long room to the other end of the table.

It was a small victory but a victory nonetheless.

Hannah beamed at them as they sat, ignoring her irritation that Andrew sat next to Lana and offered her a far too toothy smile. "I'm so glad you could join us," Hannah said. The two men flushed, just a tad, which she found gratifying. And on Dunnet, the chagrin was adorable. "I do love an intimate dinner."

"Of course," Andrew murmured through his soup.

None of them spoke as they finished the first course, except to comment on how delicious everything was. Hannah had never struggled with casual conversation, but in this she was flummoxed. As much as she wanted to get to know Dunnet, she didn't know where to begin.

As the footmen whisked their bowls away, Andrew gusted, "So, how are you finding Dunnet?" There might have been a tinge of desperation in his voice, but she could have been imagining it.

"It is lovely," Hannah said.

"Lovely." Lana offered a shy smile. "The people are so friendly."

"Aye. They are." Hannah took a sip of her wine. Her gaze clashed with Dunnet's and a sudden heat rose. There was something in his expression she couldn't quite decipher, but it seemed like appreciation. Whatever it was, it snared her. They stared at each other across the table as silence billowed. Memories of the night before, anticipation for this night, heated her blood. A flush crept up her cheeks. His lips quirked in response.

"I particularly enjoyed my visit to the stables," Lana said as the next course arrived. "Oh, famous. Syllabub." She tucked in with fervor. Lana adored a good syllabub. And this was good. Excellent, in fact. Though it might as well have been ashes, for all the notice Hannah took of it.

For some reason Lana's comment captured Dunnet's attention. Hannah hated that he turned away then, to fix his attention on her sister. It annoyed Hannah that she studied his expression as intensely as she did, searching for any hint of regret. Lana was far lovelier. Hannah would hate for him to think he'd offered for the wrong sister.

"The . . . stables?" he murmured.

Lana licked her spoon. "Aye. The puppies."

"Ah." Though he tried to hide it, his interest faded.

Surely that was not relief gushing through Hannah.

"Alexander has a passion for horseflesh," Andrew explained, shooting a blinding smile at Lana. "He has some of the most sought-after cattle in all of Scotland."

Lana took another bite of her pudding. "I dinna notice the horses. I liked the puppies."

Both men nodded and silence fell again. Hannah sought to break it, on the hope that they had stumbled upon a topic her husband might be loquacious about. "So you breed horses, Dunnet?" she asked.

He opened his mouth and then closed it with a snap, then mutely nodded.

The sounds of their spoons working on their dishes rose.

"How long have you been breeding them?"

"A . . . while."

"How fascinating." It wasn't. Not really, but Hannah was determined to draw him out. "I love to ride."

"Do you?"

She glared at Andrew for the interruption, though it was hardly that. He was probably as anxious as she to keep the waning conversation afloat.

Lana sighed. "I doona ride. Not much. It seems so terribly rude to crawl upon someone's back and make them carry you around, poor creatures."

The men gaped at her.

Her chin firmed. She leaned forward. "They really doona like it."

Andrew's lips flapped like a trout. "They . . . doona . . . ?"

"Of course not. Would you? Would you like someone tossing a nasty saddle on your back and putting a bit in your mouth and kicking you in the flank?"

"I, ah, doona believe I would."

"Of course not. And neither do they."

Andrew shifted in his seat. "Still, ah, it is a verra profitable business." He flashed a dimpled smile at Hannah and she was struck by the haunting familiarity of his features. She studied him, but try as she might, she couldn't recall where she'd seen him before. She glanced at Alexander and flinched at his frown. He shifted it to his brother, who visibly paled.

She might be imagining things, but Alexander almost seemed . . . jealous. Which was ridiculous. Andrew was a handsome man, but he didn't hold a candle to Alexander.

"The clachan seems verra prosperous indeed," she said with a reassuring smile at her husband. "I'm sure we shall be verra happy here."

His frown faded. His gaze bore into hers. He opened his mouth, as though to respond, but Andrew intruded on the moment with another conversation-saving query. "What else have you two done today?"

Lana responded, providing a lengthy dissertation on

each and every thing she'd done, each person she'd met, and her every impression. Andrew hung on her every word, which was bothersome, but Hannah found it difficult to focus on her annoyance, because Alexander caught her gaze. Snagged her attention. As Lana's monologue flowed around them, they stared at each other. Oh, it was a wordless conversation, but it spoke volumes.

When his foot nudged hers under the table, she nearly came out of her skin. She nudged him back and his eyes glimmered, but then Lana said something that ripped his avid attention away.

Dunnet stared at Lana, his mouth agape. "I . . . beg your pardon?"

Hannah glanced at her sister. She hadn't been listening. Not in the slightest.

"I said I had a delightful time in the kitchens."

"After that," Andrew urged.

Lana wrinkled her nose. "I said I had a delightful time in the kitchens. Una gave me a wonderful recipe for shortbread."

Dunnet's brow rippled. *"Una?"*

Though his question was directed at Andrew, who was staring rather rudely, Lana responded. "Aye. Una." She took a sip of her wine. "She's lovely."

"You mean Morag . . ." Andrew said.

Hannah recognized the look that flickered across her sister's face. She'd seen it many times before. Her belly tightened; she suspected what was coming.

Lana's jaw firmed. Her eyes glinted. "I mean Una. Morag is her sister."

Andrew shifted in his seat and rumpled his serviette. "I, ah . . . Una is . . . dead."

A sniff. "I know."

Hannah's bowels tightened at the two men's expressions. She'd known at some point they would discover her sister's eccentricity, but Hannah had really hoped it wouldn't be at the dinner table on the occasion of their first private meal. Still, it could have been worse. It could have been in a more public setting.

"Lana has a gift." Hannah's words were sharper than she intended, more defensive. There was nothing to defend here. Lana was who she was and Hannah would stand by her no matter what. She sent a challenging frown at Dunnet.

He cleared his throat and set his wineglass on the table with deliberate care.

Hannah held her breath. Dear God, if he mocked Lana, if he reviled her or humiliated her in any way, she would—

"Did she . . ." He swallowed. Hannah's heart stalled. "Did she mention . . . oatcakes?" His tentative smile was so sweet. It sent a wave of warmth cascading through her. It had a hint of humor but also . . . acceptance. She forced her fingers to relax; she hadn't realized they'd been clenched.

Lana's laugh tripped through the chamber. "Nae, she dinna." She winked. "Morag wouldna allow it."

Andrew, taking his cue from his brother, nodded. "Morag is rather proprietary over that recipe."

Dunnet barked a laugh. "God knows why," he murmured, and Hannah found herself laughing as well. Joy, pure joy, that they were finally engaged in an exchange, along with the relief that he accepted Lana's oddness, flooded her.

"No one tell her how dry they are," Andrew whispered, and more chuckles echoed. "Una's were always much better."

"Morag makes a mouthwatering cake, though," Lana said. Then she cracked a grin and added, "That is also Una's recipe."

The banter continued on through the rest of the meal,

but Hannah only pretended to participate. Alexander didn't even pretend.

His gaze was fixed on her, and whenever she glanced his way he smiled. It was a slow, cautious smile, but as dinner progressed it warmed into something more. Something scintillating.

It was, all in all, rather riveting, but as much as Hannah enjoyed their nonverbal interaction, she quite desperately wanted to speak with him. Preferably somewhere private. So after the dessert course was served and all the plates had been removed and Andrew had excused himself to meet with his friend Hamish and Lana expressed the desire to find some scraps for Nerid, Hannah turned to her husband and asked, "Would you show me the garden tonight? I imagine it is quite lovely in the moonlight."

She thought it charming that a red tide crept up his cheeks, that his fingers closed on his serviette, mangling it irreparably. That his gaze skated to and clung to her lips.

His Adam's apple made the long journey down his throat and up again before he spoke. And when he did, his words were whispered. "I would be . . . delighted."

She fully intended to use this opportunity to get to know him better, to establish more of a connection and perhaps talk to him about his brother's too-intense interest in her sister, but something in Alexander's expression threatened to send her noble intentions into oblivion.

~

Excitement raged within Alexander as he stood and took Hannah's arm. The fact that she'd suggested the very thing he'd been contemplating boded well for their future. And not only because he very much wanted to be alone with her, to kiss her, perhaps seduce her. But also because they seemed to be of one mind.

He had decided that walk in the garden after dinner

would be an excellent opportunity to deepen their bond, so when *she* had mentioned it his heart had soared.

The connection he felt with her was unlike any he'd ever experienced. It thrilled him to think she felt it too.

As they stepped out into the velvet night, a breeze caught her fragrance and wafted it to him, teasing his senses and making his mind reel. His body tightened; his arousal rose. "This way," he murmured, leading her along the path. There was a spot he had in mind, a secluded gazebo hidden behind the trees. It was the perfect place to launch a seduction.

"I canna tell you how much I have been looking forward to this," she said as they made their way along the moonlit path.

"Aye." Anticipation sizzled. His pace increased. It was a beautiful night. The sky was clear and the stars glimmered overhead. The scent of the ocean and the apple orchards drifted on the air. The gazebo had cushioned benches.

"It is verra important that you and I . . ." *Kiss? Now?* "Talk."

"I . . . ah . . . Talk?" He stumbled a little on the gravel.

"Aye. There's something I need to discuss with you. Well, several things, but let's begin with your brother."

Alexander blinked. "Andrew?"

"Aye." She whirled on him, her beautiful face etched with a frown. "I canna help but notice the way he looks at Lana."

"Lana?"

"Aye. His gaze is far too amorous. Lana is an innocent. A dear, sweet, gentle soul. And your brother . . ."

He didn't like the way her nose curled. "Aye?"

"He's a Lothario."

Not hardly. Oh, aye, he did kiss a lot of women and he

was far more charming than should be legal. But a Lothario?

"I should like you to warn him off."

"Warn him off?"

She shot him a smile. One that made his bowels clench. "Surely you would do that for me?" *Hell. Hell yes.* For that smile he would do anything. He nodded, though it was something of a jerky nod.

"Thank you verra much. That would be so helpful." Her smile widened and relief played across her face. He realized suddenly how worried she'd been about his brother. And he wondered if he should be worried too. He made a note to speak with Andrew forthwith. First thing in the morning. Then his thoughts scuttled when Hannah stepped closer and gazed up at him solemnly. "We're married now, Dunnet."

Something tightened in his chest. He couldn't stop his frown. *Dunnet?* Had he never given her leave to address him by his given name? He thought back. *Shite*. He had not. Well, he would rectify that now. "Call me Alexander."

Her smile was glorious. "Alexander."

Ah. He liked the sound of his name on her tongue.

"But although we are man and wife, Alexander, we hardly know each other. And I should verra much like to know you better." Her expression was warm, earnest, as she gazed up at him. "Would you like to know me better?"

Oh, would he.

He decided it was probably not necessary to go all the way to the gazebo. If he was going to kiss her, this was as good a place as any, in the middle of the roses. Deftly he plucked one. He stepped closer, intent on his target.

Her eyes widened as he neared, but he did not touch her. He stroked her. Gently, reverently, with the velvet bloom, tracing her features.

Her gaze flicked to his mouth and her tongue peeped out, wetting her lips, igniting a flame in his belly. He dropped the rose and cupped her cheek and angled her head up. Her breath caught. Her features froze as she realized his intent.

And then he did what he'd been obsessing over all day. He kissed her. He kissed her there in the moonlit garden, bathed in the scent of roses and a sweet, gentle breeze.

It was glorious.

And there was no talking whatsoever.

CHAPTER NINE

On the second morning of her marriage, when Hannah awoke to find her husband gone and another letter on her pillow, she tried very hard not to let her annoyance roil. She'd had the perfect opportunity to speak with him, to ask him all the questions churning in her head, to peek beneath the hard and fierce face he showed the world. But she'd failed. She'd allowed herself to be seduced.

It was difficult to banish her grin at the recollection of that seduction.

He'd swept her away, into a maelstrom of passion that had reduced them both to quivering lumps of flesh.

It had not taken much effort.

With a sigh, she opened the letter. There were not words on the paper; a single rose petal fluttered out. Hannah stared at it, her mind beset with the memory of the pleasure he'd drawn from her, there in the garden. The scent of the rose had weakened her knees, but it truth it was the gentleness, the reverence with which he traced her features, that had destroyed her resolve.

Surely she could forgive herself for losing sight of her purpose. Given the circumstances.

And there was always today. Perhaps she could arrange another meeting with him. And perhaps this time she would not allow herself to be distracted.

She smiled to herself. Or perhaps she would.

When she didn't find Lana in her chambers, she meandered down to the kitchens. As she suspected, she found her sister there, chatting with Morag over a cup of tea as the latter rolled out dough for a pie.

Hannah loved the hominess of the room and the smell of baking bread wafting on the air. Her stomach rumbled. "Good morning," she chirped as she took a seat at the small table.

Morag's head shot up. She stared at Hannah in horror. "Yer Ladyship," she croaked, wiping her hands on her apron and flicking a panicked look about the kitchens. "Did-did Senga not deliver your breakfast?"

"She did." *Oatcakes.* Hannah wrinkled her nose. "I was hoping for something else."

"Something . . . else, my lady?" Morag's lip trembled. Oh dear. It was rather humbling to be the cause of such desolation.

"Hannah canna eat oatcakes, either," Lana offered with a wink.

Heat crawled up Hannah's cheeks. "They were lovely oatcakes," she hurried to assure the cook, who was now wringing her hands. "But I do prefer eggs to break my fast. And perhaps some bacon? If it's no trouble, of course."

"Nae a bit of it." Morag abandoned her pie and ran to the larder to fetch some eggs, which she cracked into a bowl. She picked up a whisk and stilled. Her attention fixed on Hannah. "My lady?"

"Aye?"

"Would you care to wait in the dining room?"

"In the dining room?" She would much rather wait here. And watch. Get to know the cook a little better. Besides, the dining room was far too formal, far too enormous for one person.

"It is more . . . fitting."

Lana's smile was impish. "You are the *lady*, after all."

Morag nodded, a brisk bob of her head. Clearly, it was

unthinkable for the lady of the manor to loll about in the kitchens.

"I'd rather wait here."

Morag blanched.

"Surely there's something I can help with?"

"Help?" Practically a screech.

Hannah tried very hard not to blow out a sigh. In Ciaran Reay she'd been involved in every aspect of the housekeeping—from overseeing laundry day to planning the menu. She'd been deeply involved in the lives of all her people and had a daily routine where she checked in on the crofters, visited the shopkeepers, and met often with her factor. She spent hours poring over productivity reports and reading all the latest journals on estate husbandry.

She wasn't fashioned to be a lady of leisure. It didn't suit her to sit, alone, in a booming dining room, awaiting a plate of eggs.

"I'll come with you," Lana said, which was somewhat helpful.

"Och. I was so enjoying our talk," Morag murmured as she poured the eggs into a pan. Honestly, they would be done in a minute. Surely Hannah could wait until then?

Apparently not.

"We'll talk more later," Lana assured the cook with a cheerful grin, and then hooked arms with Hannah and led her from the kitchen.

"I feel as though I've been exiled," Hannah muttered as they made their way down the long, narrow serving hall into an antechamber that led to the dining room.

Lana's laugh was a merry ripple. "Never say it. Morag is simply old-fashioned."

"Old-fashioned?"

"In her world, the staff doesna mingle with the laird and his lady. They serve."

"She mingles with you."

"She misses Una."

As Hannah took her seat at the table, she glanced at her sister. Awkward though her ability to talk to the dead might be, it did come in handy on occasion.

"Aside from which," Lana said, "*I* am not the lady of the manor."

That would come in handy as well.

Hannah had been born in Ciaran Reay, accepted in the community from childhood. Her role had been clear. Here, not so much. Here, she would have to forge herself anew. "I *am* the lady of the manor. Not a pariah."

"Give them time. They're still getting used to you." Lana's forehead puddled. "Apparently, the last lady of the manor was something of a termagant."

"Really?"

"Also, she wasn't actually the lady of the manor. Or a lady."

Hannah shot her sister a curious glance.

Lana leaned in and whispered, "She was a courtesan."

"What?"

"Aye."

Morag entered with Hannah's plate, a pile of fluffy eggs and assorted meats. When the cook left, Lana continued. "The previous laird, your husband's uncle, was something of a profligate, if the rumors are to be believed."

"And one would assume they should be." Hannah took a bite and nearly moaned. The eggs were perfect.

"He brought in this trollop and made the staff treat her like a queen. She wasna verra pleasant to them, so you understand why they would rather keep their distance."

"I'm not like that in the slightest."

"I realize that. Once they get to know you, they'll warm up. I'm certain of it."

"I hope so. I canna bear to have every meal in this

room." She spread out her hands to encompass the long, echoey hall.

"You can have your meals in your room."

Hannah frowned. "It's brown."

"Then come and have breakfast in mine."

"Perhaps I shall. So, whatever became of this trollop queen?" she asked, taking another bite.

"Ah." Lana snagged a slice of bacon, which was hardly fair, but Hannah allowed it. It was a small price to pay for the company. "Alexander sent her away when his uncle died. There was something of a celebration when that happened."

"When he sent her away, or when the uncle died?"

"Both." Her brow furrowed. "The uncle was *not* well liked."

"How did he die?'

Her sister leaned in and whispered, "He threw himself from the ramparts."

"He *threw* himself?" *How gothic.*

"Some say that the ghosts of his ancestors tripped him. He was deep in his cups."

Hannah took a sip of tea. "An inglorious way for a laird to die."

"Och, aye. But he wasna really the laird."

"He wasna?"

Lana shook her head. "When your husband's father died, his brother, the uncle, assumed the title, until Alexander reached maturity."

Hannah's gut tightened. "How old was he when his father died?"

"Five."

Five. Poor mite. This revelation made Hannah want to find him and fold him into her embrace, to comfort the boy he had been.

He would probably not appreciate it, but she couldn't

quell the desire. She stared at her empty plate. She hardly remembered a bite. Had she inhaled it? Hannah set her serviette on the table. "Do you suppose, once Morag gets to know me better, she will let me sit in the kitchen and have tea?"

Lana grinned. "Probably not. You're the baroness."

Hannah sighed. Lana was undoubtedly right. But what did a baroness *do*? She had a new role here, one she would have to discover day by day. But in the meantime . . . "Do you suppose the castle has a library?"

Lana wrinkled a brow. "There wasna one on the tour."

"There were many things that weren't on that tour." They shared a snort. Hannah was, of course, thinking of her husband's mysterious study. Who knew what Lana was thinking? Hannah rarely did.

Her sister drummed her fingers on the pristine tablecloth. "The castle is verra large. It must have a library somewhere."

"Come with me," Hannah said, leaping to her feet and hooking arms with Lana.

"Where are we going?"

"To find Fergus. We will command him to take us to the library at once!"

Filled with a sudden trill of excitement, Hannah burst from the doldrums and into the bright light.

Until she found Fergus, that was. Until she asked about the library and he stared at her with an expression of horror and murmured something about the castle library being expressly off-limits.

Who had ever heard of a library that was off-limits?

Unthinkable.

Naturally, once Fergus had issued his dour proclamation Hannah had gone in search of her husband to flay him with her grievance. She could forgive just about anything—she was almost certain she could—but a locked library?

Her search had been fruitless, though she'd expected as much. The castle was an enormous place to hide and it appeared her husband was determined to hide from her. In truth, his reticence during the day was confusing. It was completely at odds with his scorching attention under the cover of darkness.

Hannah shivered as she recalled the glory of last night's passion. He'd been gentle and tender and then wild and brash, a tempest in bed. He'd brought her to the heights of glory and brought her down again slowly, sweetly, holding her in his warm embrace until she'd dozed off.

She'd awakened alone, of course. With a letter.

The two sides of him were so different, it befuddled her.

The man of the day avoided her and rarely spoke, locked her out of his favorite rooms as much as he locked her out of his life. But at night . . . at night he was everything she'd ever wanted, loving and passionate and utterly focused on her and her pleasure.

If she had any sense, she would confront him about the disparity, beard him with her questions, at night, before he touched her. But, no doubt, she would forget herself before she had the chance. He did that to her, made her mindless with a glance, boneless with a kiss.

Still, she needed to know. She needed to know what made him the way he was.

She feared it was a secret she would never discover.

It was far more difficult being married than she'd feared. Far too frustrating.

She decided to do what she usually did when she needed to clear her head. Indeed, it was a beautiful day for a ride. Beelzebub deserved a treat for not nipping very many people on the journey here, and it would be a wonderful opportunity to explore her new home.

Filled with resolution—about one thing she could control—she made her way to the stables.

~

Alexander put his heels to Wallace's flank and let him have his head. They tore down the road. The wild ride matched Alexander's mood. Oh, he'd awakened feeling wonderful, after that amazing night with Hannah. He'd been beset with gratitude that he'd had the good sense to marry her. Every moment they shared convinced him further that she would be an excellent wife.

She was tender and sweet and docile. And hell, a phenomenal match for him between the sheets.

But then Olrig had gone and ruined his day.

He'd ridden out to check on the Homack mill, only to discover that the bastard had sent raiders in during the night. They had stolen several bags of grain and Alexander was furious. Obviously, he was going to have to set guards on all his border properties, and that aggravated him. After he sent an entourage to Dounreay to assist with the protection of Hannah's land, his men were stretched thin. And those who remained had other responsibilities. But hell and damn, he had to.

Apparently, Olrig would not stop unless he did.

A movement out of the corner of his eye caught his attention and he looked over. His heart stalled in his throat.

It was Hannah, astride an enormous stallion, streaking over the field. Her hair streamed out behind her and she hunkered low over the horse's neck, clinging to the reins.

There was no doubt; the stallion was out of control.

The prospect of Hannah in danger made Alexander's pulse rocket and his breath stall. Beads of sweat popped out on his brow. Without hesitation he changed direction and urged Wallace after her. If Alexander could come alongside, perhaps he could snatch her from the saddle before disaster befell her. That in itself would be a dangerous move, bringing two huge beasts so close together, grabbing her from her mount, but he had to try. He had to save her.

Flying over the uneven ground in a riotous ride, he pounded after her.

The stallion was fast. Almost as fast as Wallace, so it took some time for Alexander to catch her. When he did, he guided Wallace with his knees, reached over, and plucked her from the back of the runaway mount.

She screeched and thrashed, which didn't make the maneuver easier, but Alexander had a firm hold and whipped her from danger, settling her before him. Then he pulled on the reins and slowed Wallace to a halt.

When the horse stopped, she wriggled away and shimmied off. Alexander's heart lurched as she dropped to the ground, but she caught herself. And then she whirled on him.

"What the hell were you thinking?" she screeched. "You could have killed me!"

He gaped at her. Opened his mouth and then closed it again.

She was angry? Why was she angry? He'd just saved her bluidy neck.

Fury of his own rose. That, combined with the sheer horror of seeing his wife so close to death, stole his sanity. He whipped from Wallace's back and glared down at her with his hands on his hips.

"Me? What the hell were *you* thinking?" He didn't mean to bark, but he was far beyond restraint.

"I was thinking I would go for a ride."

"On that . . . that . . . that . . ." He waved in the general direction of the monstrous equine, who, divested of his rider, had slowed to a walk. He rolled his head back and glared—aye, he *glared*—at Hannah, then whinnied and stomped his hoof, kicking up great chunks of turf.

"Aye. On *that*." She turned to the horse and clicked her

tongue. The creature obediently trotted back and she took the reins. "He's *my* horse."

Alexander's jaw went slack. She was a tiny thing and this horse was . . . hell, he was massive. There was no way she could control him. "You canna . . . canna . . . canna . . ."

She didn't allow Alexander to finish his sentence, which would have been, *You canna be serious.*

"Oh, bother, Dunnet." He flinched when she used his title. Or perhaps it was the vitriol with which she spat his name. "Never say you are forbidding me from riding my own horse." Not his intention in the slightest, but it was an excellent idea. "Because let us get one thing straight, right here and now. No one forbids me from doing anything. If I want to ride Beelzebub, I shall ride him. Whenever I wish."

"Bee-Bee-Beelzebub?" Her horse was named *Beelzebub*? Alexander glanced at the beast, who tossed his head and eyed Wallace with what looked disturbingly like malice. Wallace snorted and shook his mane, to which Beelzebub showed his teeth. "He is . . . He is dangerous." He was. Even Alexander would think twice before hopping on Beelzebub's back.

Hannah laughed. Threw back her head and laughed. And while it was an entrancing sound, it sent shivers of trepidation down Alexander's spine. "He's nothing of the sort." She cradled the creature's snout and scratched his nose. "He only nips when he's annoyed."

Bluidy hell!

"Hannah, I canna allow you to—"

Again, she did not allow him to finish. She rounded on him, her dander up. He was struck with how utterly beautiful she was at this moment, her chin tight, her body quivering, her eyes glowing with an unholy light. "You canna *allow* me? Did you no' hear what I just said?"

He frowned at her. "I canna allow you to risk your life.

I couldna bear it if you were hurt." This last bit he said softly, and somehow it seemed to reach through her anger and touch her heart. Her expression softened. Her lips quirked in what might have been the beginnings of a smile.

She stared at him for a moment and he had the unsettling impression she was analyzing various strategies of attack. In the end, she set her hand on his arm and said in a soothing tone, "Alexander, I assure you. I am perfectly safe with Beelzebub. He is a lamb."

At that moment, the beastie reached over and nipped Wallace's hindquarters. Alexander's mount jumped and shuffled away, sending him an accusing glance.

"Well, he's a lamb with me," she said, biting back her smile.

"He's . . . so large."

"I raised him from a colt, Alexander. I'm the only person who has ridden him. Now tell me." She sidled up to Alexander, hooked her arm in his, gazed up at him with wide eyes, and said, "How are we going to proceed as man and wife? Are you going to bark orders—?"

"I doona bark," he barked. She ignored his outburst.

"Or are we going to work together? As a team?"

He rather liked that idea. He nodded and grumbled something vague. He'd never been managed before and he wasn't sure if he liked the feeling. Although he didn't much mind being managed by her . . . when she looked at him in *that* way.

"And if I choose to ride my horse, and I shall, you willna sweep in and wrench me from his back each and every time?"

"Will you promise to take an escort when you ride?"

She frowned as she studied Alexander's expression. He was certain it was unyielding and firm, but he might not have gotten it right, because she nodded and said, "Of course. If I feel like it."

He opened his mouth to object, but she went up on her tiptoes and pressed a kiss on his chin and all his arguments scattered.

"And thank you for attempting to save my life," she added, patting his arm. "It was verra sweet."

Sweet?

It had been the worst moment of his life. He didn't know if he would ever recover.

And even worse? The emotions churning through his gut right now. Because he'd realized in all this, though they had only been married for a short while, she'd somehow wormed her way into his heart. She had become *necessary* to him. And if anything ever happened to her, if he ever lost her, it would devastate him.

൭൭

"Bother," Hannah grumbled to herself as she paced the terrace. Even the breathtaking view of the sparkling sea in the distance could not appease her. Annoyance prickled at her.

Her conversation with Alexander had gone well, she supposed, or at least as well as it could have gone. Though he'd seemed adamant at first that she not ride Beelzebub, he'd been willing to see reason. That was an excellent sign.

She'd had great hopes for a more in-depth interaction, perhaps a kiss or two, but then, when they'd returned to the castle, he'd disappeared. Just when she thought she was making progress with him, he retreated once more.

Although she had to allow she learned something new about him each day. He was like an onion, layer after layer of revelations that made her admire and respect him even more. She wondered if she would ever come to the core of him.

A cutting wind knifed in from the sea and Hannah wrapped her arms around herself. She turned to head inside to request some tea but stilled as she noticed a small girl standing to her left. The surly child from her welcome.

Hannah affected a smile. "It is a delightful view, is it not?"

Fiona gazed up at her with solemn eyes and nodded.

"I do love the sea."

Another nod. The girl's lips worked and Hannah could tell she was attempting to say something, so she waited patiently as Fiona worked at the words. "D-did you m-mean what you . . . said?"

Hannah quirked a brow. She had a tendency to say a lot of things, and while she generally meant all of them, she wasn't sure to which comment Fiona referred.

"Th-that everyone st-struggles with something?"

"Aye. I did mean that." In her experience, it was true.

Fiona looked her up and down, nibbling on her lower lip. "Wh-what do-do you . . ."

"What do I struggle with?"

A nod.

Hannah laughed. "I'm luckier than most. I have many challenges."

"You do?" Why Fiona sounded so surprised was a mystery. Was it not obvious that Hannah was a bundle of issues?

"Och. Aye." She set aside her desire for tea and strolled to a stone bench along the balustrade. She sat and Fiona crawled up next to her. "For one thing, I'm not terribly patient. My father despairs that I'm far too rash. Barreling in where cooler minds would wait. For another, I'm not verra pretty."

"You . . . you are v-verra pretty." The compliment sounded suspiciously like a complaint.

Hannah blew out a breath. "My sisters are much prettier. Lana is like a delicate angel and Susana is a warrior princess."

Fiona's eyes widened. "A warrior princess?"

"She is rather magnificent. I, on the other hand, have always been rather . . . ordinary." When Fiona snorted, Hannah nodded. "My eyes are too large and my mouth is crooked." She gestured at her body. "I'm . . . plump."

"He . . . he thinks you're pretty."

Her pulse stalled. "He?"

Fiona jammed a thumb up to the sky. For a moment, Hannah thought perhaps Fiona was talking about God and was about to pat her on the head and tell her how precious she was, but she glanced up, way up, and a movement in the window of the turret tower caught her attention. With a hit to her solar plexus, she realized who stood at the window, watching them.

Her husband.

She waved up at him and he jerked out of sight, as though embarrassed to have been caught spying.

"Laird Dunnet?"

"Aye." Fiona put out a lip.

"How do you know he thinks I'm pretty?" She shouldn't ask, but she couldn't not.

"He-he told m-me so."

Something pleasant trickled through her. It might have been joy. Heat crept up her cheeks. "Did he?"

"Aye."

"He told you? With actual words?"

Fiona giggled, though it wasn't meant as a joke.

"Because he doesna speak to me much."

The girl kicked her legs and smoothed her skirts. "He t-tells me lots of things."

"He must like you verra much."

"He does." She beamed and then sobered. "We . . . are verra much alike." This she said softly, with a treble of import. Hannah had the sense the words meant much more than they seemed to at face value. "Lots of p-people th-

think I'm stupid be-because I canna sp-speak well, but he doesna."

"Of course you're not."

"He gave me his quill." This in a hushed whisper, as though the quill were the Golden Fleece or the Arc of the Covenant. And he'd given it to *her.* "He-he is t-teaching me to write."

Oh, lovely. Another generation of letter writers.

"That was verra kind of him."

"S-sometimes, wr-writing is . . . m-much easier than sp-speaking."

Hannah stilled, her attention locked on the earnest little face. Her heart clenched. The breath burned in her lungs.

Lots of people think I'm stupid because I canna speak well.

We are verra much alike.

Writing is much easier than speaking.

Oh dear God.

Comprehension blossomed in her mind. Certitude filled her soul.

All of a sudden she *knew.* She understood.

Chagrin raked her. Chagrin that she had dared judge him without coming to know him.

She glanced up at the turret tower and caught him watching her again. All of her frustration, her aggravation and impatience, melted away. Something else entirely took its place, filling her chest with an ache that felt like adoration.

He thought she was pretty.

He was very kind to children.

He was a damn good kisser.

And he was hers.

She cupped her hands around her mouth and yelled up at him before he could retreat once more, "When are you coming out of your tower?"

Hannah glanced down at Fiona. "I told you I was impatient," she said with a wink. And Fiona, bless her heart, threw back her head and laughed.

When Fergus arrived with the next letter in hand, Hannah did not rip it to shreds.

And she was very glad she did not.

It was an invitation.

To a picnic.

With her husband.

It was a delightful letter indeed.

൬൭

Alexander looked up from his work, surprised to find Fergus standing nervously on the threshold of his study. After scrawling out the invitation to his wife, he had disciplined himself to return to work. If he wanted to spend the afternoon with Hannah, he needed to finish this first. In addition to urgent messages from Keiss and Feswick, which required his attention, the bitter battle in Lyth between the Dunns and the Keiths was heating up again.

The sight of Fergus nearly made him growl, because it meant the factor was bringing more to do. Indeed, he held a letter in his hand.

"I'm so sorry to interrupt, my lord."

"Come." Alexander waved him in. Whatever it was, he would deal with it, and quickly. He was beset with anticipation. Seeing her again, holding her. Perchance soliciting a kiss or two, maybe a seduction in the tall grasses of the meadow—

"Her Ladyship sent this."

Alexander's hand stilled, mid-stroke.

Her Ladyship?

Sent him a letter?

His mood took a tumble. A letter could mean only one thing. She was refusing his picnic invitation. And here he'd been so encouraged when she'd smiled and waved and called up to him, imploring him to come out of his tower. The gesture had ignited something in him, some brand of courage that incited him to ignore his simmering foreboding, the fear that she might see the truth of him and turn away. He'd been suffused with the urge to face her, share his secrets with her, unveil his myriad faults, and trust that she would be patient with him.

He couldn't bear her rejection of his gesture, but he held out his hand for the letter nonetheless.

Fergus gave it over and skittered from the study as though the hounds of hell were on his tail. Alexander had only bellowed at him once for interrupting his work—and that had been a very bad day—but Fergus had taken him at face value and rarely darkened the tower door since.

Alexander studied the letter. Her script was flowing and fine. His name was like a poem in her hand. A scent wafted up from the parchment. With trembling fingers, Alexander lifted it to his nose.

Ah. Her perfume.

It clouded his vision.

Surely a woman didn't scent a rejection?

He had no idea. Women were a mystery to him altogether.

Burning to know what she said, he sloughed off his trepidation and ripped the letter open.

Alexander,

I would verra much like to meet you for a picnic this afternoon. Thank you for suggesting it.

His lips quirked up. That was a promising start. Not like a rejection in the slightest. And she would *verra much* like to meet him.

Excellent.

I thought it would be delightful if Fiona could join us as well.

Fiona?

His grin slumped. While he enjoyed the girl's company, he'd had a very different afternoon in mind. Something romantic. With kisses.

He couldn't very well seduce his wife with a child in attendance.

He thought very seriously about sending Hannah another note, requesting pointedly that they attend the picnic alone, but was glad that he didn't when he joined the two of them in the bailey, with Brùid at his heel, and saw Fiona dancing from foot to foot, clearly delighted with the prospect of an outing.

He would have tonight, hc reminded himself.

And if all went well, he might steal a kiss this afternoon.

Or two.

Hannah looked stunning, as always. Her ebony hair flowed free and glinted blue in the shafts of sunlight. Her brown eyes sparkled and her alabaster skin glowed. She wore an alluring kirtle that hugged her curves. His mouth watered.

She reached out to his dog with great trepidation and then relaxed with a gust when Brùid lapped at her hand. She smiled up at Alexander with a look that made his bowels clench.

She carried a small basket on her arm, one that made him shoot her a curious look, but she said nothing. So, as he tucked his own basket—filled with the accoutrements of their lunch—on his arm, they set out.

It was a beautiful day. Spring was waning and summer just beginning to rumble. It was warm, but there was a fresh breeze coming in off the sea. They made their way through the bailey and across the drawbridge and out to the meadow surrounding the castle. There was a spot near the ruins of the old keep he had in mind; it was the perfect picnic spot. As they made their way up the hill, birds wheeled in the sky and the drone of insects surrounded them.

Hannah chatted with Fiona—who seemed to have no hesitation about speaking to a veritable stranger—but his wife said nothing to him. Alexander found he didn't mind. Especially when she laced her fingers through his.

It was an enchanting little walk. Just a man, a woman, a child, and a dog. One day, God willing, Hannah and Alexander would make this walk with their own children in tow. He could have kept going, could have basked in this interlude forever, but they reached the ruins. He set his basket down and picked up the blanket he'd brought, whipping it out.

It took a while to settle the blanket on the ground, because Fiona squealed and ran beneath it as it billowed. Then Hannah laughed and did the same. Brùid joined the dance, barking and bounding about, snapping at the corners. Alexander indulged them, lifting the blanket again and again, because he loved seeing her laugh. Head tossed back, eyes dancing, lips curled, wreathed in the joy of the moment . . . When finally the blanket fell, he arranged the basket on it and they all sat. One by one, he pulled out Morag's treats.

Hannah and Fiona oohed and aahed over cold chicken and fruits and tiny cakes. But they didn't ooh and aah for long. Apparently, they were both hungry. They filled their plates and all ate, enjoying this kiss of the sun, the tease of the breeze, and the comfortable company. With great glee, Fiona fed Brùid—perhaps more than she should have. But to be honest, the hound had perfected a pleading look.

To Alexander's relief, Hannah didn't pepper him with

questions. Other than a casual comment about this offering or that, there was little conversation.

In all, he felt very comfortable.

Though he still wondered about the small basket she'd brought, he didn't ask.

After they'd eaten their fill, they lay down on the blanket and stared up at the sky, with Fiona between them. Alexander couldn't help but think this was the point at which he might have launched his seduction, but when Hannah glanced over at him and smiled, a happy, contented smile, he couldn't regret the lost opportunity.

He could still steal a kiss later.

Fiona became restless and, to his delight, Hannah suggested the girl hunt for wildflowers. Alexander saw his chance. As soon as Fiona bounded up and dashed through the tall grass with Brùid at her heel, he made his move, rolling over and capturing Hannah's chin in his fingers and setting his mouth on hers. He caught her by surprise. Her mouth was open. She tasted of wine and berries and . . . Hannah.

She stiffened, but only for a heartbeat, and then she melted into him, twining her fingers in his hair and pulling him closer. She made a murmur in the back of her throat, a little growl of pleasure like the ones she'd made last night, and it sent a wave of arousal through him.

He edged closer and deepened the kiss.

Her breath gushed into his mouth as he entered her with his tongue and then, God help him, she sucked him in. His arousal raged into a boiling sea of lust.

That simply, that easily, he was on fire for her.

It was probably indiscreet to shift, just a tad, so he was over her. It was probably bad manners to press his hard cock against her hip and rub, but he couldn't help himself.

She pulled back, only enough to whisper, "We shouldna."

He grumbled a response. It was probably in the affirmative. But he didn't stop kissing her. She was far too delicious.

Phhht.

Hardly a sound that engendered romantic flights of fancy. And coming from above him as it did, from a five-year-old, it was like a bucket of cold water. Alexander chuckled and kissed his wife again, before easing away. "Tonight," he murmured, catching her gaze.

She pressed her lips together to stop a creeping smile, but it didn't work. Not entirely.

"What have you found, Fiona?" she asked, sitting up and brushing down her dress.

"Just weeds." Fiona dumped her collection on the blanket. "Wh-why were you k-kissing?" She wrinkled her tiny nose.

"Husbands and wives kiss," Hannah said matter-of-factly. It occurred to Alexander that she would be a wonderful mother. Someday. Perhaps soon. She studied Fiona's offering. "And these are not weeds. They are lovely." She picked them up, one by one, and arranged them in a bouquet. A bouquet that looked very much like the one she'd carried at her and Alexander's wedding. "If you weave them together, like this . . ."—she linked several of the stems together—"you can make yourself a crown."

"A cr-crown?" Fiona's eyes gleamed. "I should like that."

"Here. You try." Hannah handed the girl some flowers and she began weaving them together as Hannah had shown her, edging out her tongue as she worked. "Why do you no' make one for each of us?"

"I will need more fl-flowers." Without hesitation she leaped up and headed back to the meadow.

Excellent.

Alexander leaned toward his wife again, his intent clear. She stopped his advance with a palm to his chest. That her thumb stroked him didn't ease his disgruntlement. She did allow him one kiss, although it was a quick one.

"I thought we could play a game, you and I."

A game? He frowned.

He had another game in mind entirely.

"It will help us get to know each other better." She seemed so resolved, so optimistic, certainly so determined, he couldn't refuse. At his nod, she reached into her basket and pulled some things out. When his attention fell on the items, he froze.

Parchment. A quill. Ink.

What . . . ?

"I shall write down a question, and then you write down an answer. And then you can write down a question for me. All right?" She shot him a hopeful look; he saw beneath it a thread of uncertainty. Worry that he would refuse.

He would not refuse. When he nodded, she gave a tiny sigh of relief.

"Excellent." She picked up the quill and dipped it in the pot of ink. "We'll start with something simple, I think." He watched her as she scratched out her query. And he wondered, what would she want to know?

Why do you never speak? God, he hoped not. He didn't want to reveal that murky secret. Not yet. Not so soon.

When she handed him the parchment, he nearly laughed out loud.

What is your favorite color?

He took the quill and responded with *Green.* It always reminded him of spring. After a moment of thought, he added that bit as well. Then he wrote: *Yours?*

She opened her mouth, as though she were going to speak, then gave a tiny shake of her head and took the quill.

I love green too. I doona care for brown.

Why she added that part he didn't know. He hadn't asked.

Her next question wasn't as simple.

What is your favorite season?

As he thought, he tapped the quill against his lips until he caught her staring at them. He couldn't stop his grin at her fascination. And his grin incited hers. He liked that very much.

"Well, go on," she said. "Answer."

He began to write.

Spring is a reawakening. When the flowers lift their heads and smile up at the sun. When the new lambs spring forth in bleating masses. When the earth yawns and stretches after a long sleep.

But summer is delightful too. The feel of the hot sun beating down on my face and the splash of the cold sea on my toes.

Fall has her charms. When the colors change and the nights go still. When the scent of the harvest lingers in the air.

Ah, but winter, with the heavy drifts of pure white snow. When the trees lose their leaves and stretch their fingers into the sky in a bony embrace.

I love them all, I suppose.

She read his response and then stared at it for quite some time. When she lifted her gaze to his, there was a hint of tears in her doe-brown eyes. "You're a poet, I think," she murmured.

He snatched the parchment back. *Do you like poetry?*

I love poetry, she wrote. *I love all books.*

Why she stared at him with a meaningful expression he didn't know, but he didn't ask. She continued to write.

I especially enjoy histories and plays. Or scientific books.

Then she nibbled on her lip and scratched that all out and simply wrote: *Aye.* But it was too late. He'd already read the part she tried to obliterate.

He edged closer and wrote:

Scientific books?

I didn't mean to write that part. I am not a blue-stocking.

She underscored *not* several times.

I wouldna mind if you were.

He'd always had a high regard for intelligence of any kind. That his wife, who would be the mother of his children, had an aptitude for learning pleased him.

She stared at him and then scribbled:

Men prefer stupid women.

He barked a laugh.

Not true.

Quite true.

I doona. The bleating of sheep annoys me.

She chuckled and pointed to his earlier passage—about bleating sheep—then dashed off:

One would think you enjoy them.

Before he had time to think through his response, he wrote: *Not in my bed.* And then he cringed, because she stiffened at his side. Her body hummed with a certain energy, one he couldn't ignore; it set up a responding hum within him.

Their gazes locked. She looked away, but only long enough to scrawl:

What do you enjoy . . . in your bed?

He swallowed heavily.

Last night was rather fantastic.

Her smile lit a fire in his belly.

It was.

Did you enjoy that?

I verra much did.

He found he rather liked this game.

She added:

I'm looking forward to tonight.

As am I.

He glanced up at a giggle and saw Fiona returning with

an armload of weeds . . . wildflowers, and he realized his and Hannah's game was very nearly at its end. But he'd learned much about her in this short time, and through their play they had formed a bond. A tenuous one, for certain, but it was a start.

Hannah liked wildflowers. And books. And his kisses.

She had enjoyed last night . . . very much.

And he'd stolen a kiss . . . two.

Not a bad return for a lazy afternoon.

That he had to walk back to the castle wearing a crown of wildflowers was a small price to pay.

CHAPTER TEN

Oh, that had gone well. Very well.

Hannah smiled up at Alexander as they made their way into the castle. Fiona dashed off to find her friends and brag about her crown, and as much as she'd enjoyed the girl's company, Hannah couldn't help but be pleased. Because now, for a while, she had her husband to herself.

Well, with the exception of his dog, who obediently lagged at Alexander's heel. As horrifying as their first meeting had been, she rather liked Brùid now. He was very much like Alexander. Strong, silent, and fiercely protective.

"I was wondering . . ." she murmured, waiting to continue until he met her gaze and quirked a brow. My, but he was handsome. Her thoughts stalled on that for a moment.

"Wondering?" he prompted. His voice, like honey, drizzled over her.

She hooked her arm in his. "I was wondering . . . why wait until tonight?" Why not go to their room now? And begin early?

His chest swelled. His nostrils flared. Tension thrummed between them. His gaze stalled on her lips. "I—"

"There you are."

Hannah flinched at Fergus' strident tone.

Damn it. They hadn't been quick enough.

The factor bustled up, his features scrunched into a moue of distress.

Alexander sighed and raked his fingers through his hair. "What is it?" This he growled through clenched teeth.

Fergus blanched. His attention winged from Alexander to Hannah and back again. "I'm sorry, Your Lordship. A messenger has arrived from Ackergill. He needs to speak to you at once."

"Ackergill?" His expression firmed.

"Aye, my lord." Fergus leaned in to whisper, "The message is from the duke himself."

"Caithness?"

Hannah and Alexander exchanged surprised glances. Something churned in her belly. "I thought he lived in London."

"Aye. He *did*. He recently returned," Alexander told her.

"My lord. The messenger is waiting. He is . . . verra anxious."

The sound that came from her husband's throat was something like a growl, but Hannah felt the need to growl as well. Things had been going so well. She would have so loved to continue . . . in private, but it wasn't meant to be.

"You go on," she said, stroking his arm. She loved how his muscles rippled in response. "I shall see you tonight." She didn't need to add the wink to convey her meaning, but she did anyway.

She didn't expect him to take her face in his hands and hold her still as his head descended, but he did. The kiss was hard, hot, and fierce. The savage brush of his lips, his taste, his scent, sent all kinds of inappropriate urges scurrying through her. That, of course, was what he intended.

When he lifted his head, locked gazes with her, and whispered, "Tonight," her belly clenched.

Heavens, he was a glorious man.

"I canna wait."

"Nor can—"

Fergus cleared his throat.

Alexander sighed and kissed her again, quickly, before turning on his heel and storming up the stairs. But he stopped at the landing to glance back at her, a simmering heat in his expression.

Fergus, who wasn't paying attention, plowed into him.

❧

Alexander swept into the sitting room and glared at the messenger, although it was hardly his fault that Caithness had ruined what could have been one of the most amazing days of his life. The boy flinched and handed Alexander a letter bearing the impressive seal of the Duke of Caithness.

Alexander had never met the man. Had no idea what to expect, but the reports about Caithness were . . . concerning.

Trepidation—and a prickle of irritation—rose. Alexander steeled his spine and ripped open the missive. As he read the contents, a growing ire singed him.

It was a summons, a demand that he hie to Caithness Castle in Ackergill at once. And *bring his account books.* The accusation was not written in plain print, but the intimation that he'd been giving the taxman short shrift made Alexander's vision blur.

Aside from that, he disliked being called like a dog, and this from an insolent pup.

But, like it or not, Sinclair was their laird, their duke. The command was clear. Alexander was expected in Ackergill, and he had to leave at once. And take his account books.

His account books.

Bluidy hell.

Why that made him feel like a small boy being called before his uncle Alexander didn't know, but he despised the feeling. He always had.

He was not alone in his umbrage. From the conversations Alexander had had with his fellow barons, resentment toward Caithness was running rife. Word was, the duke was a pompous ass. Though he was born a Scotsman, he knew nothing of the Highlands. Yet here he came, in his gold-gilded carriage, and began spewing orders at the lairds within his aegis. Alexander had already heard the cries of outrage from his kinsmen in Keiss and Halkirk and Wick.

The chieftains of Caithness County, to a man, were all used to wielding their own power; they bowed to no man. They were all accustomed to the disregard of their duke. For him to suddenly appear, after all this time, and demand fealty was ludicrous. Suicidal, perhaps.

Caithness would be lucky to survive a month.

Which would please Stafford, no doubt.

Alexander sighed. The last thing he wanted to do was leave his bride and hie off to Ackergill to be raked over the coals about his accounts by the duke none of his friends could abide. But he would go. Because he'd been commanded to and because he wanted to meet his long-absent laird. He resolved to wait until he took the duke's measure before he made any judgments. He was, above all things, a fair man in that. He prided himself on his honor and the honor of his clan.

He dismissed the messenger and headed to his chambers to prepare for an unwelcome journey.

The hardest part of it all was facing Hannah and giving her the news that he would be gone for some time. At the same time her disappointed expression wrenched his heart, it buoyed his mood.

Because she would miss him, she whispered as she went on her toes to give him a kiss.

She would miss him.

And aye, he would miss her.

He headed for the stables with a determined stride. He wanted to get to Ackergill and return with all haste. He hated the thought of leaving his wife now, just when things were going his way. The horses whickered greetings as he made his way through the shadowed stables to Wallace's stall. He was opening the gate to saddle his mount when a strange noise captured his attention. A murmur. A rustle.

With a frown, Alexander headed toward the tack room and peered inside. What he saw caused his gut to clench. Lana Dounreay, locked in a clinch with a man.

And not just any man.

His brother.

Hannah's pretty plea of the night before rippled through him and his blood curdled. If she knew what his brother and her sister were doing right now, she would be furious.

Words escaped him. He simply issued a growl. The two sprang apart and Lana's eyes went wide. Her hand lifted to smooth her bodice. With an *eep* she hastened from the room.

Alexander turned to his brother and leveled him with a dark glare. "What the fook was that?"

Andrew blinked innocently. "That? What did it look like?"

"It looked like you were kissing my wife's sister."

His smile was incongruous, given Alexander's fury. His smile was also annoying. "She's verra lovely."

"She's an innocent. Not one of your playthings."

"Really, Alexander—"

"I'm not joking, Andrew. Above all I want to keep my wife happy, and if she knew you were trying to seduce her sister she would be decidedly unhappy. And that would make me unhappy. Do you follow?"

Andrew put out a lip. "Hardly a seduction. It was only a kiss."

"A kiss is one kiss too many." Especially with Hannah's sister.

"I needed to kiss her. Hamish and I have a bet."

Good glory. Hamish. He should have known. "What kind of bet?" But he knew Hamish. He could well imagine.

Andrew lifted his shoulder. "Just a simple bet to see who can kiss a hundred women first."

Alexander gaped at him. "A hundred women?"

"Aye." The smug grin reappeared. He thrust a thumb in the direction Lana had gone. "That was number ninety-nine. I'm verra close to winning."

"And what, precisely, do you win?"

"A dram of whisky."

"It seems like a lot of work for a dram of whisky, kissing a hundred women."

Andrew pursed his lips. "'Tis more than just the whisky. Bragging rights, and all."

Alexander blew out a breath. "You do realize at some point you and Hamish are going to have to start behaving like grown men?"

"Ah." Andrew winked. "But grown men kiss women."

"Not a hundred of them." Hell, he wanted to kiss one and only one. Shaking his head, he led Wallace from his stall.

When Alexander's brother saw his bulging saddlebags, his eyes widened. "Where are you going?"

"I've been called to Ackergill to meet with the duke—"

"Ah, hell." To his credit, Andrew's unrepentant grin faded. His gaze fell on the account books as Alexander shoved them into the bags. "Why are you taking those?"

"The duke would like to review them."

Alexander's brother narrowed his eyes. "Seriously?"

"Aye."

"We've done nothing wrong."

"I realize that."

"Why do you suppose he wants to see them?"

Alexander had been wondering the same thing himself. He was certain all was in order. Still, he couldn't stay the ripple of apprehension that skated through him. Caithness was a very powerful man. If he didn't like what he found in Alexander's books, there was no telling what he might do. At best, the man had it in mind to raise taxes, which would make things very difficult come winter, especially with all the refugees coming to Dunnet, all mouths that needed to be fed.

"I doona know how long I will be gone." Alexander frowned at his brother. "While I'm away, will you look after my wife? Make sure she has everything she needs?"

"Of course."

Alexander hefted himself into the saddle and gored his brother with an even darker look. "And I expect you to keep yer distance from Hannah's sister. Do I make myself clear?"

Andrew frowned. "Aye. But—"

"No buts," Alexander snapped. "Keep yer distance."

The last thing he needed was his brother seducing his bride's sister.

ꕥ

He'd said he would be back soon.

Ah, but he was not back soon.

Though Hannah was frustrated—she really wanted to spend time with her new husband and get to know him better—she made the best of it. While he was gone, she explored the shops of Dunnet with Lana, took leisurely walks with Brùid, and sometimes sat with Fiona, helping her learn her letters. She tried to keep busy, but none of these activities were terribly productive. She missed the constant bustle of Ciaran Reay. She missed being needed. She missed having a purpose.

It became clear, very quickly, that her help was not welcome here. The staff of the castle, a well-oiled machine, didn't want her interference. Each time she offered to help with this or that, their features would pucker up and they politely, but firmly, refused any assistance she offered. She was, in a word, superfluous.

If things didn't change, she would go stark staring mad within a week. As it was, she was bored. Unbearably bored.

Still, she'd never expected to take to her new home so much, but she had. From the far reaches of the castle, to the lively town to the west, to the surrounding fields . . . she loved Dunnet. It was so much like Ciaran Reay and the people were so very kind she felt as though she'd always lived here.

Lana loved it too. Hannah was delighted that her sister was happy here as well. But then, Lana tended to be happy wherever she went.

On the second day of Alexander's absence, Hannah and Lana convinced Fiona to give them a tour of the castle. A real tour. Brùid trailed along with them. The girl was thrilled to squire her new lady from one end of the sprawling edifice to the other, proudly showing off one chamber after another. Upon Hannah's urging, Fiona showed her the way to her husband's office in the high tower, but in his absence the door had been locked.

She tried to quell her disappointment. Seeing his private study would have told her so much about him and, at the very least, made her feel closer to him in his absence.

They discovered two other locked rooms, one on the ground floor and one directly above it, which made Hannah wonder what they were and why they were locked, but no one would tell her. In fact, whenever she asked a footman or a maid about the sealed rooms their lips would tighten and their gazes would shift away. And heaven help them if Fergus should wander by as she was peppering them for details. He would glower, as he often did, and the poor underlings would pale and melt away.

In the end, she gave up asking. There was no point. She would ask Dunnet when he returned home.

If, indeed, he ever did. As the few days stretched into several, Hannah simmered with impatience. She and Alexander had only just started getting to know each other and this interruption grated on her nerves.

As a result, her mood dipped from annoyed to dismal. Which was probably why, one evening at dinner, she decided to badger Andrew into answering at least one of her questions—one that had been bothering her since she'd spied her husband in his turret tower.

She took her place next to her brother-in-law at the long table and fixed him with a sharp gaze. He glanced at the door as though he dearly wished to escape. She wouldn't let him. His throat worked. "Lady Dunnet," he said.

As Lana sat on his other side, his gaze flickered to her. And then he paled and ripped his gaze away as though burned. Hannah had noticed, with no small delight, that since Alexander had left, Andrew had gone out of his way to avoid her sister. No doubt he'd been warned off. Satisfaction rippled. One less thing to worry about, at least.

"Good evening, Andrew."

He took a sip of his wine. And then a gulp. "Did you, ah, did you have a nice day?"

"No."

The wine spewed. Only slightly, but enough to reassure her he was paying attention.

"I . . . What?"

"In fact, I had a very trying day." They had all been difficult, since Alexander had left. Her frown darkened.

"I, ah . . . Why was it trying?"

"For one thing, the staff won't let me lift so much as a finger."

"You're the baroness." He chuckled. Unwise.

"I'm bored out of my mind."

"You should talk to Alexander."

"He isna here."

Andrew shot another longing glance at the door. "He'll be back soon."

"Perhaps." Hannah took a sip of her wine. It was a lovely red. It did not calm her mood. "Fiona took me on a tour of the castle today."

His pout reminded her very much of Isobel's. "You've already had a tour of the castle."

"A *real* tour." They both knew his tour had been sadly lacking, and his sudden flush proved it. "She showed me where Dunnet's study is."

Andrew garbled several words that might have been English.

"It doesna seem to be a very convenient location for him to work."

"He doesna like to be disturbed."

Balderdash. "Why is his office in a turret?" There had been several rooms she'd seen today that would have suited his purposes just fine, rooms that weren't up a daunting curling staircase.

"I, ah, couldna say."

Hannah stilled and fixed him with a solemn look. "You could," she said softly.

He raked his fingers through his long white-blond hair. "This is something *you* should ask him."

"I should ask him many things. However, he isna here, in the event you haven't noticed. And aside from that salient point, you and I both know Alexander doesna do well with questions. Or answers. I would very much appreciate it if you could shed a glimmer of light on this aspect of his character."

Andrew signaled the footman for more wine. Once reinforcements arrived, he shrugged. "It's quite simple. He likes that room."

Likes that room? "It's ancient, for one thing—"

"Not so very ancient. It only dates back five hundred years."

"For another, it's three hundred steps to it—"

"Three hundred and twenty-five."

"Up a spiraling staircase with no railings—"

"Those staircases were all the rage in the days of old. Quite providential for fighting off enemies."

"I am not his enemy."

Andrew stilled with his glass halfway to his mouth. Hannah saw the inner battle reflected on his features. He took a resolute swig and set his goblet down with extreme care. "It has always been his favorite room."

"It is a rather romantic spot," Lana said. "I imagine he can see for miles from up there."

"I wouldna know," Hannah grumbled. "The door was locked."

Andrew's brow rumpled. "He doesna like his office disturbed. Aside from that, the turret has always been his . . . sanctuary."

There was a tremor of something in Andrew's voice, something that captured Hannah's attention. "His . . . sanctuary?"

Andrew tossed back his wine and the footman refilled it. "The turret was always a . . . safe place."

A safe place? Alexander was the Baron of Dunnet. Why would he require a safe place?

Andrew caught the question in her eyes, but before she could ask it he blew out a breath and said, "Our parents died when we were very young. Our uncle was our guardian. He was . . . not a kind man."

Lana tipped her head to the side and studied Andrew's face. A flicker of comprehension flared. Hannah tried not to be bothered by the fact that her sister could sometimes see things that were obscured to everyone else. "Not kind?"

"He drank." Andrew set down his glass and pushed it away. It was not refilled. He flicked a glance at Hannah. "The turret was the safest place to hide, because he didn't like to bother with the steps."

Hannah closed her fingers into a fist in her lap. "I see." She did. She'd seen many brutal men doing many brutal things in her life. The thought of a young Alexander at the mercy of such a monster made her blood run cold. And it explained much. Not everything, but enough. "Thank you for telling me," she said.

He nodded. "Our . . . past is something he would rather forget."

Lana tipped her head to the side. "The past isna something you can run from. It follows you. The only way you can conquer its ghosts is by facing them down."

Andrew issued a harsh snort and reached for his glass again. "There are no ghosts here." But his tone was less than assured

If Lana's sniff was any measure, there were scores of ghosts haunting this castle . . . and Hannah's husband. Hannah vowed to do whatever she could to help him heal from that unpleasant past.

◇

Alexander made it to Caithness Castle, on the outskirts of Ackergill, in a day and a half. He'd cut across the moors rather than taking the well-traveled and rutted road.

He saw the castle, looming on the horizon, long before

he reached it. It was a desolate piece of architecture—the dream of some long-dead Sinclair—perched on the cliffs overlooking Sinclair Bay. As he came closer, he noticed the sad state of repair. In fact, parts of it were nothing but crumbling ruins, barely habitable.

Irritation rippled through him. It was the laird's place to tend his ancestral home. For his sons and his sons' sons—if not for the well-being of his people. Clearly, the duke felt no such obligation.

Though Alexander was exhausted, he handed Wallace's reins to a groom in the castle bailey, grabbed his account books, and made his way over the uneven cobbles into the keep as quickly as he could.

Whatever business the duke wanted to discuss, Alexander wanted it over and done. He toyed with the idea of sharing what he'd learned about Stafford's plan to convince the prince to grant him the duke's lands but decided to wait and see how the meeting went. He'd never met Caithness and had no idea how the man would take such news. If the duke was a complete ass and appeared to be the type who shot the messenger, Alexander might hold his tongue; it was all only supposition and rumor anyway.

It appeared the duke was a complete ass.

Despite the urgency of his missive, Caithness wasn't in a hurry. He allowed Alexander to cool his heels for several hours.

A dour butler seated him in a dour parlor in a dour wing of the castle that had been ignored for decades. Pity sake, it had not even been cleaned. Motes of dust billowed with his every move. As though that were not insult enough, a reed-thin maid brought him a delicate silver tray with tea—*tea*—and infinitesimal nibblettes of cake.

What he wanted was a slab of meat and a whisky.

One did not offer a Scotsman tea and cakes.

One offered little old ladies tea and cakes.

As he sat in the hazy parlor, belly growling and resentment boiling, Alexander fumed. By the time Lachlan Sinclair deigned to make an appearance, Alexander was ready to throttle him.

Still and all, Alexander sprang to his feet in deference as the duke breezed into the room.

He was a large man, tall and broad shouldered, but a tad pale, as though he'd never spent a day of his life out of doors. Alexander should have expected as much. The man was practically British. He was dressed as a lord—not a laird, as he should be. He wore tight breeches and gleaming Hessians with gold-tipped tassels. His tailcoat was damask and intricately embroidered with shiny brass buttons. At his neck there was a ridiculous froth of snowy linen, which made him appear to have a severe case of goiter. A flutter of lace sprouted from each of his sleeves.

Lace.

"Ah, Dunnet. Thank you for coming." Caithness held out his hand and winced as Alexander took it.

Ye Gods. Not only did he dress like one; the man was as tender as a lass as well.

Caithness pulled away and flexed his fingers, studying Alexander from beneath his lashes. "That's quite a grip."

Aye. Earned through good, clean, honest work. Not prancing about in London in breeches so tight a man's privates were displayed for all to see. But perhaps the duke felt the need to proclaim his manhood thusly. On account of the *lace* and all.

Caithness pursed his lips. Alexander wasn't sure if this was displeasure or petulance. Or perhaps a bit of both. "So," the duke said after a long, uncomfortable moment, peering at his prey through narrowed eyes. "What kind of Scot are you?"

Alexander tipped his head to the side and remained

silent. The question didn't warrant a reply, as inane as it was. A Scot was a Scot. And an Englishman was a worm.

"You know." The duke flourished a hand; his lace fluttered. "Are you of Norman stock? Or Pict? You have the look of a Viking about you. Norse?"

Alexander grunted. *Aye*. His ancestors had been ravaging brutes sweeping down from the north and planting their seed in good Scottish bellies.

"Ah yes. Norse. We're alike in that. Kin, one might say."

Bluidy fucking hell. What was he nattering on about? Of course they were kin. They were clansmen for God's sake.

But they weren't *alike*.

Not by a damn sight.

"Please. Have a seat." Caithness plopped down and was promptly surrounded by a billow of dust. He waved a hand in front of his face. "I must apologize for the condition of my parlor." A chuckle. "But in truth, this is one of the few rooms with furniture. My personal effects have yet to arrive from London and the servants have been focusing their cleaning jags on my private quarters. Not many guests coming to the castle these days." He shot what might have been an accusatory look at Alexander.

Though why the lack of visitors would put him out Alexander had no clue. The duke's thirty-year absence, and recent flurry of outrageous missives, had gone a long way toward provoking the lairds in the county. Incomprehensibly, Caithness seemed unruffled by that fact. As though he were above their disdain.

He had a lot to learn about Scotsmen, this young laird.

"I have plans to refurbish the old keep and reconstruct the east wing altogether." The duke waved his lace in a vague direction. "I had hoped to finish it all before the end of summer, but there have been . . . delays. Castles are so very costly," he added with a sigh. "But I'm sure you know that."

He peered at Alexander as though he expected a reply. None was forthcoming, so the duke babbled on.

"And servants! Don't get me started on the trials of finding good help. Didn't have that problem in London. Had them lined up out the door for the opportunity to work for a duke. But here . . . God have mercy. They see me coming and they run for the hills. But it's probably not me." His lashes flickered. "Do you know, they say this castle is haunted? Haunted!" The word ended on a high pitch. The duke's eyes narrowed. Silence bubbled and then he asked softly, "Do you believe in ghosts, Dunnet?"

Alexander opened his mouth to answer and then settled for a quick shake of his head.

"Bah. Me neither. Oh, ancient structures like this have their creaks and . . . groans. It's nothing but settling. Or the wind. I'm sure of it. Once the refurbishment is finished, everything will be just right. I'm certain. Quite certain. It will all stop." He tendered what might have been a hopeful glance, but when Alexander was not quick to concur the duke slapped his knees and fixed a composed expression on his face, one that did little to obscure the apprehension hovering beneath the surface. "Surely all old castles wail on occasion." He gored his guest with a gaze that was a tad more intent than it should have been. "Does your castle wail, Dunnet?"

It most certainly did not.

But to appease the duke, he nodded.

"Ah yes. Of course it does. They all do. What I should do is tear the whole damn thing down and start fresh. Out with the old, what?" He chuckled, as though the thought amused him, but Alexander found it a bit offensive. There was nothing wrong with the old. Scotland was steeped in old. Scotland reveled in old. And there was nothing wrong with this castle that a little attention wouldn't solve.

As for the ghosts, likely Caithness would benefit from a haunting or two. Visitations from his long-dead ancestors might put some starch in his spine, or knock some sense into his empty head.

"The overhaul will be costly of course. The coffers will need to be plenished."

Ah. The reason for this meeting at last.

The duke paused to select a cake. He chose a pink one and took a dainty bite. It was an incongruous sight. He was a handsome man, as men went, large boned and braw, with a noble brow and the dark hair of the Sinclairs of Wick. Alexander could imagine him standing on a windblown tor, hands fisted on his hips, the Garb of the Auld Gaul flapping about his legs. It was a damn shame the duke couldn't be such a man.

Somewhere along the line, Lachlan Sinclair, Duke of Caithness, had been ruined.

Life in London had turned him into a pansy.

His face was sickly and wan. In addition to his mincing ways, there was a guarded vulnerability in his eye and a troubled turn to his lips.

Alexander had known he wouldn't like Caithness. He just hadn't realized how much.

Best to end this interview quickly. Without a word, he thrust his account books at the duke.

Caithness appeared slightly surprised, but he dusted the powdered sugar from his hands and took them. He flicked through the pages, scanning the neat columns, but with such casual brevity Alexander knew he couldn't be *seeing* anything.

After a moment or two of such study, he snapped them closed and sighed. "I think it would be best," he said in that crisp, soulless English accent, "if we improve the land."

Alexander's jaw dropped. He gaped at the duke in shock.

His heart thrummed in his throat, his temples.

Surely Caithness hadn't just *said* that.

The words were a death knell. They meant the end of all Alexander held dear. Everything.

"Well, Dunnet? What do you say? How long will it take you to evict your tenants?"

Bile rose in Alexander's throat. His vision went a little red. He set his teeth. Pressed his lips together.

At times like this, times when fury took him, or when he was otherwise befuddled, he was rendered utterly speechless. No matter how hard he tried, the words would not come. His throat locked up. His tongue froze. Anxiety lashed him.

The specter of an enormous mountain of a man, towering over a small, trembling, sputtering boy and bellowing his rage with a furor that caused the rafters to shake, flooded Alexander's mind. *Idiot. Moron. Worthless lump of stuttering flesh.* His uncle had called him all of those things, before a meaty paw swung back and cuffed that boy so hard he flew across the room.

As he stared at the duke, Alexander traced the long scar on his temple, the harsh reminder, forever branded on his skin. His badge from one of those times when the blow had nearly killed him.

He had vowed to himself then and there one day *he* would be the mountain of a man. One day he would have all the power. And he would use it, every ort of his strength . . . to protect those he loved.

This was that time.

This was the time for him to stand up for his clan, if a time had ever been.

He drew in a deep, calming breath and, with excruciating precision, formed his response.

"Nae."

Caithness blinked. "I-I b-beg your p-pardon?"

There was a dark pleasure in seeing *him* stutter—the great Laird of Sinclair. To see his eyes widen. To see his gaze flick to the savage scar Alexander still stroked.

The duke paled. "I, ah . . . Whatever can you mean?"

What did he mean? For pity sake. Did the man not hear him, or did he simply not want to understand?

"Nae." This time stronger. Louder. More vehement.

No Clearances. No evictions. No bluidy *Im-fucking-provements.*

Alexander felt the urge to vomit.

Even if he'd had a silver tongue, even if he was adept at swaying men to his cause, this man—this *English* man, who was interested in nothing but the glint of gold—would not be convinced. He couldn't see past the intricate knot of his ridiculous ascot. Couldn't see the murky depths of his outrageous request. Couldn't understand what it meant to be a Scot.

Because he wasn't one.

Without another word, Alexander stood, bowed to the Duke of Caithness, collected his account books, and removed himself from the dusty castle, a betrayed relic from a time when kin meant something, when clansmen stood together and protected what was theirs like the savages they were.

Even if it meant the death of him, or the loss of all he held dear, he would fight the Duke of Caithness and his Improvements until his last breath.

A thud and a curse awoke her. Hannah shot up and stared into the gloom. After all Lana's talk of ghosts after dinner, Hannah had been dreaming about them and hence, when she awoke with a start, specters were her first thought.

Her pulse pounded as she stared at the shadows dancing through the room. She strained to hear what had awakened her, but all was still. She thought she might have imagined the noise when, of a sudden, Brùid's tail gave a whomp. Then another. And then a series of sharp whacks against the mattress.

Her door creaked open and candlelight flickered through the crack.

"Hannah?" A whisper.

Aye, a whisper. Nothing more. But it made her breath catch and her soul take wing. Not a ghost. Her husband. *He was home.* "I'm awake."

Alexander stepped into the room. He lifted the candle and a glow encased his face. Hannah stilled, stared at him. He was so striking it made her chest ache. He smiled and her heart hitched. Even as she threw back the covers to spring from the bed and run to him, he stalked to her side. In one movement he set the candle on the table, sat beside her, and pulled her into his arms.

"How was your trip to Ackergill?"

His chin firmed. "Fine."

She opened her mouth to respond, to ask for more information, but he didn't allow it. His mouth was warm on hers, hungry. The heat from his chest bathed her. But what warmed her more was his ardor.

As much as she'd yearned for him for days, apparently he'd been thinking about her as well. Thinking about this.

He kissed her with a haunting desperation and then nibbled his way down her neck to a spot that sent delicious shivers skittering through her. Tossing her head back and staring up at the ceiling, she reveled in the exquisite torture.

Ah, he worked her, tormented her, pleased her.

It was maddening. It was sublime. It was incredibly beguiling.

Surely beguiling enough that all thoughts of a prosaic nature should have been driven from her mind, excised, banished by bliss.

Not so.

As her husband's tongue drew a delightful dervish on every nerve, the incongruous thought occurred to her that, in the flickering light of the candle, the walls of her chamber looked even more like manure. The brown was slightly more brown and the hint of yellow even more . . . bilious.

She wrinkled her nose and tipped her head to the side.

Not just manure, but the manure of an ailing cow. How could it be—?

"Hannah?"

With a start she realized Alexander had stopped what he was doing. Even as disgruntlement gushed through her, so did her resolve. Oh, she wanted to continue this conversation. She wanted to very much. Just not here.

She cupped his cheek and stared into his stunning eyes. So tender. So sincere. So puzzled.

"Could we go into your room?"

His brow knit. "My . . . room?"

"Oh, aye. Let's." She wriggled free of the covers and bounded from the bed, prepared to flee the orgy of excrement, but Alexander caught her arm.

"Why not . . . here?"

She tried not to make a face. Really, she did.

He shot a glance about her chambers, a frown brewing. "Do you . . . not . . . like your room?"

She wove her fingers together. "It's verra nice. But yours is . . . larger?"

He stood and stared down at her. His throat worked.

And ah, his desolate expression raked her. "You . . . doona like your room."

Beneath the weight of his chagrin, she wanted to wilt.

He had redecorated it. For her.

Oh, she was such a petty, shallow woman. She should adore the room—despite the dismal color scheme. She should try.

But she couldn't lie. All she could manage was a shrug.

His fingers closed into a fist. "W-why?"

"It's . . . lovely." Even to her own ears, her assertion was not convincing.

"Why?"

She wrinkled her nose. "Oh dear."

"Why?" With each request, his voice became stronger, more strident.

"It's just so verra . . ."

"So verra . . . what?"

She mangled her fingers together and peeped up at him. "So verra brown?"

He stilled. "It's a beautiful color of brown."

It was difficult not to gape at him. How on earth could he ever think this was a *beautiful* color of brown? It was dowdy and dismal and it made her want to howl at the moon in—

"It's . . . the color of your eyes."

Hannah's knees locked. Her breath stalled. She struggled to keep her balance as she stared at him. Not because of the words he'd said—although those were surprising—but because of his tone. It rumbled with . . . Was that adoration?

But still—

She snatched up the candle and ran to the glass, studying first her reflection and then the hideous fabric on the walls and—

Oh dear.

Oh God.

It was.

It was exactly the same color.

No wonder she hated it.

He came up behind her and set his hands on her shoulders. The counterpoint in the glass—of his long fingers against her delicate collarbone, the way the breadth of his palm encompassed her—captured her attention. His thumb walked up her neck to her jaw. He stroked her. And, holding her gaze in the mirror, he said, "It's the most beautiful color in the world."

She nearly collapsed against him.

It was the sweetest, most romantic thing she could ever have imagined.

And he didn't stumble over so much as a word.

But it put her in quite a pickle, because clearly he had gone to extraordinary lengths to please her and honor her and show her his devotion . . . and she really hated the color.

She did the only thing she could do.

She turned in his arms and framed his face in her palms and kissed him.

And then, once he was thoroughly besotted, she led him through the parlor and into his room, where thoughts of barnyard brawls would not distract her from the delectation of his very enticing form.

CHAPTER ELEVEN

She dinna like her room.

Try as he might, Alexander couldn't banish the thought. It supplanted even his anxiety over his unpleasant altercation with Caithness, which was extreme. Upon Alexander's return home, he'd wanted nothing more than to hold her, sink into her, and forget the worry that scudded like acid through his veins.

But now . . . this.

She dinna like her room.

Even as he kissed her and caressed her and gently removed her nightdress, the thought clanged through him like a church bell.

She pushed him back against the pillows and began unfastening his belt. He helped her as she removed his boots and tugged down his breeks, but truly, his mind was beset. As much as he wanted this, as much as he'd wanted it all week, his thoughts roiled.

He should have been distracted by the curve of her breast, or her moans when he nibbled on her thrusting nipples. The silk of her skin or her scent or, for heaven's sake, her fervor as she undressed him. But he wasn't.

He couldn't bear the thought that he'd disappointed her. Worse, that he'd gone on thinking she was happy here when she wasn't. On his long ride to Ackergill, he'd done little else but think about Hannah. About their marriage and how far they'd come in such a short stretch of time. He'd thought about how contented she made him. He'd assumed she was contented as well.

Beyond all that, somewhere on that rutted track he'd realized he wanted her much more than he'd allowed himself to admit. He needed her.

This swirling tumult in his heart was, very probably, love.

It didn't feel the way he thought love would feel. In fact, it felt very much like fear, tinged with desperation and an incongruous hope. Perhaps a hint of hunger.

Or more than a hint.

She dinna like her room.

His chest ached.

He had so wanted to please her in this. He'd been convinced he had.

Where had he gone wrong? Oh, certainly she didn't like brown—he'd learned as much in the game they'd played on their picnic—but her room wasn't brown so much as smoky topaz with swirls of gold. It was a deep, rich color, one he wanted to sink into.

With that thought, he kissed her lids, one after the other, and then kissed his way along each arching brow. Kissed her cheekbones, the little dent beneath her nose, the tip of her chin.

Their eyes locked and something shifted in him. Another need rose and consumed his biting curiosity. He hauled her up his body, against him, thrilling at the drag of her silken skin against his. He set his mouth on hers, nuzzling, questing, attempting to say with his actions the words he couldn't yet utter.

She melted into him with a murmur and began exploring him with her soft, delectable mouth.

They really needed to talk about her room. He really needed to *know.*

But not yet. Not just yet.

First he needed to hold her, soak her in. Steep in her presence and rally his courage.

On a good day, constructing cogent words was a challenge. It was even more difficult with her, although he found, as he came to know her better, his raging fear that she would discover his curse and revile him for it lessened. In fact, though they had not discussed it, he suspected she already knew the truth about his struggle to speak. Even though the prospect of that discussion dismayed him, it would almost be a relief.

The game she'd devised had touched him deeply. It had been a gentle and clever way of addressing the fact that he wasn't much of a conversationalist. While her game—or the need for it at least—had mortified him in some bleak corner of his soul, the fact that she wanted to connect with him, despite his affliction, had given him hope.

Hope that maybe, when she knew all of it, she wouldn't be repulsed.

How glorious would it be to be able to speak to her . . . with no fear? No fear whatsoever?

A pity he didn't have the courage to simply tell her. Everything.

But it was far too soon for that.

She ceased her tantalizing nibbles on his neck and lifted her head to frown at him. "Alexander? Are you paying attention?"

No. He hadn't been. Not entirely.

He nodded.

"Humph." In a fit of pique, she raked him with her nails. When she hit his nipple, his attention sharpened, peaked. His cock nudged her thigh and she rubbed against it. With a murmur she nestled closer. "That's better."

He tried to stop her leg from moving, from dragging insanity on him, as each touch further addled his thinking. He tried to stop her leg from moving but succeeded only in finding another delectable place to stroke. The back of her knee was particularly tender. That and the crease where her thigh met her lush bottom.

That she giggled and squirmed didn't help.

She dinna like her room.

The nagging thought crept back to the forefront of his consciousness, scalding him. When she began nibbling her way down his chest toward his belly, he had to stop her. He just had to. He needed to know, and if she continued this play she would succeed in distracting him utterly.

She peered up at him with a question etched on her features when he stilled her busy hands. He rolled over, pinning her beneath him. While the flare of her nostrils, the sudden tight grip of excitement on her face, incited him to action, he used his position to hold her still, so he could work through the question he needed to ask without interference.

"Do you—"

Ah hell. His throat closed up.

He sucked in a deep breath and tried again, aware that she lay quiescently beneath him, that she stared up at him, patiently awaiting his next words.

"Do you . . . really hate your room?"

Her chuckle vibrated through him in an enticing rumble.

"Do . . . you?"

She wrapped her arms around his neck and leaned up to kiss him. At the very end of the sweetest kiss he'd ever known, she whispered, "With a passion."

Why he laughed he didn't know. It was truly a disaster of monumental proportions. A woman's welcome in her new home set the tenor for the marriage. And that he'd been so utterly wrong in his choices bothered him.

Because he'd been so certain.

He probably laughed because she did. Because her

revulsion twined with an amusement, an élan, he found irresistible.

"I'll . . . have it redone." He tipped his head to the side and surveyed her. "Do you like . . . puce?"

Her response was a full-bellied chuckle, one he felt compelled to taste.

When he finished kissing her, for the time being, at least, and he lifted his head, she stroked his cheek and said, "You doona have to redo it."

"I do." It was imperative. She'd mentioned she liked green. He could have it done in a bright spring heather. *Ah. An excellent idea.* Then their rooms would match.

"I could always just sleep here," she murmured.

Another excellent idea.

They kissed for a while more and his passion began to flare—and then another thought struck him. "Why . . . why do you not like the . . . brown?" It was, truly, the loveliest color on earth.

"Oh, please, Alexander." She pouted. "Let it go."

"I canna." It was like a thorn in his side, wedged right there next to his passion. "Why . . . ?"

She sobered and gazed at him for a long while before answering, "I dinna realize it, but it is, indeed, the exact color of my eyes."

He thumbed her lashes. "Beautiful."

She snorted and turned away. He grasped her chin and directed her attention back to him.

"Beautiful," he insisted.

"My eyes are no' beautiful."

"Liar."

"They are no'. Lana has beautiful eyes. So clear and blue, like a summer sky. And Susana, my other sister . . . her eyes are a stunning green." Hannah put out a lip. "My eyes are like mud."

And it hit him. Like a fist to the gut.

As incomprehensible as it was, Hannah believed she was not pretty.

Hannah, with her alabaster skin, her thick ebony hair, her delectable curves—and, aye, her exquisite, mesmerizing topaz-*brown* eyes—was the most glorious creature he'd ever seen. His chest constricted. His throat clenched. Frustration sizzled through him. Ah, how he wished he were, indeed, a poet. How he wished the words could flow right now.

He would tell her, convince her with some lyrical sonnet, some magical prose, exactly what he saw when he looked at her.

But he knew the words would not come. No matter how hard he tried, he couldn't issue forth the flood of beatitudes she needed to hear.

He would show her instead.

He would show her how beautiful she was in his eyes.

So there would be no doubt.

൬

Hannah didn't completely understand Alexander's expression as he stared down at her. There was an odd mixture of dismay and determination . . . and something else she couldn't quite name. She hoped it wasn't pity.

How mortifying to admit the truth of why she deplored her room. And to him. But it wasn't as though he couldn't see it every time he looked at her.

She was not beautiful. Certainly not as striking as Susana or as angelic as Lana.

She wasn't a troll, either, but all her life she'd known she simply didn't stand a chance of competing with her sisters' blazing presences. She'd always worried she could never truly win a man's love—that she wasn't quite pretty enough. It had been a silly, irritating fear, one she'd sloughed away whenever it niggled at the back of her brain.

She had so much to offer and she truly liked herself and, she convinced herself, she didn't need a man's love to be whole.

But now that she'd met Alexander, now that she'd come to know him, that tiny spark of a fear had ignited into a roaring blaze.

She very much wanted to win *his* love.

It was a pity she didn't know how.

It hurt to bare her soul, her fears. To him. Like this. Wound together with him in his bed, naked, his hard body pressing into hers, his heat surrounding her.

It hurt to stare into his eyes as he loomed over her; the moment was far too raw.

Frantically she searched her mind for some jest, some offhand comment, something to shatter the brittle ache inside her and ease this discomfort, but she couldn't pin down her wispy thoughts.

And then every thought scattered, whipped away by a great gust roiling in off the churning sea. Because he framed her face in his enormous hands—her ordinary, plain, *unremarkable* face—and kissed her forehead. "Beautiful," he murmured.

He kissed her brow. "Beautiful."

Her cheek. "Beautiful."

The tip of her imperfect nose. "Beautiful."

He went on, touching his lips to every inch of her face, repeating the word again and again after each and every buss. And when he had exhausted the options of her features, he pulled back her hair and started working on her ears. They were largish and poked out a bit, so it took a while to acknowledge every inch, but these he declared to be beautiful too.

When he got to her neck, he became distracted and forgot to say *beautiful*, but he mumbled it occasionally as he worked his way over the sensitive column.

Aside from the great welling in her chest at his tenderness, his devotion, his dedication to making her feel pretty, his efforts delighted her in other ways as well. Her nerves began to hum. Her skin rippled with pleasure. The tiny hairs on her arm prickled.

Oh, she wasn't some phenomenal beauty and she knew it, but the fact that he would dedicate himself to convincing her she was, was enough.

If she hadn't loved him before—if she hadn't been drawn to him physically and attracted to him spiritually and besotted with him emotionally—she certainly loved him now.

He was, indeed, the most gorgeous, captivating, fascinating man she'd ever met.

And he was her husband.

A bubble of joy welled up. The urge to laugh, crow, rejoice, filled her.

But she did none of these things. Instead she threaded her fingers through his hair and gripped tightly until he, perforce, raised his head. He gazed at her with a curious look on his face.

"You," she said in a tight voice that threatened to fail her, "are the beautiful one." And she pushed him away, tipping him off her and onto his back. He was much larger and stronger than she, but he allowed it. Perhaps he'd been stunned by the ferocity of her tone.

He opened his mouth to respond, but she didn't hesitate. She straddled him and kissed him silent. His lips moved warmly, wetly, beneath hers. As she devoured him, she settled on him more fully, rubbing against him where their bodies touched, entranced by the feel of his hard belly on that aching spot between her thighs.

She lifted her head and smiled at him. His eyes were glazed over. His jaw slack. His fingers played restlessly over her hips.

With great deliberation, she leaned down and kissed his forehead. "Beautiful," she announced.

His brow, his cheek, the tip of his crooked nose.

"Beautiful, beautiful, beautiful."

His scar.

He winced as she kissed him there. Tried to turn away. "Hannah . . ."

"Hush."

From the place it began on his temple over his cheek to the puckered end near his chin, she peppered the wound with tiny kisses, murmuring her acceptance of him, of his perfect imperfections. All of them.

She trailed her lips over the muscled column of his neck and nuzzled him there, as he had her. Then she licked her way over his collarbone and the flat slabs of his chest, riffling her fingers in the wiry hairs, dabbing his nipple with her tongue, glorying in his taste, his scent, the response of his skin.

He lay beneath her silent and still, but he watched with glittering eyes as she explored him. His hold on her hips was gentle, but his fingers drifted in languid circles, awakening her, inciting her.

When he shifted, restlessly, something nudged her bottom. Something insistent and hard.

A shaft of need lanced her.

She stared at him, at the hunger etched on his features.

As delightful as this was, this slow, lazy, lingering discovery, she wanted more.

Holding his gaze, she braced her palms on his chest and edged back, just a tad. She rose up and settled her silken cleft over the length of his cock as it lay across his belly, engulfing him in the damp embrace of her folds. When she rubbed against him, back and forth, he shuddered. His lashes fluttered.

"Lord . . . have mercy," he breathed.

Mercy?

Not a bit of it.

It excited her that she could stir him.

It thrilled her that she could make him writhe and pant.

Slowly, teasingly, she bathed him in her arousal, stroked him in a relentless massage.

Ah, but she tantalized herself as well. With each movement, the hard bundle of nerves at the center of her being scraped against him. And with each nudge, shards of pleasure blossomed.

It wasn't long before she had to have more.

As she lifted up again, his nostrils flared. His gaze locked on her hand as she searched for and found him.

His cock was heavy and full, slick and hot in her fist. His pulse thrummed along his length. Her fingers drifted over him, caressing and testing his girth, but not for long.

She'd never been a patient woman.

With a small adjustment in her position, she guided the head of his cock into her weeping channel. Every nerve awoke and sang as she slipped down and down, impaling herself on his glorious length. She didn't stop until he was fully seated in her. He filled her so perfectly, so completely.

Testing the fit, she edged forward and back; she gasped as new sensations, new bursts of pleasure, exploded in her. Thusly encouraged, she tried a new movement, and yet another. She rose up and dropped down. She circled him. She rode him.

One particularly glorious lunge made her body seize as a wave of delight took her. She clenched around him and the wave swelled. She wasn't sure if the groan echoing through the room was hers or his or a twining of the two.

Though sweat formed on her brow, though her breath caught and her heart raced, she worked him relentlessly, pleasuring herself—and him—in a lazy, languorous ride.

But her need grew. Hunger raged within her. Some

inexorable force compelled her to move faster and faster still. She planted her palms on his chest, glorying in the feel of him beneath her, around her, and in her. She allowed her instinct, the savage, knowing woman within, to direct her thrusts.

He hissed out a breath as her pace, her intensity, increased; his fingers tightened on her hips. "Hannah," he growled. His body tensed, his muscles quivered. She had the sense he was yearning to flip her over, to cover her and take her and slake his passion. But he did not.

It was clear his discipline cost him.

She resolved to make this worth his sacrifice.

His attention locked on her breasts, bobbing with her every move. He loosed his hold on her hips and took them, one in each hand, thumbing her nipples and then, to her shock, pinching them.

It was a gentle pinch, but the scream of sensation it sent through her was not gentle in the least.

Ach. Had she thought she'd been savage before?

With a growl she sank her fingers into the flesh of his chest and raked him. He hissed and tightened his hold. Something wailed within her, screamed, clawed for release.

As though he could no longer hold back, his hips began to arch, to thrust into her, meeting her movements with an urgency that bordered on ferocious. Slick with sweat and arousal, bound in an insanity she'd never experienced, they battled against each other and with each other and for each other.

Her grunts and his groans echoed through the room, along with the sharp slap of flesh against flesh.

Faster and faster, tighter and tighter, wilder and wilder she pummeled him, each lunge on the knife's edge. Barreling toward oblivion, but going there together.

It was magnificent torture. She was stretched on a rack

of bliss, poised between pleasure and some grating, aching need. She kept reaching for it, but it danced away, just beyond her grasp.

And then, just when she thought she could bear it no more, just when she thought she might expire from the agonizing frenzy of unfulfilled need . . . he swelled inside her. The added pressure, the tightness of his fit, the sudden jolt of his cock, scraped at her sanity, loosening her grip, catapulting her up and away and beyond this bed, this room, this consciousness. Lights exploded behind her lids; glory rained through her.

He snarled something that might have been her name as he closed his fingers on her thighs in a pinioning clasp; holding her tight, he thrust up and up and up, though he was already as deep as he could go. Each manic lurch sent new waves of delight through her, but none so much as the hot stream of heaven that filled her as he released.

Instinctively she clutched at him, but as she reached her bliss—as she succumbed, dissolved, melted—her muscles lost their vigor; her deliberate clenches became no more than feeble squeezes and then uncontrollable ripples.

A shudder racked her from head to toe and she collapsed on his chest. His arms came around her, strong, tight bands. He cradled her close, pressing tiny kisses on her brow and murmuring into her hair. He tipped up her chin and stared at her, then thumbed at the tears on her cheek.

Hannah blinked in surprise. Was she crying?

Why?

Ah, but she knew why. This joining had been so much more than a physical tangling. It had been something ever so much more.

She knew, because there was a tiny tear in the corner of his eye as well.

CHAPTER TWELVE

He awoke her with a kiss. An enthusiastic swab of his tongue over her mouth. And then her cheek. And then the shell of her ear.

It wasn't romantic as much as . . . slurpy.

And drooly.

Hannah opened her eyes to glower at her husband for making her so damp first thing in the morning and . . .

Well, it wasn't his handsome visage that greeted her.

Unless he had grown fur. And a snout. And a lolling tongue.

With a growl, she pushed Brùid off her—he was looming over her with a paw on either side of her head, the better to lap her with. He didn't make it easy for her, tipping his great head this way and that so he could continue slathering her with canine adoration.

Or perhaps he was hungry.

She finally managed to wrangle the hound off of her and sat up, glancing at Alexander's side of the bed.

It was illogical to be disappointed that he was already gone. She should have expected it.

It was illogical to be annoyed to find a letter on the pillow where his head should have been.

Hannah picked it up with a sigh and waggled the parchment in Brùid's direction. "This better be good," she muttered.

Brùid grinned.

In something of a snit, she ripped the parchment open and began to read.

Her heart skipped a beat at the first line and then, as she read on, her fingers went numb and her body softened. Her annoyance drifted away like smoke on a breeze.

Because he had written her a love poem.

Well, not a love poem, per se, but close enough.

Hannah
I love her hair, like ebony silk
Her skin, so soft, like mother's milk
Her gift, a smile
Her laugh, a song
A kiss for which my heart does long
She speaks to me with dancing eyes
In their warm depths the answer lies
With a glance, she does my heart cajole
For there I see her pure bright soul

Hannah sighed.

Romantic? Most certainly. And it rhymed. She preferred poems that rhymed. In fact, it should be written into law that they all did.

There was something scribbled beneath the verse in tiny print. She held it closer to read it and a laugh burst from her.

He'd written: *And I do love brown.*

Of course he did.

The thought flittered through her mind that she should go find him in his tower and . . . thank him for this poem, but she remembered the ferocity on Fergus' features when he'd declared that no one bothered His Lairdship in the mornings and she decided against it. She could be patient. She could wait for him to finish his work.

Ballocks.

She was his wife.

If she couldn't distract him from his work, what was she good for?

Alexander frowned at the report before him.

It wasn't bad enough that he'd received a truly concerning report from his men in Dounreay, one that he needed to respond to immediately.

It wasn't bad enough that reports were coming in from Olrig, that the bastard had started clearing his land. Hell, homeless refugees had already begun showing up at the gates.

It wasn't bad enough that Alexander's mind was beset with worry over Caithness' demand that he do the same in Dunnet.

It wasn't bad enough that as he struggled to concentrate he very much wanted to be elsewhere. Preferably in bed. Making love to his wife.

But now he could smell her.

Smell her.

She had, indeed, sunk into his soul.

It surprised him that it had happened so quickly, but then again, it was Hannah. He'd wanted her on sight. That she continued to delight him, enthrall him, as he came to know her better should be no great shock.

But bluidy hell. He couldn't make love to her, couldn't find her and yank her into his arms as he so yearned to do—until he finished his work.

He had several reports to review and matters that required his attention, including the new wool mill in Brough and another squabble in Lyth . . . not to mention the evergrowing flurry of letters from the neighboring barons urging him to join their ranks. Beyond that, he'd lit upon a plan to propose to Caithness, an option to the Clearances the duke seemed so intent upon, and Alexander wanted to sketch out the details. There was so much to do, and so much depended on his effectiveness as a manager. Especially now.

This was no time for distraction, even as delectable as she was

With a sigh he pushed away from his desk and stood, stretching his neck with a crack. He'd been working for hours. Answering letters, writing out orders for supplies, and plowing through these endless reports. He was exhausted and—

He stilled as his gaze snagged on a movement by the door; someone was perched on the landing just outside his office.

He took a step closer to investigate—though he knew who it was; he could *smell* her, after all—and she glanced up. A smile flooded her face.

"Hannah, what . . . are you . . . doing there?" He didn't intend for his voice to be so sharp, but it must have been, for her smile dimmed. He held out his hand to her in recompense. "Come in."

She hesitated. "I doona want to bother you."

Ah, but she did. Bother him. But only the best possible way. "Come in."

"Fergus said I shouldna."

Alexander took her hand and pulled her to her feet and then, because he couldn't resist, he yanked her into his arms and kissed her. He intended it to be a quick kiss—he did have a lot of work to do—but it lingered.

Ah, he was glad she'd come. He'd needed her.

And Fergus be damned.

Though he did mean well.

Fergus had always been Alexander's champion, although, nowadays, he was often more diligent than he needed to be. Old habits did die hard. Besides, there had been a time when that diligence had saved Alexander's life, and he would never complain about it.

When the kiss ended, Hannah sighed and looped her arms around his neck. "Will you be working verra much longer?"

Alexander glanced back at the desk and winced. "Aye."

"You should let me help you."

He tried not to snort, but it escaped. She had no idea how difficult his work was, what a burden. It was a weight he would never want her to bear, and as he was her husband, it was his responsibility to protect her from the worry it all entailed. He would do whatever it took to protect her from that onus.

But it was sweet of her to offer.

Her brow rumpled. "I can help you," she insisted. She opened her mouth to add more and he kissed her again, although he shouldn't have, because she was distracting.

"You . . . shouldna be here," he sighed. He kissed the tip of her nose to soften his words.

"I'm bored."

He gaped at her. *Bored? Lord in heaven above.* He would love to be bored. "You could ride."

"I canna ride all the time." She put out a lip. "The servants won't let me do anything—"

"You are . . . a baroness."

"I'm used to being busy. For heaven's sake, Alexander, at Ciaran Reay I did everything."

He chuckled. *Surely not* everything. When she frowned at him, he cuddled closer. "I can think of . . . something for you to do." Again, not wise to even jest about it. There were several pressing issues on his desk that had to be handled at once. So he amended, "Tonight."

While he invested the word with a sultry tone, she

wasn't mollified in the slightest. "I want something to do now." She sucked in a determined breath. "Alexander—"

"Aye?"

"There is . . . something that has been bothering me."

His throat tightened. "Aye?"

"Fergus said the library is *expressly off-limits*."

His bowels clenched with a ferocity that stunned him. Why it hit him so hard he didn't know. Or perhaps he did.

He did not like to think of that library.

Ever.

Once, it had been a magical room, filled with his father's prized collection, each tome lovingly acquired and attended to. The very smell of it evoked memories of hours spent at his father's knee, learning to read and exploring the treasures on those shelves. But when his father died, all that had changed. His uncle had wasted no time in turning that sanctuary into his own depraved haunt.

A shudder rippled through Alexander as a cold finger traced his spine. Now the room held only repulsive memories. Nightmares. Alexander had locked the doors when his uncle finally met his maker and hadn't opened them since. No one was allowed in there, not even to clean. The room had housed Dermid's squalor for years.

Hannah wrapped her arms around Alexander's neck. "I should verra much like to visit the library. I should verra much like something to read. Surely that isna too much to ask."

"H-Hannah . . ."

"Alexander." She nestled closer.

She was warm and soft in his arms. He knew damn well what she was doing, and while he didn't much mind being seduced, the thought of unlocking that room was beyond him. He very much wanted to give her everything she desired, but he couldn't give her this. At least, not yet. He wasn't ready to brave his ghosts in that library. He doubted he ever would be. The thought alone made his gut churn.

"What-what kind of . . . book would you like?" He glanced over at the shelf on the wall, filled with almanacs and dusty volumes about crop rotation and animal husbandry.

She fluttered her lashes. "Do you have any . . . poetry?"

"Not . . . I. . . . Not here."

"Hmm. I read a verra pretty poem this morning." She nestled against him. His cock stirred.

"Did you?"

"Umm-hmm."

"Did you . . . like it?"

"Aye." A whisper.

"I shall have to write you more."

"I would like that." She leaned back. "In the meantime, is there something else I could read? A room, perhaps full of books, I could visit?"

He winced.

He could just hand her the key, he supposed, but the room had been closed up for years. He had no idea what manner of disaster she could find. Mice at best. Dermid's howling ghost at worst.

Indeed, though it was not a logical thought, the locking of the doors had been akin to trapping the specter of his uncle in a hell of his own making, locking the memories away. Alexander despaired of letting them rage free.

He waved at the shelf of boring tomes. "Help yourself."

She sauntered over and surveyed the meager offerings. She picked up one and flipped through it in a desultory fashion. Her sigh was heavy as she set it back on the shelf. "I've already read this one."

Really? He leaned closer and checked the title. *Agricultural Tenancy* by Harlan Arbruthnot. No wonder she'd sighed. That one had been deadly dull.

She tapped another on the spine. *The Beauties of England and Wales*. "This one as well."

"This one?" He indicated another, his newest, a treatise on the impending industrial revolution.

She wrinkled her nose. "I found his conclusions rather simplistic."

Hell. So had he.

Alexander studied his wife. She'd told him she liked to read histories and scientific books, but he'd never imagined she would want to read books like these. "What did you think of Cantor?" He lifted the slender tome on the use of fertilizer in field regeneration.

She tapped her lip. "Interesting. But not as interesting as a piece I read on the methods used by the ancient Mayans."

Alexander blinked. "The . . . ancient Mayans?"

"They used fish. Fascinating."

He loved the way her face lit up as she told him more, though he remembered reading something about that as well. He was enthralled by the animation of her features, the way her eyes glowed . . . the way her lips moved.

It occurred to him he should probably buy her some books. Or he could brave the library and bring her more.

And he would. Just not yet.

For now, he just wrapped his arms around her and occupied her with other pursuits.

∾

Hannah bit back her smile as she strolled through the bailey, hugging to her chest the book Alexander had given her. After they'd made glorious love—in his sanctified office—he'd hunted through his shelves to find her something she had not read. Oh, it wasn't one she particularly wanted to read, but that was hardly the point.

He'd given it to her. With a kiss.

She had it in her mind to spend the rest of the morning in the garden, reading or pretending to read. She'd probably be thinking about him.

Their relationship really was warming, if the tryst in his office was any indication. He'd let down his guard enough to allow her in . . . at least a little. The thought thrilled her.

A flurry of activity, a familiar face, in the stable yard captured her attention and she changed her course. "Rory!" she called.

The lad stalled in the act of tightening the straps on his saddle and glanced up at her. His usual tranquil smile was replaced with a gloomy frown.

"How are you doing?" she asked as she came up to him. She had seen neither hide nor hair of him since they'd arrived in Dunnet, and she was so pleased to see him she decided to defer the lecture she'd been planning—about how he really should keep his distance from Lana—until later.

He rubbed his palm over the back of his scalp. "Fine," he said, a low grumble. He shoved several items into his saddlebags.

Unease trickled through her. "Are you going somewhere?" she asked.

His glance, twined with surprise and pain, shocked her. "Ye doona know?"

Her stomach soured at his bleak tone. "Know?" *Know what?*

"There have been . . . troubles in Reay. Yer husband is sending me back, along with his brother and more men."

"Troubles?" Her blood went cold. "What kind of troubles?"

Rory flushed. "Maybe ye should ask your husband."

"Maybe I shall." She whirled on her heel and stormed back to the castle, anger making the back of her neck prickle. If Alexander had heard something—anything—

from Reay, she should be the first to know of it. Not the last.

Fergus was the first unfortunate soul she spotted. He was bustling through the foyer as she entered. "Where is he?" she barked.

Fergus froze and stared at her, eyes wide.

"He, my lady?"

"Where is Dunnet?" Who the hell else would she be looking for?

Fergus twined his fingers and cleared his throat. His eyes flicked hither and yon. "My lady . . . His Lordship is . . . busy right n—"

"I doona give a good goddamn if he is busy or not. Where is he?" Her snarl echoed through the hall.

Fergus had the good sense to blanch. "My lady—"

"Where. Is. He?"

"In the great hall, my lady."

The great hall? Where was that? She searched her memory, but it failed her. "Take me there."

"But—"

"Now."

To his credit, he did, although Hannah could tell he was reluctant to do so. He slumped, like a dog with his tail between his legs, dragging his feet with every step.

Hannah heard the bustle before they reached the room. The shifting of many feet, the clink of weapons . . . and her husband's booming voice. "Andrew will oversee the defenses. Hamish, the investigation. And I want daily reports, do you understand?"

Oh, certainly he could speak to *them*. This only made her angrier.

She burst into the room and silence fell like a boom. Twenty-five men, all outfitted for travel into a battle zone, turned to stare at her. But she had eyes for one man only. Her husband.

And those eyes, they blazed. "What the hell is going on?" she snapped.

He whipped around and stared at her. His mouth opened. Then closed. "Hannah . . ." he finally managed.

"What the hell is going on? Is it true that you received a message from Reay?"

"A-aye."

"And you didn't tell me?"

Energy crackled between them. Alexander glanced at his men and she knew what he was thinking. *Not in front of my men.* She didn't care.

"How dare you? How dare you keep this from me? Reay is *my* land."

"Hannah—"

"What is it? What is going on? I deserve to know." She knew her demand was shrill, but the anger and the panic and the worry for her family, for her people, overcame her.

Her brother-in-law stepped forward, holding out his hands, as though that simple gesture could calm her down. "Another croft was burned down."

Hannah's stomach clenched. Her pulse raced. "Which one?"

Andrew shrugged and Hannah nearly smacked him. Of course he wouldn't know. No one knew, no one cared, as she did. "And there was . . ."

His hesitation made her knees knock. "There was what?" Despite her vehemence, he didn't answer. He glanced at Alexander.

Her husband stepped closer, slowly, as though approaching a wild animal, which, frankly, she felt like. He made a soothing sound and set his hands on her shoulders. "There's been . . . an attempt on your father's life."

Thank God Alexander was holding her, else she would have collapsed. Her breath caught. Her heart clenched. A silent wail rang through her head. "I . . . Is he . . . ?"

"He's fine." Alexander bussed her brow. "He's fine. They caught the villain."

A howl of panic whipped through her like a winter wind. Her father in danger. Her sister, dear, sweet Isobel. If she'd been there, this would not have happened. She was certain of it. Determination coiled in her gut. "I'm going home." She whirled to leave.

Alexander stopped her with a hand to her arm. "Nae."

She attempted to pull away but couldn't. She frowned at him. "I must go. I have to protect them." *Dear God, no one else could.*

"You must . . . stay." Alexander tucked a curl behind her ear. In another circumstance, she would have found that charming. Now she just wanted to slap his hand away. "My men will protect them."

Andrew grinned, although it was an anemic offering. "Our men are verra good at what they do."

Hannah glared at him and then swung back to glare at her husband. Somewhere, beneath the worry for her family, there was a deeper fear. She hated the fact that he hadn't bothered to share this with her. They'd just been together. Surely he'd known then. But he'd said nothing. He'd promised to be her *partner*, for pity sake. A bitter taste filled her mouth. "You should have told me," she hissed.

"I dinna want to . . . worry you."

"Worry me? These are my people, Dunnet. My life. I deserve to know. I deserve to be included in the discussion, in the decision. You canna keep everything to yourself."

His throat worked, but he said nothing more.

And aye, he probably would not.

Ever.

It rained down on her then, the fruitlessness of her hope that they could ever be partners. The hopelessness of wanting more with him.

It wasn't only that her husband wasn't a *bletherer* or that words were a challenge for him. This was something more. Something deeper.

He didn't want to share anything with her. He didn't see the need.

That was the desolation that gripped her, tore at her.

How could she have a real marriage with a man who thought her too frail, too stupid, too worthless, to handle anything?

Her heart formed a hard ball in her chest. Without another word she turned and swept from the room.

CHAPTER THIRTEEN

The door was locked.

He should have expected as much, but it still surprised him when Alexander tried the knob to her bedroom and found it wouldn't budge.

He'd never seen a woman so angry. Or hurt. The wounded look in her eyes had confounded him.

He should have followed her when she left the great hall. He should have found her then and soothed her, tried to explain.

But the men had been waiting for orders. There had been much to arrange before he sent them off.

And what, really, was there to explain?

He'd made the decision not to tell her about the letter, at least until he'd made all the necessary arrangements. He hadn't wanted to worry her. He hadn't wanted to have to form the words until it was absolutely necessary.

So he hadn't.

Cowardly of him?

Perhaps.

He hoped it hadn't cost him everything. Everything he'd been trying so hard to build with her.

Softly he knocked on the door. "Hannah?"

No response.

He knocked again. "Hannah, let me in."

Nothing.

He tried knocking louder. That worked . . . after a

fashion. He heard a rustling on the other side of the door. "Hannah, please. We need to talk."

A snort.

"Hannah." He attempted a commanding timbre. This succeeded in bringing her closer. He heard the shuffle of her feet, felt her presence as she stood on the other side of a wooden barrier. But it was more than a wooden barrier, wasn't it?

It was a chasm.

"I'm sorry."

Another snort. More of a grunt.

"Won't you let me in?"

"What's the point?"

His heart leaped at the sound of her voice, until her words sank in. And her tone. It was desolate. Damp. As though on a sob. "Please. Let me explain."

"Go away."

"I willna." He stiffened his spine. "I will stay here all night long."

Silence. And then a muttered, "Good."

"Hannah Lochlannach, let me in."

"You should have told me."

"I . . . know." Damn, it was hard, admitting it. To her. Through a door.

"My father was in danger, for pity sake."

"He's fine now. And Andrew is going to protect him."

"I should be there."

"I . . . need you. Here." He did. That was the harsh truth of it. He couldn't bear to let her go, and certainly not into harm's way. They had caught the villain who had tried to poison Magnus, but Andrew's quest was to ferret out any others and to bolster defenses. "Hannah. Please."

"Go away, Dunnet. I doona want to talk to you," she growled through the door. His gut clenched when she used his title. He was no longer Alexander to her. He was Dunnet. The laird. The thought crushed him. He'd never felt as utterly alone as he did at this moment.

Although, if he was being honest, he could hardly blame her.

She was probably right to be angry with him.

It was a pity he had no idea how to make things right with her.

With a sigh, he plodded back to his cold and empty room.

And it *was* cold and empty. Because hell, she'd taken his dog.

ᘓ

As silence fell on the other side of the door, Hannah threaded her fingers through Brùid's thick fur. He gave a little whine and snuffled at the door, although they both knew, with cold clarity, Alexander was gone.

He'd left. He'd taken her at her word and left.

A ribbon of regret wove its way through her. Maybe she should have opened the door. Maybe she should have spoken to him, but she was far too furious. So furious, she was afraid of what she might say.

It was better this way.

She needed some time to grapple with the emotions roiling through her, the worry for her family, the anger at her husband, and the sheer frustration with the entire situation.

Still, it crushed her that he'd left. And so soon.

Maybe he really didn't care.

Maybe there was no hope for them.

She couldn't let herself think on it.

Instead she closeted herself with her sister in her brown room—oddly, now the color was fitting; at least it fit her mood. She summoned Senga and had her bring up a dinner Hannah didn't eat. Then, after railing to Lana until her voice was worn out, she curled up in her bed with his dog and cried herself to sleep.

Alexander stood before the great double doors to the library, his hand hovering over the knob. His heart pounded and his palms were damp. He hated this room. Hated it with a seething passion.

It was filled with horrible memories, so much so that Alexander had not darkened the door for years.

But today he needed something from this room, wanted it enough to brave the shadows of his youth.

Redemption.

It occurred to him that if he wanted to appease his wife the gift of a book might do. The library—if memory served—was filled with them, although Dermid had never so much as cracked a spine.

The past few days had been sheer hell. Not only had it been very difficult sending his brother away—although he trusted no one more with the mission to protect Dounreay—but also Hannah had locked him out, out of her life, her heart, her bedroom. He'd tried everything—flowers, gifts, letters. Nothing had worked. She'd returned the letters in shreds. His flowers had not fared much better. Braving the library was his last hope.

A shudder passed through him. Now that he was here, poised on the threshold, he found the old trepidation creeping in.

It was ridiculous for a grown man to feel the scuttle of fear . . . for a room. It was only a room—a room in his *home*—but it was a room that held secrets and memories and a hint of horror.

He'd sworn to forget it, block it out. Overcome the past, but that was easier said than done. Entering this room, facing his ghosts, would be an excellent step in that direction.

He supposed.

"Are you going in there?"

Alexander started as a soft lilt intruded on his deep contemplation; he glanced down. His wife's sister Lana stood at his side gazing up at him. She looked nothing like Hannah. Lana's hair was a gossamer froth and her eyes were a bright and shining blue, slightly unfocused. She was a tiny thing with delicate bones, of reserved nature, and maybe even a little fey—given to flights of fancy about puppies and dead cooks—but she was his bride's sister. It behooved him to befriend her. She might just be able to help him with his quest to win Hannah's forgiveness.

He tendered a bow. "Miss Dounreay."

She folded her fingers and peered up at him with a sharp gaze. He had the sense she was examining his soul. It was probably silly to be relieved when her lips quirked. "Your Lordship." And then, "Well? Are you? Going in?"

"I, ah, was going to."

"You've been standing here quite some time. And glaring."

Surely he'd not been glaring.

She waved at the door. "What room is this?"

"The library."

Her eyes widened. "Fergus said it was expressly off-limits."

He tugged down his shirt and grumbled, "I am the laird."

"So you are."

"I can go in if I like."

She tipped her head to the side. "So . . . are you going in?"

"Ah. Aye. I was . . . hoping to find a . . . gift for Hannah."

Lana's eyes danced. "She would like that."

"She's . . . rather upset with me."

A snort, but Lana softened it with a smile. "So I heard.

You really should keep her apprised of the goings-on." And then she added, as though in afterthought, "My laird."

Heat rose on his cheeks. "She found out about the troubles in Reay before I could tell her."

Lana patted his hand. "She does that. In the future, you'd best tell her things as soon as you know them."

Not bad advice at all.

"At home, she knew everything. Did everything. You can see how frustrating it would be for her to have no role here."

Alexander gaped at her. "She has a role here!" She was his wife, for pity sake.

Lana's response was a reproachful look. "She's capable of so much more. You should trust her."

"I do." He trusted her. Aggravation and chagrin slashed him. All right, he probably should have told her immediately about the letter from Dounreay, since it affected her family, but it honestly hadn't occurred to him to do so. He was used to managing things on his own without gaining counsel from anyone other than Andrew.

However, he wouldn't make that mistake again.

He would share everything with her—or attempt to do so.

"She managed the entire estate, you know."

Alexander stilled. "The entire estate?"

Lana's expression firmed. "Everything." She glanced at the sealed door once more. "So you think to calm her ruffled feathers with the gift of a book?"

"I do." Alexander swallowed. "Do you think it will work?"

"It would help." Lana's eyes twinkled. "The entire library would work better." *No doubt.* "Shall I help you choose?"

Relief gushed through him. Not only because she probably knew her sister better than anyone. But also because he wouldn't have to brave the room—and its memories—on his own.

"Please." He marveled at how easy it was to speak to her. Perhaps because she had the aura of a child, innocent and pure. And peaceful. It was easier with some people than others, he found.

"Well?" She glanced at the key in his hand. It was only a hunk of metal. Surely it didn't *mean* anything more than a means of opening a lock.

Ah, but somehow it did.

Alexander drew in a deep breath and fit the key into the lock. As though she understood his apprehension, Lana set her hand on his arm, bolstering him as it turned.

It had been a long time and the mechanism stuck. It issued a grating whine as it gave.

He pushed open the door. A familiar musty scent surrounded him. His knees locked, his gut clenched. He stood at the entrance staring in; it was dark, though not nearly as dark as his thoughts.

The room was long, running the length of the wing, with windows facing the east and west. It reached up two stories high and had a balcony ringing the second floor. With the exception of the hearth and the draped windows, shelves marched along the walls. A thick mahogany desk dominated the far corner. Alexander did not look in that direction.

The chamber was littered with filth. Old plates covered with desiccated food, tipped-over whisky bottles, tumblers strewn here and there. It looked exactly as it had all those years ago. As though Dermid would storm in and begin railing at any moment. As though he would bend a boy over that desk and proceed to bloody his back with a cane until one of them collapsed.

Alexander hovered on the threshold, but Lana was not so tentative. She marched into the room and over to the east wall and whipped the curtains open. Sunlight flooded in. Dust motes danced on the bright skeins. Like a miracle, the shadows shrank. "Where shall we begin?" she asked.

Alexander sucked in a breath, focused on his mission—books for Hannah—and stepped inside. "I do believe the histories are over here." He led Lana to the right, away from the desk.

"Ah, aye." She studied the spines, running her fingers along them, stopping every now and again and then shaking her head. At length, she pulled out a thick and dusty volume and opened it, reading the table of contents. "This one looks verra dull." She thrust it at him. "Hannah will love it."

She continued on, pulling book after book from the shelves. Many of them ended up in the growing pile in his arms. Histories, dramas, Shakespeare, and several of the scientific volumes, although, Lana averred, they were far too old to be really interesting.

"That should do," she said when his arms were piled high with tomes. "What do you—?" Her gaze locked on something on the far side of the room. Her eyes narrowed and her chin firmed.

Alexander looked over his shoulder. There was nothing there. "What is it?" he asked.

Lana nibbled her lip. Her eyes flickered from the corner to Alexander and back again. "It's . . . nothing."

It wasn't nothing. "Miss Dounreay?"

She wrinkled her nose. "I doona . . . like that man in the corner," she said.

Alexander glanced at the corner. The empty corner. He blinked. "Ah . . . What man?"

"Och, the angry one."

A shudder rolled through Alexander. For nearly two decades, this room had been Dermid's haunt. Even now, years after his death, the very air seemed to seethe with his vitriol.

Incongruously, Lana laughed, a melodic trill. "Why is he so angry? Does he no' know no one can hear him shouting?"

"He's . . . shouting?" Alexander's eyes narrowed. Dermid had shouted. A lot. "What . . . does he look like, this shouting man?"

"He's verra tall, though not as tall as you. He's quite ugly, though it's mostly his scowl. And he's got a red bulb of a nose." She tittered another laugh. "He doesna like that I said that at all."

Saints have mercy. She'd described Alexander's uncle to a T. Right down to the bulging proboscis. He'd killed a man for making fun of his nose once, just gored him with a dirk over dinner.

"You . . . see *him*?" Bile swirled in Alexander's gut. He'd always sensed, felt, his uncle's presence in the castle, but he'd convinced himself it was only the memories that haunted him, not the man himself. That Dermid could be here, now, sickened him. The sudden urge to run possessed him. But he didn't. He was a grown man, not a frightened boy.

"Of course I see him. And hear him. Although who could ignore that racket?" She leaned in and whispered, as though in confidence, "The weak ones are always the loudest."

Alexander blinked. "The weak ones?" *Weak* was not a word he would ever use to describe his uncle. He'd been vicious and brutal . . . and strong. Strong enough to knock a boy from one end of this room to the other.

She smiled at him, and again her eyes took on that faraway look, the one that seemed to pierce through all shadows. "He has no power over you. Not anymore, you know."

His heart stalled. His breath locked. Thoughts whirled. *He has no power over you. Not anymore.*

"No one has power over you unless you grant it. Especially ghosts. Och, he thinks he does, but he doesna. That's why he's so angry." She gave a little sniff, as though in response to something a bellowing ghost said. She fixed her attention on Alexander. "We should just ignore him."

He has no power over you.

He has no power over you. Not anymore.

The thought gushed through him in a wash of exultation. The claws of the past loosed their hold on his soul. He felt it in a wild rush of relief, release, and an odd brand of vindication. His head went light with a sudden rush of euphoria.

His worst experiences had occurred in this room at the hand of a truly malicious man, but somehow, now, it was just a room. The desk was just a desk.

The monster was just a man.

Alexander glanced around the chamber again, studying each and every corner, each and every mote. If Lana was not completely insane, if she did, in fact, see ghosts, his uncle's spirit was *here*, apparently ranting and raving and raging. Yet Alexander felt nothing. Not even a dribble of fear.

He blew out a deep breath and gloried in the moment; then he turned to Lana with a smile. "Do you . . . often see ghosts in libraries?" he asked.

She gusted a weary sigh. "Oh, everywhere."

"Do they often bellow?"

"On the contrary, most of them are verra pleasant. I rather enjoy them. That one, though." She waggled her fingers in Dermid's direction. "That one I shall ignore."

"Excellent idea," Alexander said with a chuckle. If anyone deserved to be ignored throughout eternity, it was Dermid Lochlannach.

Dermid would have hated being ignored.

"Are you ready to go?" Lana asked, taking several of the books from the top of Alexander's pile, as though she could lighten his load. Oddly enough, she had.

He grinned at her and lifted the books. "Do you think this will do?"

"Oh, aye," she said with a nod. "This will do verra well."

And as she closed the door on the library, he had the distinct impression she was not referring to the books.

That very day, he gave orders to have the library thoroughly cleaned. Windows thrown open. Doors unlocked.

It wouldn't scour away his uncle's fetid spirit, but at the very least, it would irritate the bastard.

∾

The knock on the door was an annoyance. Hannah was busy. Far too busy to answer a door. She was pouting. Oh, she realized she was pouting—which was odd, because she'd never been much of a pouter. And she realized it was childish and pointless and probably a waste of time, but she was enjoying her martyrdom.

She'd received a letter from her father and one from Susana and Isobel as well, which had gone a long way in easing her worry for them, but her anger at Alexander had not waned.

At some point, she would need to speak to him, educate him, perhaps, on how to handle her, but she wasn't ready yet. She wasn't ready for the world to intrude on her misery, so she didn't answer the door.

The knocking persisted.

It was probably Fergus with another letter. While she wasn't in the mood to speak to anyone, she was in the mood to shred something, so she plodded to the door and opened it.

It wasn't Fergus.

It was Alexander . . . which surprised her, because usually when he knocked on her door it was the one from the sitting room, where he could plead with her in relative privacy. It occurred to her that he'd tricked her by coming straight at her, rather than from the side. As a tactician, she appreciated his finesse. Still, upon the sight of him, she closed the door.

Or she tried.

His foot blocked the slam.

He winced. "Hannah—"

"Go away, Dunnet." She made it a point to spit his title, so he would know she was using it on purpose.

"I brought you books."

She stilled, noticing the pile in his arms for the first time. For some reason, the glimpse of his face—weary and wan—had blurred out everything else. With a frown, she focused on the spines of the books. One of them caught her attention, and then another. A sprig of interest burst through her melancholy.

"May . . . I . . . come in?"

Regarding him askance, she sniffed and opened the door wider. It was the books that lured her. Surely not the deep lines around his mouth or the tight set of his jaw. Though the smudges beneath his eyes were particularly concerning.

He blew out a sigh as she stepped back, allowing him entrance. "Thank you. "I . . . Lana helped me choose them. I hoped . . . they would serve as an olive branch."

He held out his offering. An armful of books?

She raked them with a disdainful gaze. "A library would have been better."

"It-it is available to you. At . . . your convenience." This he said with a small bow. "Once . . . it's been cleaned."

"Cleaned?" *Who on earth didn't* clean *a library?* It was the most important room in any home.

He didn't respond to her squawk. He set the books on a table by the hearth and raked his fingers through his hair. She tried not to be distracted from her pique. His hair was tantalizing. Long and silky and inky black. Her fingers curled into a fist.

She'd missed him these past few days, more than she'd ever imagined possible. She'd even considered breaking down and storming into his room in the dark of night. It took every ort of discipline she had, but she'd managed to resist.

Now, in the power of his presence, her resistance flagged. She wanted to toss herself into his arms and kiss him. Crawl up his body, feel his warmth.

She turned away.

"Hannah . . ." His voice was low, resonant. "I'm sorry."

"So you said."

"Please forgive me."

She whirled back. "You should have notified me immediately."

"I realize that now."

"You shouldna have kept things from me."

"I agree."

"And for God's sake, you shouldna have ordered your people to shut me out."

He blanched. "What? I did no such thing."

"They won't let me do anything. Anything! Help with laundry? 'Oh, no, my lady. You're a baroness, my lady.' Plan the meals? One would think I had suggested sedition against the Crown. I'm not even welcome in the stables when the mares are foaling."

He turned an odd shade of green. "Of course not. You're a baroness!"

She growled. "If I hear that again, I may be incited to violence."

He blinked. "I, ah . . . What do you want?"

Honestly. How could he be so obtuse? "I want to be happy here."

It was a shaft to her heart, the bleakness that settled on his features. His body seemed to shrink in on itself. "You're no' happy here?"

Oh, bother. She hadn't meant it that way. She softened and stepped closer, set her hand on his arm. "I am happy, Alexander. With many things. But I'm not the kind of woman who can simply loll around and *be*. Even if I am *being* a baroness. I must have things to do. I must have responsibilities and chores and a say in the matters of the estate."

"I willna work my wife like a servant."

She issued a dismissive snort. "I was raised for this, Alexander. Trained for this. My entire life has been a preparation for managing lands. Do you understand? I can read and analyze reports, make orders on crop rotation, manage stock, conciliate disputes. I can certainly plan a meal or oversee wash day."

A peculiar look flickered over his face. "You *like* those things?"

Oh dear heavens. "I love those things. I thrive on those things. This . . . sitting around and *baronessing* is driving me mad."

"I suppose . . . I could find some things for you to do." His smile held a tinge of relief. She had the suspicion it was not only because they were coming to a meeting of the minds.

"Do . . . do you enjoy those things?" she asked.

He made a face and said in a small voice, "Not really."

"Why do you do them?"

"I'm the laird."

"A laird can hire people, Alexander."

"Aye, but the onus is on me."

His tone made his position clear. Though he disliked much of the work that gobbled up his day, he did it because he didn't want to burden others. There was probably the desire to maintain control in there as well. He did seem like something of a controlling sort, when it came to his lands. She recognized the same proclivity in herself.

She crossed her arms and fixed a resolute expression on her face. "Well, now the onus is on *us*."

He stared at her, a cascade of emotions flickering across his features. "Us?"

"We are a team. We work together to make a go of it. On everything. Agreed?"

"Agreed."

"We shall spend the morning tending to the business of Dunnet . . . together." Oh, she liked this idea. She liked it very much. He appeared to like it as well. His smile broadened. And then he chuckled. "What?" she asked.

"Together? In my office?"

Where else? "Of course."

"We likely willna get . . . much work done." He pulled her into his arms and tried to kiss her, but she pushed him away.

She wouldn't give in so easily. Not yet. "We still have the issue of your keeping things from me to discuss."

He put out a lip. "I apologized."

"That isna enough."

He frowned.

"I require a promise from you."

"A promise?" The way he said it, one would think he'd never heard the word before.

"A promise to *talk* to me."

His horrified expression made her chest ache. He stared at her in silence for a long while; his lips worked.

And then, at long last, he lowered his head. "I doona like to talk."

She smiled softly. "I've noticed. But Alexander, we have to talk sometime."

He frowned. "I have . . . trouble speaking sometimes." Naught but a murmur.

Ah, lord. She cupped his cheek and made him meet her gaze. "I know."

"I doona want you to . . . think less of me."

Ach. As though she could. She shook her head. "I wouldna. Not ever."

"Sometimes it . . . takes a while for . . . the words to come."

She smiled encouragingly, brushed the bristle of his beard with her thumb. "I'll wait."

His cheek bunched. He swallowed heavily. A glimmer appeared in his eye. "Hannah . . ."

"Alexander, I doona care about any of that." She took his hands in his. "I just want to *talk* to you. Promise me. Promise me that you will never again keep something from me. Nothing. Not even the tiniest thing."

He didn't respond right away, though she could see the thoughts sifting through his mind. She waited. At long last, he nodded. "I . . . All right."

"You promise?"

"I do. But Hannah . . ."

She frowned. "What?"

"There are . . . many tiny things. Boring things."

No doubt there were, but they would forge through the sea of details together. The thought elated her. "We shall begin working together in the morning. Oh, and rule number one, when you awake, you willna sneak off—"

He bristled. "I never sneak."

"You willna sneak off without waking me first. And you shall do so with a kiss."

He complied immediately. The kiss was soft and sweet and nearly impossible to resist. Nearly. She pushed him away again. "And no more letters." Her brow wrinkled. "At least, not in the morning. I doona mind the poems, but waking to a barked missive on my pillow is—"

"I doona bark."

"You rather do, darling." She patted him on the chest, a consolation. Why he stilled, why his muscles locked, was a mystery.

"Did . . . you . . . just . . . call me darling?"

Oh dear. She had. "Perhaps."

"Does that mean . . . you forgive me?"

"Perhaps."

He whipped her into his arms again and kissed her, this time with a savage passion. It occurred to her that if she allowed this to continue she might lose ground. So when he lifted his head she added, "If you agree to my terms of surrender."

"Och, aye, I do."

She evaded his questing mouth, so he settled on kissing her neck. It was rather scintillating, but somehow she retained the wherewithal to add, just to underscore her point, "And tomorrow we begin working together. We shall spend the morning in your office. Together."

His smile was a slow quirk, but he said, "Nae."

Aggravation dribbled through her. "What do you mean, nae?"

"I have a better idea." His expression was mischievous and lighthearted. It sent a gust of elation through her soul, a ripple of delight. He pulled her closer and she nestled against him, allowing his warmth to soak in.

She tipped her head to the side and said in a teasing tone, "Is this the same idea you always have? The one that invariably leads to tangled limbs?"

His chuckle rumbled through her. "Nae, Wife, but we

could do that tomorrow instead, if you like. I was thinking of taking you on something of a wedding journey."

"Hmm. Tangled limbs indeed," she teased.

"A tour of the borders. To help you become acclimated for your work. I should like to show you everything."

"I would love that."

"All the way round, it's a two-day ride. We can stay at the inn in Bower."

"Ah. The tangled limbs."

"Indeed." He grinned. It was a beautiful, carefree offering and she loved it.

In fact, she very much suspected she loved him.

They started their ride as dawn broke because Alexander explained they would need to get an early start if they were to make it to Bowermadden Inn before dark. At the last moment, they decided to take Brùid, because his large brown beseeching eyes could not be resisted. He loped along beside them, glorying in the run, his tongue a'loll.

Hannah was entranced as she and Alexander rode side by side—he on Wallace and she on Beelzebub—but she was not just entranced with the beauty of Dunnet. Alexander's glances and smiles bedazzled her as well. For a while, as they rode up to Gutteregoe and turned for Loch Dunnet, he held her hand, which was a challenge because the two horses didn't care to be so close.

When Beelzebub took a swipe at Wallace and Alexander's mount retaliated, both Hannah and her husband laughed and released hands. They could touch tonight.

They followed the Burn of Ratter through Greenvale and then he gave her a tour of the Barrack mill. It was much like every other mill she'd ever seen, but it was fascinating . . . because he was there.

After a lovely lunch on the banks of the Loch of Scister, they headed south, toward the village of Hartfield. Just beyond that they stopped at a small croft on the border of Olrig's land, where Alexander introduced her to Agnes, the elderly woman who was now confined to her bed. Though she was ailing and weak, her mind was sharp as a tack, and Hannah enjoyed the riotous tales of the adventures Agnes had had in her youth. It warmed Hannah's heart when Alexander produced a shank of ham and some bannocks for Agnes.

Evening was just beginning to fall as he and Hannah reached Bowermadden Inn, south of the Dunnet border, on the road that ran from Wick to Castletown. It was a simple collection of buildings on the heath, just the inn and the stables, but it was bustling. There were not many roads crisscrossing Caithness and fewer posting houses. Any traveler seeking shelter for the night and a warm meal would stop here.

As they rode into the stable yard, Hannah frowned. "It looks busy," she said.

Alexander shot her a grin as he dismounted. "Not to worry. I sent a runner yesterday to reserve rooms for us." He reached for her and she allowed him to help her down. Not because she needed it, but because she enjoyed the slow slide of her body on his.

"That was verra thoughtful of you," she said softly.

His eyes twinkled. "Not thoughtful so much as prudent. If the inn was full, there would be no . . . tangling."

She gusted a sigh. "I do love a man who plans ahead."

His humor faded. He stilled and their gazes locked. A flush rose on her cheeks.

He leaned closer. "Do you?" A murmur.

She swallowed. "Aye. I do."

The coming kiss set her blood on fire long before their lips touched.

"Perhaps," he suggested when he came up for air, "we could have our meal served in our rooms."

"Mmm. An interesting suggestion."

"I am a wealth of interesting suggestions."

"You most certainly are." She shot him a mischievous glance. "So, sir, am I."

His responding grin was wicked. He opened his mouth to say something, but the words stalled as his name echoed through the yard.

"Dunnet!"

He winced. "Blast," he whispered beneath his breath. Then he fixed a smile on his face and turned. "Bower, old friend."

Bower was a tall man with a kind, though florid, face. He welcomed Alexander with a slap to his shoulder. "It's damn fine to see you, but what the bluidy hell are you doing here?" he asked.

"I've been showing off my lands to my bride." He pulled Hannah forward and slipped his arm around her waist. "Ranald Gunn, Baron of Bower, meet my wife. Hannah Lochlannach, of Reay."

Ranald's eyes widened on her. "Of Reay?" He barked a laugh and slapped Alexander on the shoulder once more. "You dog. Why was I not invited to the wedding?"

Hannah leaned forward and answered for her husband, "It happened . . . *forthwith.*"

"Ah. I . . . see. Well, congratulations to you both, and welcome. You're just in time for supper."

Hannah set her hand on her stomach as it growled. It had been a long time since their impromptu picnic by the loch.

As the ostler took their mounts, Hannah and Alexander fell in beside Ranald and made their way into the inn. Brùid loped at Alexander's heel.

"So, what are you doing here, Bower?" Alexander asked. "The inn is quite a ways from Hestigrew."

"Aye. Aye. I'm just returning from a hunting trip with some of the local lairds. We decided to stop for a tankard or two before we all return home."

"Well met then."

"Aye."

As they stepped inside the inn, a loud, harsh laugh barraged them and Alexander stilled. When Hannah glanced at him, she was surprised to see his face had become a mask, his jaw tight and his lips pale. He flicked a glance at her. His hold on her tightened.

Curious, she scanned the crowd . . . and her pulse stuttered.

Niall was here. And he was staring right at her.

ᘓ

Alexander's gut churned.

Damn and blast. He'd wanted to have a romantic evening with Hannah, a nice dinner and then perhaps some . . . tangling. The last thing he wanted to do tonight was rub elbows with the local lairds. Especially the ones who were here.

Niall Leveson-Gower for one, especially given the look on his face as he *ogled* Hannah. He was, no doubt, put out that he'd lost her to Alexander. It was clear from Niall's expression he intended to be unpleasant, and Alexander didn't want to expose her to his malice. He certainly didn't want her to witness his own temper, which was beginning to stir.

The other two men lounging beside Niall at the table in the corner—Olrig and Scrabster—were also on the list of men Alexander would least like to spend an evening with. He considered taking Hannah's arm and tugging her back into the stable yard, leaping with her back on their horses and scurrying home in the dark, but before he could, Olrig spotted him.

"Dunnet!" he bellowed, opening his arms wide. He tipped in his chair, as though it was a challenge to stay seated. It was clear he'd had more than a tankard or two. In fact, all the men looked decidedly foxed. "Jus' the man I wanted to see."

"Aye," Niall said with an insincere smile. He stood and pulled up two more chairs. "Won't you join us?"

Alexander was about to decline when Bower gusted, "Oh, please do." His tone was so desperate, Alexander hesitated. No doubt, after days in the company of these men his friend was despairing for some rational conversation.

Alexander glanced at Hannah. "Perhaps for a moment?" When she nodded, he acquiesced and settled her in the seat farthest away from Niall. He sat beside her and shot a dark look around the table. "But we canna stay long. My . . . bride and I have plans for this evening."

"I'll bet you do," Olrig muttered with a smirk. Niall and Scrabster laughed. Alexander glared them all down.

"I suppose congratulations are in order," Niall said, fixing his brooding gaze on Hannah. Bless her, she met his eyes without a flinch.

"We're verra happy," she said, tucking her arm in Alexander's.

Alexander pulled her closer and kissed her brow. And not just to annoy her former suitors, but because he wanted to. "Aye. We are."

"You bested us all in the pursuit of the elusive Hannah Dounreay," Olrig said, lifting his tankard and taking a healthy snort. A splash landed on his tunic, but he barely noticed.

Alexander frowned. His uncle had been a deep drinker, and Alexander had never cared for the trait in other men.

Aside from which, Olrig looked very much like Dermid, from his portly silhouette, to his reddened, bulbous nose, to his narrow, mean eyes. Alexander forced his attention elsewhere.

Niall took a healthy quaff as well. "Aye. Snagged the prize, as it were." His gaze flitted to Hannah and he proffered a reptilian smile. "Oh, and the *lovely* Hannah, as well."

Alexander's hackles rose at the implication that the lands were worth more than the woman. He hated that Hannah flinched at the insult. It wasn't true. *She* was the true prize here. But he said nothing. His ire was too high for him to speak with any prudence. Aside from which, his throat was clogged with irritation. Instead he tightened his arm around her in a show of support and affection. He drew his thumb along her shoulder to make his point. She glanced up at him and he smiled down at her. And then, because he couldn't not, he kissed her. Gently. Briefly. Reverently. On the brow.

"You know, it's odd that you should arrive just now," Scrabster said into the breach. "We were just talking about you, Dunnet."

"Were you?"

"Aye." Olrig motioned for another drink. "You know, you and Bower, and Dounreay of course, are the only lairds who havena joined with the other barons."

Alexander glowered at him. "This is not the time to discuss politics," he said.

"Ach, bah! Because your *bride* is here?" Olrig shot a belligerent look at Hannah. "She can sit there and be silent as men discuss their business, as all good wives should."

Olrig really was an ass. And a fool. If he didn't sense Hannah's growing annoyance, Alexander did. He stroked her arm in hopes of calming her. It would probably be awkward if she grabbed one of the forks on the table and stabbed a baron. Which, judging from the glimmer in her eye, she seemed wont to do.

"Dunnet is right," Niall said with a glance around the room. "We shouldna talk about *that* right now." He leaned in and added, "There are far too many ears."

Aye, and their plot to betray Caithness amounted to treason.

"But these are changing times," Scrabster said. "It behooves us to change along with them."

"Aye. But there are right ways. And there are wrong ways." Alexander's gaze fell on Niall. "Clearances, for example." He shouldn't have brought it up. With the exception of Bower, the men around the table bristled.

Niall frowned. "Clearances improve the land."

"At what cost?"

"At what gain?" Olrig bellowed. "Stafford has cut the deadweight and brought in a profitable business."

"At the cost of his crofters and tacksmen. At the cost of his vassals."

"Bah! That is the old way of seeing things."

"It is the Scottish way," Hannah snapped. The men glared at her interruption.

"Stafford's efforts have been so successful, I've begun doing the same with my lands," Olrig said.

Alexander gored him with a glower. He shrank back. "I know," Alexander snapped. "Where do you think your refugees turn?"

Olrig smirked. "More fool you, for taking them in."

"He is hardly a fool for showing mercy," Hannah said.

"He's a fool for resisting the inevitable," Scrabster rejoined. "It is going to happen. Both Stafford and Caithness want it. So let it happen. These Improvements are a chance to make more money. For ourselves. For our laird."

"A chance to decimate our land."

Niall shrugged. "It's only a few sheep."

Hannah bristled. "Nae. It is more than a few sheep. It is murder."

"Murder?" Scrabster chortled. He lifted his cup. He was clearly deep in it.

Hannah appeared stalwart and strong, but Alexander could feel the tremble of her hand on his arm. "It is the murder of our people. The murder of our way of life." Her voice was cold and clear.

"Bah." Olrig stood. He teetered to the side. "This conversation is pointless. And I need to take a piss."

Hannah flinched at his vulgarity. When she met Alexander's gaze, he could see her thoughts in them. Though they had rooms for the night at the inn, he had no desire to stay here. Not with those men in residence. And he sensed Hannah felt the same. The evening had been ruined. "Perhaps we should go home," he murmured.

She nodded. "Aye."

He whistled to Brùid, who scrambled to his feet and loped to Alexander's side. He riffled his fingers through the hound's fur and tried to calm himself. As unpleasant as this altercation had been, he had no desire to carry this bile with him.

Bower rose with them and walked them to the door. "I'm verra sorry about that," he murmured, bowing to Hannah.

"It's all right," she said with a smile.

Alexander clapped his friend on the shoulder. "You had no way of knowing, but there is bad blood between the lot of us."

"Still, I fear I have ruined your wedding trip." Chagrin wracked his countenance.

Hannah trilled a laugh. "Never say it. It has been a lovely day."

"You must let me lend you my carriage. It is a long ride back to Dunnet on horseback."

Alexander glanced at Hannah. He could ride the rest of the way with no problem; he knew this land like the back of his hand. But she was tired. Besides which, a carriage ride would allow for . . . tangling. At least of some sort. "I would appreciate that. Thank you, Bower."

"Excellent. I will arrange it." Bower shot him a relieved smile, and together Alexander and Hannah stepped outside.

The stable yard was quiet and cool after the cacophony of the inn. As they made their way to the stable, a noise from inside caught Alexander's attention. A snarl, a thud, and a yip.

At his side, Brùid stiffened. His hackles rose. A growl rumbled from his throat.

"Goddamn you!" a yell wafted from the stable, along with a pained howl.

And ah, Alexander's hackles rose as well. It was a collection of sounds he'd heard before. Hannah called after him as he sprinted toward the broad open doors, with Brùid at his heel. Alexander's muscles tightened as he took in the scene, though he'd known. He'd already known what he'd find.

Olrig, drunk and red-faced, had cornered his dog in a stall and he was whipping her. Though the animal tried frantically to escape, the furious man would not allow it. One lash fell and then another. Olrig cackled with glee.

Aye, he was very like Dermid indeed.

Swamped with rage, the remnant of years of helplessness, Alexander lunged for him, grabbing his arm. Olrig snarled and lashed at Alexander's face with the whip. The pain barely registered.

"You bastard," he growled.

Olrig growled back and hit him again and again.

With a hair-raising snarl, Brùid attacked. He lunged across the stable and tackled Olrig, knocking him to the ground. The bastard issued a shrill scream as Brùid planted his forepaws on Olrig's reedy chest and snapped and snarled at his face. Olrig lifted his fist and slammed it into Brùid's muzzle. The dog whimpered but didn't budge.

When Olrig lifted his fist again, this time clutching the handle of his whip, Brùid took his hand in his mouth and bit down. Olrig howled and writhed and then fumbled for something on his belt.

Though stunned to silence by the drama playing out before him, Alexander barked, "Brùid. Heel."

With a glance back at Alexander, his dog whined and then released his prey.

Olrig reeled up; something glinted in his hand. Alexander saw the danger, even if his hound did not, but there was no time to warn his faithful friend before the blade came down hard, sinking deep into Brùid's shoulder.

To Alexander's horror, his dog fell.

Alexander's vision went red.

A memory assailed him. A memory of another man, another dog. Another time.

He launched himself at Olrig and, without thought, plowed his fist into the other man's fleshy face. Blood spattered as the man's nose crumpled beneath the blow. It was extremely satisfying. So satisfying, Alexander wanted to continue the pummeling.

Hannah's call reined him in.

It wouldn't do to kill the man before her very eyes.

He forced himself to retreat and bent down beside his panting dog. He was relieved to see the knife had glanced off his dog's ribs, but there was a long gash in his side. Brùid whined and winced as Alexander slipped the blade out.

"Dunnet, are you insane?" Olrig trilled. He fished for a handkerchief and blotted his nose.

Alexander glared at him, too furious to form words.

"You are a maniac." Olrig turned to the grooms who had run to investigate the commotion. "He's a maniac. He set his dog on me. And then he hit me." He turned to Alexander. "You broke my nose!" He struggled to his feet, gesturing to the onlookers. "You can see. You can see what he did!"

"Nonsense." This from Hannah; the word dripped with disdain. "Alexander dinna set his dog on you, you cretin. And he only hit you after you pulled a knife."

"Shut up, you whore."

Ah. Olrig was going to die. Alexander rose to his feet and stepped forward, the knife, providentially, fisted in his hand.

"Alexander." Her voice was calm, composed, though there was a tremble of rage in it. It forced him to meet her gaze. "It doesna matter. What matters is Brùid, and the other poor creature this man has wounded." She glowered at Olrig. The other dog, a bitch, was curled into a ball, quivering and staring at the men, wreathed in fear. "How dare you beat a helpless animal."

"It's my dog. I do what I want," Olrig had the gall to pronounce.

"She isna your dog anymore," Alexander growled.

"What?"

Alexander's fists tightened around the knife. "Go. Go now."

"But I—"

"I suggest you leave, if you want to walk away from this undamaged." Hannah's fury was like a cold wind whipping through the stable.

It even seemed to sink through Olrig's cloud of outrage. He paled and then took a step back. And another.

"Go," Alexander barked, and he did. He whirled and scampered from the stable, lucky to escape with all his body parts attached.

~

With Bower's help, Alexander and Hannah bound the dogs' wounds and wrapped them both in blankets and eased them into the carriage as the grooms tied the horses' reins to the back of the conveyance. Alexander suggested an immediate departure was in order and Hannah agreed. For one thing, she wanted very much to put distance between herself and Niall. Aside from that, the altercation in the stable with that hideous man had soured her stomach and her concern for Brùid and the other sweet pup was high.

Thankfully, it wasn't a very long ride home. Still, Hannah worried that, with his wounds, Brùid would not make it. Neither she nor Alexander spoke much as the carriage made its way along the road to the north. Hannah, cradling the other dog in her lap, as Alexander cradled Brùid, cringed with each jolt.

The carriage was nearly in full dark before Alexander spoke a word. "I'm verra sorry for that." She hated the anguished lilt to his tone.

"Sorry for what?" She didn't intend to speak so sharply, but mercy, he had done nothing wrong.

"I shouldna have lost my temper."

She gave a snort. "I would have done a sight worse." Flailed Olrig with his own whip, for one thing. She trembled with outrage for that poor helpless hound. It always infuriated her, the inequity of the world. That some men were so large and had so much power, while others suffered beneath their thumbs.

"I shouldna have lost my temper." Alexander's sigh was audible. "Only weak men resort to violence."

Her chest tightened, ached, at his desolation. "Nae. There is a difference between a man who chooses violence because it is the easy way and a man who uses violence because it is the *only* way. Today, it was the only way to get through to that savage."

"But—"

"And beyond that, there is a difference between a man who uses violence to dominate weaker creatures and one who uses it to save them." She petted the fur of the dog in her lap; the hound whined and nestled closer. "Can you see the difference, Alexander? Because I see it in you."

"Thank you, Hannah." He was silent for a long moment, then said gruffly, "I just regret—"

"You have nothing to regret. Nothing."

"I shouldna have hit him."

"He deserved it. What he did was heinous. But you stood up to him. I love that about you. You doona back down without a fight."

He stilled. She could feel his pulsating energy, all the way across the carriage. "You . . . love that about me?"

Ah. Aye. Dare she admit it? She did. And much more. "You are verra brave."

He barked a harsh laugh.

"You *are*." She fiddled with the hem of her sleeve.

Alexander was silent for a long while. Then he said rather softly, "He reminds me of my uncle. Perhaps that was why I lost my temper."

"Or perhaps you lost your temper because he is an ass."

He chuckled and fell silent again.

"Andrew . . . told me about your uncle." *Oh dear.* Maybe she shouldn't have mentioned it. His retreat was cold and quick. "Not a lot," she hurried to say. "Just that he was . . . not a pleasant man."

Alexander snorted. "That's putting it mildly."

"Was he . . ." *Oh.* Could she ask? Should she? But if they were ever to be close, she needed to know. She needed to know *him*. "Was he the one who gave you the scars on your back?"

Silence crackled, and then, into the shadows, he murmured, "Aye. He . . . beat me daily."

"Why?"

His laugh was harsh and held no humor. "No reason. He also gave me this." He touched the side of his face. "But the beatings were the least of it. I did what I could to protect Andrew, but in the end, I had to send him away. I feared Dermid would kill him in one of his drunken rages."

"See. You are brave. You stood up to him."

"I was only a boy. I wasna verra good at fighting him, I fear."

"He was a grown man. The point is, you tried. Many a man would have been destroyed by his brutality. You used it to become stronger." She glanced away from the denial flickering over his face. "I canna imagine what it was like growing up with a guardian like that."

"It was . . . horrendous."

"But still, you protected your brother." She was fishing for information but willing to take what minnows she got.

"Aye. But there were others I couldna . . . protect. . . ." He trailed off as though lost, buried, in the memories of those devastating failures. He riffled Brùid's fur. "He murdered my dog." His voice was soft, but she heard.

"That is awful." She wished they weren't sitting so far apart, that they didn't each have an animal cradled on their lap, so she could comfort him, but she sensed he needed the distance.

"Her name was Eoeith. She was my salvation. My best friend. One night . . . Dermid took her to the river. He . . ."

Hannah clenched her teeth. She didn't want to know. Didn't want to hear. But she didn't stop him.

When Alexander glanced at her, his expression was tormented. "He killed her, and made me watch, Hannah. I couldna stop him."

"Of course not. You were a boy."

"I was fifteen." He scrubbed his face. "I was taller than him. I could have . . . done something. But he was in a rage because I'd sent Andrew away . . . to relatives in Perth. Dermid was furious. And in retribution, he . . . killed Eoeith." He stroked Brùid's fur once more. "Brùid was her pup. I didn't let Dermid know I cared for him. I pretended nothing mattered after that. Anything I loved Dermid destroyed."

Hannah shuddered. She could imagine it, see it, that poor sad boy cut off from everything that mattered, forced into a prison, forced to hide his feelings. Brutalized. Her chest ached at the thought. "He was an evil man."

It was as though Alexander didn't hear her, as though he were somewhere else, wrapped in the thick, choking cloud of memory. "Fergus' scar? The burn?"

Something clutched Hannah's gut, a tight fist. "Aye?"

"Dermid did that." A whisper. "Held his face to the fire. Because Fergus defended me. He nearly died. I can still hear his screams." Alexander's laugh was harsh. "You would think, after that, Fergus would have abandoned me. But he dinna. He stayed by my side. Defended me, protected me."

Ah. Her heart wept. *Poor Alexander. Poor Fergus.* She cringed now as she recalled all her uncharitable thoughts about the dour man. It was a harsh reminder that one never knew the true depths of another soul. A caution against passing judgment over another. "You are lucky to have such a fine man at your side."

"Aye. Indeed. Without him . . ." She waited, patiently for Alexander to finish, as she knew these words were difficult. "Without him . . . I would be dead." He attempted a smile, but it was wreathed in shadows.

Glory, he was a magnificent man. Stalwart, resilient, and brave. How she loved him. How she longed to bring him peace, comfort him, protect him from every hurt, past and future. She didn't have such power, but she could give him what she could. "I'm so sorry you had to go through that, Alexander . . . but I canna help be thankful for it."

"Thankful?" Incredulity wove through his tone.

"As difficult as your childhood was, it made you the man you are. A man who is strong, yet gentle. Powerful, but caring. That is what I see in you." She dandled her fingers in the scruff of the wounded pup's neck and then, after a while, added, "But I'm glad he's dead."

Alexander's smile flashed. "Me too, God save me. I'll probably rot in hell for it, but I am glad."

"Lana told me he fell from the ramparts . . . or was pushed by ghosts."

"There are many who would have cheerfully pushed him . . . dead and living. I couldna say, as I missed the . . . happy event." He tipped his head to the side. "Lana . . . ?"

Hannah nearly flinched at the question in his tone. She wasn't certain how to answer it. "Aye?"

"She had an . . . altercation with Dermid. Does she . . . ? Can she . . . ? Is she . . . ?"

Hannah sighed. "Aye." To all the unasked queries. "She speaks to the dead." *Frequently.*

"Hmm."

A trickle of unease skittered through Hannah. She'd worried over her husband's reaction to her sister's gift, and while he'd seemed to accept it that night at dinner, he and Hannah had never discussed it directly. His murmur was not illuminating. She wished she could better see his face.

Relief washed through her at his chuckle. "She doesna care for him."

"She wouldna. He doesna sound like a restful spirit."

"Not in the slightest."

Hannah swallowed. "How . . . How did you take the news?"

"That Lana can speak to my dead uncle, or that Dermid still haunts the library?"

Oh dear. Not the library. Thank heaven *she* was oblivious to specters.

"At first it bothered me greatly . . . the knowledge that he might still be there. I'd felt safe from him for so long. But then Lana said something that . . . freed me from his onus. More so than mere death."

The dog on Hannah's lap shifted position and groaned a bit and Hannah soothed her. "What did Lana say?"

"That ghosts only have as much power as you give them. That no one has power . . . but what you give them. I had never . . . thought of it like that."

"Lana can be verra wise."

"Indeed. I believe she is right. By locking the library . . . I was attempting to lock away the past. In truth, I was confining myself there."

"Hmm. Methinks you are verra wise yourself, my husband."

His soft laugh danced to her. "A wise man makes his library available to a wife who loves books."

"Now that I know Dermid is in there, I doubt I should enjoy it as much."

"Lana gave me some verra good advice on that point as well."

"Did she?"

"Aye. She suggested I ignore him. And I think I shall."

"An excellent strategy."

He chuckled. "I agree. Aside from which, it is high time I put the past where it belongs. Behind me."

Ah, aye. An excellent strategy indeed.

They rode then in a companionable silence as the carriage wound its way toward Lochlannach Castle. Hannah couldn't help but reflect on the past day and how illuminating it had been. It filled her with hope for their marriage and anticipation for the days, and nights, to come.

It was a pity the trip had been cut short, but she couldn't regret it because in that experience she'd had the opportunity to see clear through to his soul. And she liked what she saw.

Beyond that, it warmed her heart to know her husband was as adamantly opposed to the Clearances as she was. The altercation with his peers had shown that. But . . .

"Alexander?"

"Aye, Hannah?"

"What did Olrig mean when he said you had not joined the other barons?"

His sigh was heavy. "Hannah, we shouldna discuss this."

Her welling pleasure deflated. "Why? Because I am but a *wife*?"

"Nae. 'Tis not that."

"Because you made me a promise. You made a promise to share. Everything."

He stared at her across the carriage. His eyes glittered in the darkness. "This is dangerous business."

"Then we should face it together."

He didn't respond for a while, for so long Hannah was certain he would refuse to answer. The prospect nearly broke her heart. But then he raked his fingers through his hair and blew out another sigh. "Aye. You are right. But Hannah, you canna discuss this with anyone."

"I willna."

"When I was in Barrogill . . . Olrig and Scrabster approached me with a proposition. Apparently, Stafford is in line for a dukedom—"

"A dukedom?" The thought appalled her. He was power hungry enough as a mere marquess.

"Aye. And he is planning to petition the prince to grant him all the lands in Caithness. He is attempting to . . . gain the support of all the barons in this endeavor."

"Those lands belong to the Duke of Caithness."

Alexander lifted a shoulder. "Hence the danger. Siding with Stafford is a betrayal to our oath. Supporting Caithness could result in disaster if Stafford has his way."

"Yet you have remained loyal to Caithness."

"He is my overlord."

Ah. Of course. Alexander was, in all things, a loyal man. But . . . "I doona understand. Why would the prince even consider such a request?"

"He would if Caithness were dead."

Her heart stilled; her breath locked. "Dead?"

"There are whispers that the duke will no' live much longer."

"I thought he was a young man."

"He is. But all of the Sinclair men die young and, according to Scrabster, the duke is ailing. If he does die, without an heir, there is a very good chance the prince will grant Stafford's request."

Horror crawled through her at the thought. "But Stafford has cleared his lands."

"Aye. And he will likely do the same in all the northern parishes if he has his way. Dunnet. Reay. All of it." The devastation he would wreak was unthinkable.

"It occurs to me it would be a wise thing to make sure Caithness doesna die."

"Aye. It would indeed, but . . . it may be a moot point." His tone was grim. So grim, it made apprehension skitter along her nerves.

"How so?"

"Because Caithness is considering clearing the land as well."

Revulsion roiled. "Nae."

"Aye. And if he does, we will lose everything we've worked so hard to build."

He sounded so disheartened, she ached to soothe him, but what could she say or do to ease his mind? There was, indeed, a sword hanging over their heads.

But sword or no, she was his wife. His partner. His other. She steeled her spine and forced a chipper tone. "Whatever happens, Alexander, we shall face it together."

He didn't respond, but she thought she heard him sigh. It sounded like, *"Ah, Hannah,"* and the words were wreathed in gratitude.

CHAPTER FOURTEEN

They arrived home in the middle of the night and, though they were both tired, Alexander and Hannah spent several hours with the surgeon as he saw to the dogs' wounds. Only when they were convinced the animals were as comfortable as they could be, nestled together in a stall in the stables, did Alexander and Hannah head for bed themselves. Hannah liked that Alexander took her hand as they walked to their suite of rooms, twining his fingers in hers. His palm was warm against hers. And though he said not a word, it was a comfortable silence.

It surprised her that he passed the door to his chamber and led her to her own. Her mood slumped at the thought he might kiss her good night at the door and hie off to sleep alone. Aye, she was tired and wanted to sleep, but she very much wanted to sleep with him. She needed it, his presence, after this very trying day.

He took her in his arms. His lips were soft on hers. "I have a surprise for you," he said.

She glanced up at him, trying to read him. "Do you?"

His lips tweaked as he turned the knob and pushed open the door to her room. As curiosity swirled, she stepped inside . . . and then she froze.

The lamps were lit, limning the chamber in a soft glow. As she stared, her heart swelled and then overflowed with delight.

"Alexander . . ."

"I had it redone while we were gone."

And oh, he had.

Gone was the shite-hued fabric on the wall. Gone were the dreary bedcoverings and the doleful drapes.

It was green. A glorious spring green. Everywhere. Her room looked like a garden. Except for the wall next to the hearth. There he had constructed shelves. They were filled to the brim . . . with books.

She launched herself at him. He caught her. "I adore it!"

"Do you? Do you really like it?"

"I love it!" She framed his face with her palms and kissed him, long and deep. "Alexander, you canna know how happy this makes me."

"I can hope."

"Ah." She stared at him, soaking in the beauty of his deep brown eyes, the dear features of his face. And it hit her. It hit her hard. All that he was, all that he had been, and all that he had become—she loved. To the depth of her being. To the deep well of her soul. Her chest ached with it. She longed to say it, claim it, bellow it from the rooftops, but she couldn't yet. The feelings were far too raw. She hoped her expression spoke for her. "You are the best husband ever."

A rosy tinge blossomed on his cheeks. His gaze heated until it scorched her.

When he took her lips, it was with a blazing passion. In that kiss she tasted his desire, aye, but also something far more significant. Something like vindication. And she gave it back, full force.

Thank heaven he thought to kick closed the door before he walked her back to the bed, else they would both have forgotten the need for privacy completely. He laid her down on the mattress and kissed her again, his hand roving over her bodice, sending spirals of ecstasy through her each time he swept over her pebbled nipples.

She groaned and wriggled beneath him, tugging at his shirt, his pants, his hair.

In a tumble of limbs, with a fumbling of fingers, they tore at each other's clothes until they were bare, though it took some time, as Alexander felt the need to kiss each spot he uncovered and Hannah reciprocated . . . with glee.

She gave back as good as she got. Her palm ranged over his ravaged back, delighting in the ripple of his flesh at its passing, loving each and every inch of him. She raked his scalp, thrilling in his shudders. She tested the strength of the muscles on his arms and, though she'd tested them before, nearly swooned, as though it were the first time. She'd never had the urge to *consume* a man as much as she ached to consume him. She wanted his all. Everything.

Their mutual fervor rose as he teased her and she teased him. When she wrapped her fist around his cock, hard and rampant and ready, he stilled and lifted his head from his nibbling of her neck and stared at her.

"Hannah."

A question, but not.

"Aye, Alexander." *I am ready.*

She shifted her legs farther apart and he settled between them, nudging in without delay. At first touch, delightful sensation exploded in her. It was as though she'd been saving up, waiting, holding her passion in abeyance for the moment they could be alone, like this.

It all rushed back in a heartbeat, swamping her. Drenching him.

He groaned as he pushed deeper. His cock filled her, stretching her, inciting a fresh wave of delight. He groaned again as her body, of its own accord, closed on him.

New pleasure raged. It was wild and savage and tender and sweet, all at the same time. As splendid as their lovemaking had been, and always was, this was something else entirely. And Hannah knew why.

Love.

Heart wrenching and soul feeding.

She knew him in ways she'd never suspected. She had glimpsed his essence and loved that too. She loved who he was as a man, as a husband, as a leader.

It didn't matter that he wasn't a *bletherer.* His body spoke well enough for him.

And ah, if it was saying what she thought, he loved her too.

At the very least, she knew he respected her and cared for her and wanted to make her happy. She suspected, she hoped, his heart was hers until it ceased to beat.

He made a fierce movement with his hips and all thoughts flew. He hit a spot, deep within, that made her eyes cross and her mouth water. Bliss, unlike any bliss she'd ever known, rained through her and she gasped, groaned, clutched him tighter.

His breath stuttered. He gave a growl and pulled back to hit her there again and again and again. Pleasure screamed through her.

Hannah went wild. There was no other word for it. Some ifrit slipped in and claimed her sanity and she lost all control. Scraping at him with her nails, she fought against his thrusts. It frustrated her, aggravated her, ached, until she got the rhythm right. And then, ah, and then they moved in concert.

He increased his speed and intensity. His lungs worked like a bellows as he pounded into her harder, deeper, faster. His cock swelled and, with it, the insanity consuming her. The tension between them mounted to near unbearable heights.

She broke first, shattering beneath him, shuddering and wailing and succumbing to his demanding plunges. Her calamity incited his. It could have been the tight hold she had on him, or the heat, or the gush of welcoming arousal, but he stiffened over her, lunged in once, twice, thrice . . . and he released.

He flooded her, inundated her womb. She hoped, prayed, that his seed would take hold, that they would make a child this night. Because it was the most perfect melding she could ever have imagined.

And she dearly wanted his child.

A boy, perhaps with Alexander's tumble of curls and shy smile. A boy they would adore and spoil and surround with all the security and love his father had never known.

That would, perhaps, help to heal him.

That would, perhaps, make him whole.

෴

Alexander felt as though he were walking on air as he made his way up to his study the next morning. He'd spent the whole night in Hannah's room, making love to her off and on until dawn. Something had changed between them. He liked to think it was his gesture of redecorating her room, but he knew it was probably something more profound.

The fact that she knew the truth about his past—or the bits he could bear to share—had lifted a weight from his shoulders. He'd been living in fear. Fear that she would discover how weak he'd once been and that the truth of it would shatter her esteem for him.

But that hadn't been the case at all. If anything, the knowledge of the trials of his past had made her respect him more, or at least that was how it had felt. It was certainly what she'd said, and he believed her.

How freeing it was. How glorious. As though the specters that had shadowed him his entire life had wafted away, like morning mist burned off by the kiss of the sun.

And how odd—and wonderful—that with Hannah's

advent in his life his uncle's memory had lost all power over him. He even found it easier to speak.

When he'd clipped a chipper, "Good morning," to Fergus, as he'd passed on his way to the stables to check on Brùid, the factor had jumped and gaped at him, as though the suit of armor in the hall had suddenly burst into song.

He would have woken Hannah and taken her with him, but, poor thing, he'd exhausted her the night before. He'd left a note, which would probably annoy her . . . at least until she read it.

Come join me, he'd said.

He hoped it would be soon. If he got through his mail and she had not yet appeared, he planned to head back to their suite and rouse her. The thought filled him with exhilaration and an even more trenchant resolve.

His footsteps stalled as he rounded the curve on the narrow staircase leading to his study. Maybe he shouldn't wait. Maybe he should rouse her now. *He* was certainly roused.

With a chuckle he pushed into his office and headed for the desk. While he loved this room, and he always had, it was a long way up, and it could be tiring for Hannah if she was truly to work with him every day. He should probably find a room closer to the ground floor. He certainly didn't need a sanctuary anymore. Indeed, he didn't want one. He felt no urge to separate himself from the world. Not anymore.

The mail on his desk was high. He regarded it with a frown. They had only been gone a day. He flipped through it quickly, separating out the pieces he thought Hannah might want to tackle. Although, if he was being honest, many of those were the ones he dreaded.

His hand stilled as he came upon a letter with a seal that made his throat clog. His heart gave a painful thump.

The Duke of Caithness.

Hell.

He ripped it open and scanned the contents. His bowels clenched.

Hell and damnation.

So soon?

He was still staring at the letter when Hannah breezed into the room with a bright smile on her face.

God, he loved her smile. It was a balm to his soul. He opened his arms to her—because he needed her touch—and she settled on his lap, dropping a kiss on his forehead. "Good morning, my husband," she purred.

A pity she was in this mood, because he no longer was.

"Hannah—"

"Did you sleep well? Because I dinna. Something kept me awake to the wee hours."

"Hannah—"

"Why did you leave so soon?" She put out a lip. "I was hoping we could . . ." She wiggled illustratively on his lap. Despite his misery, his cock rose. His cock had a terrible sense of timing. Or maybe not. Maybe making love to her would wash away the panic, the worry, the cold—

"What is this?" She took the letter from him.

"It came while we were gone. From Caithness."

She wrinkled her nose. "Oh, bother."

"Read it."

Something in his voice, something desolate and weary, captured her attention and she focused on the letter. He knew—*knew*—when she read *that part*. Her entire body stiffened. She crumpled the letter in her fist. He took it from her and smoothed it out.

She leaped to her feet and paced from one end of the solar to the other. "That ass. That bastard. That—" She ran out of invectives.

He'd thought her capable of more, but he understood. Caithness' letter had rendered him mute too.

"To speak to you in such a condescending tone—"

" 'Tis a letter."

"To *write* to you in such a tone. As though you are a witless child who needs to be *educated*. Oh, I could throttle him."

Aye. It had been a patronizing letter. But that wasn't the worst of it. Caithness was coming *here*. To *speak* with him. And, likely, to discuss the Clearance he had in mind. The Clearance Alexander had, in essence, refused.

It would likely not be a congenial meeting. No doubt the duke would be . . . displeased with him.

"We should probably notify the staff that he's coming."

She snatched the letter back and read it again. "He doesna say when."

"Soon, I imagine."

Hannah stiffened her spine. "We need to prepare." But rather than turning on her heel and leading the way downstairs to assemble the staff, she took her seat at his side and folded her fingers. "How shall we approach this?"

He blinked. *Approach this?* How did one approach potential disaster?

She tapped her lip with a finger, a militant look in her eye. "The best tack would be to show him the true effects of the Clearances, do you no' think?"

"Show him . . . ?" What was she talking about? Had they not read the same letter? Caithness was not coming here to negotiate.

Hannah rose and began to pace once more. "The man spent his entire life in England, poor wretch. I doubt he has a clue what devastation this policy has wrought. How could he, and still make such a demand?"

"Greed is a powerful motivation."

She pinned him with a resolute frown. "So is understanding. If he could *see* what clearing the land really means to his people, speak to the ones who have been affected, realize that this is a dagger in the heart of all Scotland, surely he would change his mind."

It was adorable how naïve she was, but she'd never met Lachlan Sinclair. She had no clue what a heartless prig he was. "He wears *lace*, Hannah."

Her face scrunched up. "Lace?"

"Aye."

"Well, there's the problem right there. We need to get that man into a kilt. Who wouldn't cleave to Scotland wearing the Garb of the Auld Gaul?" She paced some more, her expression adorably fierce. "We shall begin with the orphans."

"The . . . orphans?"

"The orphans of the Clearances." Her smile was fiendish. "What man with a soul could look into those eyes and not be moved?"

"You are assuming he has a soul."

"Of course he has a soul. And if he isna moved, we shall lock him in a room with Lana—"

"I doona think that would be wise—"

"And she can tell him what his ancestors think of these *Improvements*."

Perhaps the lack of sleep had made Hannah dotty, but he liked where she was going with this. "He did seem rather obsessed with ghosts the last time we spoke."

"Excellent. Because I can tell you, the Scots of old are turning over in their graves at this new policy."

"*You* can tell me?"

Though she was on a roll, she stilled and shot him a contrite glance. "*Lana* can tell you. The point is, we can convince him, Alexander. I'm sure of it."

He waved the letter. "Did you read this?"

"I did."

"He doesna seem . . . pliable." Not in the least.

Hannah set her fists on her hips and glared at him, but it was a lovely glare, because it was lit with her determination to go to battle . . . for him. "We shall convince him. I know it. And now, as much as I was looking forward to spending the morning with you, my love, I must get to work. There is much to prepare and verra little time."

Alexander didn't respond, other than to stare after her as she whisked from the room with a swish to her skirts. He couldn't. Couldn't so much as utter a word.

She'd called him *my love*.

It was the sweetest moment he'd ever known.

Hannah was certain their plan would work. She was convinced they could change the duke's thinking.

Until she clapped eyes on him.

And suddenly she understood Alexander's reservations.

It was early morning when word came that the duke's entourage was near. Hannah met her husband at the gates, where he was stationed to greet his overlord. As all the men had, Alexander had donned a kilt. Her heart clenched at the sight of him. He was so handsome in the formal dress. She brushed her hand over his shirt to smooth it, adjusted his sporran, and gazed up at him. "It will be fine," she said.

He wrapped his arm around her. "Aye."

But when the gilded carriage rolled to a stop before the gates and his footmen swarmed around to help the duke alight, Hannah's optimism deflated.

He was, indeed, a dandy.

And an English dandy to boot.

He wore the most ridiculous costume. His white breeches looked as though they had been painted on . . .

and he clearly wore a codpiece. The ensemble was finished by a pink tailcoat with gleaming buttons. His boots were nice, but for the tassels that blew in the breeze. As Alexander had warned, there was lace. Everywhere. And he wore a cravat.

Hannah had never liked cravats. She felt they looked unnatural. And this one was unnatural, so tight the man could barely move his head. He looked around with odd, sharp movements, like a bird, blinking incessantly as though surprised to find himself in such surroundings.

Aside from all of that, he was a strikingly handsome man, tall and broad shouldered, with a bold jaw and piercing blue eyes. It was a pity he had the pallid white skin of an Englishman. Had he been more robust, he would have been bonny indeed.

On cue, as the duke set foot on Dunnet soil, the pipers lit in, playing "When the King Enjoys His Own Again." The duke stood still and politely listened, though the shuffle of his feet betrayed his impatience. Hannah had the suspicion he'd never heard the traditional tune before and had no idea of its meaning.

When the final skirl of the pipes wafted away on the breeze, Alexander stepped forward and tendered a bow. "Your Grace," he said. "Welcome to Dunnet."

The duke didn't respond, except to wave a large man with a grim visage forward. "Please know my cousin Dougal. Dougal serves as my second in command." The duke's voice was clipped and cold.

Alexander shook Dougal's hand. Hannah noticed the man pulled away quickly, as though burned.

"My brother, Andrew, is my second in command. He's in Dounreay at the moment. I've, ah, written you about those issues."

The duke glanced at Dougal, who nodded.

Hannah bristled at the implication that the duke had not

read the letter himself. Alexander must have noticed the same, for his jaw bunched. "Perhaps we could . . . discuss the situation in depth while you are here."

"Perhaps."

Nothing more than that. *Perhaps.* The duke's indifference scraped at Hannah's nerves.

Alexander forced a smile and eased her forward. "This is my wife, Hannah Lochlannach, of Reay. Her father is Magnus, Laird of Reay."

Hannah curtseyed. The duke responded with a tight nod. It could have been interpreted as rudeness, but Hannah decided to blame the cravat. "Welcome, Your Grace."

"Lady Dunnet." He made the gesture of kissing her hand, though it was only a gesture.

"Won't you please come in? I have arranged for some refreshments after your journey."

It was not her imagination that the duke reared back. His sharp gaze fixed on Alexander. "I need to speak with you immediately." His glacial tone did not bode well; it made something slightly acidic squirm in her belly.

Hannah and Alexander exchanged looks. In his eyes, she saw a similar trepidation. "Would you care to settle into your rooms first?" she offered.

"No."

Oh dear. Just no.

"Is there somewhere we may speak? In private?"

Though Alexander swallowed heavily, he nodded. "Of course. The library."

Hannah glanced at her husband in surprise. Granted, he could hardly lead the duke up three hundred narrow steps to his study and the library was on the ground floor, but she knew how much Alexander disliked that room. From his expression, she gathered that he expected this meeting to be a trial, so it might as well take place in a room where he'd faced many trials before.

He'd survived them before.

He would survive them now.

She flashed a smile at the duke—it was not returned—and hooked arms with Alexander, leading their guests to the castle doors. She gestured to Fergus. "Please bring whisky to the library," she murmured. If this interview was indeed unpleasant, likely someone would need it.

She had every intention of staying by her husband's side and he seemed inclined to have her there, but the duke did not. As they reached the library doors, he turned to her. "Lady Dunnet. If you don't mind."

Hannah shot a glance at Alexander, who, with a tinge of resignation, nodded. She stepped back and allowed the men to enter without her, though it was highly contrary to her nature.

As the door closed on them, she couldn't ignore the cold finger tracing down her spine. Foreboding clutched at her heart. Clearly, the duke wasn't pleased with Alexander and intended to give him a set down. She wanted nothing more than to be there with him, to protect him, defend him if she could.

Not for the first time in her life, she was swamped with frustration.

Sometimes it was exasperating as hell being a woman, being excluded from important conversations.

It was a damn good thing the duke didn't know the library balcony, accessible from an alcove on the second floor, was the perfect place to eavesdrop.

CHAPTER FIFTEEN

Alexander's feet felt like stones as he followed the duke into the library. When Alexander had met the man before, he'd been friendly, almost pleasant. This was a different man. His demeanor was distant, his expression hard and his eyes cold.

Something had changed.

It didn't take a seer to figure out what that was. It was no secret that the duke favored the Clearances. No secret that Alexander resisted them. And neither of them was prepared to budge.

He regretted not having Hannah at his side to bolster him. She—and all his people—counted on him to lobby eloquently. He hoped to God he could do their faith justice.

Caithness strode across the room and took a seat at Dermid's old desk. Dougal followed, taking his place at the duke's shoulder, radiating hostility. The duke waved at the chair before the desk. "Have a seat."

Alexander ignored the ripple of unease the room itself brought to the fore. More than once he'd been called before this desk. Although never once had Dermid invited him to sit. He forced all that away and dropped into the chair, fixing his attention on the duke.

Caithness seemed disinclined to speak. He spent long moments rearranging the lace at his cuffs. Alexander saw this for what it was. A ploy to make him nervous. It didn't work.

Though his gut churned, he leaned back in his chair and set his features in a deferential arrangement. When Fergus scratched at the door with a tray of whisky, he accepted a tumbler and sipped it. Long after his factor left, the duke remained silent, his drink ignored. Alexander tried not to let his annoyance simmer. He focused on the burn of his whisky and the sunlight shafting through the window. He glanced at the shelves and pondered which book his wife might read next.

If Caithness wanted a war of no words, so be it. Alexander was a past master at that game.

When the duke finally spoke, it was almost a surprise. His voice, with that cold British accent, snaked through the room on a sibilant whisper. "I cannot tell you how disappointed I am in you, Dunnet."

Though the words hit him and hit him hard, Alexander forced a blasé smile and quirked a brow. "Disappointed, Your Grace?"

"First, your failure to respond to my order for the Clearances of Dunnet."

"I did respond. My answer was nae."

"It is your obligation to obey me."

"My obligation is to my people. They depend on us—on you and me—to protect them." He leaned forward. "It is our sacred oath, passed to us by our ancestors."

This seemed to befuddle the duke. He stared at Alexander without reply. So he continued.

"It is my position that these Improvements will destroy the county. As they are destroying Scotland."

The duke fluffed his lace and offered a petulant frown. "It is my position that I need the funds."

Hope flared. This was the opening Alexander needed. "You . . . need the funds?" There was money in the Dunnet treasury. It was for emergencies, but if there ever was one this was it. If it proved necessary, Alexander was willing to use the money, every penny, to buy them some time.

"It is my intention to renovate Caithness Castle before . . . Well, as soon as I can."

Alexander's hope deflated. The Dunnet treasury was healthy but not healthy enough to renovate that pile of stones. Still, he asked, "How much do you need?"

"This conversation is beside the point."

Alexander could have planted one in Dougal's face. At his interruption Caithness seemed to recall himself. His resolution firmed. "True. True. The point of this conversation is my disappointment with you, Dunnet."

"Your Grace, surely you see that the Clearances—"

"I refer to the other source of my disappointment, Dunnet." Judging from Caithness' tone, it was a greater source of disappointment, although Alexander couldn't fathom what it might be.

"Your Grace?"

Caithness lanced him with a sharp blue stare. "Did you think I wouldn't hear of it?"

"Hear of what, Your Grace?"

"Your treason," the duke's man snapped.

A lead weight settled in Alexander's belly. *Hell.*

Caithness sent his minion a quelling glance, and then he turned back to Alexander, his expression harsh. "I really liked you, Dunnet. Silly of me, but I thought on some level we were cut from the same cloth."

Where on earth had he gotten that impression?

"I thought you, of all my lairds, would be loyal."

"I am loyal."

Dougal snorted.

"I'm not a fool. I know Stafford has been courting my barons. When I heard about your meeting with his son, I was wounded. Wounded to the core." He set his hand to his heart. Where his lace cascaded in a snowy waterfall over his coat.

Alexander swallowed heavily. "That was a chance meeting at an inn. There was no discussion of politics. And it doesna signify. I have no intention of joining with Stafford."

"That's not what Olrig said—"

"Olrig?" Alexander nearly came out of his skin. Fury lashed him.

"Is it true or is it not that you called a meeting of *my* barons to plead with Olrig and Scrabster to side with Stafford?"

"Nae. It most certainly is not."

Caithness seemed surprised by Alexander's denial. His eyes widened.

"That's not what Olrig said." Dougal again.

Ah, fury. Alexander had always been wary of his temper, wary of becoming like his uncle, but at the moment he had no control. It raked him with scorching claws. He leaped to his feet and planted his fists on the desk. "Olrig is a stinking pig."

Though Dougal leaped back, Caithness was undaunted. He studied his nails. "Is that why you beat him up? Or did you beat him to a pulp because he opposed your plot?"

Oh. Holy. God. Olrig was worse than a stinking pig. He was a *lying* stinking pig. "It isna my plot—"

"Ah, so you admit your involvement?"

Really. Dougal needed to be silenced. For his own safety.

"Nae. I doona." Alexander's growl rumbled on the skeins of air. Even Caithness was taken aback by his vehemence. "Regardless of what you have been told, I have never even considered siding with Stafford. Olrig is another matter entirely. In fact, he is the one who approached me."

The duke sat back and considered this information. Alexander was hopeful that his vehemence had convinced Caithness, but there was a hint of doubt in his eye. As he thought, he drummed his fingers on the desk. It was oddly reminiscent of the way Dermid would drum his fingers on the desk. Alexander attempted to ignore the similarities. "You say you are my loyal man."

"Aye. I am." And the duke had few left, it seemed.

"Well then, my loyal man, surely you will have no difficulty acceding to my wishes."

"Your . . . wishes?"

His gaze hardened. "Consider it an ultimatum, if you will."

Alexander's blood went cold. A slither of unease snaked through his veins. "And that is?"

"You shall clear your land, or I will strip you of your title and your property. It is as simple as that."

Alexander's gut clenched and clenched hard. His breath froze in his lungs. His pulse rushed in his ears.

Clearly, he'd misheard the duke.

"I beg your pardon?"

Caithness' features tightened, his chin jutted forward. "Clear your land or I shall have the new baron clear it for you."

Ach, aye. That was what he thought he'd heard.

Alexander collapsed in his seat and stared at the duke through burning eyes. Never in his life had he been so stunned. So devastated. So speechless.

He *was* Dunnet. He always had been, and he'd assumed he would be until the day he died.

And now this.

Now he was forced to make an unimaginable decision. Destroy everything he loved or lose everything he was.

Either way, he would no longer be Laird of Dunnet. Because if he cleared the land he would be naught but the laird of a herd of sheep.

Either way, his people were lost. He had failed them utterly.

But beyond his horror, beyond his shock, one thought winged through his mind.

How on earth was he going to tell Hannah? How could he survive losing her respect? Her love?

Her?

She had married a baron, a powerful warrior who could protect her and her people. How could he hope to keep her if he was a nothing more than a shell of that man?

~

Hannah shook. With fury, of a certainty, but with outrage as well. Perched in the gallery overlooking the library, she'd heard every word of Alexander's interview with the revolting Duke of Caithness and decided that she really didn't like him very much at all. He was a cold, stubborn, stupid man. And a popinjay to boot.

But as odious as the duke was, his minion was worse. It had taken everything in her not to reel out of her hiding place and rain hell down upon the man as he battered Alexander with accusation after accusation.

Her husband, she decided, was a saint. He'd only bellowed once. Or maybe twice. He hadn't pummeled anyone. Through it all, he'd managed to retain his composure.

Hannah, not so much.

Even now she wanted to find the duke and smack some sense into him. But she feared it was too late. For sense.

After Caithness' proclamation, Alexander had spun from the library without a word. Hannah had directed Fergus to show the visitors to their rooms, because she couldn't bear to face them and she suspected her husband was far too overwrought to think of it. Indeed, he'd disappeared. Hannah had searched for him everywhere and could find neither hide nor hair of him. He hadn't been in the tower or his bedroom or in the stables. His horse was gone, though, so she assumed Alexander had gone for a ride to clear his head.

She wanted, needed, to speak with him. Worry for him wracked her.

She couldn't imagine what he was going through, being commanded to give up everything he believed in—or lose everything that mattered.

Och, just thinking of it again made her furious. She stormed through the bailey and headed for the terrace overlooking the sea, to the one view that always calmed her.

How naïve they'd been, she'd been, to think they could reach such an obdurate man. Nothing could reach him. She was certain of it.

She passed through the arbor and turned onto the terrace and stopped short.

Oh, bother.

He was there. Leaning against the balustrade and staring out at the bay. Wreathed in lace. Perhaps if she backed away quietly—

But no. He saw her and straightened.

Hannah blew out a breath and stepped forward, ignoring his little bow. She saw it for what it was, a pointless gesture.

"Lady Dunnet."

"Your Grace." She tried not to spit the words. Really, she did. She was still shaking with ire over the conversation she'd witnessed. "Have you . . . settled in?"

"Ah. Yes."

"And your accommodations are to your liking?" They had housed the duke's party in the east wing. His Grace's rooms were opulent and grand, indeed fit for a king. Though they were, by far, the finest in the castle, Hannah understood why Alexander had not taken them as his own, as they had once belonged to his uncle. Her and Alexander's suite was situated in the west wing, far away from old ghosts.

"The rooms are comfortable. Thank you."

"Excellent." She wound her fingers together. It was a challenge holding a civil conversation with a person one wanted to throttle. With all her heart, she wished he would return to England and never come back. "Well," she gusted. "I suppose I should see about dinner—"

"Lady Dunnet. A moment if I may?"

She fought back a grimace. The last thing she wanted to do was *talk* to this man.

"Certainly."

"I, ah, have a question about your husband."

Hannah narrowed her eyes. She didn't like the duke's tone in the slightest.

Was there a capital punishment for smacking one's overlord? Probably.

Pity, that.

When he seemed disinclined to continue, she prompted him with a cold, "Aye?" Although encouraging the conversation was probably unwise.

"Something has been perplexing me."

"Aye?"

"When I met your husband in Ackergill, he seemed like a reasonable man."

"He *is* a reasonable man."

"Yes. Of course he is." The man's crisp English accent was starting to grate on her nerves. Hannah tried very hard not to grit her teeth. "He didn't seem like a man who was prone to disloyalty—"

"Alexander is the most loyal man you will ever have the good fortune to meet."

"Or violence—"

"He is as gentle as a lamb."

The duke ignored her interjections. She was not surprised. When one was exceedingly stubborn, one recognized the same in others.

"Yet he battered Olrig—"

"Olrig deserved it."

"And he met with Stafford's son to foment insurrection."

"Nonsense. Dunnet explained that was a chance meeting."

The duke's sharp gaze landed on her. "How do you know this?"

Hannah gulped, realizing her mistake at once—she'd been excluded from the discussion. She should have no knowledge of what had transpired. She decided to be truthful because she didn't want Caithness to labor under the misapprehension that Alexander had scurried back to her telling tales. Aside from which, she no longer cared much what this man thought of her. She tipped up her chin. "I was eavesdropping."

For some reason this made him smile. She disliked his smile. It was far too charming and she wasn't in the mood to be charmed. "Do you eavesdrop often, Lady Dunnet?"

"As often as I need to." She crossed her arms and glared at him. His smile widened and irritation trickled through her. She tried to hold her tongue, but the urge to take him down a peg overwhelmed her. *Ah well. In for a penny, in for a pound.* "And frankly, you werena fair in the least."

Caithness' eyes widened. "I beg your pardon?"

"You dinna give Alexander a chance to explain his side. For heaven's sake, you have a handful of loyal barons left,

Dunnet and my father to name two, and this is how you treat them? Given that and this"—she waved disdainfully at his person—"it is no wonder your lairds are turning to Stafford."

He frowned. "What do you mean . . . *this*?"

"Your costume."

He tugged on his waistcoat. "Whatever is wrong with my costume?"

Jesus, Mary, and Joseph. "You are wearing *lace*."

"It is the fashion in London."

"Aye," she snarled. "But ye are no' in London. This is Scotland, where men dress like men."

"This is perfectly manly." He fluttered a frilly cuff.

She nearly snorted. "Ye should try wearing a kilt when you meet with your lairds."

"How on earth would that help?"

"They would see you as one of them, a Scottish laird, rather than as an English lord."

He frowned. "I *am* an English lord."

"Aye. And therein lies the problem. You've spent your life in another country, another world. You know nothing of Scotland, of our way of life. What we value, what we deplore. How can you lead men you doona understand? How can you expect them to follow? How can you demand their loyalty?"

"I'm . . . the duke." A simple statement, one wreathed in his hubris and naivety. But there was, threaded in it, a hint of contemplation. Then the glimmer flitted away and his expression darkened. "You say your husband remains loyal to me?"

"Aye. He is."

"Yet he has refused my order to clear the land."

"Aye."

He barked a laugh; it held little humor. "In the face of

that evidence, how on earth can you insist he is a loyal man?"

"Because he *is* loyal. To his people. To his home. To his title. As baron he is responsible for making sure the clachans doona starve in the winter. He's responsible for making sure the clans doona fight. He's responsible for keeping his people safe from all threats. And this, Your Grace, is a threat. If you had any idea what horror and desolation the Clearances have wrought, you would never command them. No man with a heart and a soul would."

A muscle in his cheek bunched and Hannah wondered if she'd gone too far. But she hardly cared. There was nothing left to lose.

"You realize every lord in London has ordered them. Are you implying the House of Lords is soulless?" Infuriatingly, his eyes danced with humor. *Humor.*

"Aye," she snapped. "It is easy for *English* lords to clear the land. They doona care. They doona see the impact this policy has on people. On families. On children. Why, there are twenty Clearance orphans living here—"

"Clearance orphans?"

"Children. Babies. Orphaned when their crofts were cleared." When the confusion still clung to his features, she added, "The children of the people killed in the course of these *Improvements*."

The duke shook his head, a refusal of the cold, hard facts.

Anger and frustration swelled. Hannah forced it down. If she was to be the voice of reason here, if she had any chance of convincing him of the sheer immorality of his plans, she needed to remain calm and rational. It cost her, but she drew in a deep breath and said, "For example, Fiona's mother was evicted from her home in the winter.

She and her newborn and the wee lass of five. When she refused to leave, they set her home on fire. Destitute and starving, she brought her family here. She died at the gates, and her baby with her."

The duke made a slash of denial with his hand. "A woman with small children tossed out in the snow? That could not have happened."

"It did happen."

"Her tale must have been embroidered. No man in good conscience would burn a woman out of her home."

Hannah snorted. "Yet there are hundreds of like stories. *Hundreds*."

His chin firmed. "Those were brutal men. Our Clearances will be orderly. No one will be harmed. I promise. On my honor."

"Still, even if they are not harmed, where will they go?"

He shrugged. "To the cities, I suppose."

"To live in filth and squalor? Having left everything they know behind? With nothing to sustain them? Only imagine how devastating that would be to one person. One family. Much less an entire parish. The county. How many souls are you willing to sacrifice for your profit?"

This question made him visibly uncomfortable. Hannah didn't care. She pressed on.

"Your Grace. You are a powerful man. You have the ability to make a difference. Your decision will affect thousands of lives—"

"Surely not thousands."

"Thousands. Because you are creating a legacy here. One that will ring through the ages long after you and I are gone." He paled. His fingers clenched. She thought she might be reaching him, but whether she was or not, she had to continue. "Your one decision can save your homeland, or destroy it. Please." She set her hand on his arm. "Please think about it."

Hannah's heart lifted as a flurry of emotions flicked over his face. She thought he might be softening, thought he might be willing to relent, just a little. He opened his mouth to respond, but before he could, a harsh voice rang out from the garden.

"Your Grace! Where have you been?" Dougal strode toward the duke, as though a man on a mission to save his lord from a vile villain. The look Dougal shot at Hannah made clear *she* was the villain.

She offered him a glowing smile. Just to be contrary.

"Ah, I was just taking a walk. I needed it after our journey."

Dougal's brow furrowed. "Are you . . . feeling all right, Your Grace?"

"I'm feeling fine. Fine." He swept out his arms. "What do you think of this view, Dougal?"

Dougal glanced at the bay and frowned. "It's water."

"Ah, but it's a magnificent view, is it not?"

"Your Grace, you really must rest."

Hannah nibbled on her lip. Dougal was treating the duke as though he were an invalid. Which made no sense. He seemed healthy as a horse.

The duke clapped his cousin on the shoulder. "If you need a rest, do go on, Dougal. Lady Dunnet and I are having a chat. And I fancy a stroll. Will you accompany me, Lady Dunnet?" He offered his arm.

Why Dougal sent her another blazing glare she had no clue. She responded with an even more brilliant grin. "I would be honored, Your Grace. May I show you around the castle grounds?"

"I would like that."

As they walked away, Hannah shot a look over her shoulder at Dougal, who had clearly been dismissed. She didn't imagine his glower. And oddly enough, it wasn't aimed at her.

It was aimed at the duke.

"So something else has been plaguing me, Lady Dunnet," Caithness said as they made their way into the bailey.

"What is that, Your Grace?"

"If Dunnet is not a violent man . . . why on earth did he beat Olrig?"

"Have you met Olrig?"

Caithness chuckled, perhaps his first hint of humanity. "I have. But still . . . Englishmen do not resort to savagery to resolve their conflicts."

"Do they not?"

At her frank assessment his ears went pink.

"Aside from which, it was hardly savagery. Alexander punched him once. That was all. T'was Olrig who came at him first."

"I expect better than petty squabbles from my barons."

"The Scots doona live by the same rules as the English, Your Grace." *Thank God.*

"I've noticed."

"But we do have our codes. Verra strong and deeply rooted traditions. Scots are passionate men, but reasonable at their core."

"Like your husband?"

"Aye."

"And about your husband . . . What happened to make this reasonable, nonviolent man break Olrig's nose?"

The stables came into view just as he asked; a sudden resolution flooded her and she shifted her course to head in that direction. "I shall show you."

Caithness shot her a curious glance but followed.

The stables were cool and shadowed. Hannah made her way to the back toward the stall where Brùid and the bitch were healing. Several steps in, she realized she'd lost the duke's attention. He'd stopped at the first stall and was patting a mare on the muzzle.

With a sigh, Hannah headed back.

"This is a beautiful beast."

"Aye, she is. Alexander has some excellent horseflesh."

The duke glanced at her. "Arabian?"

"Aye. And a mix of his own. Horses need to be strong and fleet in the Highlands. One of his hobbies is breeding them."

"I shall have to discuss this with him."

"Do." She took his arm and guided him farther in, though it was a challenge, as he wanted to stop at each stall and inspect the stock. He was particularly entranced with Beelzebub, who was not flattered by his attention in the slightest. In fact, the horse took a swipe at the duke. It was probably beneath her, that trickle of glee as Caithness leaped back.

They finally made it to the last stall and Hannah opened the gate. "Here."

The duke peered inside and froze. His cheek bunched. His eyes glimmered.

Aye. What Olrig had done to these poor creatures was truly monstrous. Hannah stepped in behind the duke . . . and froze herself. The animals were in there, curled up in the straw, but something else was curled up with them. Or someone.

Lana lay next to Brùid with her arm wrapped around him. Incomprehensibly, Nerid was nestled in the curve of the great hound's body. It appeared, somewhere along the way, the two had made peace.

A delicate snore riffled through the stall. It was not Brùid's snore.

"Oh dear."

"She's . . ." The duke's lips flapped. "I . . . Who is she?"

"My sister Lana," Hannah said. "She's been looking after the dogs."

Apparently, sleeping with them as well.

The duke's gaze flicked from one dog to the other. "What happened to them?"

"Olrig beat the female. With a whip. When Alexander tried to stop him, well, that's what caused the altercation between them. And then, when Olrig turned the whip on Alexander, Brùid attacked and Olrig stabbed him. Fortunately, both animals survived."

The duke's brow lowered. "He beats his dogs?"

"He beat this one. Quite badly. She nearly died."

Caithness knelt down to inspect the female's wounds. She whined a bit and licked his hand. His gaze flickered over to Brùid. Then to Lana. It stalled on her.

Considering he was a heartless man who wanted to destroy their way of life, the heat in his gaze as he surveyed Hannah's sister was concerning. When Lana's lashes flickered open and she smiled at him, a red tide crept up to his ears.

"Hullo," she said.

"Hullo." Though he managed the word, the duke was clearly befuddled. But Lana's beauty did that to men. Hannah made a sudden vow to keep her sister and the duke far apart for the remainder of his visit.

She stepped between them. "Lana, darling, have you been sleeping in the stables?"

Lana smiled at her as well. "Oh, hullo, Hannah. I didn't see you there."

Really? She was standing right next to him. Hannah refrained from rolling her eyes, but just barely. "Have you? Been sleeping here?"

Lana frowned and ruffled Brùid's fur. "They get lonely at night."

"They have each other. And it's the middle of the afternoon."

"Is it?" Limpid blue eyes blinked.

"It most certainly is. Have you had anything to eat today?"

"No. I've been here."

Hannah shook her head. "Come along then, darling." She helped her sister stand, which was difficult—because the duke didn't seem inclined to move out of the way—and then she brushed the hay from her skirts.

When Hannah straightened, she realized that the duke was still gaping at Lana. Her bosom, in fact. Hannah glared at him.

He ignored her glare. "Would you . . . introduce us, Lady Dunnet?"

Hannah set her teeth. It was the very last thing she wanted to do, especially given the gleam in his eye. But he was a duke. And he had asked. And he would be here for at least a day or so before he hied off to destroy other lives; the two were bound to come into contact at some point.

"Your Grace," she muttered, "this is Lana Dounreay. Lana, this is His Grace, the Duke of Caithness."

Lana's eyes widened. She surveyed the duke—and his costume—with curious eyes. She glanced at Hannah. "He's a duke?"

The duke tugged on his waistcoat and then, noticing Lana's attention to his cuffs, put his hands behind his back. "I am."

"I see." Lana's lips tweaked and then she executed a deep curtsey. "Your Grace."

"Miss Dounreay." He kissed her hand. Really kissed it. Not the mere hovering he'd bestowed upon Hannah.

Apprehension licked through her. Hannah took hold of her sister's arm. "Let's go get you something to eat."

"I'm not hungry," both Lana and the duke said at the same time.

Hannah tugged. "Come along. We need to get you inside."

"But the dogs . . ."

"They will be fine. Fetch Nerid and let's go."

Lana put out a lip. "Nerid wants to stay here." At Hannah's frown, she added, "They feel safer with Nerid protecting them."

Hannah nearly snorted. More likely, they wanted to nibble him when no one was looking. Although—she shot a glance at the ferocious cat—no doubt he could defend himself.

"I did assure them that horrible man shall not bother them here." She bent to riffle the female's fur and she nuzzled closer. "But I can understand their concern."

Hannah nodded and tugged again. "Fine. Shall we go?"

Lana resisted her urging and fixed her enormous eyes on the duke's. "Can you imagine, that poor thing? A terrible man beat her. She dinna do anything to anger him. He just beat her."

The duke tipped his head to the side and arranged his features in a sympathetic moue. "That is a terrible thing."

Blech. Hannah wanted to retch at Caithness' tone. As sticky as honey. And nearly as sweet.

The mounting impulse, to whisk her sister away from the duke, raged within Hannah. For one thing, Lana was far too innocent and trusting to recognize that this man could be a threat. Powerful men tended to take what they wanted.

Hannah didn't want her sister to become the duke's plaything.

Aside from that, Lana was unpredictable. One never knew what might come out of her mouth. She often saw things and knew things that made people uneasy, even nervous. Despite the potential disaster of sharing this information with the people involved, she often did. God forbid she should say something untoward to the duke and absolutely scuttle whatever progress Hannah had made with him—if any.

Urgency screamed through her. She needed to separate these two immediately. Before it was too—

Ah. Too late.

"I do like your mother," Lana said with an angelic smile.

Caithness reeled back. His jaw locked. Shock drifted across his features.

"My . . . mother?"

"She's verra nice."

The duke drew himself up to full height and tugged down his waistcoat once more. "Madam. My mother died long before you were born."

Lana chuckled and patted him on the cheek. *Patted him on the cheek.* The duke. "I know," she said. And then she turned on her heel and made her way from the stables and into the sunlight.

Bowing to the gaped-jawed duke, Hannah hurried after her.

Lovely. Just lovely.

Judging from his horrified expression, that was the end of that.

That was the end of everything.

CHAPTER SIXTEEN

He shouldn't have left. Certainly not on a three-hour ride to the far-flung clachans and back. But Alexander had felt the need to ride. To run.

The horror of the duke's ultimatum rang in his soul, and, wrapped with it, a bone-chilling panic.

It was over. All he'd built. All he'd fought for. All he'd struggled to protect.

All gone.

With one decision, the Duke of Caithness would wipe it all away, along with a thousand years of Scots history. And there was nothing he could do or say to stop it. Change it.

And it hardly mattered which decision he made. To clear the land and remain laird or lose his station. Both were untenable.

As he passed his people on the road and they lifted their hands in cheery greetings, Alexander was stultified by the knowledge that he'd failed them. Utterly failed them all.

And worse, he'd failed Hannah.

How could he survive the look of pity or, worse, the contempt in her eyes?

Even if she didn't repudiate him, if he lost his title and his lands where would they go? Where would they live?

What would he *be*?

It was a death of sorts.

It took him time to process it.

But before he gave Caithness the answer to his ultimatum, Alexander needed to find his wife and talk to her. He had promised to share everything with her and, as distressing as this news was, she deserved to know. It would crush her. As deeply as he felt for his land and his people, her passion met and matched his. Beyond that, they would need to discuss which of the two untenable decisions they would make and how they would deal with the consequences.

He knew which he would choose, but he wanted her input as well. This affected her as deeply as it did him.

He didn't want to have that conversation, but he had to. She was his partner. His mate . . . if she still wanted him after this.

He was still not resigned to it when he returned to the castle. That he found Caithness lurking in the stables as he unsaddled Wallace didn't help. Caithness was the last person he wanted to see at the moment. Still, he bowed. "Your Grace."

"Dunnet." The duke ran a hand over Wallace's withers and checked his teeth.

Assessing the goods already? Alexander had not even given him his answer. Although, in truth, the point was probably moot.

"This is a beautiful beast. All your horses are."

"Thank you. It's . . . something of a hobby of mine."

"Quite an enviable assemblage. No doubt, these animals would be in great demand in London."

London.

Aye. It was the only thing that mattered to the duke, after all. What they thought of him in London.

"They are not for sale."

"Hmm." Caithness patted Wallace on the neck. "A pity. He would make a fine stud."

Alexander didn't respond. What was the point?

He was possessed of the urge to hop back on his stallion's back and ride away, but he'd had enough riding, enough running away. It was time to face this. End this. End it all.

"Have you made your decision?" the duke asked.

Alexander frowned. "I need to speak with my wife before I give you my answer."

"Ah. Your wife." He had no idea why Caithness smiled like that. "I just had an interesting conversation with her."

"Did you?"

"She is quite outspoken. Not at all what I'm used to in a gently bred lady."

It took some effort, but Alexander restrained his snarl at what could be a thinly veiled insult. His fingers curled. "She's a fine Scottish lass."

"I'm certain she is. Relax, Dunnet. I did not mean offense. I appreciate frankness in my dealings. And your wife was . . . frank."

Alexander quirked a brow.

"She seems to be of the mind that I have lived in London too long. That I do not understand my people."

Aye. Hannah had the right of it.

"She suggested I . . . dress like a *man* while in Scotland."

"She . . . did?" A curl of laughter bubbled up inside him. Good God, he loved her.

"What do you think, Dunnet? Would it help in my dealings if I dressed the part of a Scottish laird?"

In all likelihood, his perusal of the duke's outfit was disdainful, but Alexander didn't try to hide it. The man had said he preferred frankness. Well, he was happy to oblige. Aside from which, he had nothing left to lose. "You look like a dandy."

"I most certainly do not. I know many dandies in London. I assure you, I am rather circumspect in my dress."

"Ye are no' in London."

To Alexander's astonishment, Caithness smiled. "That's what she said."

"You would look more like a proper duke in a kilt."

"I shall have to find one."

Alexander gaped at him. "You doona *have* a kilt?" It was unthinkable.

"There is little call for them—"

"Aye. In London." He snorted a laugh. "We shall have to get you a kilt forthwith."

"I would appreciate that."

"What else did my wife tell you?"

The duke leaned against the stable wall and crossed his arms. "Your wife assures me, despite your recalcitrance, you are a loyal man."

"I am." Alexander pursed his lips. "Did *she* say I was recalcitrant?"

"I added that part."

"Much obliged."

"Yet loyal though you may be, you refused to obey my orders."

"Only because you asked me to choose between loyalties. And when forced into such a choice, I must choose the one that protects my people."

"Ah, loyal to the bitter end." The duke made a sound, something like a laugh. "You know, I do like you, Dunnet. I think, perhaps, we got off on the wrong foot. Shall we begin again?"

Begin again? Alexander gaped at him. His mind whirled. The man had arrived in his gold-gilded carriage, barked out his ultimatum—one that was intolerable at every turn—and now he wanted to be friends?

But as he stared into the duke's eyes, Alexander saw something there he didn't expect, and it wasn't just the hint of hope and vulnerability. It was a flash of the man's soul.

He knew, in that moment, that in other circumstances he and Lachlan Sinclair would have been friends.

A flicker of regret washed through him.

At the same time, he realized if he was to have any chance to convince the duke to change his mind—if indeed he did—it would not be if they were at odds. And damn it all, he did like the man. Despite all his best intentions not to.

He thrust out his hand and said gruffly, "Aye." They clasped hands, and for the first time in hours Alexander's gut calmed. A handshake. It was a small thing, but it was something.

As they turned in tandem and strolled from the stable into the bailey, Alexander glanced at the duke. "May I ask you something, Your Grace?"

"Certainly."

"Why is it you are so set on clearing the county?"

"I believe I answered that. I need the money."

"Surely there are other ways to assure prosperity."

"The Improvements are proven. And the rewards immediate. I need the money now if I am to restore the castle before . . ."

At his hesitation, Alexander studied him. They were hardly friends. Certainly not confidants, but something urged him to ask. "Before what?"

Caithness raked his fingers through his hair and stared out at the busy bailey. Then he murmured in a very soft voice, "I'm dying, Dunnet."

Alexander's chest tightened. "I . . . I'm sorry."

The duke grunted. "Me too."

"Are you ill?"

"Do I look ill?" His hint of indignation was perplexing.

"Not in the least."

"Ah. Good." He brushed down his waistcoat. "No. Not ill."

"Then . . . what?"

"A family curse."

Alexander stared at him. *A family curse?* Alexander didn't believe in curses, just as he didn't believe in ghosts . . . or hadn't, before he'd met Lana Dounreay. Still, the question of the duke's sanity flickered through his mind.

Caithness caught his expression and chuckled, but there was little humor in the sound. "Centuries ago, one of my ancestors incurred a curse which, according to the legend, condemns the firstborn males to die before their thirtieth year."

What rot. "This is Scotland. Everyone curses everyone." There were many curses floating around. "No one pays them any mind."

"Yes. This is true. But in my case, the curse has borne true. My father died on the eve of his thirtieth birthday, and his father before him. Throughout our history, no one has escaped."

"No one?"

"Not one man since the reign of Longshanks, thanks to my ancestor the second Baron of Rosslyn. And while I'm not a believer in such things, it would be irrational, given the evidence, to assume I will be the only one to evade my fate. It would be foolhardy not to prepare."

"What did the baron do to earn such ill will?"

"He aligned with Edward the First for one thing. And betrayed his people for another. He traded the family's relic, the MacAlpin Cross, to the enemy in exchange for the title of Duke of Caithness." The title the duke nearly spat. "Edward smashed the relic and tossed it into the sea and, with her dying breath, the Keeper of the Cross levied the curse on Rosslyn and his descendants."

"Of which you are one."

The duke nodded. "I suppose some men would consider

it a horror to know the approximate date of his death, but I see it as a blessing." He said this with a little too much conviction. "It gives me time to set my estate in order. To reclaim the glory that was once Caithness Castle. I owe it to my ancestors." He fell silent for a moment and then muttered, "They do . . . plague me."

"I beg your pardon? They plague you?" *His ancestors?*

"Every night."

Which explained the dark rings beneath his eyes.

As insane as it sounded, Alexander understood completely. He'd suffered his share of ancestral plagues as well. And with the incontrovertible evidence that some people—such as Lana Dounreay—could truly see the specters, maybe even speak to them, he had to belie logic and assume Caithness was more haunted than deranged. So instead of marking the duke off as a madman, he nodded. "Again, this is Scotland. Ghosts abound."

Caithness' tension visibly released. He even smiled, though it was a wan effort. "You have your ghosts as well?"

"I do."

"How do you silence them?"

"My wife's sister gave me some excellent advice. She told me ghosts have only the power over you that you grant them."

"I wish that were true." His expression took on a contemplative aspect. "Your wife's . . . sister? Would that be Lana Dounreay?"

"It would be. Have you met her?"

"I have. She . . . she mentioned my mother." His tone was befuddled.

"Your mother?"

"She died when I was an infant. I never knew her."

"I'm sorry."

Caithness shrugged off his sympathy. "Miss Dounreay

spoke of her . . . as though she were still alive. Do you think . . . ? Do you think she can actually speak to the dead?"

"Anything is possible. Perhaps you should ask her about this. Maybe she can help bring you peace."

"Perhaps I shall." He sighed heavily. "I should love some peace. Even a small shard of it, in my final days."

"She certainly brought me peace." And how blessed it was. Too bad it had been followed so quickly by the likelihood of losing everything he was. He glanced at the duke. "How . . . long do you have?" No doubt, it was rude to ask, but it was relevant to the conversation.

Caithness pinned him with a bleak glance. "I'm twenty-nine now. I have six months."

"Ah. And this curse . . . is there any way to break it?"

"There is. But it's impossible."

"Nothing is impossible."

The duke sent him a wry look. "I like that about you, Dunnet. Your optimism."

Alexander didn't think himself optimistic, not in the slightest. "I prefer to think of myself as stubborn."

"I like that too. But sadly, the only way to break the curse is to reunite the pieces of the cross."

"The one that was tossed into the sea?" The sea was very large and did not give up its treasures easily.

The duke snorted. "Yes. My family has searched for it for centuries but never found so much as a hint that it still exists. If it ever did."

"That is a pity."

"Yes, it is."

Their conversation was interrupted as a tiny bundle of muslin wearing a crown of woven wildflowers ran across the bailey and flung herself into Alexander's arms. He lifted her up and swung her around and she squealed her delight.

"And who is this?" the duke asked, not bothering to hide his grin.

"Ah. This is Lady Fiona." Alexander set her on the ground. "Fiona, make your curtsey to the duke."

Fiona wrinkled her nose, as though she'd never been asked to do such a thing before. Which she probably had not. Still, she made a credible curtsey, and then she asked, "Do you like my crown?"

The duke blinked; his gaze settled on the wildflowers. "It is very . . . elegant."

Fiona preened.

"Say 'thank you, Your Grace,'" Alexander said on a chuckle.

"Thank you, Your Grace." She peered up at him. "You are verra tall."

"I am indeed. And you are very pretty."

The poor girl turned scarlet, then dipped her head and darted away.

The duke stared after her. "Is she your daughter?"

An ache shafted through him. "I doona have any children . . . yet. Hannah and I were married little more than a month ago."

"Ah, newlyweds. And here I am interrupting the honeymoon."

"Not at all. We are delighted to have you." Oddly enough, this wasn't a complete lie.

The duke's eyes glinted with humor. "I appreciate that." Alexander had the sense he was referring to the fib. "So who is the girl?"

"She's one of the orphans we took in." Alexander cleared his throat. "Her family came to us when their land was cleared."

"Ah yes. Your wife was telling me about the orphans."

They passed a group of men sorting bales of wool by the mill. They all raised their hands in greeting. "We have many refugees here," Alexander said. "These men, for example, came to us from Castletown."

"Yes. Olrig has been aggressively clearing."

"Verra aggressively. In the past week, refugees have been pouring over our borders. Some of the stories are . . . heartbreaking."

Caithness' lips quirked. "Do I detect a hint of censure in your tone?"

Alexander shrugged. "I canna hide how I feel and I willna lie to you. I truly do believe these Clearances are morally wrong."

"I do appreciate your honesty. I do." He sighed. "It's a pity things couldn't have been different. . . ."

Silence crackled between them as they watched the busy denizens scuttle about the bailey, the way men had hurried about their work in Lochlannach Castle for ages. Watching them, Alexander had a sudden sense of timelessness. As though the past and present and future were, in some strange way, one. "It makes me wonder. . . ."

The duke glanced at him. "Wonder what?"

"How men like Stafford and Olrig will be remembered by future generations. I'd wager they willna be lauded by their descendants."

"I daresay you are correct in that."

Alexander pinned the duke with an intense scrutiny. "And how do you want to be remembered by your descendants?"

Caithness' frown was sharp. "I believe I mentioned I shall not have them. The Sinclair line ends with me. And the curse with it."

"And that will be it?"

"Yes. That will be it." The duke smoothed down his waistcoat, although it did not require smoothing.

Though he knew the answer, Alexander had to ask, had to try, just one more time. "Is there any chance you might be willing to reconsider your decision about the Clearances?"

Caithness sighed. "No."

Odd, how this blatant confirmation of his worst fears didn't decimate him. Indeed, an acceptance bloomed within him. A peace, of sorts. What would be would be.

The duke tipped his head to stare at the sky. "I'm determined to leave something of myself behind, Dunnet." He pierced Alexander with a bright stare. "I shall return Caithness Castle to its former glory before I pass."

"Even at the cost of all of Caithness?"

Though Alexander's words were mild, the duke set his teeth.

"Even if it costs lives?"

The man bristled. "As I told your wife, no one will be harmed."

Alexander tried to stifle his snort but was unsuccessful. "And what happens to this gloriously restored castle when you die?"

The duke stared at him as though he hadn't ever considered the question, as though he hadn't thought that far ahead. "It shall revert to the Crown, I imagine."

"You have no heirs at all? No relatives to steward this great treasure?"

"Only Dougal." It was odd, the trickle of regret in his tone.

"Will he become the duke?"

Caithness shook his head. "Unlikely. For one thing, he was born on the wrong side of the blanket, and for another . . ."

"Aye?"

"The Prince Regent doesn't like him."

Hardly a shock.

He was an utterly unlikable creature.

They continued their stroll in a somewhat tenable silence. When they reached the castle walls, they climbed the steps until they reached the lower battlements. From there, the vista of Dunnethead stretched out, the sea to the north and the town to the west. The village was awash with colors and flapping banners. From their vantage point, they could see the people bustling about.

A great wash of pride gusted through Alexander as he looked down on his holdings. He endeavored to cling to the feeling, because once he and Hannah made their decision, once he gave his answer to the duke, none of this would belong to him anymore. None of this, but the tenuous memory of what it had been like to be the Baron of Dunnet.

~

After he and the duke parted ways, Alexander went in search of Hannah, to have the conversation he dreaded since the moment the duke had issued his ultimatum. He found her in the kitchens, marshaling the staff to prepare dinner for their visitors. He leaned against the doorjamb with his arms crossed and watched. Just watched. It was glorious, and daunting, witnessing her crack the whip over his people. And, judging from their expressions, she frightened them a little as well. Even Morag was in awe.

If nothing else, it looked as though Hannah had found her place in this household at last.

When she spotted him, her frown blossomed into a bonny smile. "Dunnet, darling," she said as she made her way to his side. Though they were all there, all the household staff, he kissed her. He couldn't not. She was far too exquisite, far too alluring, to resist. "Where have you been?"

"Riding. I needed to think."

She patted his chest. "Of course. How do you feel?"

How did he feel? What kind of question was that? His

stomach hurt. His head ached. His pulse pounded. Nausea bubbled. And hell. Now that the moment was here, his trepidation rose to new heights. Though he'd been mulling over this for hours, he had no idea how to approach it. Certainly no idea how to *tell* her.

"I feel fine. Could I . . . speak with you? In private?"

"Certainly. Where would you like to go?"

"Our suite?"

Her grin became minxish. It lit an inappropriate fire in his gut. That wasn't what he'd had in mind, but now that the thought had taken root, he had trouble banishing it. How tempting it was, to make love to her one last time before telling her the truth.

But he wouldn't do that.

He owed her better.

They made their way to their rooms through the servants' staircase, because it was faster than winding through the main halls. Alexander couldn't help noticing the bounce in her step, the glow about her. He hated to think he would steal all that from her with a few small words.

When they entered his bedroom, she wrapped herself around him. It was delightful . . . and agonizing. Because he had to gently untangle her. "Hannah, we need to talk."

"I doona want to talk. I want to kiss."

"I want to kiss too but—"

His words were muffled. By her mouth.

Ah, heaven. Though he knew he should stop this, he didn't want to. In his heart of hearts, he really didn't want to. He allowed her to kiss him, and aye, he kissed her back. But when she came up for air, he said before she could distract him again, "Hannah, I have something I must tell you."

She stilled and gazed up at him with limpid eyes. "All right."

"I . . . ah . . . It's . . ."

"The duke?"

"Aye. It . . . has to do with the . . . duke."

"And your meeting with him?"

"A-aye."

He broke away and strode to the window, staring out, though he saw nothing. God, this was hard. The hardest thing he'd ever had to say. He couldn't bear to look at her. Couldn't bear to see her crumble. "He . . . has issued . . . an . . . ultimatum."

"Aye. Clear the land or lose your title. I heard."

Alexander froze. He wasn't sure what stunned him more, the fact that somehow she'd already found out or her blasé tone. He whipped around. "You heard? How did you hear?"

Inexplicably, she grinned. "I was eavesdropping."

He winced. *Hell.* She'd heard . . . "Everything?"

"Most of it. That Dougal is a fine piece of work."

"Aye. He is." But Dougal was the least of it. Truly he was. Alexander stared at Hannah, his heart aching, his stomach sour. It had to be said. It had to be. "Perhaps . . . you should have married Stafford's son." He attempted something like a chuckle and failed.

Hannah's brow wrinkled. "Never say it. Oh, Alexander. Never say it."

"Perhaps then you could at least have saved Reay."

She blew out a snort. "Stafford would have gobbled it up in a trice. My people would be homeless already had I married that beast. Aside from which . . ." She wrinkled her nose. "*Eww.*"

His chuckle was real this time. He liked that she didn't have second thoughts about her decision to marry him. Even if it might cost her everything. He stepped closer and cupped her cheeks in his palms. She tipped her face up for his kiss. But he couldn't kiss her. Not yet. "Hannah, we need to decide which answer to give him."

Her chin firmed. "They are both untenable choices."

"Aye. They are."

She nestled in, closing her arms around him and staring up at his face. "Which would be best?"

He snorted. "Neither. But I canna in good conscience agree to clear the land."

She held him closer. Nodded.

"And if I refuse to clear the land, I will no longer be the laird. Could you . . . could you bear that?"

Her smile warmed him. "Oh, Alexander. I could bear anything. So long as I'm with you."

His heart gave a great thump. God, he loved her.

"Besides . . ." Her grin was wicked.

He thumbed her lips. "How can you be smiling?" It was the end of the world.

"I believe we can still change his mind."

Ach. His mood dipped. Sometimes inappropriate hope served only to delay the eventual heartbreak. "No, Hannah. We canna. He is set on this course."

"Of course we can." She went up on her toes and kissed the tip of his chin. "There is something women know that men doona."

"And what is that?"

"If I told you, then you'd know."

Seriously? Was she teasing him? At a moment like this? "Hannah . . ."

"Oh, all right. The secret is this. No man is *ever* completely set on his course. Not ever. It is always possible to change his mind . . . if you can figure out what really motivates him."

Of all the times Alexander had been utterly flummoxed and rendered speechless in his life, this was the most confabulating. He gaped at her.

She ignored him and rattled on. "I had a conversation

with him this afternoon and it started me thinking. He seems like a caring man, and a rational man—if one doesna take his sartorial misfortune into account. He was bothered by the tales I shared with him, and seemed moved by the plight of his people. His reaction wasna that of a lord who wants to destroy, but one who wants to protect those weaker than he. He is very much like you in that, my husband." She stroked his cheek. "Though he was raised in England—and, clearly, that has addled his thinking—I have the sense he really wants to do what's right. We just need to . . . provide him with options." She shrugged, as though it were that simple.

"Options?"

"If Caithness wants sheep, we shall give him bluidy sheep. We have wonderful weavers, ships to share our wares with the world. And then there are your magnificent horses. With verra few changes, your hobby could become a thriving business in itself. And that doesna even take into account the bounty of Reay. Surely, once we show him the possibilities, he will see reason." She tapped her lips with a finger and paced. "Perhaps we could take him on a tour of Dunnet tomorrow and point out all the lovely prosperous possibilities. We can do this, Alexander, you and I. We can show him there is a better way than clearing the land."

"He needs the money, Hannah."

"For what?"

"He plans to refurbish his family home before he dies."

Her brow wrinkled. "How much would that cost?"

"You havena seen his family home. It's practically rubble."

"Well, for heaven sake, it can hardly cost the price of the entire county. And what do you mean, before he dies?"

"He's convinced he's cursed."

"Oh dear. Is he mad?"

"That was my thought, but he seems rational enough. And, to hear him tell it, every member of his family has died right on cue. He believes he has six months to live."

"Then we shall have to work quickly."

Alexander tried not to sigh. She was so hopeful, so certain, so resolute. He hated to dash her optimism. But the truth couldn't be ignored. "And if that doesna work? If he canna be convinced? What then? When Caithness insists on his answer, and I tell him I willna clear the land, we will have to leave Dunnet."

"Then we leave." Her chin firmed. "Together."

"Where shall we live?" When he was not the baron? When he was no longer the laird? When Lochlannach Castle was no longer his home?

She tipped her head up and stared at him. "It doesna matter." Her voice was so soft, so calm, so sweet, he almost believed her.

"It does. It matters verra much."

"Nae, my husband." She set her palm to his cheek. "As long as we're together, we will be fine."

"I willna be a laird."

"You will always be *my* laird."

Silence filled the space between them. It had a weight. A potent presence. A tight ball formed in his chest. It was the most pleasurable ache he'd ever known. He stared down at her as long as he could bear it and then he pulled her into his arms and held her tight. God help him, he loved her, this woman he'd taken to wife. She was his heart, his life, his everything. With her, he was . . . complete.

"I am so glad I married you, Hannah Dounreay," he murmured.

Her smile nearly split her face in two. "Hannah Lochlannach," she responded softly. He loved the pride ringing through those words.

"Aye. Hannah Lochlannach."

In that respect, she was right.

The castle, the lands, the treasury . . . none of it meant anything without her.

And with her, he had everything that mattered.

Although a roof over his head and food in his belly would be nice. And maybe a horse.

But he'd worry about that tomorrow.

CHAPTER SEVENTEEN

"How do I look?" Lana twirled, though it was hardly necessary. She looked stunning from all angles. She wore a baby-blue gown festooned with lace—His Grace should love that—and her hair was piled in a frothy creation that made her look whimsical and delicate.

But then, Lana always looked stunning.

"Perfect, darling." Hannah sat back and soaked in her sister's glee. How wonderful it must be not to have any worries at all.

Though she'd tried very hard to appear otherwise before Dunnet, Hannah was a bundle of nerves. This evening was crucial in their campaign to sway Caithness. While Hannah had every confidence that things would go well, there was no certainty that the duke would be amenable to their pleas in the slightest. She hoped she wasn't being naïve to think that sharing her ideas on how he could make money without clearing the land would make the tiniest difference. But it was all she had.

Beyond that, she was worried for her sister. Hannah didn't care for the way the duke stared at Lana. As though he wanted to eat her up. With his advent in Dunnet, all Hannah's overprotective instincts—which had calmed when Andrew had left—bubbled up once more. And the duke was a much greater threat.

She flicked a look at Lana, to which her sister responded with a mock frown. "What is it?" she asked.

"I . . . ah . . . What do you think of the duke?"

"He really is verra handsome, isn't he?"

Hannah's heart lurched. She fiddled with the hem of her sleeve. "Aye. He is . . . handsome."

Lana laughed. "Why do you say it in that tone?"

"What tone?"

"As though it tastes bad."

It rather did. She sighed. "He's a duke. And practically an Englishman."

"What does that mean?"

Hannah shrugged. She saw a pleat on Lana's skirt that needed smoothing, so she did. "Just that men like him are used to taking what they want."

Lana's snort rounded the room. "Have you yet to meet a man who dinna take what he wanted?"

"You know what I mean. You need to steer clear of him." And then she added, just to underscore her point, "Alexander tells me he is cursed."

"He doesna seem cursed . . . other than his unfortunate choice in clothing." Lana wrinkled her nose.

"It hardly signifies. I doona like the way he looks at you."

Lana sighed. "Are we having the rabbit and the flower conversation again?"

"If necessary."

She sighed again, this time with much more melodrama. "Honestly, Hannah. You doona need to protect me from everything. I'm not a child."

"I know that, darling. But I canna help worrying. I doona want you to be seduced by the duke."

"Seduced by him?" Lana chuckled. "Have you *seen* what he was wearing?"

"It is all the rage in London."

Lana sniffed. "I sincerely doubt I could be seduced by a man who wears lace."

"There's a relief. Still and all, do be careful around him.

Lana, he's a powerful man, and powerful men tend to believe that women were put on this earth as playthings and nothing more."

"Och, Lachlan's not like that."

Hannah blinked. "Darling, who is Lachlan?"

"Why, the duke, of course."

Lachlan?

Horror crawled up Hannah's spine. "How . . . Why . . ." *Oh for heaven sake.* "How do you know his given name?"

Lana's laugh was light and merry. Of course it was. She had no concept of the danger powerful men could pose to an innocent girl with a pretty face. "His mother told me."

Relief whooshed through Hannah. "His mother?"

"Lileas. She told me he's a good man at heart."

Hannah crossed her arms. "Hasn't she been dead for years?"

Lana gored her sister with a wounded look. "She's been watching him."

"Well, *Lachlan* has given orders for Dunnet to clear the land. And if he refuses, he will be replaced as baron. Most likely, *Lachlan* has sent the same orders to Papa."

Lana gaped at her. "He has?"

"Indeed. Do you still think he is a good man at heart?"

Her sister put out a lip. "And you think I could be seduced by a man like *that*?"

Hannah tried not to wince at her wounded expression. "You did say he was handsome."

"There is more to a man than a pretty face."

"Aye." T'was true. Much more. Hanna blew out a breath. "Well, then next time you speak to Lileas, ask her if she knows how to change his mind." She meant it as a joke, but Lana's eyes went a little cloudy and she tipped her head to the side. Her resultant smile, inscrutable as it was, made Hannah rethink such nonsense. Lana did know things. She often had information she couldn't have gathered on her own. That in itself had convinced Hannah long ago that whatever gift her sister had—even though she didn't understand it—was real. This prompted her to ask, "Does she? Does she know how to change his mind?"

"She has some ideas." Lana tapped her lips and surveyed Hannah's costume. She was wearing her favorite green, the dress she'd been married in, as it was her finest. Obligingly, she held out her arms and gave a little twirl as well.

"What do you think?"

"Charming. But you need something more."

"More?"

Lana's fingers fluttered at her neck. "Some jewelry, perhaps?"

Hannah made her way to her jewelry box in the wardrobe. There wasn't much in it. She selected the piece that had been her mother's and held it up before herself, gazing in the glass. "This one?"

Lana wrinkled her nose. "Not that one. Not grand enough for a baroness dining with a duke."

Hannah tried another, and another, all with the same response.

Her sister studied her for a long moment, then said, "Why do you no' wear my mother's necklace?"

"You brought your mother's necklace?"

Lana put out a lip. "I wore it to your wedding. Did you not even notice?"

Oh dear. "I was rather distracted."

"Well, I did bring it and it would be perfect with your dress." Without another word she bustled across the hall to her rooms and brought back the necklace that had been her mother's. It was a lovely piece hewn of gold on a thick-linked chain. It was intricately carved and had a small stone mounted on the bottom. "Here. This is much better."

"It is quite nice."

"Perfect for dinner with the duke."

It was, indeed, much grander than the others. "Help me put it on."

She should probably have thought about jewelry before she'd done her hair, but together they managed to get the necklace over her coiffure without too much damage. It fell, a cool and heavy weight against her breasts in the vee of her décolletage.

"Oh, aye," Lana cooed. "That is perfect."

"Do you think?" Hannah turned this way and that, observing herself in the glass.

"It is lovely. You are lovely." The deep voice coming from the doorway made her start. She whirled around.

Her heart swelled as she set eyes on her husband, dressed as he was in his kilt. He was always handsome, but never as handsome as he was like this. Something about the costume made his shoulders seem impossibly broad, his legs sturdier, and his visage more savage. He was terribly striking tonight. She clasped her hands and gazed at him. "Dunnet."

"You look verra much the laird," Lana murmured.

"Does he no'? So handsome."

Was it her imagination, or did he blush? "Not so verra handsome," he grumbled.

"Verra handsome." She sauntered to his side and kissed his cheek.

He kissed hers.

Then her lips.

"Ahem. I will meet you downstairs, shall I?" Lana said with a twinkle in her eye. As she headed for the door, she waggled a warning finger. "Doona get distracted."

Hannah sniffed. Surely there was no call for such a comment.

Oh, but there was. They became very distracted indeed.

They were almost late for dinner.

~

Lana was the only one present when Alexander finally led Hannah into the parlor. She stood by the window staring out into the falling shadows. So absorbed was she in the view, she didn't turn around when they entered the room, for which Alexander was grateful. He paused at the door to give Hannah another quick kiss and tucked a curl behind her ear. Sadly, her hair had become . . . mussed. But her cheeks were rosy and her lips bee-stung. She looked ravishing.

He certainly wanted to ravish her.

Even though he already had.

It was a damn shame they had guests.

But they did and this dinner was important, so he fixed a credible smile on his face, linked his arms in Hannah's, and entered the room.

"There you are," Lana said with a gust when she finally noticed them. "I was beginning to think I would have to have dinner all on my own."

Hannah flushed charmingly. "Nonsense. We came straightaway."

Lana nodded, but her mischievous smile showed she knew the truth. "I just feel honored that you remembered at all—" Lana stilled. The smile froze on her face. Her lips parted and her throat worked.

Alexander followed her stunned gaze just as the duke, dressed in the Dunnet-hewn kilt he'd found for him, entered the room. He could understand why the sight had addled Lana's thoughts. Caithness looked very fine in the deep Sinclair red. It set off his dark hair and striking features. In fact, suddenly, miraculously, he looked like a Scotsman. And a duke to boot.

It was very annoying, then, when Hannah espied him. Her body tensed. Her eyes widened and she murmured,

"Oh my." Alexander tried not to be annoyed at the awe in her tone. *Damn.* Maybe he shouldn't have given Caithness the plaid after all. Not if the look of him in it made Hannah gape so. He couldn't resist the urge to nudge her with his elbow.

She turned to him, her eyes wide. "Oh my," she repeated.

When he glowered at her she grinned, but when she caught sight of Lana's dewy-eyed look at the duke her eyes narrowed. She grumbled something beneath her breath and then burst forward with a strident, "Good evening, Your Grace."

Caithness seemed to find it a challenge to rip his attention from Lana's face, but at length he did, probably because Hannah thrust her hand at him. He stared at it for a moment before he took it. "I . . . ah . . . Good evening, Dunnet. Lady Dunnet."

When the duke bent over his wife's hand, his gaze stalled. Alexander couldn't help but notice it stalled on her cleavage.

Aye, Hannah was in fine form. The dress she wore was stunning; it hugged her curves and highlighted her eyes. But nothing was more alluring than that shadowed crease. That another man was ogling it—with what looked like glint of avarice—made his fists curl.

He had to forcibly open his fingers and remind himself this was his overlord. One did not, as a general rule, plant one's fist in the face of one's overlord.

Dougal, on the other hand, he could pummel, and Alexander wanted to, because when the duke's cousin ambled into the room behind his liege, his gaze locked on Hannah's bosom as well.

Irritation snaked through Alexander, making the little hairs at the back of his neck stand on end. It took every effort not to growl. The last thing he wanted to do was ruin the dinner Hannah had carefully planned.

But he would, if it became necessary.

Though he'd always been a fiercely loyal man, never in his life had he felt this. This sense of belonging in something and to something. This feeling of partnership . . . and the scorching possessiveness that seemed to come along with it, fist in glove.

Hannah was his. His wife, his love, *his*.

Other men should never be allowed to ogle her bosom. He would have to remind her of that later. Perhaps a new party dress was in order. One without a plunging neckline.

These thoughts flickered through his head, but he said nothing—certainly punched no one—as they made their way into the dining room for their meal. Hannah and Lana chatted with the duke about, well, whatever it was they were chatting about—Alexander found it difficult to focus on the conversation—and while Caithness seemed to divide his attention politely between the two, more often than it should his focus returned to that which Alexander considered his own.

Not growling was becoming a challenge.

The duke took the place of honor at the head of the table, and because they were a small party and had agreed to suspend formal protocol Hannah sat on his left and Lana on his right. Though it appeared Dougal seemed inclined to take the space next to Hannah, Alexander elbowed him out of the way. With a grumble, he headed over to the other side of the table to sit next to Lana.

Alexander realized his error at once. From that vantage point, both men had an unimpeded view of Hannah's décolletage, whereas Alexander had to lean forward to enjoy it. Or to glare at them. Whichever proved most necessary at the moment.

Sadly, neither of them noticed his displeasure.

They were far too preoccupied.

In truth, it wasn't a very plunging neckline. As the conversation swirled around him, Alexander mentally compared the two sisters and decided Lana's dipped far lower. Though Hannah's breasts were fuller. That was probably the attraction.

The necklace she wore only drew attention to the rise and fall of those milky swells. It cradled between them like a golden lance, sending lurid visions through his mind, visions of things a man should like to try when his woman had breasts as splendid as these. Tantalizing explorations . . .

His rising lust was an annoyance, because it was twined with the knowledge that Caithness and Dougal were likely thinking the same things.

Hannah, of course, was oblivious to the attention. But then, she would be. She was utterly absorbed with painting a picture of Scotland—true Scotland—for their guest. She and Lana shared stories of rollicking fetes and heartbreaking struggles, of ancient traditions and amusing anecdotes from their family history. Their tales were peppered with examples of men, women, and children affected by the Clearances, but it was so subtle, Alexander almost missed it.

When he allowed himself to ignore the too-frequent glances toward her chest, he was surprised to find he discovered much about his wife he didn't know, and it occurred to him that though they had become very close, they had not had long lazy conversations about their lives and their beliefs and their hopes and dreams. He resolved to rectify that. He wanted to know it all. He wanted to know everything.

The fact that her mother had died giving birth to her surprised him. She made a comment about being a large baby and, though she didn't say it, he sensed a long-buried wound. She blamed herself.

Her sister Susana's mother—who married Magnus shortly after Hannah's birth—died bringing Susana into the world as well. And while Lana's mother didn't suffer the same fate with her first child, she did with the second, a babe who followed her quickly into the afterlife. After the loss of this third wife, Magnus never tried again.

Alexander shot a look at Hannah. Though she chatted unconcernedly as she nibbled at her dinner, he had to wonder if the fear haunted her that one day she would be heavy with child and the birthing of it might kill her. His first thought was a swelling tenderness for her. Childbirth was dangerous, but she was strong and sturdy. No doubt she would prove more than worthy of the challenge.

His second thought was sheer terror.

At the prospect of losing her.

His appetite fled. The food in his mouth turned to dust. The beef in his belly churned.

How on earth could he face the future without her?

Laird or not?

No matter where this journey led him, he wanted her, needed her, at his side.

"Dunnet?"

He must have made a noise, perhaps that growl he'd been holding back. He had certainly stiffened. His hands were fists, but he had no desire to punch anyone at the moment. All he wanted was to hold on. Hold on to her forever.

"Dunnet? Are you all right?" Her voice was a balm, the sweet caress of a cool breeze over his spirit.

No point in borrowing trouble from tomorrow. They had plenty today.

"Aye," he murmured. "I'm fine." He was. As long as she was at his side.

She smiled. The sight of it danced down to his core, releasing something held tight. "Shall we order dessert?"

Dessert?

He glanced down at his empty plate. He didn't remember eating so much as a bite. "Aye. Shall we?"

She gestured to the footman who disappeared into the kitchen. "You will love Morag's cake, Your Grace," she said, patting the duke's arm. "It is delicious."

Lana nodded. "It is the traditional Dunnet wedding cake, but we loved it so much, we convinced Morag to make it again."

"For you." While he disliked the smile his wife shot at the duke, Alexander understood it was really for him. She was determined to help *him* achieve his goal. This fact calmed his aggravation when the duke smiled back . . . and his eyes, once more, flickered to her breasts.

"I look forward to tasting it."

Alexander felt the bite of displeasure at what might have been a double entendre.

"I do love cake." The duke rubbed his belly.

Hannah's laugh rippled through the room in a delicious wave. Her bosom rippled with it. Caithness' gaze locked on.

"I say," he said. His tone was casual, but something murky and disquieting simmered beneath it. "I've been noticing your . . . necklace all evening. It's . . . rather stunning."

Dougal's head, which had been nodding, snapped up.

Hannah touched the necklace. It was probably an instinctive gesture, but it made Alexander's nerves fizzle and spit because it drew all eyes to her chest. "This? Thank you."

"Where, ah, where did you get it?" To Alexander's ears, all pretense of nonchalance evaporated. The acquisitive glint in the duke's eyes stunned him.

It was gold, to be sure, but certainly not the Crown Jewels.

"It's Lana's."

The duke's attention swiveled to her. *Thank God.* "And . . . where did you get it?"

Lana shrugged. "It's been in the family for ages. My mother gave it to me. Her mother gave it to her, and her mother before her."

"Interesting," Dougal said. It was an odd thing to say, because that was generally how heirlooms worked. The glance he and Caithness shared was odd too.

"It's said to have belonged to the MacAlpin," Lana said.

Dougal stilled. "Which one?"

Lana shot him a frown. "*The* MacAlpin. Kenneth. The first king of Scotland."

The duke went a trifle pale. His lips worked. He cleared his throat. "May I . . . see it?"

"Of course." Hannah leaned closer. The hair on Alexander's nape rose as the duke reached for the necklace. Though he was careful not to touch her, he was far too close for comfort.

Alexander found himself leaning closer as well, and not just because he wanted to remind her he was behind her but because, now that he noticed, the necklace had strange, rune-like carvings on the surface.

"It does look verra old," he murmured into Hannah's ear.

"It is," Lana said. "Ancient."

The duke said nothing as he stared at the gleaming gold. With trembling fingers, he traced the markings; then he caressed the stone embedded at the tip.

Dougal leaned forward; his eyes glinted. "Is it the one?" he asked in a hushed voice. "Is it the piece you've been looking for?"

Caithness nodded. His lips worked. "It is." A sigh. "This is it."

"This is what?" Alexander asked.

"It's a piece of the cross. The one I told you about."

"What cross?" Hannah murmured. She pulled back and reluctantly the duke let go, but still he stared at the necklace longingly.

"The MacAlpin Cross. The one that belonged to my ancestors. The one Longshanks broke into pieces and tossed into the sea. The reason for the curse on my family."

Alexander shook his head. "How can you be sure?"

"There's a portrait in the castle of it. It is very distinctive. I've been searching for this. Searching my whole life." The duke's features were fierce, his eyes red rimmed. "It is my duty to reunite the cross," he whispered. "May I . . . have it?"

Hannah glanced at Lana, who tipped her head to the side. She studied the duke for a long moment. "I doona think so."

The duke gaped at her. "I beg your pardon?"

Lana fluttered her lashes. "It's been in my family for ages," she said. "I'm no' eager to give it up."

"Miss Dounreay. I don't think you grasp the consequence of this piece."

"Oh, I think I do. Correct me if I have this wrong. It's a piece of the MacAlpin Cross. The one you believe might break the curse on your family—if indeed such curses exist—and it could, in your estimation, possibly save your life." She smiled sweetly. "Did I get that right?"

The duke narrowed his eyes. "You did."

Her eyes took on a Machiavellian glint. "How badly do you want it?"

Caithness firmed his jaw. "I want it very badly."

"Excellent." Her tone was threaded with resolve. "Then perhaps we can discuss concessions."

A muscle worked in his cheek. "Concessions?"

"Aye. Most importantly, you agree to reconsider the Clearances of Dunnet and Reay."

Oh holy God. Alexander stared at Lana, a woman who, until now, had always struck him as charming, demure, and . . . pliable. She was nothing of the sort. He'd had no idea she had it in her to be so ruthless.

Caithness sat back and fixed Lana with a daunting stare. She was undaunted. She shot him a cheery smile back. It was not a sign of weakness. It was a sign of certitude.

Then again, Caithness' pose was intractable as well. "My dear, I am a duke."

"I'm aware of that."

"Do you realize how much power I have over you? Your circumstances? Your livelihood? Your very life?"

Lana blew out an incongruous derisive snort. "Your Grace. You canna threaten me."

He reared back. His nostrils flared. "B-but I'm a duke!"

Her eyes narrowed. Her charming, demure, and pliable expression faded, replaced with something hard, cold, and wounded. "You have no power over me. You have already threatened everything I value in this world. My family, my clan, my way of life. I have nothing left but this necklace, and I would sooner throw it back into the sea than give it to a man who is bent on destroying the lives of everyone I love."

Caithness' features tightened as he studied her obdurate expression, searching for weaknesses. There were none. Lana was indomitable. Magnus had mentioned his daughters were all stubborn, but in truth, Alexander had not seen the trait in Lana . . . until now. Apparently, she held it at bay until she really needed it and then wielded it with the skill of a master swordsman.

The duke didn't stand a chance.

At long last, Caithness sighed. "I could just take it."

"You willna."

"How can you be so sure?"

"Your mother told me you are a man of honor. And a man of honor would not stoop to such villainy."

Caithness stilled. "My mother . . . ?"

"Aye. Lileas."

He paled. His throat worked and then he huffed out something that might have been a laugh. "You, Miss Dounreay, do not play fair."

She fluttered her lashes. "Life is unfair."

"Yes. It is at that." The duke was silent for a long while, occupying his attention with the aspects of his fork. When he spoke, his voice was low and soft. "If I can reunite the cross and break the curse, there will be no need for me to clear the land at all."

"So you will reconsider your decision?"

"Yes." The duke nodded. His gaze locked with Lana's and they stared at each other for a long moment. "Yes. I will reconsider my decision." His chin firmed. "But I make no promises, Miss Dounreay. I make no promises at all."

It was agreed that in light of the duke's concession, Alexander would arrange a tour of the neighboring lands, so Caithness could witness the effects of the Clearances for himself. Olrig had just begun the process, so the impacts there were still raw. It would allow Caithness to see the true horror of the decision he'd made.

Hannah hoped the evidence would change his mind, and though Alexander tried to talk her out of coming—claiming things were too unstable in Olrig's land right now—she would not be deterred.

They planned to ride out at first light, the three of them, Hannah, her husband, and the duke. Lana didn't ride and professed she had no desire to see the destruction. Dougal had elected to stay behind as well.

Alexander looked magnificent in his kilt, with his sword at his side as he strode through the bailey to the stables. The duke was impressive as well, kitted out in full kilt. Although his sword was much smaller. In fact, when Alexander saw it he gave a snort and asked, "What the bluidy hell kind of weapon is that?"

The duke bristled. "It's an épée."

"An épée?"

Caithness pursed his lips. "It's French."

Alexander narrowed his eyes and leaned in to peer at it. "It's verra small."

"I assure you, it is quite deadly. And I am an accomplished swordsman."

To which Alexander grunted.

They mounted up, Hannah astride Beelzebub and Alexander on his beloved Wallace, while the duke selected one of the stallions he fancied in Alexander's stable, and they headed through the misty morning to the southwest. As they passed through Dunnet land, Alexander showed the duke some of the prosperous crofts, mills, and villages. There was great pride in his voice as he described all of the improvements they had made to the land—improvements that did not involve evicting tenants. Though Caithness seemed engaged and interested, he was reserved in his responses.

When they crossed over onto Olrig's land, the contrast was sharp. The first evidence that all was not well was a blackened field. It was a harsh and visual reminder, juxtaposed to the verdant bounty of the land they'd left. The desolation reached as far as the eye could see.

"What has happened here?" Caithness asked as they picked their way through the seared remains of a once-productive croft.

“ ’Tis common practice to burn out tenants who willna leave,” Alexander said between his teeth “This croft belonged to Jamie Kirk. He inherited it from his father, who inherited it from his father before him. He and his wife lived here with three small children.”

Hannah’s heart lurched as her gaze fell on the scorched remnants of a cottage and barn. The duke was similarly affected. He paled and a muscle worked in his cheek. “Where have they gone?”

Alexander shrugged. “I doona know. But away from here. He was a good man. A loss for certain.”

They continued to the south and came to the village of Tain. It was eerily quiet. A shiver walked down Hannah’s spine as they passed through the deserted streets. Some of the cottages were burned and the inn showed damage. Not a soul greeted them.

Caithness said nothing, but he blew out a breath and his brows knit. While Hannah was hopeful this desolation would show him the truth of the Clearances, the sight of such bleak wreckage, the knowledge of the pain and suffering that had occurred here, made her chest ache.

“I’d like to stop by one more croft before taking you to see Castletown,” Alexander said. “I often visit Agnes when I’m on my rounds and I’d like to check on her.” It was clear from his tight tone that he was worried all would not be well when they arrived.

And it was not.

As they emerged from the woods near Agnes’ croft, Hannah’s pulse stalled. A large angry plume of black smoke curled high into the sky. There was no doubt Agnes’ croft was on fire.

Hannah glanced at Alexander. He frowned at her. A muscle worked in his cheek. In tandem, they charged forward. Hannah’s heart hammered as Beelzebub flew for the croft, pounding as though the hounds of hell were on his heels. The old woman was bedridden; she couldn't escape from a blazing hut if she crawled.

Fear clutched at Hannah, making her breathless. The dear woman was aged, and but for her son, who came to work the land, she was all alone in this remote spot.

Ah, but she wasn't alone.

As they barreled into the clearing Hannah saw a group of burly men and horses milling about. Relief gushed through her as she realized it wasn't the house that was ablaze but the barn. At the same moment, she noticed the men were doing nothing to stop the licking flames.

The panicked lows of the cattle were a testament to that. Above them, she could hear Agnes' pleas coming from her tiny house.

Alexander threw himself from his horse and stormed up to one of the men. He was a muscled brute, with craggy features fixed into a scowl. "What are you doing?" Alexander snarled. "Set those animals free."

The brute's response was naught but a chuckle.

As Hannah dismounted and made her way to his side, with Caithness behind her, a fat ginger cat darted from the barn, the singe of smoke trailing from its fur. The man scooped it up and, to Hannah's horror, he hauled back, as though to toss it back into the flaming structure.

Oh. Hell no.

She dove forward, even as he prepared to make a fatal throw, and snatched the yowling cat from his hands. In its panic, the frightened creature scratched and clawed its way free and leaped to the ground; it was clever enough to skitter away from that vile man and disappear into the woods.

Hannah was not.

Clever enough.

To skitter away.

The man rounded on her, and before she had a chance to react he snarled a word—one she'd never heard before and, from the sound of it, wouldn't care to hear again—and he landed his meaty fist in her cheek.

Agony exploded. The impact blinded her.

She flew back, into the hard dirt. The shock of the landing was a mercy because it distracted her from the searing pain in her face. She was certain he had shattered her jaw until she managed to make it move.

A sound, low and feral, something that caused a shiver to walk up her spine, echoed through the croft. It took a moment for her to realize this terrifying sound came from her husband's throat.

The second sound that registered on her dazed brain was the unmistakable hiss of his sword sliding from the scabbard.

"I will fooking kill you for that," he roared, charging the man who had hit her.

In response, all the men drew their swords.

Hannah watched in terror as her husband threw himself into battle. The other men were large, and there were more of them. Indeed, three of the men rushed Alexander with their weapons raised, as another three rushed Caithness. Her heart lodged in her throat as frustration roiled. She had no weapon, other than her dirk, which was pathetic in contrast to their great swords. Still, she unsheathed it. She needed to be ready if there was a chance, any chance, to help.

The battle raged in the yard, hidden at times by the great roiling clouds of black smoke. Hannah desperately tried to see what was happening, but the occasional glimpses she caught were not forthcoming. Grunts and howls and thuds and great clashes of metal hung in the air. They gave her no clue to what was happening, either.

Acid churned in her belly. She couldn't bear it if Alexander was hurt. She would simply curl up and die. He was her heart, her everything. And the duke . . . with his dainty little épée? What would become of them, of all of them, if the curse held true and he died today?

They should never have come. They shouldn't have risked it. Alexander had been right; it was too dangerous. Ah, she only hoped she would have the chance to tell him so.

A gust of wind blew through, wafting the smoke away, and Hannah scraped her hair from her face and focused on the scene. Her heart lifted as she saw two of the brigands had fallen, and then the breath lodged in her throat as she realized Alexander was still battling two large men. Though it was clear he far outclassed them, her heart still pounded with worry.

Hannah's gaze was drawn to his body, his powerful muscles, the unrelenting swing of his sword arm. His movements were like a magnificent, savage dance. The men he was battling didn't stand a chance. A glimmer of delight glinted in Alexander's eyes as he beat the second man to his knees and sent his sword flying out of reach. Then he turned to his final rival.

Caithness was still in play as well. The duke was as large as his opponent but far more fleet of foot. He danced around his foe with elegant parries and thrusts that made the other man dizzy. Occasionally he whipped his slender blade around and jabbed at the man he was fighting, resulting in a yelp and a blossom of red on his shirt. What stunned her was the smile on Caithness' face. It shocked her to realize he was enjoying this ferocious battle.

In fact, they both were, the duke and her husband.

Hannah set her hands on her hips and glared at them—though neither was paying her any mind. How like a man to enjoy something so—

A movement out of the corner of her eye caught her attention and her blood went cold. One of the men had slunk over to the burning stable. As she watched, he picked up a flaming cudgel and tossed it onto the thatch of Agnes' home.

It burst into flames.

With Agnes still inside.

Hannah screamed, though she had no intention to do so. The sound wrenched from her in a feral howl. "She's still in there!" she bellowed, and launched herself toward the cottage.

The man caught her. His hands were bony and hard and they cut into her flesh. "Damn her, the old witch." His snarl rumbled through Hannah even as the foul skeins of his breath surrounded her. "She has lived too long. Let her burn."

Something bitter and nasty tickled the back of Hannah's throat. Her pulse thudded in her temple. Her vision blurred. She wasn't quite certain if this scorching emotion was panic or fury, or both.

Frantic to break free, to save Agnes, whose frightened cries were rising, Hannah fought his grasp, and when that didn't help she turned and plowed her knee into his groin. He sucked in a pained wheeze and sank to the ground, releasing her.

She bolted into the burning hut.

It was dark and a pall of smoke hung heavily on the air. Hannah covered her mouth with her shawl and made her way through the murk; Agnes' cries were a beacon. Still, it seemed to take forever to reach the bed.

The crackling overhead, the occasional drop of embers as the fire consumed the thatch, was like a ticking clock. Sweating, quivering with fear, Hannah lifted Agnes from the bed. She was old and frail but heavy. Hannah staggered under her weight.

Making her way to the door, blinded, choked, she stumbled and nearly dropped her fragile bundle. She despaired she wouldn't have the strength to carry Agnes to safety, though it was not far. It was not far at all. Yet it might as well have been a league.

Oh, how she wished she were stronger.

The flames had spread now. They licked at the walls and gobbled up larger and larger chunks of the roof. The scent of baked dung and scorched hair clung to her nostrils. Heat singed her cheek. Glowing embers fell all around them, catching her clothes with a sizzling sear. Hannah ignored it all and fought her way for the door. So far. So far . . .

Panic tightened in her gut. Certainty.

Death was upon them.

Her only regret was that she had never told Alexander she loved him. Bless him, she did, and he deserved to know.

But it was too late—

A looming shadow appeared through the smoke. Relief swamped her . . . and then her pulse snarled with trepidation. *Alexander.*

He'd run into a *burning building.* Was he insane?

"What are you doing here?" she snapped.

He didn't answer, other than to say gruffly, "Let me take her." With great ease, he cradled the old woman in his arms and herded Hannah out the door.

They barely made it. As they burst through, into the fresh, clean, sunny morning, the hut folded in on itself with a great whoosh.

Hannah whirled to watch, although she didn't know why. It was a tragedy. Everything Agnes had, including the timbers she might have sold for a bite of food, everything, was gone.

Alexander sank to his knees and set Agnes gently on the ground. He himself was gasping for breath. There was a slash on his cheek and his hair was singed. His face was pale. The sight made her belly clench.

Agnes moaned, commanding her attention. *Poor dear.* She was pale and shaking. Hannah rolled up her scorched shawl and eased Agnes down, tucking it beneath her head. Her heart still pounded in her chest, but *doing* something helped.

A cursory scan of the yard showed that the men who had incited this mayhem were gone. But for the four of them, the clearing was deserted.

The hut and the barn were gone as well.

There was nothing left.

Absolutely nothing.

The thought devastated Hannah. Agnes had spent her life in this croft, and her mother's mother before her. It had taken centuries of hard work, scraping by, to build what little she had. It was all gone. In the blink of an eye.

"Is she all right?" Caithness asked, sheathing his sword.

"Aye, but she needs water," Hannah said. She made her way to the well—thankfully that was still standing—and drew out a cup, which she carried back and gently fed to the old woman as Alexander and the duke went to collect the cart standing in the field. Hannah and Alexander would bring Agnes home. To live with them in the castle. It was the least they could do.

When the men returned with the cart, Hannah watched as they carefully lifted Agnes in. The horror of the morning descended, filling Hannah's belly with bile and rage. Her mind flitted through it all. The brutal fist to her cheek, the men's cocky attitudes, the heartless manner in which Olrig's minions had destroyed Agnes' croft, uncaring even if they took a life.

There was a special place in hell for men like this.

If there was a God in heaven, they would pay.

Hannah's gaze fell on her husband, on the burn marks on his plaid, and a fresh fury rose, spurred by an unaccountable panic.

She'd nearly died, but she didn't give a whit about that.

He had nearly died.

She'd nearly lost him forever.

Dread scoured her soul. Dread, panic, and a biting annoyance.

Which was probably why, when he approached her, arms extended to fold her into a hug, she smacked him.

~

Alexander blinked and glanced down at his chest. Being smacked by Hannah was akin to being batted by a kitten, but it had still shocked him. His body was shaking with reaction. The absolute terror of seeing his wife run into the flaming hut had liquefied his bowels. His alarm had given him inhuman strength and he had quickly vanquished his opponent, and then, without thought, he'd run in after her.

Why she was angry with him—as she clearly was—was a mystery.

"What the hell were you thinking?" she spat. "You could have been killed."

Exasperation rose. "Me? *You* could have been killed. Bluidy hell, Hannah. Do you know what it did to me seeing you hie into that cottage?"

"I would have been fine. You should have stayed outside. Where it was safe."

"*You* should have stayed outside. You should have waited for me to save Agnes."

"There wasna time and you know it."

"Children. Children," the duke interrupted. They both ignored him.

Alexander glared at Hannah. "You are far too reckless."

"Reckless? I saved a woman's life."

"And nearly lost your own. I couldna bear it if I lost you, Hannah. You are my life." He hated the way his voice cracked, hated the weakness, the vulnerability, in his tone. But something in his anguished words reached her.

She stilled. Blinked. Tipped her head to the side. "Did you say, 'You are my *wife*'?"

"Nae. My *life*." And she was. God help him. His wife, his life, his love. "Hannah . . ." Though she was still humming with anger, he yanked her into his arms. The feel of her body, hale and whole against his, was a joy. He stared down at her face; smudged with soot though it was, it was the most beautiful face in the world. "Hannah," he whispered, and then he kissed her.

He kissed her with all the love and hope and relief in his soul. It was not a tender buss. It was a wildfire, as savage and raw as the blaze that had taken Agnes' home. Hannah's response was just as fierce. Alexander didn't want the kiss to end.

But Caithness cleared his throat.

"We should probably head back. Agnes will need tending."

Aye. He was right. With great regret, Alexander released his wife, but he couldn't resist one last quick buss. He stared down into her wide, beautiful brown eyes. "When we get home, Hannah, we are finishing this conversation."

"I look forward to it." Her grin was impish and wicked and it sent a lance of lust through him.

~

When they returned to the castle, Alexander handed Agnes into Fergus' care and the three trooped inside. Hannah was exhausted and aching but couldn't still the trill of relief to be home.

Home.

Aye. That was what Lochlannach Castle was to her now. Home.

Lana met them in the foyer. "How did it go?" she said

with a bright smile. Then her gaze lit on Hannah and her eyes widened. She stopped stock-still and stared. "What happened to you?"

Unbidden, Hannah's hand rose to her hair. Aye, it was a tangled nest—likely singed off in places—and her cheek was still an aching mass. No doubt she looked horrible. Alexander stepped up beside her and curled his arm around her in a show of support that warmed her. She nestled closer.

"Olrig's men burned down a crofter's cottage," he said in a dark voice.

"While she was in it," Hannah added.

"How horrible. Is she all right?"

"She's fine." Alexander frowned down at Hannah. "Hannah ran in to save her."

Lana gasped. "You dinna!"

Caithness chuckled. "And then Alexander ran in after her. You were both very lucky. I shudder to think what could have happened." His gaze rounded the company. "I don't know about you, Dunnet, but I should very much like a drink right now."

Alexander grunted his assent and they made their way into the parlor. Hannah collapsed on the divan while her husband poured three healthy draughts. When Hannah tried to refuse the one he offered, he insisted. "You've had a shock."

She frowned at him. "Caused by you."

"Me?"

"When I realized you'd followed me into that inferno. Honestly, Dunnet. What were you thinking?"

He sat beside her and glowered. "I was thinking perhaps I might save my wife from burning to a crisp."

Caithness sighed. "Are we going to start with this again?"

In tandem, they glared at him. But when Alexander

covered her hand with his and squeezed, her ire faded. How could she stay mad? He'd saved her after all. She stared into his eyes and her heart fluttered. "You were wonderful in the fight," she murmured.

"Ooh. There was a fight?" Lana leaned forward.

"A ferocious battle between Dunnet and Caithness, and Olrig's men. They trounced them."

"Did they?"

"Aye." Hannah turned to Caithness. "You were rather impressive as well, which was a surprise."

The offense on his face was comical. "A surprise?"

"Your sword is quite tiny."

"It is nothing of the sort," he grumbled as he resettled himself. "I'll have you know, fencing with an épée is a time-honored sport. And I'm known to be one of the better swordsmen in England."

"As I said. You were impressive."

He tugged on his plaid. "Thank you."

Lana's contemplative gaze landed on the duke, causing his ears to go pink.

"As awful as it was, I'm glad we were there," Hannah said. "I canna imagine what would have happened to Agnes had we not been there to rescue her."

Alexander nodded and squeezed Hannah's hand. His thumb made a distracting foray over her palm. "So, Caithness, what do you think of the Clearances, now that you've see the truth of it?"

The duke tore his gaze from Lana's and scrubbed his face with his palms. "It is a horror. Not what I imagined it would be. Not what the lords in London claimed it was. Not in the least. But then . . ." His attention flickered back to Lana. "Nothing here has been."

"Have you . . . reconsidered your decision?" This Lana asked in a soft voice.

"Yes. Indeed I have. I cannot be a part of what we saw

today and I certainly do not want to be the cause of such suffering. I shall have Dougal send missives to all my barons, ordering them to cease and desist all Clearances immediately."

Hannah nearly deflated as relief gushed through her. Her family, her lands, her people . . . all safe. It was a glorious moment. She glanced at Alexander and they shared a smile.

"And Dunnet?" she asked the duke, though her gaze still tangled with her husband's. "Will he remain as laird?"

The duke took a sip of his drink and sighed. "I must say, I owe you an apology for that, Dunnet. I came here so arrogant. So full of myself. So sure I knew everything. But I didn't. I didn't know anything."

"You owe me nothing, Your Grace."

The duke blew out a breath. "Please. Call me Lachlan. If we're to be friends moving forward, it is only fitting."

A warm glow rose on Alexander's cheeks. "I would like that."

"Well," Lana said. "Since we're all being so charming and friendly, I have something for you, Your Grace." She stood and crossed to the sofa where he sat and perched next to him, pulling something from her pocket. The necklace. With a smile, she handed it to him.

He stared at it for a moment, a somber expression on his darkly handsome face. When he took it from her, he covered her hands with his and gazed into her eyes. His throat worked. "Thank you," he said.

She fluttered her lashes. "For the record, I would probably have given it to you anyway. Because it meant so much to you."

He narrowed his eyes on her, but a smile played on his lips. "Minx," he murmured.

The two stared at each other for a long while and, to Hannah's surprise, the familiar trickle of annoyance did not skirl through her belly. Upon reflection, she rather liked the duke. He'd proven himself to be an honorable and fair man, and though his sword was rather tiny, he certainly handled it with flair. And he had eschewed his lace. Indeed, he looked fine in his Sinclair kilt with a manly smudge of soot on his face.

Should some romance happen to flare between him and her sister, it might not be so terrible. In fact, it might come in handy having a duke in the family. So when Lachlan stood and asked Lana if she would like to take a walk in the garden with him, Hannah didn't squawk as she once might have done.

But she did send him a narrow-eyed warning glare.

She wasn't a fool.

Once they were alone, Alexander pulled her into his arms. "Shall we go to our rooms?" he asked. "I believe we have a conversation to finish."

She rumpled her brow. *A conversation?* His saucy expression reminded her. *Oh. Aye.* "Let's," she said, tugging him to his feet. Together, they made their way up the grand staircase of their home, his arm around her and her head tucked against his chest.

"I'm so pleased with the way everything worked out," she said.

"Mmm." His murmur rumbled through her.

"That he changed his mind about the Clearances, certainly, but also that he willna be replacing my baron." She went up on her toes and kissed the underside of Alexander's chin. "I have a fondness for my baron."

His eyes glinted. "And I have a fondness for my baroness."

This was hardly a declaration, but then, she had vowed to herself that she would not expect too much of Alexander. And fondness was, indeed, a start.

When they entered his room, she turned to face him.

"Alexander, I'm sorry I frightened you by running into the cottage. I shouldna have been so rash. I promise to be more circumspect in the future." Surely there was no call for him to chuckle. "I am a baroness. I shall endeavor to act like one."

"And how does a baroness act?"

"She is reserved and elegant. Remote, perhaps."

He snorted. "But I love you the way you are."

Her heart stalled. She gaped at him. Her lips flapped. "You . . . you . . . you l-love me?"

"Ach, Hannah Lochlannach. I do. I love you." His arms tightened around her and he kissed her on her nose. "I love everything about you from the top of your head to the tips of your toes and everything in between."

"B-b-but . . ." she sputtered. "I'm plain."

"Not a bit of it."

"And plump."

He nestled closer. "I enjoy that verra much."

She narrowed her eyes. "I am stubborn," she offered in a warning tone.

"Aye." He kissed her lips. "You are. And willful and fierce. I adore all those things too. Even your rash, reckless spirit." He winked. "I can only hope our sons will inherit that."

Sons!

Oh mercy. The thought sent a bolt of excitement and anticipation and hope through her. "Ach, Alexander," she sighed. "I'm so lucky to have you." She stared up at him—at his harsh, craggy face, at the eyes she adored beyond bearing, at the lips that had always fascinated her—and something swelled in her chest. An urgency, a need.

She cupped his cheek and captured his attention, though it had not wandered so very far—just down to her cleavage. "Alexander Lochlannach?"

"Aye, my Hannah?"

"I'm so pleased you are my husband. So honored to be your wife. I know I've never said it, but I love you too, with all my heart."

His grin was wide and wicked. "Aye," he whispered. "Aye, my sweet. I know."

"You know?" Surely there was no need for this feeling of pique.

"I can tell in the way you look at me, the way you smile. The way you warm in my embrace."

She nibbled a lip. "There are those things, I suppose." She'd experienced the same with him.

"Hannah, *mo ghraidh,* some things doona need words. Some things will always speak for themselves."

How convenient then, that no more words were necessary.

All through the night and far into morning.

EPILOGUE

"We'll be there soon." Alexander pulled Hannah closer and nuzzled her brow. Poor thing, she was sheeted in sweat. He'd suggested they stop at an inn, so she could rest comfortably until she was ready to travel again, but his wife had refused. She was too anxious to arrive in Dounreay and see her family to stop for something as insignificant as a stomach upset.

But it didn't seem so insignificant at the moment. Hannah moaned and clutched her belly. Caithness, sitting across from her in the carriage, looking fine and manly in his kilt, widened his eyes. "Maybe we should pull over again," he suggested.

More than once on this journey, the Baroness of Dunnet had voided the contents of her stomach on Lachlan's Hessians. Fortunately, he was an understanding and patient man, for a duke.

Alexander knocked on the roof and the carriage rolled to a stop. Hannah reeled through the door, not even waiting for Alexander to help her down. He followed her, concern limning his brow. He held her hair back as she retched in the unfortunate bushes on the side of the road.

It was gut-wrenching, watching her heave, because there was nothing he could do to help her.

When she finished voiding, she gazed up at him with a watery smile. "Not verra . . . not verra *baronessy* of me, is it?" she asked.

He handed her a fresh handkerchief and she wiped at

her mouth. "You missed the duke that time," he offered, and was rewarded with a chuckle.

"I wasna aiming for him," she insisted, taking Alexander's hand and struggling to her feet. "He just happens to be sitting across from me." Her eyes held a hint of humor beneath the misery.

Alexander wrapped his arm around her shoulders and led her back to the carriage. Lachlan peered out the open door; concern wreathed his expression. Most likely, concern for his Hessians. "Are you feeling better?" he called.

"Aye, much better," Hannah replied, but Alexander suspected this was a lie. She still looked a little green around the gills, but he said nothing.

Lana beamed at him as he helped Hannah into the carriage and took his seat. He tried to respond, but it wasn't an entirely sincere offering. In truth, he was very worried about his wife and determined that, at the next town, he would summon a doctor—no matter what Hannah said. It was not natural for a woman to retch like this. It couldn't be.

Lana patted him on the knee. "Doona fash yerself," she said. "It will all be fine." And then she shot a wink at her sister. Lana's cavalier attitude prickled him. Hannah often complained that Lana hadn't a care in the world, and now he was beginning to understand her exasperation about that.

Though it was true Lana did *know* things sometimes. Perhaps, in this, she was right. Perhaps it would be all right. He hoped.

Hannah settled herself more comfortably and cleared her throat.

Lachlan's eyes widened. Alexander noticed that he edged his boots back under the seat. "Ah . . . Have you . . . always had trouble traveling?" he asked in a cautious tone.

Hannah blew out a breath. It was . . . bilious. "Nae. I've always loved traveling. Haven't I, Lana?"

Lana sniffed. "Aye, Hannah, but you've never traveled quite like this before."

"Like this?" Hannah tipped her head and gazed at her sister. "In a carriage? With three other people? I've done so many times."

"Aye, but not with . . . a husband." Lana's gaze flickered over him. The look Hannah shot Alexander was a trifle accusatory. Though this was hardly *his* fault. He'd done nothing to make his wife ill. In fact, he'd gone out of his way to—

Lana's attention shifted to Hannah; it settled on her belly. Her knowing grin widened. When their eyes met, she gave Alexander a tiny nod.

His pulse skipped a beat. His head went a little light. He turned to his wife and studied her through narrowed eyes. It could have been his imagination, but were her breasts fuller? Her belly slightly rounded? Could it be? Could the grandest miracle of all have happened? A shiver of excitement shot through him.

"Dunnet?" she muttered. "Why are you gaping at me like that?"

"Ach, I do love you, Hannah Lochlannach."

She frowned. "I know that. And I love you too." This she snapped, but he didn't mind. If his wife was truly with child, there were many cranky days in his future. He didn't mind at all. His heart was too full, his spirit too unfettered, to care about a cranky day or two.

He was the luckiest man on earth. He had a beautiful wife—who might be even now carrying his son—a prosperous and happy clan, and a secure and shining future laid out before him.

Best of all, there were no more shadows wreathing his soul. She had banished them all. His Hannah. His love.

Ach, he yearned to kiss her. On the cheek, perhaps—her breath was rather . . . bilious. But as he leaned forward to do so, the carriage lurched into motion.

And his wife threw up again.

All over Lachlan's boots.

Read on for an excerpt from the next book by Sabrina York

SUSANA AND THE SCOT

Coming soon from St. Martin's Paperbacks

Susana was annoyed. There was no doubt about it. The swish of her hips as she led him across the bustling bailey was a dead giveaway, that and the dark glowers she shot over her shoulder. But Andrew couldn't help but be amused. For one thing, she was damn alluring when she was annoyed.

Hell, she was damn alluring altogether. The curve of her waist alone could drive a man insane, much less that silky tumble of hair. He wanted to wrap it in is his fist, wind it around his body. A certain part of his body.

At the thought, his cock rose.

It was difficult to remind himself that he'd vowed to eschew seduction, but try as he might, he couldn't banish the fantasy of stripping those breeks from her lovely body and laying her down in the heather. Visions of that twitching backside—bare before him—danced in his head.

But he'd made a vow. A sacred vow. And as tempting as she was, he would control his baser urges. He could. Probably.

These thoughts whirled in his head as she led him into the stables, past his men—who were unpacking and seeing to their horses—and through the kennels. Though he was perplexed, Andrew followed. He would probably follow anywhere she led. It was a fact that should have scared him to death or, at the very least, concerned him. But it didn't. However, when she started up a staircase at the very end of the long hall, he had to stop her.

She glared at the hand he set on her arm. He tried to ignore the sizzle that raged through him at their first touch. It was ridiculous how much that touch affected him. And how much he enjoyed her glare.

He edged closer. "Where are we going?" he asked in a purr.

Judging from her frown, his tone irritated her. He rather enjoyed irritating her, he found.

She ripped her arm away and continued up the stairs. He followed and found himself in a narrow loft that ran the length of the kennels. It was dim and a little dusty. Motes danced on the air. The roof was so low he had to duck his head to miss the rafters.

"Your men will stay here," she said.

Andrew gaped at her. The room was swept clean and empty. A thin shaft of light from the far window illuminated it with a murky light. But the yipping from the kennel and the stench of excrement wafted up from below. For some reason, all thoughts of alluring backsides dissipated. Disbelief gushed through him. *"Here?"*

She crossed her arms and offered what could only be described as a smirk. "Here."

He tipped his head to the side. "This is a kennel."

"I am aware of that."

"I have twenty-five men."

"The room is quite large."

"There are no beds."

She blew out a breath. "We'll bring in pallets."

Andrew blinked. He set his teeth and tried to remain calm. His men were warriors. They did not sleep on pallets. In a kennel. "This will not do." Surely she saw that. Surely she understood . . . He caught a glimpse of her smug expression and it dawned on him.

She did. She did understand. She knew damn well what she was doing. Her response only verified his suspicions.

"I'm sorry, but you have descended upon us with no warning whatsoever with a large group of men. I'm afraid this is all we can offer you at this time." Her smile was deferential, but hardly sincere. The light dancing in her eyes lit a flame in his belly. "Of course, if our accommodations are unacceptable, you can always return to Dunnet . . ."

Oh, she'd like that, wouldn't she?

The minx.

Rather than the exasperation her self-satisfied look should have sparked, Andrew found himself filled with another emotion entirely. Anticipation. Exhilaration. The thrill of a challenge.

For that was what she was, Susana Dounreay. A challenge.

And it appeared she reveled in provoking him.

A pity she didn't understand he was a dangerous man to provoke.

The tumult her presence sparked within him flared again, burning the edges of his resolution; his inconvenient lust blossomed, and with it, an unruly resolve.

He wanted, very badly, to kiss her. He wanted to wrench her into his arms and cover her sweet mouth with his. He wanted to taste her, consume her, possess her.

And he would.

Clearly he wasn't the kind of man who could swear off women. Clearly he wasn't the kind of man who could keep a vow.

So be it.

Damn to hell his ridiculous vow.

Damn to hell the fact that she was his sister-in-law.

He was going to seduce this vixen, and he would start right now.

Desire, like a snarling, snapping beast, rose within him, and he stepped closer.

~

Susana's eyes flared as Andrew advanced on her, like a skulking fox that had spotted a plump rabbit. She didn't mean to retreat, but she had to. She'd seen that expression in his eyes before and she knew what it meant. Something within her howled: *Run*.

Perhaps it was the expression in his eyes, or the knowledge that she was playing with fire, or the sudden realization that she'd foolishly come here, to this deserted loft with the most dangerous man she'd ever met, but she couldn't still the urge to whirl and pace to the far end of the room to peer out of the smudged window. She was aware he followed. She felt his presence like a fire in a forge.

Desperation prompted her to continue their conversation, to put some space between them, to raise a shield. "The room is perfectly habitable," she proclaimed. "And once we have pallets brought in, it will serve you well."

"Will it?"

His voice was low in her ear, a whisper almost. And far too close. She wanted to turn, to confront him, but she knew if she did, they would be face to face, perhaps lip to lip, and she could not allow that. She could never allow that.

The last time he'd kissed her, it had been her undoing.

A pity he didn't remember.

"My men *willna* like being housed with the dogs." *Holy God.* Was that his hand on her hip? His thumb tracing her waist? "*Nae* doubt they will all want to find . . . other beds to welcome them."

Susana stilled as his words sank in. The threat was clear. And it was rather horrifying. A horde of randy warriors set loose on the innocent maidens of Dounreay? That his hand had slid over to toy with the small of her back, to tangle in the skeins of her hair, didn't help.

Her pulse thudded and her knees went weak. She couldn't have it. She couldn't have this man *touching* her. She sucked in a breath and slipped to the side, out of his grasp. When she was far enough away for some measure of safety, she turned to face him, a reproachful look fixed on her face. "Are your men so lacking in discipline?" She hoped her frown, her reproving tone, would bring him to heel. She should have known better.

He grinned and stepped closer. His eyes glinted, as though needling her was an amusing sport. "They are *verra* disciplined . . . when their needs are met."

She crossed her arms, as though that could protect her, and pretended to study the room. Pretended she wasn't aware of his thrumming presence, his heat, his intent. "Well, I shall hold you responsible for any . . . improprieties." She took a step toward the staircase, only a tiny one—surely not an attempt to escape.

He chuckled—*chuckled*, the bastard—making it clear he recognized her cowardice for what it was. And he paced her.

"They're all good men. They all volunteered to come with me. Each and every one of them is dedicated to the cause of protecting Reay from the villains who have been plaguing you. However . . ."

The way he trailed off derailed her retreat. She stilled. Glared at him. "However, what?"

"However, they do have . . . needs. Surely you can find better lodgings."

She blew out a breath. "In time." In time.

In time, he would be gone, God willing.

He stepped toward her again, although nonchalantly, as though he were not chasing her across the room. It occurred to her they were engaged in something of a macabre dance. It set her nerves on edge. She hadn't realized what a long room this was, or how far it was to the stairs.

"*Doona* leave it too long." His smile was heinous. It made all kinds of shivers dance over her skin. "My men are . . . restless." She had the chilling sense he was talking about himself.

"I shall . . . do my best." Like hell. "And now, if you will excuse me, I have things to do."

His brow quirked. She tried not to notice what a perfect brow it was. "Ah, but I thought you and I could . . . talk."

"Talk?" She didn't intend to squawk, but she could tell from his predatory stance, a conversation was not the primary urge on his mind. At least, not one with words.

He nodded. Though his features were patently earnest, the sincerity was patently affected. "About the defenses you have in place . . . so I can decide what needs improvement."

Aggravation rippled. It displaced her concerns about being here, with him, all alone. Fury did that, she'd often found. Overrode common sense and led one into dangerous waters. Her hands curled into fists. She strode toward him until they were nearly nose to nose. "Nothing needs improvement," she snapped. They didn't need him. Or his men. Or his stupid ideas.

"Nonsense. Now that we're here, we intend to make a statement to Stafford, or whatever miscreants are lurking out there thinking Dounreay is an easy target. But before I set my plans in motion—"

"Your plans?" *He already had plans? Och!* He was so exasperating.

She barely noticed that he stepped closer . . . until their chests brushed. He was hard and hot; the touch made her tingle. His voice, low and luring, made her tingle as well. His gaze skated over her face, then stalled on her lips. "Let's meet and discuss—"

Her pulse skittered. "I *doona* have time to meet with you. Not today." She took a step back. He followed.

"*Nae*?" A whisper. And his caress over her shoulder, that was a whisper as well. Like a panicked fawn, Susana eased back again. And again. He matched her, step for step.

She swallowed heavily. "I . . . You have descended upon us with no warning—"

"My brother sent a letter."

He was too close. Far too close. She swallowed heavily. "Twenty-five men that now need to be housed and fed. On top of that, I have many other duties that need attending."

He cocked his head to the side. "Which duties?"

"*Many* duties." She frowned and glanced toward the staircase. Ah, lord. It was so far . . . He was too warm. Too broad. Too alluring. Though she didn't intend to, she took another step back and—

Oh hell. He'd backed her against the wall. That he couldn't stand straight in the low-ceilinged room was a small consolation.

"Susana," he said as he leaned closer. His breath was a tantalizing trail over her face.

An unholy thrill snaked through her. Surely that wasn't anticipation? Hunger? Need?

She could not allow him to kiss her. She could not—

Her knees nearly melted at the touch of his lips. His warmth, his taste, his scent made her mind whirl. Thank God he had his hands on her waist and was holding her steady, or she might well have collapsed.

It occurred to her that she should push him away, fight him, but she couldn't. Something, something deep within her, resisted. Something deep within her needed him. Needed this.

And ah, it was glorious. As glorious as she remembered.

His lips were soft, gentle, questing as they tested hers, and then, with a groan, he pulled her closer, melding their bodies together. He deepened the kiss, sealing his mouth over hers and dancing his tongue over the seam.

She opened to him. She couldn't resist. He filled her senses with his presence, his heat. With tiny nibbles, sucks, and laps, he consumed her, enflamed her. All sanity fled. All logic and resolution and anger flitted away as Andrew tasted her, tempted her.

His hands were not still. They roved over her body from her shoulders, down her arms to her waist. They tangled in her hair and stroked her cheek and chin.

Heat blossomed, skittered through her veins. Her body softened, melted, prepared for him.

She should not have responded the way she did. She should not have pressed against him, rubbed against the hard bulge on his belly. She should not have explored the hard flesh of his back, cupped his nape, raked his silken scalp. She should not have moaned.

Surely all these things would only encourage him.

He lifted his head and stared at her, an odd mixture of befuddlement and awe in his eyes. His tongue peeped out and dabbed at his lips, snagging her attention. Surely she didn't lean toward him in a mute plea for more.

Was she truly so weak?

Aye. She was.

Get more Highlanders with Suzanne Enoch and her
Scandalous Highlander Series

The Devil Wears Kilts
Available Now

Rogue with a Brogue
Available Now

Mad, Bad, and Dangerous in Plaid
Available Now

Don't miss the next *Scandalous Highlander*...

COMING OCTOBER 2015: ***Some Like It Scot***
Visit SuzanneEnoch.com

If you enjoyed this novel by Sabrina York,
you'll love Julianne MacLean's Highlander series!